Samantha King is a former editor and also a qualified psychotherapist. After her childhood in the south-west of England, teenage years spent in the north-east and student days somewhere in between, she finally settled in west London, where she enjoyed a career publishing other people's books before going freelance and surrendering to a long-time urge to write her own. She lives with her husband and two young children, who inspired her to write *The Choice*, her debut novel.

An English graduate and lifelong bookworm, Samantha is always fascinated to hear readers' opinions. You can share yours with her at:

Facebook: www.facebook.com/samanthakingbooks
Twitter: @SamKingBooks

The Choice

Samantha King

piatkus

PIATKUS

First published in Great Britain in 2017 by Piatkus

3 5 7 9 10 8 6 4 2

A CIP catalogue record for this book
is available from the British Library.

ISBN 978-0-349-41465-2

Typeset in Garamond by M Rules
Printed and bound in Great Britain by
Clays Ltd, St Ives plc

Papers used by Piatkus are from well-managed forests
and other responsible sources.

MIX
Paper from
responsible sources
FSC® C104740

Piatkus
An imprint of
Little, Brown Book Group
Carmelite House
50 Victoria Embankment
London EC4Y 0DZ

An Hachette UK Company
www.hachette.co.uk

www.piatkus.co.uk

For Paul, Hani and Rafi – you are my world.

For in that sleep of death what dreams may come

—WILLIAM SHAKESPEARE
Hamlet, Act 3, Scene 1

PROLOGUE

My daughter's curls are red-gold. They glint in the morning sunshine as the fine silken tendrils dance away from my searching hands, and I stand transfixed as I watch them drift upwards in a fiery cloud. I wasn't reaching for her hair – I was aiming for her body as it flew backwards, a slow-motion tableau implanting itself in my brain – but my arms flail uselessly, hugging only dry summer air to my chest as I try to stop her from falling and instead catch just the floating wisps of her coppery ringlets, the ones she's been pestering me to trim so that she can straighten them and look less cute, more grown-up.

She will never look more grown-up; she will never grow up.

The thought jolts deep inside me, echoing the thud of her body hitting the ground. I drop to the garden path, ignoring the bone-crunching impact of concrete against my kneecaps as I crawl, clawing my way towards her beneath the rose bushes. My shaking fingers scrabble through stony soil, skin tearing as I reach frantically ahead of me, nausea burning my throat at the sickly smell of blood on my hands and wrists. So much blood. My shoulders almost dislocate as I overstretch my arms, plunging my hands into the halo of Annabel's hair, twining the soft coils around my fingertips as if that will tie her to me. I rest my cheek against the clammy soil and hope to die too.

No release comes; instead, my mind is stuck in a loop of horror and memory . . .

Annabel is small for her age. Her frame is slight, her legs surprisingly long for a girl barely four feet tall, and her arms are skinny. *My chopsticks*, she always calls them. Her hair is the biggest thing about her – a fine, sugar-spun gossamer crown of untameable auburn curls. I've always thought Annabel's personality grew to complement her hair: ethereal, restless, impossible to behold without smiling in delight.

Aidan's would be the same, if Dom hadn't made me get it cut short nine months ago. I'd felt like a criminal taking him to the barber on the high street, the Saturday before their first day at the new school. I remember the tears he'd tried to hide behind his encyclopaedia, and then later my tears as Annabel impatiently waved me away at the school gate, pulling her younger-by-two-minutes brother behind her across the lush lawn towards the grand red-brick building. I looked around at the smart purple blazers and my heart squeezed for Aidan as he self-consciously reached up to rub his shorn hair.

Dom had been right to complain: the barber had gone too far and I should have stopped him, but I'd hesitated too long when he insisted that *all* the boys were wearing it that short. I consoled myself that it might help Aidan fit in rather than stand out. The poorest kids at the posh school: I couldn't bear to think of the gibes they might suffer, no matter how small the class sizes and how amazing the facilities. Dom had been wrong about the school, though: the twins were far happier at their old state primary, with their old friends, kids who didn't expect iPhones and private ski lessons in their party bags. But I'd lost that particular argument, as I've lost most arguments over this last year, especially when it comes to the twins.

Aren't they so terribly alike? the gym-kitted nannies always gushed, before racing off to their Pilates classes.

Well, yes, except that they're not. My son always clung to me, wanting to hold my hand as long as possible, but my daughter was forever shrugging me off, longing to fly high, soaring towards freedom.

Was that why you chose him? Because he needed you − loved you − more?

My children both needed me! They both loved me. And I loved them equally.

The gritty soil grinds deeper into my cheek as the argument in my head spins endlessly, pointlessly: Annabel will never need me again, and Aidan won't admit it even if he does. That is my punishment for allowing a killer to enter my home, for shielding my shy, sweet, overcautious son and allowing my vivacious, spotlight-seeking daughter, who always faced life so fearlessly, to race headlong to her death.

'I'll get it, Mum. You carry on; you're doing a great job.' Aidan ambled towards the front door at the sound of the buzzer, but I raised a hand to stop him.

'Hang on a minute, love. You know I don't like you answering the door to strangers.'

'Who says it's a stranger?' Annabel said, leaping up from the sofa. 'It might be Uncle Max. He said he had an extra-special surprise for us.'

'Huh.' I rolled my eyes. 'Just give me one more sec.'

There. Perfect. Unaware of tragedy lurking round the corner, a malicious spy watching our safe, ordinary family, I actually smiled as I inserted the last of the candles into the blue icing on top of their huge, swimming-pool-shaped birthday cake – ten purple ones for Annabel, ten red ones for Aidan. It would make a stunning centrepiece for their pool party that afternoon.

'I'll be right there!' I called out, licking a smudge of icing from my fingers and hurrying to the door.

But Annabel got there first. 'It's the postman, bet you – look at that giant shadow through the glass. He must have the most humongous stack of presents!'

'Hope one of them is a new Xbox,' added my gaming-obsessed son, moving to stand at his sister's shoulder.

'You know your dad's not keen on video games,' I said, doing my best not to sound snippy.

'That's because he always wants to win and hates getting shot,' Aidan said sagely, his eye-roll so like mine, and I laughed again.

It was uncanny, though, because the next few seconds felt exactly like we'd stepped into one of Aidan's trigger-blasting games. I watched my daughter, two steps ahead of me, pull open the front door and look up at the giant shadow wearing army fatigues and a balaclava but bearing no gifts, blotting out the perfect summer morning, looming larger still as he grabbed hold of both children and dragged them down the side of the house into the back garden, gloved hand pointing a gun at each of their almost-identical, birthday-shiny faces and then at my stricken one as I caught up with them.

'Choose one, bitch.'

Now there is darkness.

PART ONE

ONE

Three months later

My son's hair needs cutting. It hangs over his eyes and he peeps through it like a nervous actor scanning the audience through a chink in the curtains before daring to make an appearance on stage. It's only me he's hiding from, though. He turns his head when I walk into the room, twists his slim body away from me when I go to cuddle him. My fingertips tingle with longing for the almost forgotten feel of Aidan's milky-soft cheeks, and I wrap my arms around myself to stop them aching with the heavy emptiness of having no child to hug.

For thirty-six weeks I carried the twins inside me, our heartbeats a triple echo of each other's, first from the inside and then against my chest as I nurtured their tiny bodies, physically and emotionally, skin against skin. An invisible knot of mutual need and love bound us together; we were as one, and for the first ten years of their lives the knot tightened. Now it has been ripped apart, and my beautiful girl is gone.

Missing her somehow keeps Annabel's presence alive, and I cling desperately to that. I abandoned my daughter in that one dreadful moment; I will *never* let her go for all the moments hereafter. But the pain of loss is paralysing – for me, for my husband Dom, and for my son who doesn't know how to be in this world without his twin.

Pressed into one corner of the sofa, eyes fixed on the Nintendo DS in his hands, Aidan looks like he wants to disappear into his surroundings. I notice he's wearing the jeans and shirt again, the ones I bought him to wear to their tenth birthday party, and I wonder how he can bear to – how the very fabric of them doesn't hurt his skin with painful reminders. Or maybe that's the point: wear the same clothes, remind Mum of what she did. It's working, and I know I deserve it, yet it feels . . . unexpected.

I'm not quite sure what I did expect; just not this . . . this *void* of silent recrimination. Aidan has never been a cruel boy; he's gentle and caring. I remember holding him for hours when our pet cat Disco was run over, stroking his hair, his three-year-old body shuddering beneath my hands, while Annabel patted his hand curiously, looking uncertainly at me with questions she didn't know how to ask. Eventually, his tears stopped and he cuddled her and she smiled again.

Aidan was the only one of us who could make Annabel smile when she didn't get picked for the lead role after a dance audition, or when she had to miss a swimming gala because of a cold. He adored her as much as he now clearly hates me. No, hate is too strong, too *active*. I simply don't exist for him any more, and he is barely existing. He was always Annabel's shadow, but now he's a shadow of himself, adrift without the twin who curled against him in the womb, wrapped herself around him as a baby and held on tight to him for the rest of her too-short life.

My precious, extraordinary twins.

They were always inseparable and I see Annabel's face every time I look at Aidan's. I would speak to him – I *long* to – but the words won't come, and I know he won't answer, anyway. *Aidan, I'm so sorry, my love.* The apology – so inadequate – fills my mind and vibrates through every nerve ending. It seems like the only thing I ever say these days, and I only say it in my head; the words never actually pass my lips.

I don't need a doctor to tell me that post-traumatic shock has stolen my voice. *Selective mutism* – the term floats towards me from university psychology lectures, oh, so many years ago. I know this explains my silence, and I understand that trauma has created an anxiety disorder that is suppressing my memory – along with my appetite, physical sensations, energy levels . . .

I know all this but I'm powerless to change it. Every day I feel like I'm walking through clouds; everything is hazy, deadened. Everything except my emotions; they have never felt so raw. I keep mentally listing them on the imaginary whiteboard in my head – anything to keep some kind of grip on reality, to retain some sense of myself. I already feel like I've half vanished.

That whiteboard. It's in my mind most days now, with all kinds of notes, diagrams and commentary jotted across its gleaming surface. My own personal textbook. My eyes feel strained, myopic, but I have no trouble at all picturing my old uni whiteboard, complete with handsome failed-actor-turned-lecturer Seamus Jackson striking a pose in front of it. I suppose it's to be expected; I spent enough hours staring at them both.

Seamus Jackson. I haven't thought of him in years, but now his dulcet Scottish tones have become the voice in my head. In today's imaginary lecture, my memory has dredged up the image of Seamus-call-me-Shay-guys in his usual spread-legged stance, theatrically squiggling a drawing of a brain after severe trauma – scattered neurotransmitters, the lot. Hands on hips, Shay carves a dramatic tale from a dry explanation of how, after trauma, an overstimulated amygdala can become 'jammed in fight-or-flight mode, guys, often completely freezing a person's capacity for speech'. A dramatic pause, then he continues: 'Excessive anxiety, or trauma, can crank up the amygdala's sense of danger to *such* a heightened extent that it effectively, like, short circuits, creating an ever-present sense of danger that, put bluntly, causes the sufferer simply to *clam up!*'

Yes, I understand my silence, but I hate it. I hate that I can recall lectures I attended when I was barely out of my teens, but I cannot remember what happened in my own back garden on the morning of the twins' tenth birthday, a day that changed all our lives completely and for ever. I remember Shay's piercing blue eyes yet the exact details of my daughter's murder – the last moments of her precious life – are a complete blank. Such is the paradox of the mind; and people always think it's the heart that's so complicated.

I hadn't even realised I was paying that much attention to Shay. We'd shared just one illicit week together (*Dating a student is a lecturer's self-destruct button*), yet I remember every word he taught me. It's only now that I recall them, though: at the lowest point of my life. I have lost my darling daughter – worse than that, I gave her up – and it is unfathomable to me.

Choose one, bitch.

Why would anyone want to force me to make such a choice? It's like something out of that old Meryl Streep film my flatmate and I used to weep buckets over on rainy Sunday afternoons. *Sophie's Choice* – that was it. But this isn't a movie; this is my *life*. How dare anyone do this to me – to my daughter?

Anger. Here it comes again. I've learned not to resist it. Instead, I jot it conscientiously on my mental whiteboard, allowing the wisdom of Shay to surface once more: 'Rage can grip many a bereaved person, guys. Don't make the mistake of thinking loss is a passive experience.'

Instinctively I know my mind is protecting itself by blotting out everything the police must have told me about the gunman; the trauma of losing Annabel has brought down a shutter in my mind, and no matter how many times I try to recall that awful day, those appalling moments, all that emerges is jumbled, fractured memories. But in truth, it isn't agonising over who did this or even *why* that has stolen my voice along with my capacity to sleep, think or even move very far. What keeps me frozen in shock is not *his* guilt, but *mine*.

I try for the thousandth time to make sense of it. Did it mean I love Aidan more because I *saved* him? Or that I loved Annabel more because I *chose* her? They were twins; I always vowed to love them equally, to show no favouritism. So what was I thinking? Did I sacrifice Annabel for her brother's sake? Or did I save her from the torment of existing in this dark place where the three of us drift like shadows, tiptoeing silently around the gaping hole in our lives, together but no longer a family?

No answer comes; my mind is a closed book.

Dom has been a glacier of impassive calm, and I know I've left it to him to speak to the police, the lawyers, the journalists, the neighbours ... He's never blamed me – and he's never, in my hearing at least, told Aidan that I'm to blame. I know he won't turn our son against me; he won't force him to choose between his parents in the way that I was forced to choose between my children. We disagreed passionately about the twins' school, but those arguments are long forgotten.

Life simply drifts on – the same, yet totally changed. We live in the same comfortable home, on the same quiet street in Hampton village; the usual domestic routine ebbs and flows: school, clubs, homework, playdates with Aidan's friend Jasper. But I don't leave the house any more. I spend my time now watching my son and my husband prowl restlessly through each room, unable to settle. They stare right through me, pretending they're busy just getting on with everyday things, while I glide like a ghost on the periphery of their lives. I can't speak, I barely sleep, and I don't know how to look forward; all I seem able to do is look back and wonder: *How did I get here? Why did this terrible thing happen?*

Dom hasn't looked up from his laptop, and Aidan's eyes are still glued to his DS. They're oblivious to my presence. So I look at Dom, really look at him, at the man I have loved so much but who can no longer bring himself to look at *me*. His face is creased in a frown. Didn't he used to be bigger? Has he lost weight? These last weeks and months will have taken as much of a toll on him as they have on me, I know. His face is leaner and he looks desperately tired, his blue eyes glazed over.

And then I notice the little crinkle at the corner of his eyes and it takes me back, all the way back to the first time I met him.

TWO

'If your eyes get any wider, they'll pop right out of your head.'

'Excuse me?' I blushed as I noticed the tall, good-looking guy leaning against the A-to-C bookshelf of the serial killer section, his own blue eyes fixed on me. I had the sense he'd been watching me for some time.

'You haven't blinked for at least three minutes. Are you trying to break some kind of record? Or maybe you're just a beautiful freak of nature. I'm Dom, by the way. Dominic Castle. And you are . . . ?'

'Deeply offended. *Freak?* Gee, thanks.' I made a show of checking my watch even though there was a clock on the wall right in front of us. 'Library closes soon. I'd best make a move.'

'Without even telling me your name? But how can I spread the word about this extraordinary talent of yours, if I don't know who you are? And I said beautiful, in case you didn't notice. So don't run away. I won't bite. Unless you ask me to.'

He strode towards the desk where I'd been camped out for the last two hours, staring at my psychology textbooks but really spying on Shay. Then he pulled out a chair and sat down next to me, grinning as he folded his arms behind his head. His black T-shirt strained across his broad chest and I felt the hairs on the back of my neck prickle.

'Sorry?' I said, even though I'd heard him perfectly.

'I said pleased to meet you, Madeleine Hartley.' He thrust a big hand towards me.

Heat surged through my body, already flushed from the balmy evening. London was collectively sweltering in the sultry oppressiveness of a late-summer heatwave, and I longed for the cool, crisp autumn days that surely lay ahead. I wanted to swap my jewelled flip-flops for soft suede boots, lacy vest tops for cosy cardigans; I wanted summer to end and my university days to be over.

'How do you . . . ? Oh.'

He abandoned the handshake offer I'd ignored and held up my Child Psychology binder, rubbing his thumb slowly over the name label. His fingers were lean and tanned; I wondered what it would feel like to be touched by them.

'Are you a Madeleine, Maddie or, uh, just Mad?' he said, grinning again as he swivelled his body so that his legs were spread either side of mine, trapping me in my seat.

'Depends.'

Distracted by sudden movement in my peripheral vision, I glanced towards Shay. He hadn't spoken to me for three whole days now, and revision tutorials for the exam resits started on Monday. It was going to be cringingly awkward sitting in the small lecture theatre with just him and the two other students who, like me, needed to retake our final paper. I wished for the hundredth time that I'd spent less time daydreaming about my lecturer and more time concentrating on studying for my finals, then I could have graduated and moved on to my teacher training course and—

'Depends on . . . ?' Dom queried, reaching out to pinch my chin lightly with hot, rasping fingertips, turning my head back to face him.

I deliberately closed my eyes, resisting his command to make me look at him, but the image of his dark brows and sharp cheekbones remained imprinted behind my eyelids. He was far too cocky; he was probably laughing at my gawky shyness. *Damn*. With a huge effort I forced myself to open my eyes. I wasn't going to let him see that his nearness flustered me.

'Well, my mum used to call me Madeleine. Mostly when she was telling me off. My flatmate calls me Mads. Otherwise I'm just plain old Maddie.'

'Nothing plain about you, Maddie.'

'I wasn't fishing for compliments.' I bravely held eye contact with him, despite feeling myself blush.

'And what does *he* call you? Your man there?' He nodded abruptly at Shay.

'He's not my man. He's my psychology lecturer, if you must know. Not that it's any business of yours.'

'Ah, I see.' His deep voice softened, and his big hands were surprisingly gentle as they took hold of mine and squeezed.

'What do you *see*?'

'Oh, nothing in particular. Just that it's his loss. Definitely my gain.'

There was the tiniest, sexiest crinkle around his blue eyes when he grinned. For some reason, that irritated me; I didn't want to be charmed by this big, overconfident man invading my space uninvited. I pulled my hands away.

'I'm not anybody's to lose. *Or* gain. I'm not an object to be passed from one man to another. In case *you* hadn't noticed, this is a university library. You know, for borrowing books? Not, uh, girlfriends.'

I was being snippy, but mostly because I was annoyed with

myself for finding the hint of possessiveness about him perversely exciting. I'd seen my dad lay down the law for most of my parents' married life, and after his death I'd watched my mum flounder helplessly without the husband who had defined her. Bossy, controlling men held no appeal for me, and Dom struck me as exactly the kind of guy who liked to be in charge. I wasn't sure why his arrogance was giving me butterflies; it was making me uncharacteristically prickly.

'Not even on short-term loan? Shame. I'd better check out some textbooks instead, then. Nowhere near as fascinating or pretty to look at, though.' He cocked his head and quirked an eyebrow.

'You do that. Since you're so obviously here to study.' I glanced pointedly at the empty desk in front of him, then back to my own books.

'You have amazing hair, by the way.' He lifted a strand and stroked it.

I pulled back sharply. 'Did no one ever teach you to ask nicely before you touch?'

'Are you a natural redhead?' he said, ignoring my prickliness.

'Strawberry blonde, actually. Anyway, I'm thinking of getting it cut.' I twirled a long strand around my finger, telling myself that I wasn't flirting, just being friendly. Polite. Nothing more than that.

'Don't. It suits you long.'

'I'm not asking for your permission,' I said, lifting my chin. 'I go running a lot, as it happens, and it just gets in the way. And it's too thick. Makes me hot. That's all.'

'You keep in shape. I can see that. Which means we have even more in common than where we choose to hang out on a Friday night.'

My cheeks burned fiercely as his eyes wandered brazenly over my white gypsy skirt and sleeveless turquoise blouse. I wanted to hug myself to cover my pale arms that never seemed to tan, no matter how many hours my friend Gabrielle and I propped ourselves on the tiny balcony of our rented first-floor flat in Kew, bodies angled to catch every last ray of sun, yearning for our fair skin to turn golden brown. Her long, skinny legs had at least been toasted a more toffee-coloured shade of pale, but all I'd achieved after spending almost my entire summer break sunbathing while pretending to revise was a freckled nose and sore, pink knees. At least running kept me reasonably trim, I thought, pulling self-consciously at the hem of my skirt as I saw Dom check out my legs.

'Don't you have something useful you need to be doing? Maybe a few sit-ups, checking your abs in the mirror ...' I huffed and rolled my eyes.

'Well, there is this thesis on the economic aftermath of globalisation I need to finish. I *guess* I could be getting on with that.' He sat back, relishing my reaction.

'Oh.'

'Let me guess. You thought I was a trainee PE teacher, right?'

'No, I just thought ... I wasn't expecting ...' I trawled my brain for excuses but my mind emptied.

'Currently working on my MBA to top up my first in Business Studies. First rule of dating Dominic Castle? Expect the unexpected.'

I couldn't believe he'd just said that; I should have laughed in his face. But I didn't. I was young; I was impressionable. I swallowed every word.

'Er, who said anything about *dating*?' I was so flustered that it was impossible to hide it.

'This *is* our first date, right? I'm pretty good at reading people. Especially curvy strawberry blondes with huge blue eyes and cute freckled noses. I don't generally misread the signs.'

'Curvy!' I glared at him. 'And I'm not *giving* you any signs.'

'Oh, but you are, Maddie. Your body is sending out all kinds

17

of exciting signals. Your brain just hasn't caught up with them yet. But it will.' He leaned towards me and my mind spiralled off into a fantasy of him scooping me up off my chair in those strong arms of his, throwing me over his shoulder and carrying me off into the sunset.

Shay walked past us on his way out; I didn't even look up.

THREE

After that first meeting in the library, Dom and I spent almost every waking hour – and most of our sleeping ones, too – together in the very tiny attic room of the elegant four-storey Georgian house on Richmond Hill where he lodged, having charmed the landlord into giving a discount on his usual rent. We happily squandered time lying on his narrow single bed, talking late into the nights, his textbooks piled neatly on one bedside table, candles and wine on the other. He was the first person I'd ever met who, like me, had lost both his parents. I didn't generally talk much about it, but it was easy to open up to Dom. He knew exactly what I meant when I described my life as walking a tightrope without the safety net of parents to catch me if I fell. He was the first man who'd really listened to me, and the feeling was intoxicating.

Even though Dom was only a year older than me, he seemed a lot more grown up, and that was as seductive as his powerful body and the intense blue eyes that never left my face as I talked. About how I'd started running when my flatmate challenged me to take part in a half-marathon; about how studying child psychology had made me want to become a teacher; about how my parents being so aloof and career-obsessed had made me long to have a happier family of my own one day. I'd expected him to run a half-marathon of his own – in the opposite direction from me – when he heard that. To begin with I'd had him down as a serial flirt who would break out in hives at any mention of the word 'commitment'; the wistful way he too spoke about wanting a family surprised me, until he opened up about his own upbringing.

'My only real regret is that my mum and dad never got to see me graduate. Cancer has the worst sense of timing. They died before they got to see me make something of myself. Not many kids off our old estate go to uni. A lot don't even finish school. My brother certainly didn't.'

'I'm sure your parents were incredibly proud of you, all the same.'

'It's not about pride. It's about *vindication*.'

'Sorry?' His choice of word surprised me; it was a cocktail of passion and fury.

'I always told them I'd do it, but they had Max down as the clever one. He is too, I don't deny that. First-class brain. Academic stuff came easy to him; he just never bothered. Spent most of his time at school telling teachers they were idiots, then walked out at fifteen and lied about his age to get a job labouring on London Underground.'

'Sounds like he wasted his potential. What a shame.'

'You think? Actually, it made Mum and Dad's day. A son with a real job, bringing home an actual pay cheque, not dossing around as a student.'

'No one gets a first dossing around,' I said, indignant on his behalf. 'I always wanted a brother or a sister. Maybe I had a lucky escape after all. No sibling rivalry to contend with. They really should give parents a textbook in the maternity ward. With "Treating Your Children Equally" as chapter one.' I rolled my eyes.

'Can't always blame the parents. Max was determined to rule the roost from the day I was born. It probably wasn't his fault, either, to be fair. I came along ten years after him, so I guess the three of them had already formed their little club. I just didn't fit in to it. The baby of the family who didn't want to end up working on the trains like his dad. My brother isn't a bad man. Just … lacking in self-awareness, shall we say. He's rubbed plenty of people up the wrong way, not just me. I've tried to stick up for him. Got the battle scars to prove it.'

'Scars?' I said faintly, hoping he never invited me to visit his old estate. 'So when do I get to meet this intriguingly complex big brother of yours?' I snuck my fingers between the buttons of Dom's shirt, enjoying the soft tickle of his chest hair.

'We don't see much of each other these days,' he said, suddenly sitting upright and hunching over.

'Why not? He still lives round here, doesn't he?'

'Yep. Took over our parents' council house tenancy after they died.'

'Ah. That must be a bit weird for you.' I could see the tension locking his jaw and turning his body rigid.

'I guess. He hogged pretty much all their attention the whole of his life, then he gets their home as well. *Our* home, I should say. I wasn't exactly a cuckoo in the nest. But I know when I'm not wanted. Still, Dad left his savings to me. That's something. Max just gets on with his life now, and I get on with mine. And that's the way I like it.'

'Well, whatever your parents thought, *I'm* incredibly proud of you. It's *amazing* what you've achieved. My father was a judge; my mum was a lawyer. I had my own pony. And trust fund. But still I'm only just scraping through my degree. I wonder how many guys applying for jobs in the City had as tough a start in life as you did.'

'Yeah, I bet most of them have more in common with *you*. Not too late to find yourself a nice posh Surrey boy, you know.' He finally relaxed and lay back on the bed, wrapping his big arms around me and pulling me close, confident of my response. But beneath his teasing I could hear the sting of sensitivity about our different backgrounds.

'As if.'

He grinned in reply, slipping a finger through a gap at the front of the 1940s-style tea dress I'd bought especially for our first *properly official date*, and tickled my ribs until I squirmed and laughed, then he worked his way downwards, flicking open more of the tiny pearl buttons, his big hands surprisingly nimble.

'Ah, there's the Dom I know and—' I stopped and bit my lip.

'You were saying?'

His fingers stilled and he pulled me on top of him so that I was lying full-length along his much taller body. I rested my cheek against his chest, listening to his steady heartbeat as I waited for my blush to subside. Despite how intimate we were becoming I'd never told him I loved him. I hadn't been close to my father, right up until he died of a heart attack when I was sixteen, and over the following two years my mother became increasingly distant, preoccupied by her own grief until she just seemed to give up on life. They were socially well-connected but emotionally distant people, and I'd grown up feeling shy about outward displays of affection. I was glad Dom's relaxed, unselfconscious passion compensated for my natural reserve.

I pressed closer against him, hoping he'd be able to read my mind as well as my body. 'You know. Do I have to spell it out?'

'Maybe you can mime it for me. That might be fun.' He winked and kissed the tip of my nose as I smiled up at him. 'And I'm proud of you, too, honey. You're going to be a fabulous teacher. Just as long as you don't go running off with some smarmy PE hunk.'

'Only if he's tall, dark and handsome and turns out to be studying for an MBA.'

Dom grinned. 'I might know someone who can satisfy your requirements.'

As it turned out, both Dom's MBA and my teacher training had to be put on hold. I finally managed to graduate, even though Shay never returned to the psychology department to coach the stragglers through our resits, instead moving to Brighton to become a dinner-theatre performer; I guess he'd never really given up on his real vocation in life.

Nine months later, I discovered mine: I became a mother.

Dom always swore that finding out I was pregnant with the twins was the happiest day of his life. It didn't matter that we'd only been dating a few weeks; he'd fallen in love that very first night in the library, he said, and all he wanted to do was take care of me and make our shared dreams of a happy family home come true. Twelve weeks after we met, Dom borrowed a suit from his ever-obliging, clearly besotted landlord, scrounged every spare penny he could and booked dinner for the two of us at the Oxo Tower restaurant. With the exquisite, almost surreally beautiful London skyline as a backdrop, he proposed to me with his mother's old engagement ring.

'*This* is the life I want to give you and our babies,' he said, his arms spread wide, encompassing our plush surroundings, and I looked around at the white-clothed tables, chrome champagne buckets and well-dressed diners before gazing wistfully out at St Paul's Cathedral, lit up so majestically against the indigo night sky. It was a different world to Dom's little bedsit.

'It's beautiful. But very expensive,' I cautioned.

'Who cares? It's only money.'

'Easy to say when you've got plenty. Which we haven't,' I pointed out.

'It doesn't matter if I have to work twenty-four hours a day, seven days a week, I'm going to give you the best of everything, babe. No more shared flats and poky attics for us. And *definitely* no more charity-shop dresses for you.'

'I like my dresses,' I protested, laughing. Dom favoured crisp preppy smartness whereas I adored a kookier vintage look. 'But what about your MBA? There's no way you can do a full-time job and still study so hard. I'll pick up my teacher training as soon as the babies are settled, but till then—'

'Where there's a will there's a way. And you're looking at a man with a plan. One more meeting with the bank manager next week and Castle Consultancy will be born. Before our babies.' He grinned.

'Consultancy?'

'Yep. It's always been my ultimate goal. Had my business plan ready for ages. It just means setting the ball rolling sooner rather than later, which is no problem. Far less painful than putting myself through the City recruitment grinder. I'm going to set up on my own. Be my own boss. More lucrative in the long run, too.'

'You make it sound so easy . . .'

'It is. No need for you to worry about a thing other than taking care of *this*,' he said, his big hand gently spanning the bump pushing against my sleeveless black chiffon shift dress, the one I'd splashed out on for my graduation ceremony, little knowing that its generous A-line style would come in handy for a rapidly expanding waistline. I couldn't believe how fast my body was changing.

'But I *do* worry. And I have no intention of being a kept woman.' I attempted a smile, not wanting us to squabble, especially in such exquisite surroundings. Especially when Dom had just asked me to marry him.

'You want to be at home for the kids, don't you? Isn't that what you've always dreamed of – a proper family?'

'Yes. Yes, it is,' I conceded, remembering all the times I had let myself in to an empty house after school, the walls echoing with loneliness. I wanted to be there for my children; I just didn't want Dom to insist on it.

'Well, then. That settles it. So what's your answer? Will you be my wife, Maddie?' He sat back in his chair, beckoning the waiter for more champagne, never doubting my response.

It was all happening so fast. I was still reeling in shock from the pregnancy test Gabrielle had bought for me the third time I'd thrown up my breakfast. Locked inside a toilet cubicle upstairs in Kingston's Bentall Centre, I'd thrown up once more for good measure. Gabrielle had come to meet me afterwards, her willowy height and cropped black hair cutting a distinctive figure as she swung jauntily through the crowds of shoppers, arms full of shopping bags overflowing with baby clothes, nappies and cuddly toys: she'd never been in any doubt that the test would be positive. As I'd wept on her shoulder, hormones and mixed emotions ran riot through me. I was desperately sad that Gabrielle was about to return to Paris, having completed the placement year of her languages degree, and I was a bag of nerves at the prospect of telling Dom I'd fallen pregnant. His reaction, and his proposal, had astonished, thrilled and ever so slightly terrified me.

'Yes. Yes, I will.' I had butterflies at the thought of the babies growing inside me. They were all I cared about now, all I wanted; *Dom* was all I wanted. 'But the teaching is just on hold, mind. Soon as the babies are old enough, I'll go back to it.'

'One step at a time. Let's see, hey? You're the most beautiful woman I've ever met, Maddie, and I'll never, ever let you go. I just want you at home,' he said, reaching across the table to squeeze my shaking fingers, pressing down on the sapphire ring that still felt odd on my left hand.

'Barefoot and pregnant, you mean,' I teased.

'I can't think of anything sexier.'

FOUR

The sound of a long, slow sigh draws me out of my memories, but when I look up, Aidan is still curled up on the sofa while Dom remains hunched over his laptop, his head in his hands. It's like he's drifted off into his thoughts, too, and I wonder if he ever thinks of those early days. I remember them as clearly as if they were last week. I remember his proposal, and I remember giving birth to the twins, their first steps, *their last words* – I remember every second of those things, but not a single moment of other life-changing events.

I don't remember my wedding night or honeymoon. I don't remember who the police said came to the door on the morning of the twins' birthday, their face hidden beneath the black balaclava . . . And I have absolutely no idea why he asked me to choose between my children. All I know is that he's stolen my daughter's life and destroyed my family, and that I can't forgive myself for letting him. Beyond that nothing seems to matter. My guilt, my heartache: nothing can make either worse – or better.

Perhaps if I force myself to confront the details, maybe then

I'll be able to work out how to start living again and look forward rather than eternally backwards. I glance at Dom and my heart pounds as I steel myself to ask him everything I've forgotten. I have to try, I have to stop burying my head in the sand, but even as I move towards him, I feel my mouth dry and the words lodge deep in my throat. I try to force them out and my eyes begin to water, panic crushing my chest.

Before I can pull myself together, I hear a metallic buzzing noise, a long, shrill command, and it takes me a second to realise that someone must be at the front door. I spin around, wondering if I should go to answer it, and when I turn back to where Aidan and Dom were sitting moments before, they are gone.

Minutes, hours later – I have no idea how much time has passed – I find myself sitting on the stairs, taking deep breaths and trying to calm my thumping heart and racing mind. I need to focus, to gather my skittering thoughts.

Aidan and Dom were right next to me, and now they're gone. *Where* have they gone – to the pool, the park? Why didn't they say goodbye? And didn't I just hear someone at the door? But no finger pushes the buzzer a second time. No distorted silhouette darkens our hallway; there is only the hint of figures passing by on the street as they go about their daily business. Daylight pours uninterrupted through the frosted-glass of our front door, flitting in a dappled dance over the parquet floor.

Shouldn't it be getting dark soon?

I keep losing track of time, of life around me, and it dawns on me that I may be having blackouts. Or perhaps it's nothing physical, nothing so dramatic as fainting fits or losing consciousness. Maybe I'm just so buried in thought these days that I've been sucked too deeply inside my inner world. I'm not sure whether this is another side effect of post-traumatic stress, or whether I'm deliberately floating in this muffled state of vagueness because it's far, far less painful than confronting reality. Only it's proving confusing. Great chunks of time constantly seem to go astray, not to mention my son and husband.

Then I hear the sound of Aidan's recorder, the clear high notes scaling upwards until the tune ends with a hasty grating squeak, and moments later Aidan drifts past me on his way back into the living room. *My darling boy.* He always loved it when I called him that, his nose crinkling as he smiled shyly; Annabel used to laugh and punch my arm: *Don't be soft, Mum!* She never waited for goodbye kisses at the school gate; Aidan wouldn't leave me without a last cuddle. At least I got to spend those moments with the twins – chats on the walk to school, hot chocolate and toast afterwards as we sat at the kitchen table, comparing our days . . .

I've never regretted my decision to stay at home with the twins. A teaching salary would have been helpful, especially at first, and sometimes I regret not using the degree I struggled to pass. But while I may not be teaching a class of children, I've found incredible fulfilment helping the twins learn, develop, grow into such clever little people. Maybe at some point in the future I would have gone back to teacher training. Maybe once, but not now. Now I can't bear the thought of ever leaving Aidan again.

Every time I look at my son now, it feels like I'm seeing him for the first time after a long absence. Like I've just stepped off a train after a trip and I'm racing up the platform towards him, tears in my eyes and my heart pounding with excitement and eagerness to hold him. It's like a continual sense of joyful reunion – only it's one-sided, because he still refuses to acknowledge me. He looks so pale. He's barely left the house this summer. He needs some sun on his skin and fresh air in his lungs; he needs to run and play, to see his friends and get up to all the mischief that ten-year-old boys love. Only Annabel was the mischievous one. She made endless

29

dens in Bushy Park, little hidey-holes and secret lairs. I'm not sure if Aidan has even been back to the park without her; he doesn't tell me anything these days.

And every time I open my mouth to ask, the pain in his eyes silences me and I retreat into my shattered inner world, a heavy weight of guilt pressing down on my chest, paralysing me. So I stay hidden in the shadows, a guilty bystander, listening, longing.

'Dad, you said you'd take me to Bushy Park.'

My heart jumps; it's like Aidan has read my mind.

'It'll be dark soon,' he continues after a long pause.

Aidan's unusually abrupt tone sharpens my attention, and I trail after him. He never used to be snappy; he was always so laid-back when Annabel was around. I want to cry as I see how hard he's trying to act tough; I can see in his eyes that he's torn, not sure whether it's appropriate to go and play football in the park while his sister lies dead in the ground.

I yearn to reach out to him but he's angled his body away from me. His legs are crossed; one trainer scuffs the other; hands are deep in his jeans pockets. I try to speak but still no words will come, and Aidan keeps his sad eyes focused on Dom, avoiding me. I try not to let Aidan see that it hurts when he ignores me, that he doesn't even bother to suggest that *I* take him out to play. He knows I've become frightened of the outside world, yet his acceptance of that somehow hurts more than if he were to yell at me, openly blame me. He's not letting me off the hook; he's allowing me to sink under the weight of my own guilt. He's angry with me, and he has good reason to be. I let his sister die.

'Sure. Just let me finish this email then we'll shoot.'

I see Aidan's face tighten fractionally at the ill-chosen words, the casual reference to a weapon that blew his sister halfway across our back garden. But then he shrugs. 'I'll get my boots. They're in the shed, aren't they?'

Aidan's expression is uncertain. He's not sure his dad has a clue where football boots and scooters and bikes are kept, but he doesn't want to upset him by drawing attention to the fact. He doesn't want to point out that it's Mum who puts these things away; he doesn't want to have to ask me – to *need* me – and he's showing his dad that he doesn't.

I still understand my son.

I allow the realisation to soak through me, reminding myself that Aidan is still my child, and although we are both lost in grief and don't know how to talk to each other, we are still *connected*. He is still part of me, and no matter how hard he's trying to cut me off, I'm still part of him. I know how he sleeps on his tummy with his right hand hooked under his chin, his right leg tucked up as if he's climbing a ladder; I know that he prefers white chocolate to dark; I know that he's scared, and missing the closeness we used to have, and that he thinks if he shows any of this it will be disloyal to his dad.

Guilty relief takes my breath away: I don't deserve this comfort but I cling on to it. Aidan might try to erase me from his life, but I'm still *here*. I'm still his mum. No one can take that away from me.

Can they?

I glance fearfully towards the hallway, the front door, then I turn my back on the terrifying unknown of the outside world and watch Dom lock his briefcase and set it down on the coffee table. He looks up at Aidan with a broad smile, his thin mouth bracketed by creases I don't remember seeing before under each sharp cheekbone. I wonder again if he's lost weight; I try to put my finger on what's changed. His hair is as thick and spiky as ever, neatly trimmed and still richly dark brown. Visibly, he hasn't aged; he just seems . . . different.

'Tell you what. Let's head over to Kingston and I'll buy you those football boots,' Dom says, slapping his knees before standing up and resting his hands on Aidan's shoulders.

'They cost over a hundred pounds. Mum says designer boots are an extravaganza,' Aidan says dutifully, but his legs uncross and one foot begins to tap against the floor in an excited jitter.

'An extravagance. And they're not. Only the best for my boy. So stop worrying, you sound like your mum.' He grins and pulls Aidan roughly against him.

A memory stirs, but I can't place it. Instead, I think with sudden irritation: That's right, talk about me as if I'm not here.

'Mum worries a lot.'

'That's what mums are for, son. But we still know how to have fun, hey?'

Suddenly Aidan grins, sunshine breaking through the clouds, and I want to kiss his sad face that, just for a moment, has remembered how to look happy. I want to hug him and tell him that he's right, I do worry too much, but it's just because I care – because I don't want things to get worse, so much worse . . .

I puzzle over what that means: another memory just beyond reach. I have a sudden sense that I don't want things to go back entirely to the way they used to be – but how *did* they used to be?

I look around the living room in search of clues to help me decipher the mysterious gulf between *Life Before* and *Life After* Annabel. I see the brown leather Chesterfield that dips more on the left side than the right, because that's where Annabel and Aidan always curled up together so they could stare in unison at the same book or comic, hands dipping in synchronised rhythm into a shared bowl of snacks. I see the upright piano and ornate walnut grandfather clock Dom bought at an antique fair, both incongruously grand in our modest 1930s semi.

I grew up in a sprawling detached Edwardian house full of

austere antique furniture and would have preferred a homelier, more cottagey look, but Dom was always trying to turn our house into a downsized version of an English stately home. We've never managed to find a compromise, I reflect, and the house has become a hotchpotch of mismatched styles. And as my eyes linger on each familiar object, my thoughts turn inwards once more and I remember the day we moved in – our first night as Mr and Mrs Castle.

FIVE

I remember Dom clowning around as he carried me over the threshold, pretending to stumble beneath my weight.

'Put me down!' I giggled.

'All right, if you insist. You're getting chubby, Mrs Castle.' His grin was infectious; I never tired of seeing it.

'Idiot! I'm pregnant, not fat.' All the same, I glanced down at the smock top straining over my belly. I'd long since had to give up going for a run in the evenings, and my natural curves were growing more generous than usual. At five foot seven I wasn't exactly short; lately, though, I'd begun to feel almost as wide as I was tall.

'And you ate *how* many slices of wedding cake this morning?' Dom set me down on the kitchen floor like a sack of potatoes.

'Not as many as your brother, that's for sure.'

'Huh. You noticed. He also drank most of the float I put behind the bar. Good job we went for a pub reception, not the Petersham Hotel. It's always been the same with Max. My moment in the spotlight – he's got to jump in and steal it with a rambling speech full of ludicrously long jokes without a punchline in sight. My wedding cake – he'll scoff the lion's share.'

'He seemed sweet to me. Bit random, but then being best man is probably terrifying. I didn't think his speech was that bad, actually. I heard a few laughs.'

'They were laughing *at* him. Not with him,' Dom pointed out.

'Surely not? I'll have to have words. It's not easy standing up in front of a bar full of people. He probably got stage fright.'

'Don't be fooled. Max isn't frightened of anything. And he wouldn't have noticed anyway. He's oblivious to other people's feelings. Too wrapped up in himself.'

'Really? And I was just thinking how uncannily alike you and your brother are.'

'Max and I are *nothing* like each other,' he said, moving away from me to lean against the worktop, long legs crossed in front of him, arms folded rigidly across his chest.

'Well, you both looked very handsome next to each other,' I said quickly, realising I'd touched a nerve. 'The registrar definitely noticed.'

'So *that's* why you were glaring at her. I did wonder. Thought you were getting cold feet for a second.' A grin broke out across his handsome face.

I sighed in relief. It was less than twelve hours since our small, simple wedding ceremony at Richmond Register Office; I didn't want to provoke our first row before the ink was even dry on our marriage certificate.

'Think I'd struggle to be a runaway bride at this size. I can't quite see myself doing a Julia Roberts and leaping on to a horse. Sadly, my pony-riding days are well and truly over. For now, at least,' I said, fondly remembering the hours I'd spent riding as a child.

I'd hacked through Richmond Park a couple of times during uni holidays, too, and I wondered if children's riding lessons were ridiculously expensive. Those kinds of luxuries couldn't be a priority now; my jaw had dropped at the price of the double buggy, and needing two of everything really bumped up costs. It was a good job I still had some money left in my trust fund; a huge chunk of what I'd inherited from my parents had gone on university tuition fees and student accommodation. Education mattered a lot to me, though; I valued the choices it gave me and I wanted to pass that on to the twins when they were older. I'd checked out the local schools before we settled on the house, and I was really happy with the local state primary down the road.

'You were a stunning bride, and I'm the luckiest man in London. England. The world.' He laughed, pulling me into a slow dance around the kitchen.

'Me too. Woman, I mean,' I half whispered, half laughed, tucking in close, allowing myself to be swept along. 'And you're right. The house is perfect. The garden too,' I said, peering out of the kitchen window as he finally released me. 'Hampton's lovely, really pretty and quiet, and I'm going to check out that teacher training college in Strawberry Hill next week.'

'Hmm. You might change your mind once the babies are born. Once I've signed my first client. There's no rush for you to work. Just put your feet up, enjoy being a lady of leisure for a while.' He pulled out a chair at the kitchen table and, with a dramatic flourish of one arm, invited me to sit.

'Are you *kidding*? I'm not sure looking after two babies is going to be a walk in the park. You did listen *some* of the time in those antenatal classes, didn't you?' I teased, trying to get comfortable on the wooden chair; my back was aching after all the standing around chatting and celebrating with my friends. Max had actually been the only guest Dom had invited.

'Of course I did!' Dom mimed a massive yawn and laughed. 'I can't believe there are only five months to go.'

'Um, I hate to break it to you but I think it's nearer four,' I said, although the midwife had seemed puzzled by the dates of my cycle when I'd had my booking-in appointment. I was never very good at keeping track of those sorts of things. The bump felt enormous already, though, and was pressing down heavier with each passing day.

'We'd better make the most of being newlyweds, then, hey? Let's go and check out the upstairs,' he murmured, bending over to nuzzle against the nape of my neck, cupping his hands suggestively around my hips. 'But first ...' He opened the fridge and pulled out a bottle of champagne, two glasses and a punnet of luscious-looking strawberries. 'Here's one I prepared earlier,' he said with a slow smile, deftly popping the cork and pouring the sparkling wine without spilling a drop. 'I nipped round yesterday,' he explained when I gasped in happy surprise. 'Go on, half a glass won't hurt. Here's to us.'

'To us. And our new family,' I added, clinking my glass to his.

For all he joked about nodding off in the antenatal classes, I knew Dom would make a great dad. He was working every hour there was to make a go of his management consultancy, and when the time was right I was confident he'd support me getting back into teacher training. Everything was perfect, and we were going to be the perfect family.

Perfect but small.

The birth was difficult and there were 'complications', the doctor said, offering me a tight smile. There would be no more babies.

'Your twins are perfect, though, Mrs Castle. Congratulations.'

'Look, Mads, this one's eyes are open.' Dom's deep voice squeaked boyishly.

He actually held the twins before I did. They were so tiny, so fragile, that I could hardly bear to leave them. Dom was the only person I would trust to take care of them, and he held them both for two whole hours, hardly moving, hardly breathing, just sitting alone with the miracle of new life in the darkened delivery room while the doctor wheeled me off to see the surgeon, to be put back together and stitched up.

'That's your daughter, Mr Castle. Gorgeous, isn't she?' The pretty young midwife smiled as she watched Dom proudly, wonderingly, stroke his brand-new baby girl's velvety forehead.

'Happy birthday, darling Annabel,' he said, touching the tip of his nose to her tiny one. Her sleepy blue eyes opened a fraction, capturing all our hearts before she closed them again.

I tried to lift my head to peer at my son, my second-born, feeling anxious about him being forgotten, overlooked in favour of his bewitchingly beautiful sister who came out first, cried first (*died first*) and drew all eyes to her from her very first breath. I vowed there and then that there would be no favouritism between them. They were twins but each was unique; I wouldn't expect them to be carbon copies of each other. I would encourage their differences, and I'd love them equally. Tearfully I made this promise to them both as I was trundled out of the room like a piece of meat on a butcher's trolley, straining for one last glimpse of my little family – so new but already so precious.

I would have no more children, so, brimming over with a need to nurture, I took up gardening. I planted the roses that autumn, and as the years passed I filled the garden with flowers, wind chimes and cute wildlife statues to amuse the twins and create a peaceful sanctuary. I called it my tranquillity garden, and Annabel and Aidan bought me a chubby bronze Buddha one year for Mother's Day. It was one of my greatest treasures: a gift of peace from my children. But the roses struggled, only blooming properly for the first time this year.

Just in time to hide Annabel beneath their flouncy skirts.

I look out of the French windows now, watching the breeze catch the delicate white petals, making them shimmy in a silent dance.

Keep her safe for me, until I can see her again.

Something shifts in the back of my mind, nudging at my awareness, another memory just out of reach. I stretch to grasp it but it slips away from me. I look up and realise I'm alone again in the living room. What time is it? I glance at the grandfather clock and notice it isn't ticking, the hands frozen and the pendulums hanging like paralysed limbs. I'm surprised Dom hasn't noticed; that clock is second only to his golf clubs in his ranking of precious objects. I look towards the bay window and see that the heavy green velvet drapes are closed. Is it dark already?

What time is it? I wonder again, panicking now. Dom was taking Aidan to the park, wasn't he? Or were they going shopping, heading into Kingston? Or was that yesterday? I feel dizzy. My head is muzzy and I can't think straight, can't even see clearly. Suddenly I can smell roses and it reminds me that Annabel must feel cold, so cold. I must ask Aidan if he's done his homework yet – but where is he? And how can I ask him anything when he won't even look at me, when every time I look at him the words die in my throat?

I'm numb, mentally and physically, lost in the middle of a frozen wasteland. And with every day that passes, Dom and Aidan drift further away from me and I feel more alone – barely a wife and only half a mum.

SIX

'Hi there, you. Hug?'

I'm on the landing upstairs waiting anxiously for Aidan to come home from school, mentally counting the steps from the bus stop at the end of our street, when I hear Lucy's voice in the kitchen.

Lucy March has been my best friend since we met on the twins' first day at primary school, when Lucy's son Jasper was starting in the same reception class. We clicked immediately and since then she's become like part of our family. I missed seeing her at the school gates after we defected to the posh prep school, but Lucy continued to pop round whenever she could rope in an extra pair of hands to help out at Lucy's Place, the organic deli she owns in Teddington. In the past she used to let herself in through the back door and flick on the kettle before calling out to announce her arrival, then we'd spend a happy hour or so catching up over a cuppa while the kids did their homework together, Aidan and Annabel complaining in recent times that they had far more to do than Jasper.

I shake my head to clear my hazy thoughts as I realise I can't actually remember the last time Lucy came round. Instinctively

I know she'll have been a huge support to me lately, and I feel tearful with gratitude without knowing exactly what she's done. I just can't *remember*. Any of it. But she's here now, and I feel a smile spread across my face. I make my way downstairs only to freeze when I hear Aidan's voice in the kitchen. He must have let himself in through the back door too, I think, but how is he home so soon? Or is it later than I realised?

'Are those cookies for me? *Thanks*,' I hear Aidan say.

'No probs, hon. I put in extra chunks of white chocolate especially for you.'

'Wicked. They're awesome.'

I peep round the corner of the banister, reluctant to interrupt them; it's the most relaxed I've seen Aidan in ages. I watch as Lucy ruffles my son's hair, wishing I could trade places with her, wishing I could be more like her and bound in to my own kitchen, hug Aidan and start chatting away.

I've often wished I could be more like Lucy: strong, easy-going, effortlessly glamorous. She's raised her son Jasper all by herself, abandoning her bullying first husband in Devon and fleeing to London with Jasper soon after he was born. *Useless waste of space*, she always calls her ex, and Lucy doesn't do waste. She crams more into her days than I've ever managed in a week, running Lucy's Place and qualifying as a yoga instructor in her spare time, yet still managing to look immaculate as she turns up bang on time for the school run. She organises every fundraising cake sale, every school fair, almost single-handedly, and half the dads at the school gate are in love with her.

Lucy must really have turned heads today, I think, watching her glide between the worktop and the kitchen table. Only a teenager should look that good in skinny jeans, and her long silky hair falls like a golden curtain around her slim shoulders. Guiltily, I remember that when I first saw Lucy dash across the playground, with her long legs and perfect tan, I assumed she would be at best slightly vain and at worst a stuck-up yummy mummy. But I've never heard her utter a bad word about anyone. I've probably spent more time with her over the last few years than I have with Dom, the two of us waiting endlessly outside classrooms for the kids to be released, or hunched together on low benches in the school hall, waiting for Annabel to twirl on to the stage while Aidan and Jasper skulked towards the back row of the orchestra with their violins. So much waiting, but Lucy's relaxed chattiness always made it fun.

I realise how much I've missed our school-gate chats, and I recall how she was the only one to give me a tearful hug on the twins' last day at the primary school they loved and Dom despised. His words float back to me from a year ago.

'We can do *better* for our kids. What am I working so hard for if not to give them a step up in life? You're too complacent. Second best just isn't good enough.'

I remember the row and am niggled by a sudden sense that there were others. What did we used to argue about? Was it always about the twins' education? What else could have provoked discord in our happy life, our nice ordinary home in our nice ordinary street – the fulfilment of everything Dom and I had both dreamed of? I watch Lucy and Aidan sit together in companionable silence, and I think back to the first time I can remember feeling the cold edge of my husband's disapproval.

It all started with my walks. After the difficult birth, I wasn't able to go running for a long time, so I lost the habit and started going out walking instead, not only to burn off the baby fat but also for the sheer pleasure of seeing the twins look at the world around them and know that they were part of it.

'But where do you *go*?'

'Oh, just around. Nowhere special.'

'Such as?'

'Well, the twins love Bushy Park. There's a sandpit there, and a café—'

'So you just wander around. For hours. Every day.'

'I do other stuff as well. Clothes don't wash themselves, you know. And funnily enough this isn't a self-cleaning house. But it's good for the twins to have fresh air, and—'

'Look, I know we agreed you'd put work on hold for now, but I thought you might do something a little more productive with your time than hang out in the park all day.'

'Where do you *suggest* I hang out with two lively toddlers?'

'Perhaps you could join some kind of . . . oh, I don't know, club, or something? Baby group. Coffee mornings. Isn't that what stay-at-home mums do?'

'Perhaps you could try to be just a *little* more patronising?'

I remember my prickle of irritation; I remember thinking that Dom had no idea what it was like being at home with the babies all day. It took every ounce of my energy to look after them; there wasn't a lot left for anything more productive. *Productive*. What did that even mean? What was more productive than teaching our children to eat, walk, talk, play with other children and—

'Just being honest. You've changed, Maddie. You even look different.'

'I've become a mum. What did you expect?'

'A little adult conversation every now and then? You know, about something other than baby milestone charts and weigh-ins at the health centre. Which reminds me, I thought you were ditching those smock tops now you've stopped breastfeeding. I thought you'd been dieting,' he said bluntly.

'We don't all get to spend our evenings playing golf or going to the gym,' I said, trying to remain upbeat but pulling self-consciously at the supposedly loose-flowing tunic top that was still clinging too tightly. I caught sight of myself in the mirror over the mantelpiece, acknowledging that my heart-shaped face was rounder these days, that my new, practical shoulder-length bob needed a trim, and I couldn't remember when I'd last worn jewellery, perfume or make-up. I'd swapped my favourite dresses for leggings and hadn't worn anything on my feet other than Birkenstocks or soft Ugg boots for months.

'Sure. Well, just so you know, I took on two new clients last week. Booked us a holiday in Cornwall next month to celebrate.'

'Oh, that's *wonderful*,' I said, giving him a quick hug, overlooking his hurtful digs in my excitement. This would be our first family holiday.

'Let's hope so. I've found a hotel right opposite the beach. Five star. It'll do us good to get away. Do *you* good to get back out into the world a bit.'

I put Dom's cutting remarks down to worry about me being lonely, but I was far from it. Somehow I seemed to have lost touch with my old uni friends since getting married. Gabrielle had come over for our wedding, but she'd returned to Paris immediately afterwards, becoming immersed in her career as a translator, and Dom always raised an objection to anyone else I suggested inviting round. I got the feeling he wanted us to mix with different people now. I teased him about wanting to reinvent himself, but I was so busy adjusting to being a mum that I didn't argue too strenuously. The twins were my focus, and teaching them to be part of the world around them made me happier than I'd ever been.

'Sky. Tree. Flower. Dog. Ha, yes, woof woof,' I remember saying, laughing as Annabel sat up in the double buggy on one of our walks and did her best puppy imitation. She was always a little performer, right from her very first word lisped into the cool evening air as I wheeled the twins out for a last stroll: '*Star!*'

'Yes, darling, it's a star! Just like you.' I laughed again as she waved her hand, stretching her tiny fingers in imitation of a twinkling star.

I laughed a lot in those early days. Life was perfect; and then suddenly it wasn't.

After Dom's comments, I hesitated to mention to him that I was beginning to struggle. I called the health visitor, thinking she'd brush it off as a bout of delayed baby blues and tell me not to worry. Instead, she said that my increasingly frequent hallucinations of bad things happening were undiagnosed symptoms of postnatal depression – that the nightmarish visions of death and disaster that began to grip me every time I took the twins out were just nature's way of helping me to rehearse what might go wrong, to prepare for potential dangers around me: a bus driver that might plough into the buggy, not seeing us crossing the road; a passing stranger who might steal the twins if I turned my head for just a split second. All I knew was that every time I looked at my children, I started to feel terror instead of love. For a time, the outside world became a place to be feared.

I remember that dark place; I feel like I've gone back there now.

Baby steps. That's what the health visitor taught me. 'You're very young, you got married in a whirlwind, it's all happened so fast – give yourself time! Just walk to the end of the road, to the post box at the end of the street. Then, tomorrow, go a little further. Maybe visit a friend for a coffee, buy a newspaper and sit in the park, let the twins enjoy the sunshine.'

Obediently, I complied. Without telling Dom. Or was it that he didn't ask? He was so busy preparing endless business plans for expanding his consultancy, and stalking round the house when he got a phone call saying his latest client pitch hadn't been successful. He was preoccupied dealing with his problems, and I just dealt with mine. I didn't want to see that look of disappointment on his face again, the one that said: *I married a strong, happy woman, and now you've turned into a frumpy, frightened mess.*

Then, one day, weeks later, I wasn't frightened any more. The worst thing imaginable had happened on that first family holiday in Cornwall. Annabel and Aidan, fascinated by their first experience of the sea, toddled away from our picnic blanket and within seconds fell face down in the waves rippling on to the shoreline. The twins were only small, but they were *fast*. I saw them jump up; I reached out, too late to grab them. I couldn't prevent their excited headlong charge into the foamy white froth that beckoned irresistibly; my frantically grasping hands weren't quick enough to stop their tiny bodies being swallowed by the cold water that tossed them around and filled their lungs, turning their skin a mottled blue in seconds.

Dom had barely put his mobile phone down for the entire week, but for the first time in days I was glad of it, because the ambulance arrived within minutes of us scooping up the twins and working desperately to massage life back into them. They had almost drowned, but they'd survived. *I'd* survived. I'd stared tragedy in the face and defeated it. My hallucinations stopped overnight. It was as if, having been a whisker away from real-life tragedy, my fears evaporated. Having survived my worst nightmare, I'd banished it. I pulled myself together, enrolled the twins in swimming lessons, and vowed I'd never let them go beyond my reach again. And with each swimming trophy they won, each increasingly confident step they took, I relaxed and trusted that lightning wouldn't strike twice.

But falling face down in the sea is one thing; a masked killer shooting my ten-year-old daughter is a lightning strike, thunderbolts and earthquake all rolled into one. Nothing can make that go away. Somehow, I have to live with it – Dom and Aidan have to live with it. And they need me. They *need me.* The reminder pricks my conscience: I must try harder. Yes, I really should try to leave the house. Do the school run once in a while. Walk in the park. Maybe that would help. The park – the twins always loved it . . . Sitting on the swings, flying down the slide . . .

For a moment, I feel stronger, almost up for the challenge, and then I look at Aidan's slight body and shadowed eyes as he sits silently next to Lucy, building his Lego model at the kitchen table, and I feel fear crushing me once more. I don't want to go out, and I don't want anyone to come in. I don't want visitors, not even Lucy. I just want my children back: the one who stared into my eyes as she died, and the one who lived but refuses to look into my eyes ever again.

SEVEN

I'm not sure how many minutes pass as I remain in my hiding place on the stairs, listening to Lucy chat about Jasper joining Annabel's drama club and the school disco in a few weeks' time. I watch as Aidan, tongue poking out of his mouth in concentration, wiggles some kind of bright-red detonator device on to the base of his astonishingly elaborate construction. I have no idea where he gets his dexterity from. Technology and gadgets are beyond me, even plain old Meccano. Christmas mornings have always seen a queue behind Dom's armchair, waiting for his help to insert batteries, decipher instructions and 'please enter your password to add a new device to the network'.

At least, that's how Christmases used to be. Aidan looks up and I feel a surge of pride in my son, banishing the thought that Christmas will never be the same again. He's such a clever boy. Annabel always came top in every test, but Aidan has the deft fingers and logical mind of an engineer. 'He'll reinvent the world, one day,' Dom loved to say. 'Yes, and Annabel will mess it all up and paint it a different colour,' I'd always reply.

My ears prick up as I hear Lucy say how unhappy Jasper was on the first day back at school, starting yet another new term without the twins, and I wonder what other parents are saying about me. I'm sure most of them thought it was *my* decision to send the twins private. I saw the hastily averted glances at the school gate; no doubt they thought I was being a snob. I would have felt disloyal saying that changing schools had all been Dom's idea, just as I'd felt awkward about explaining that shyness, not snobbery, kept me from joining in their cake sales and coffee mornings. Lucy sailed through that world; I was happier in my own little bubble.

Aidan and I have always had our shyness in common. Annabel had my laugh, my blue eyes, my snub nose and pointy chin; but her irrepressible confidence, incandescent prettiness and desire to throw herself at life were all her own. I remember how Aidan and I both watched in awestruck admiration as Annabel would swing across the playground through a chorus line of eager high-fives. She was Daddy's princess and Mummy's angel, and she never doubted for a second that her princess status at home was viable currency in the outside world.

Did I envy her? I'm gripped by a sudden dreadful thought. Does that explain my choice – that I was secretly jealous of my daughter? Annabel was so confident of her place in life. She never waited to be invited; she simply joined in, took over, with Aidan in tow. She was always picked first for teams, but she would never leave her brother behind. Except for that one time. How bitterly ironic that being *unchosen* saved Aidan's life, in the end . . .

Perhaps that's how other parents are judging me – as a heartless, jealous mum. I wonder if Lucy finds the playground an awkward place now. Guilt by association; tragedy might be contagious. *Don't speak to any friend of* that woman *in case a killer comes knocking on your door, too! She handed her daughter over without a second thought. What kind of mother does that?* They will be whispering about me in corners, but they couldn't possibly judge me more harshly than I do myself.

Lucy hates any kind of clique or bitchiness, though, and I reassure myself that she'll either zone out the gossip or gently chide the scandalmongers so charmingly that they won't be offended by her disapproval. She never gets mad; she always looks on the bright side of life, and her positivity is one of the things I love about her; she's sunshine on a cloudy day.

'That yellow blouse is dazzling, Luce. You're like a bowlful of sunshine.'

The coincidence of the compliment jolts me and my heart starts hammering as, for a second, I don't recognise the voice, having assumed Dom wouldn't be back from work for ages yet. He rents an office in Teddington, just round the corner from Lucy's deli, and although it's mainly for admin – as he spends most of his time either out meeting prospective clients or working in-house with teams already under contract – it dawns on me that he's been spending more and more time at the office lately.

I peep round the corner to watch as he cups Lucy's face with his big hands, planting a kiss on each of her smooth cheeks.

'Good job you've got your shades on, then.' I can hear the smile in Lucy's voice as she stands on tiptoe to receive his greeting. She's taller than I am but Dom still towers over her. 'Why *are* you wearing Ray-Bans inside, incidentally? Just out of interest.'

She's always teased Dom for his fashion obsession, and he always takes it in good part. I smile at the familiar repartee.

'Because they make me look cool. What else?' he says, not embarrassed in the slightest at sounding vain. He swipes one of her home-baked cookies out of Aidan's hand. 'These are amazing.'

'Thanks.' She checks her watch. 'Which reminds me. I've got a delivery from the wholesaler coming, and I've still got to pick Jasp up from drama club. Will you be around later?'

'Should be. Why?' He takes off his sunglasses and stares intently at her.

'I just wanted to pick your brains about something. I've been toying with diversifying the deli. Thought you might have some bright ideas to help me out.'

'Always happy to help a good friend. You know that.' He smiles at her, and she smiles back.

'It's been a crappy year, to be honest. Interest rates, losing a couple of my best suppliers. The bank was all over me when I first set up. Not quite so helpful now.'

'I know what you mean. I lost one of my biggest clients last week. Poached by a consultancy just down the road, would you believe?'

'Sadly, I would.' They are in full flow now. 'A new café opened up three doors down from me and they've already poached my Saturday girl. She only started two weeks ago. The cheek of it! And my skinflint landlord has just put up the rent on my flat. I need to find a bigger place anyway, but it looks like Jasper and I will be out on our ears if I don't get a move on. Sorry, I didn't mean to cry on your shoulder. You have far bigger things to worry about.'

'Don't be daft. You're welcome to cry on my shoulder any time.'

Slowly, I poke my head around the banister again and see Aidan with his head bowed, eyes fixed on his Lego model, nimble fingers twiddling bricks. Dom and Lucy stand either side of him, and I watch as Lucy scoops the last cookie out of her tin and pops it on to the plate. She brushes crumbs from her hands and licks honey from the tip of her left thumb. Dom watches her.

'These are your mum's favourites, too,' Lucy says to Aidan, and I wonder if she's deliberately mentioning me.

'Mum doesn't like honey.'

I want to weep at the affirmation that I'm still in Aidan's thoughts. I know this is my cue to show myself, to stroll into the kitchen and pop the kettle on again for a fresh brew, to sit down at the table and chat with them all. But that's just it: I can't chat. I can't *speak*. I can't bear to look at Lucy's face and feel her sympathy but also her confusion: *Why did I do what I did?* I'm scared because I can't answer her questions, and I'm on edge because I never used to feel worried about the easy friendship between Dom and Lucy. But for some reason I am now. Very worried.

So I stay where I am: hidden, watching. Listening in the shadows.

Dom sits down next to Aidan, leaning across him to steal the last cookie from his plate. 'I think she's actually allergic to it. Honey, that is. Well, to cooking in general,' he jokes.

'Oi! That's mine.' Aidan glares at his dad and I remember how he would always give Annabel his last cookie, his last sweet, his favourite book or toy. No matter what, he'd share anything with his twin. Then again, Dom hadn't waited to be invited – he'd simply taken what he wanted.

'Don't be greedy. And remember who puts food on your plate in the first place,' Dom says, reaching out to cuff Aidan round the ear.

Aidan's shoulders hunch and his mouth is a wobbly line. Something shifts in the depths of my memory, looming heavily behind my mind's eye, pulsing hotly before it vanishes beyond reach. What is it? *What?*

'It's all right, hon. Here, have mine,' Lucy says, diffusing the tension. 'Mr Grant was asking after you today. Says he still misses you at chess club.' She ruffles his hair. 'Jasper misses you in class, too. Though I bet you've made loads of new friends at the prep.'

'I should hope so. It's costing me enough,' Dom chips in, resting a hand on Aidan's shoulder.

'Not really. No one's into the stuff I like.'

My chest hurts as I watch Aidan angrily break his amazing model apart, systematically separating all the bricks into little piles of different colours.

'It'll get easier. Change is always hard,' Lucy says softly.

'Exactly,' Dom echoes. 'I know your mum isn't a fan but trust me, in years to come that school will look amazing on your CV. You should listen to what Lucy says, son. She runs her own business too. She knows what she's talking about.'

'I liked my old school better. So did Annabel,' Aidan mumbles, his head bowed.

No one hears him but me. I watch as Dom hands Lucy the empty cookie dish, their fingers accidentally brushing. I don't see her expression because she quickly turns away to scrape crumbs into the food-recycling tub. When she turns back to the table, she stands behind Aidan's chair and flicks back her hair as she glances up at Dom.

'We should take the kids over to Bushy Park with their kites. Before it gets dark. I'll pick up some snacks for a picnic, shall I, and head over there once I've got Jasper.'

'It's a date,' Dom says.

Oh, hello: this is a new feeling. *Paranoia.* I scribble it dutifully on the mental whiteboard, adding it to the growing list. My best friend and my husband of ten years, chatting comfortably at my kitchen table with my only surviving child, kettle on, planning a picnic. They look like a family. Dom, Aidan . . . Lucy.

A warm smile spreading across her face, Lucy rests a hand on Aidan's other shoulder and gives it a gentle squeeze.

Don't you dare lay a finger on my son!

EIGHT

My head is bursting with confusion and suspicions I can barely acknowledge, even to myself. I need to see Lucy; I have to try to talk to her and feel that everything is all right between us. But as I make my way down the hall the house is quiet, and when I reach the kitchen doorway I see that the room is empty. The table has been cleared, the dishes washed up and put away. There's no trace left of Dom, Lucy and Aidan having even been here.

They must have gone out through the back door. Perhaps they decided to leave straight away; perhaps Dom offered to take them to the twins' favourite café on Hampton High Street instead of having a picnic. He seems to do that more often, lately. It's kind of him, I suppose, to spare me the trouble of cooking – he knows I don't enjoy it – and to give me some time alone. He's allowing me to bypass the questions and small talk from the local shopkeepers, and to avoid the strained sympathy of neighbours or other parents from school that we might bump into.

Maybe today I could have gone with them, though, I think with mounting frustration. I wanted Aidan to tell me about his day at school; I wanted to hear news of old friends from Lucy. Only they're gone; I've missed them – *and I miss them*. I may not take part in their conversations, but their voices comfort me. Without them the silence expands into an endless vacuum. And even as I tell myself to stop being so silly, the coil of suspicion tightens into a solid lump of fear: Lucy is replacing me, and it's my fault for letting her, for allowing grief to weave its web of sadness ever tighter around me until I feel paralysed by it.

Or had Lucy already been inching her way into my shoes, and I just never noticed? The easy familiarity between the three of them felt *normal*, unquestioned, as if it has been that way for a long time. I feel like I'm the one on the outside – the intruder in my own home.

I stare at the kitchen table, forcing myself to focus on happier thoughts, smiling as I think of Aidan methodically building his Lego model. I remember Annabel sitting next to him, just there, so many times, the pair of them painting or drawing, giggling and whispering. The three of us were always together. Even if we were each engaged in our own separate activity, we spent most of our time in this house within feet of each other. It filled my heart with such joy to see them happy, and I'm suddenly consumed by the hope that the ten years I had with them were as wonderful for the twins as they were for me.

The ache of longing intensifies into a deep pain inside me. My whole body hurts and I feel a powerful urge to lie down on the tiled kitchen floor and howl in agony that I will have no more years with Annabel; I want to beat the walls in angry protest that Aidan won't, either. It was so easy being with my children; it's so impossibly hard being apart from them.

Being apart from Annabel.

Aidan is still here, I remind myself; I *must* find my way back to him. I close my eyes and try to conjure up a burst of energy, to force myself to leave the shadows, to leave the *house* and follow them, to take my place alongside my son. Dizzily, I make myself keep moving, trailing round the kitchen, examining every corner as if the three of them might suddenly jump out and surprise me.

I notice that my favourite wedding photo is on the kitchen windowsill rather than in its usual place in the living room. I try not to torment myself that I will never see Annabel as a bride; I will never get to watch her try on wedding dresses or chat about where to go on honeymoon. She will never introduce me to the love of her life; she will never cry on my shoulder over the boys she's loved and lost. I try to make myself smile as I imagine what kind of crazy boys she would have brought home as a teenager. I can't manage it; the thought bites so painfully.

I glance one last time at our wedding photo, deciding to leave it where it is. I wonder if Aidan moved it; maybe he's worried about Lucy's presence, too, and wanted to drop a subtle hint. I take comfort from that thought, even though I know I'm deluding myself. Then I scan the kitchen looking for a note: it occurs to me that I have no idea when Dom and Aidan will return, and I feel a moment's panic before remembering that they won't be late – it's a school night, after all. Dom is being a *good father*; he's being a *good husband*.

I wander out of the kitchen and back up the stairs to our bedroom. I'm tired, so very tired. If I could just rest for a while . . . But as soon as I close my eyes, my thoughts return to the easy familiarity between Dom and Lucy, the hint of flirtatiousness, and I wish I could remember if that's old or new – if they've always had this closeness, or whether since Annabel's death their friendship has become more . . . intimate. The word shocks me, and I wish I could remember . . .

I wish I could remember if I've been happy as Dom's wife . . .

NINE

'Are you sure you don't want me to ask Max to babysit?'

It was our ninth wedding anniversary, and the first one we'd actually contemplated celebrating since our milestone fifth. Life had got so busy – Dom's business was really taking off; school life had taken over. There was always another play for Annabel to rehearse; always another swimming gala, football tournament or violin recital. Our half-hearted attempts to instigate a regular 'date night' had fallen at the first hurdle when the twins both came down with chickenpox. We'd postponed our planned dinner date; neither of us had got round to making another reservation.

'Yes, I'm sure. I told you, he's round here too much as it is.'

'The twins need *some* family. They don't have grandparents, remember? It's good for them to have a relationship with their only uncle. Maybe it's time you two made your peace. I realise things weren't easy before, and you clearly have your differences, but Max has always been really good with the twins. I know he'd like to see more of them.'

'You know, do you? And how do you know?'

'He told me.' I sighed. We'd been over this a hundred times.

'Like I said, he's round here too much. Why do you invite him?'

'Because he's *family*. And because the twins have fun with him.'

'Meaning they don't with me?'

'I didn't say that. But you've got a lot on your plate with work, and—'

'And while the cat's away the mice need to play? Jesus. I'm working this hard for *us*. Not just so you can hang out with my useless, waste-of-space brother.'

'That's not what I meant, and you know it. I appreciate how hard you work, and I know you'd love to spend more time with the twins too. I don't want you to feel *guilty*. I just want you to see that Max has actually been a big help. After-school clubs clash, sometimes. I can't be in two places at once. And if Max can walk Annabel to drama or Aidan to football, that's a good thing, isn't it?'

'No. It's not.'

'Then what do you suggest?'

'Ask Lucy. I bet she'll be happy to babysit.'

'No, I meant generally. Are you saying you don't want your brother round here at all? *Why?*'

'Because I don't like him very much.'

'Still? After all this time? That's just so sad.'

I'd always known Dom resented his older brother, and I could see that Max was a strong personality; he talked nineteen to the dozen and told those long, rambling jokes that never had any punchline. But he'd shown only kindness to me and the twins. Nothing was ever too much trouble. It wasn't that I actually asked him for help; he just seemed to *know*. The faulty lawnmower was suddenly fixed; the broken bathroom latch was mended. And he was as happy hanging out playing board games with the twins in our living room as he was flying kites with them in the park.

I could see he had a particular soft spot for Annabel. Perhaps

Dom was jealous of that: his princess enjoying the attention of someone who wasn't *Daddy*. He needn't have worried. Lately, Annabel had started saying she would rather hang out with her friends than her crackpot uncle. She'd started arranging her own lifts back from drama club with friends' mums.

'It's a fact of life, that's all. I've helped him as much as I can. I got him started as a personal trainer, sorted him out with that job at the gym. I've done my best to get along with him when he's round here. I realise the kids like him, and I know he dotes on them. He's always very generous to them, but—'

'But he had all the attention from your mum and dad, and now it feels like he's getting it from your kids. Getting the cuddles they should be giving *you*.' The penny suddenly dropped. It wasn't about Annabel. Not specifically. It was about Max always hogging the attention of anyone Dom loved.

'Don't psychoanalyse me,' he bit out. 'I just don't want him muscling in on my family, that's all.'

'Muscling in? Or being part of it?' I refused to let it go. The children *did* need family around them. Dom was overreacting.

'I didn't invite him. *You* did. *Come for Sunday lunch, Max. Come over and have coffee while Dom works his fingers to the bone.*' The finger jabbing in my face underlined his accusation.

'The kids love seeing him, but they adore *you*, Dom. You're Aidan's hero, you know that. And Annabel's always been a daddy's girl. You have no reason at all to be jealous.'

It was a bad choice of word, and if I'd known the reaction it would provoke, I would have kept my mouth shut. The slap to my left cheekbone sent my body tumbling to the living-room floor and my whole world crashing around me.

'Don't you *ever* say that to me again,' Dom said through gritted teeth, looming over me. 'I'm not the jealous one here.'

'What on earth do you mean?' My voice was hoarse with shock;

I could hear it echoing in my ears. I reached for the coffee table, shakily pulling myself upright. Gingerly I pressed my throbbing cheek with trembling fingers. I wanted to stand up, but Dom was blocking my way, leaning over me to continue the tirade I'd unknowingly unleashed.

'You're always tougher on Annabel than you are on Aidan. Always picking little faults, letting him off lightly but coming down hard on her. You're soft on that boy, and you're jealous of Annabel. Her spark. Her exuberance. She's the angel on top of the Christmas tree, and she outshines you every single day of her life. And you can't *bear* it.'

'That's rubbish. Utter nonsense. I've no idea what you—'

'You want to throw your psychology degree at me? Well, two can play that game. I see right through you, sweetheart.'

'I love them both the same,' I insisted. 'I don't favour *either* of them.' My chest was painfully tight. He was going to bring up our holiday; I just knew he was.

'Oh, come off it. Who got your attention first that time in Cornwall?'

Oh, God.

'I told them to go to Annabel,' Dom went on, 'but oh, no. You said help *Aidan*.' His voice was low, but every word sounded like gunfire in my head.

I knew exactly what he was talking about; I would never forget that awful day. But Dom was wrong: I didn't direct the crew to Aidan first because I favoured him. I saw his little face turning blue and I knew he had less than a breath of air left in his tiny lungs. It was a split-second impulse. The paramedic looked to me, and I gestured to my son.

I picked Aidan.

TEN

I can hear beeping, like the sound of a lorry reversing, and it's driving me mad. It must be Mr Cooper next door having his shopping delivered, I think. I wish they'd hurry up and park the van, stop that infernal beeping. I'm trying to remember what happened after that row, what else Dom said to me about Max coming round to our house all the time, and about Annabel. The jealousy he accused me of feeling. But I can't concentrate with that repetitive high-pitched sound: *beep, beep, beep, beep* ...

I'm beginning to remember that after the thrill of our whirlwind romance and the joy and excitement of our early married life, seismic cracks had begun to appear between me and Dom. That first slap created a fault line that destabalised everything. It shocked me, and I thought it would also have schocked Dom into changing his ways. It didn't. I realise that the strained atmosphere in the house now isn't only due to my grief, my post-traumatic stress: it was like this *before*. Dom looks right through me now, but his aloofness isn't entirely due to the choice I made; we were drifting apart long before we lost Annabel ...

I feel like a stage curtain has been lifted after the interval, only for me to realise I've been watching the wrong play. I thought Dom was being so calm, so caring after the death of our daughter. I thought he was being so understanding of my guilt, patiently giving me space to deal with my pain and remorse. It's bewildering to realise that I've completely misinterpreted it – or that it might all be an act . . .

Where does the truth lie? I need to carry on trying to remember. I know I'm getting closer . . . I can see a little more clearly through the clouds in my head now. I can remember that Dom and I really weren't getting on well, and that our marriage was floundering and that I was feeling . . . *what* was I feeling?

I try to pin down my emotions but there it is again, that beeping sound. It seems to be coming from the back garden, though, not the street at the front of the house. How odd, I think. And then I notice that I'm downstairs again, in the back sitting room, which is supposed to be the formal dining room but we've always used it as more of a playroom because it has French doors that open on to the garden. I look around in panic. I can't remember coming down here; I have no idea how long I've been standing, looking out at our neat lawn with its vibrant evergreen borders. The swing, the slide, my tranquillity garden with its quirky diminutive population of statues, the sprawling wisteria winding lustrously, lazily along the fence towards the laurel hedge at the back.

I must have blacked out again. I wonder if Dom has noticed this happening to me; I wonder if he thinks I'm not safe to leave in charge of Aidan, and that's why he's taken him off with Lucy – why he's *always* taking him off. Dom has assumed responsibility for everything now, I realise. Everyone is treading on eggshells around me. They're too worried about my state of mind to engage with me – perhaps the pressure would be too much, they think; perhaps I will fall apart if they expect me to take up my usual duties: housework, shopping and cooking, making Aidan's packed lunches, washing his uniform, listening to his moans about the volume of homework.

Or perhaps it's just that they simply can't bear to talk to me.

Unneeded. They're coping perfectly well without me. Dom, Aidan, Lucy, Jasper. I've become irrelevant, sidelined. Maybe this is how it always was and I just needed to *believe* I was important, because if I wasn't the centre of my family's world, what was I?

I remember longing for the twins to say my name for the first time: 'Mum-my. Mmm-mum-my.' I would say it over and over, trying to coach them into giving me the ultimate affirmation – the recognition of my importance in their lives. Lucy laughed when I confessed my frustration that 'Dad-da' popped out months before 'Mum'.

'Seriously, it's got nothing to do with who they love best. It's all about speech development, which sounds are easiest for their little mouths to make first.'

'I know that *now*. At the time, though, well . . . '

'Besides, you don't need them to say your name to know they love you,' she said. 'Jasper barely calls me Mum even now. He doesn't need to, though, does he? I'm always right there. It's a continuing conversation. Who else would he be talking to? We're part of each other, as you are with the twins.'

'Part of each other. Yes. The twins do just seem to *feel* what the other's thinking. I *guess* it's the same with me. I hope so. They certainly take it for granted that I'm always here, always listening. Is that a *good* thing, though?'

'Good thing or not, we're part of the furniture, hon, you and me. Aidan and Annabel will only really notice you when you're not there. Take my word for it!'

They'll only notice me when I'm not here.

Well, I'm still here, but I might as well not be, I think; I'm not the mum I used to be, and it doesn't seem to bother Aidan in the slightest.

'Dad. *Dad!* Can you come and practise keepy-uppies with me?'

As if thinking about him has conjured him up, I hear Aidan calling out to Dom in the garden. They're back from the café, then, I think, puzzled, until I notice that the light is fading and the hazy summer evening swathes the garden in an orange and gold sunset. I must have slept the afternoon away, locked in my dreams, my stuck memories. I hear the wind chimes clang eerily and I feel unsteady and displaced, like I'm trying to walk across the deck of a ship that's pitching and rolling on ocean waves, even though my feet feel rooted to the spot. *I'm really losing it*, I think desperately.

Don't go near the roses.

My heart beats faster as I suddenly worry they will kick the ball into the rose bushes and disturb Annabel.

Please, be careful; please let her rest in peace . . .

'Mummy?'

I freeze.

'Mummy, where are you?'

I glance frantically out at the garden but Dom and Aidan have disappeared; it isn't my son calling to me.

'Annabel? *Annabel?*'

And then I'm running, blood pounding in my ears, chasing a glimpse of a white shirt and a grey school skirt, and suddenly I'm in my daughter's bedroom, eyes darting around the messy room (I've left everything exactly as it was; not a dress has been hung up or a book put away), wide eyes staring back at me from pop-star posters on the walls, a sharp pain in my heart and my breath choking in my throat as I see that her duvet is still half off her bed where she always kicks it to the floor during the night. Her bed is empty. Un-slept-in.

I sink down on to the edge of the mattress and then swing my legs up, lying down, head resting on Annabel's rose-printed pillow, the scent of her shampoo teasing me, making me believe she could be right here, lying next to me along with her panda bear, his huge glassy eyes staring knowingly at me: *You poor deluded soul. She's not here. She's never going to be here again.*

I feel my throat closing up and I cough suddenly, air shooting up into my nose and mouth. My body feels heavy and lethargic as adrenalin surges through and then ebbs out of my bloodstream.

'Annabel, angel, where *are* you?'

I know I haven't conjured up her ghost; I don't believe in spirits wandering the earth. I know my daughter isn't going to twirl into the room, kick off her slippers and snuggle up next to me on the bed and rest her head on my shoulder, as she's done thousands of times before. I know that no matter what I promise the universe, there is no deal to be struck.

She won't ever come back, but she will always be here – in this room, her private sanctuary, the theatre of her secret dreams that played out as she lay in bed each night, staring at the ceiling. I *feel* my daughter inside me always, but I *see* her here, in this tiny bedroom with its view over the back garden. Preening in front of the mirror, making up funny little plays with the china animals she loved but pretended she'd outgrown, practising her latest dance by hooking up her dressing gown on the wardrobe door and hold-ing on to its outstretched arms. In this gold and cream bedroom Annabel slept as a baby, played as a toddler and threw tantrums as a pre-teen. Every inch of the space is a reminder of her; I visit it every day and each time a new memory wraps itself around me.

I pull one closer and surrender to its comforting magic.

ELEVEN

'Read me a story, Mum. The one about the magic ballet shoes.'

There is no ghostly apparition except in my imagination. All I'm left with is silvery, flickering memories of sitting next to her, perched on the edge of her bed, the soft evening lamplight catching the contours of her pretty face that seemed to be changing in front of my eyes, inching away from the baby softness of childhood and towards the angles and hollow planes of a teenager.

Too fast: the twins were growing up way too fast.

Too soon: I lost her far, far too soon.

'Aren't you too old for bedtime stories?' I smiled as I teased her.

'Never too old.' She smiled back, allowing me to squeeze her hand.

I smile now at the familiar conversation, remembering how our bedtime chats always ended with Annabel opening the book at her favourite page, the scene she liked best in the story. The one where the little dancer girl pirouettes so fast that she is lifted into the air and flies away, hair floating through the night sky and getting tangled round the stars, her magic ballet shoes whisking her away to a beautiful land full of giant flowers and talking animals.

'Wouldn't it be lovely,' I said, 'to be able to fly?'

'I wish I really believed in magic shoes. Magic isn't real, though, is it, Mummy? Nor is Father Christmas. Or the Tooth Fairy. Or the Easter Bunny. Or—'

'Hey, hold your horses, darling – where's all this come from? For magic to be real, you have to—'

'Believe. Yes, I know. That's what Aidan says.' The sparkle was gone; her eyes looked sad and tired.

'And you don't believe your brother? If you really, really want your dreams to come true, angel, they will. You'll find a way. Anything is possible.' I stroked her cheek, wondering how long it would take her to shrug me off; she wasn't really one for kisses and cuddles. But she didn't move, staying crushed against my side like a baby lamb.

'The other night I dreamed about Matthew Jones getting squashed by a giant enormous bug. Will that dream come true?'

One day those beautiful, flashing, clear blue eyes, full of defiant spirit, will torment boys like Matthew Jones – and Jasper March – in quite a different way, I thought.

'Oh, Bel.' Tentatively, I cuddled her, feeling the fine silk of her hair tickle my cheek, inhaling the scent of apple shampoo, squeezing her delicate shoulders that were far too tiny to be carrying the weight of any worries. 'Is that boy still bothering you? I did have a word with the teacher about Matthew what's-his-name. What's happened now?'

'Nothing, really. Just, you know. Stuff.' She buried her face in Panda's tummy.

'Bel, is there anything you want to tell me? Because, you know—'

'Yeah, I know, Mum. Everything's OK. Don't worry. You have *enough* to worry about,' she said, sounding far too grown up.

'Do I?' I laughed but realised with a sinking heart that she must have heard me when I yelled those very words at Dom the night before. *Stop going on at me about that school. There's nothing more I can do about it, and I have enough to worry about!*

I allow the painful fragment of memory to drift away. Softly, I close the door of my daughter's room behind me.

Nighty night, darling. Love you.

But I can't close the door so easily on the sudden worry that's surfaced; I can't shake off my guilt that the constant rows between me and Dom had made the twins unhappy. Because we *had* started rowing a lot of the time. I realise that now. Had Annabel been scared in our home? Were the last hours of her life full of trembling anxiety? Dom accused me of being too hard on my daughter, and the barb lodged deep. Is that really what Annabel thought – that I chivvied her too much? That I wasn't the mum she needed, wanted me to be?

I take deep breaths until the pain of this thought passes then I force myself to think back to the past once again, desperate to reassure myself that my beautiful birthday girl didn't die without knowing that her ten years on earth were the absolute best of my life, and that Mummy loved her.

TWELVE

'Please, darling, can you stop leaning over the railings. Step back just a little, *please?*'

I remember I'd taken the twins down to Brighton for the day on the train during the May half-term break, and Annabel was deliberately provoking me by hanging over the railings at the end of the pier. The wind lifted her hair, and her body was so slight I was terrified she would be carried off, too. Or fall in.

'Look at me! I can fly!'

'Annabel. *Enough*, now. Please. Just don't push it.'

'Spoilsport. I'm not going to fall in and drown, you know,' she said, reading my mind. 'I'm not a little kid any more. I'm a better swimmer than you *or* Daddy. So you can stop freaking out every time we're near water. Bull's-eye!' she added, picking up a stray crust dropped by a toddler and throwing it at a pigeon.

'Let's go and skim some stones,' Aidan said. 'I challenge you, Bel. Winner gets to sit by the window on the train home!'

Aidan. Always the peacemaker. He wanted to pacify; Annabel wanted to provoke.

But she was right. I had to stop worrying. They were both excellent swimmers now, I'd made sure of that, and since that one terrible incident when they were toddlers, we'd been to Cornwall every year for our summer holiday and nothing bad had happened. I needed to lighten up.

'Come on, love,' I said more gently. 'Let's get some candyfloss. Bet you can't eat it without licking your lips!' I ushered them towards a stall selling every kind of unhealthy snack I usually tried to persuade the twins to avoid.

'I thought you said candyfloss is bad for your teeth!' Aidan said, laughing as he took hold of one enormous, fluffy pink cloud of gooey, sticky sugar.

'Sugar gives you spots.' Annabel was trying to stay grumpy, but I could see her eyes twinkling.

'It sure does. Huge pink ones.' I pulled at a soft strand of candyfloss and dabbed it on the tip of my nose where it stuck like an enormous hairy pimple.

'Look, I've got measles,' Aidan said, joining in, sticking little fluff-balls to his chin.

'No, you've got a humongous pink *beard*, Aid!' Annabel crowed, grinning at last as she tore off a huge handful and shoved it in her brother's face.

'Well, let me just wave my magic pink fairy wand and I'll transport us all in the blink of an eye all the way down to the shore where we— *Oi!* Cheaters!' I called after the twins as they beat me to it and scampered off the end of the pier and down the steps towards the pebble beach.

'Last one to the sea is a stink bomb!' Annabel called out, her hair flying behind her as she sprinted ahead of Aidan into the water.

'You're crazy, Bel,' Aidan said, shaking his head. 'You too, Mum!' he added, laughing as, seconds later, I slipped off my Birkenstocks and joined Annabel.

'Come on in. It's lovely and warm, honest!' I teased, luring Aidan into the water and chuckling at his horrified expression as the cold turned his skinny calves pink.

'You *tricked* me!' he called out indignantly, his teeth chattering.

'Makes a change,' Annabel said, her smile suddenly dropping. 'Dad's usually the one who plays tricks.' Scooping her legs through the water, she dragged herself back on to the beach and started heading back up the shingle slope.

'Hey, hang on, sweetie. Not so fast.' I hurried after her, grabbing my things and trying to ignore the sharp stones cutting into the soles of my feet. 'What was that about? Have I done something to upset you – or has Daddy?'

'I don't want to talk about it,' she said, pausing only to shove her feet back into her trainers, not bothering with her socks.

'Talk about *what*, darling? Do you know what this is about, Aidan?' I asked him as he appeared, panting, at my side.

'Is it because Dad didn't come to watch your show when he said he would?' Aidan slipped an arm through Annabel's and matched her stride for stride as they set off in their own three-legged-race back to the promenade.

'Yeah. That's it,' Annabel said. 'Can we go shopping now, Mum?'

'Well, if you're sure, love?' I said, not completely convinced. 'You know Uncle Max loves coming to watch you in all your plays. I bet he asked if he could go instead of Daddy. I expect it was supposed to be a surprise. Not a trick.' I hooked an arm round her shoulder and pulled her against me.

'Mum, it's fine. Shopping?' she reminded me after a few moments, pulling away and rolling her eyes.

'Sure. Shopping. You can each choose a new outfit then I just have one more stop to make – a quick appointment – before we get the train home.' I frowned and checked my watch before pressing the button at the pedestrian crossing.

'Cool,' Aidan said, linking arms with his sister again.

She never pulled away from Aidan; ever since they were little, I'd often looked at them and found it hard to distinguish which skinny arm belonged to which tiny body. They were entirely comfortable being entwined; I wondered if that would change as they grew up, and my stomach clenched at the thought of them turning into teenagers, then adults. My babies; they'd *always* be my babies, and as we ambled through the sunny streets of Brighton, I hoped we'd always be this close.

'How about this?' I asked, holding up a gorgeous blue velvet mini-dress that I was sure Annabel would love. She adored anything dramatic and sophisticated. 'The navy really brings out the colour of your eyes, love.'

'It's too short, Mum. And the neck's really low. It'll show everything. No. I don't like it.' She pushed it away and strode off to the next section.

'Oh, are you sure?' I held on to it, surprised that she'd rejected the dress. 'You could wear your black leggings underneath, and—'

'*No*, I said. I just want a new hoodie.' She stalked off towards a rack of black sweatshirts, back ramrod straight.

'Not like you to be self-conscious, darling?' I said softly, shoving the dress back and helping her flip through the jersey tops, raising my eyebrows as she picked out a sweatshirt at least three sizes too big for her. It would hang down around her knees.

'Hey, look. Let's get this for Dad as a surprise,' Aidan said, grinning as he held up a white T-shirt with a logo of giant black sunglasses on the front.

'Hmm, funny. They do look a bit like your dad's, don't they?' Shall we get it, do you think?'

'Yeah. Dad *loves* surprises,' Annabel muttered as I juggled debit cards and finally handed over the one for my small savings account. We only had one credit card, and Dom kept hold of that. Household finances were his responsibility; childcare was mine. That was what we'd agreed, although it did sometimes occur to me that Dom treated himself to far more new clothes than the three of us put together.

'Uncle Max does too,' Aidan added, trying to be reasonable. 'He's always bringing us new DVDs and video games and stuff.'

'You're his niece and nephew. He likes you. It's not a crime.'

'Daddy said he's surprised Uncle Max isn't in prison by now,' Annabel said.

'*What?* That's silly. He was probably joking. It's just that where they grew up was . . . Well, I think lots of the kids used to get in trouble. You two are lucky you have such a nice home.'

'Is that why Uncle Max is always coming round?' Aidan hooked his arm through mine as we left the store.

'Probably, love. But family is important. Don't you think? We all need to look after each other.' I squeezed his arm and automatically reached for Annabel's hand as we crossed the road.

Once we were safely on the other side, I paused to look at each of the twins in turn. Aidan was eyeing up football boots in the window of the sports shop, but Annabel had her head down, scuffing her feet.

'OK, am I just *missing* something here? What's up, darling?' I said, squeezing her hand encouragingly. But whatever it was, she refused to say, and I felt a pang of nostalgia for the old days when the children blurted out every thought they had the second they had it. They were closer to turning into pre-teens than I'd realised.

'Can we get an ice cream now?' Aidan asked when there were no more football boots left to admire.

'Yes. You *may*. When you've told me what's going on,' I said. 'Something's happened. Or something has upset Annabel. And I'd like to know what it is, please. Is it something about Daddy?'

'Why didn't he come with us today?' Annabel asked, looking up at me, a frown on her pretty face. 'He didn't come last time, either.'

'He's working.' Aidan poked his sister in the side. 'He's *always* working.'

'Holidays at the seaside don't pay for themselves, you know.' *Nor do school fees*, I added in my head.

'We could have just stayed at our old school. That was free,' Aidan mumbled, reading my mind.

'Nothing's completely free, and you haven't even finished a whole year at your new school yet. Let's just wait and see how things go over the next few weeks, hey? Now, we've just about got time for an ice cream before my appointment, *if* we get our skates on.' I forced a smile, feeling worried but not quite sure why.

'Yay,' the twins both said in unison, and I wasn't deaf to the irony in their voices.

'Come on, darlings. It's been a lovely day. I know it's a shame for it to end, but we'll come back again soon. You like being by the sea, don't you? I know you love Cornwall best, but Brighton's lovely, don't you think?'

I try to remember what the appointment was, but I have no recollection of who we were meeting that day, or why. The next memory I have is of Annabel's tiny feet stamping up the stairs the following evening after I told her that she couldn't go for a sleepover at her friend's house because it was miles away and I didn't know the parents.

'But it's half-term, Mum. I want to hang out with Davina for a couple of days. What's wrong with that?'

'Don't you want to have time at home, though? I told Daddy last night that you missed him in Brighton, and he said he'd take a couple of days off.' I didn't tell her that Dom's agreement only came after almost two hours of me carefully cajoling and him irritably deriding my inability to drive, my lack of appreciation of his work schedule, and generally acting like I'd asked him to fly us to New York for the weekend. 'I thought we might all go to the cinema tomorrow. That film you and Aidan wanted to see is on in Kingston. Or we could take your bikes up to Richmond Park and invite Uncle Max. Yes?'

I hesitated in the doorway of Annabel's bedroom, feeling torn. I wanted to sit down and have a proper chat with her, but I knew if I didn't have Dom's dinner ready when he came home he'd be in a foul mood.

'I'd rather stay at Davina's. *Please*, Mum?'

'Oh, Bel. I'm sorry, I—'

'Fine!' Annabel snapped, leaping up and slamming the door in my face.

'Darling, don't be like this,' I said, leaning my head against the door, wishing I knew what to do for the best, annoyed that I couldn't discuss these things with Dom.

Aidan had been right: their dad *was* always working. Dom didn't seem happy about it, either, often complaining that all he was good for was a pay cheque at the end of each month, and that I spent more time with the twins than with him. We seemed to bicker about it constantly, and I knew I was guilty of finding excuses to avoid going out alone with him. After dashing between school runs, after-school clubs, the supermarket, cleaning the house and keeping the garden in order, the last thing I felt like doing was dressing up and sitting in a noisy restaurant. I knew I needed to make more effort, but it didn't help that every time we went out we just ended up arguing about the kids or Dom's work.

It felt like we'd started to live on different planets, and it was turning into a war of the worlds. Dom said he missed having a wife who didn't have Lego bricks in her handbag and baked beans on her shirt. And I couldn't remember the last time I'd felt able to talk to him about the things that worried me – about Annabel growing up and wanting more freedom, about me not feeling ready to let her go off into the big bad world. I didn't even dare to raise the issue of the school again. Dom had apologised profusely after the slap on our ninth wedding anniversary, but he'd lifted a hand to me several times since then. So far, he'd just about managed to keep his temper under control, but I was forever on tenterhooks, trying not to provoke him into unleashing it.

I shared some of my anxiety with Lucy, and I bottled up the rest, not wanting to admit to my friend that Dom had struck me. Nor that Annabel had actually shut me out of her room. I almost felt sadder and more hurt about that than about Dom's creeping aggression, and I remember my fear at the thought of letting Annabel sleep over at someone else's house, not knowing who was tucking her in at night, giving her a last kiss and cuddle; not being able to keep her safe.

A sudden thought surfaces and refuses to be ignored . . .

Does *that* explain my choice?

Did I want to clip Annabel's wings? Keep her as a child – my baby – for ever?

Daddy's princess; Mummy's angel.

That's what she will be forever more, now. She will never grow up, and I ask myself if, deep down, that's what I really wanted. Did I choose Annabel because death ties her to me for all of eternity? She can never become an adult and leave me now; my beautiful darling will always lie beneath the rose bushes, close to me, frozen in time.

Maybe I chose my daughter because I believe that my son – gentle, home-loving Aidan – will always choose me, but one day Annabel would have chosen to leave me. All I would have left would be a room full of her swimming trophies and dance medals, her story books and teddy bears. She would have taken flight and perhaps never returned to the nest.

Having unlocked the thought, painful as it is, I force myself to consider it: did I punish Annabel for not needing me enough – for craving the big wide world more than the welcoming home I'd tried so hard, and endured so much, to create for my children?

I can't breathe as the possibility hangs in the air: did I push my daughter away before she could reject me? It's a thought far too painful to bear, especially because in choosing Annabel, I have lost Aidan anyway.

THIRTEEN

Aidan is dancing round the living room. His whoops of glee pull me to him like a magnet and I drag myself away from tormenting memories to seek him out, finding him bouncing around holding some kind of shiny gold figure above his head.

It's a trophy, I realise. A swimming trophy. It must be Sunday, then; swimming galas are often on Sundays. Have I lost an entire day, locked inside my thoughts? Time still doesn't seem to have much meaning for me, but I cling on to this one small detail: it's the weekend, Aidan will be at home. Perhaps today I'll find my voice again, find a way of closing this awful chasm between us.

He must have won a gala this morning, I think, smiling at the joy I haven't seen on his face for so long, feeling sad that I wasn't there to support him. I wish Dom had told me about it rather than leaving me to sleep. I wonder if he is deliberately keeping Aidan away from me. Maybe he *wants* me out of the way; maybe he's intentionally withholding our son – to protect Aidan from the distress of seeing his traumatised, confused mum, or to punish me for what I did?

Or perhaps it's nothing so calculated. Maybe he simply left me sleeping this morning because I look exhausted. I am feeling so dreadfully tired, it's true. So tired that it's an effort to move. Dredging up my memories has left me wrung out by emotion; everything aches and my nerve endings feel like they're buzzing, my fingertips tingling hotly and a headache taking hold.

This is new, I acknowledge in surprise. For so long, I haven't felt much in the way of bodily sensations at all, my physical senses numbed by grief. Now, at least, I'm aware of pain – which is progress of sorts, although I worry that, my immune system weakened by stress, I might have developed some kind of debilitating illness. I'm still losing chunks of time, and mostly I feel confused and disoriented. I should probably see my GP, but I still can't face leaving the house. I wonder if she does house calls . . .

I'm diverted from the thought as I notice the bright halo of afternoon sunshine spotlighting Aidan in the centre of the room. He looks thinner, I think, and his hair is shorn again. I wonder if he decided to get it cut for the swimming gala, or if Dom took advantage of my mental absence to get his son's crowning glory clipped – to make him look less prissy, more manly, as he always insists. Did Aidan glance anxiously over his shoulder, waiting for me to save him as his father dragged him protesting into the barber's?

Did he stretch out his arm beseechingly when I chose his sister?

The question blindsides me, and I can't stop my mind spiralling into even darker thoughts . . . Did I signal to Annabel with a nod or a gesture? Did she look at me with confusion in her eyes, the agony of my betrayal tearing her heart to pieces even before the killer took his shot? Did Aidan watch, his whole world crumbling in horror, then run for his life to escape the woman who should have given *her* life to save theirs?

Stop. Don't go there. I order myself to resist being dragged back into the past; I must stay in the moment. Today Aidan is a winner, and I'm fiercely glad to see his joy. I just wish I'd been there to cheer him on. Selfishly, I wonder whether, in his excitement, he might actually have turned to me, sharing his surprise and pride with his mum just as he would have done before. When Annabel was here.

She would have been so proud.

I long for Aidan to meet my eyes and read my thoughts without needing to hear me say the words I'm unable to speak – a smiling conspiracy between us, both of us remembering how Annabel would have pirouetted around the room along with her brother, and then teased him that he'd only beat her time because she let him.

Just for a second, Aidan pauses and his eyes seem to meet mine. They are bluer than the Cornish sea with tiny flecks of gold in the irises; his pupils are black pinpricks in the bright sunshine that fills the room. *I'm so sorry, my darling.* The thought ripples through me. I try my absolute hardest to say the words but they are stuck in my throat; I try to smile but it won't come.

I close my eyes and instantly I see a balaclava, big gloved hands, a gun pointing at my face; I see Annabel's eyes so wide the whites all around the sapphires of her irises are bone-china bright; I see Aidan's eyes dull with shock and fear, terror transporting him somewhere else. He looks right through me, as he has done every day since.

Why did you choose Annabel, Mum?

I see this question in his eyes constantly. My gentle, sensitive boy who was always a step behind Annabel; my shy, loving son who used to be so much more openly affectionate and needful of me. And I still can't give him an answer, I think wretchedly. I can't explain it to him because I don't even have an explanation for myself. The whispering parents at the school gate are right: what kind of mother chooses one child over another?

I force myself to listen to the voice in the back of my mind torturing me with one more possibility I can't bear to confront: *Did I love Aidan more than his sister?*

I stare at him in mute anguish but he spins away from me and in the next moment his flying arms catch the tip of a glass trophy on the Art Deco mantelpiece, the heavy object tipping and falling to crash in a shattered pool of glistening splinters on the tiled grate below, the shiny victorious glass golfer figure decapitated, his bronze golf club rolling to one side.

Dom appears as if from nowhere, his right arm raised like an axe above Aidan's cowering head. I stare down in fear at my son, crouching now on the carpet, and my mouth opens in a silent scream.

Run!

Aidan darts to the left and I see a wet patch darkening his jeans. His small face crumples, toffee-coloured freckles standing out more prominently against his white skin, his eyes dark with embarrassment, shock and distress.

Don't look back!

He throws himself to the ground, arms shielding his head, and the world seems to spin. I feel like I'm suspended upside down and a surge of nausea chokes me, blood rushing to my head. My arms feel like dead weights and I cannot lift them. I feel powerless to protect my son. Dom is taller, stronger. He could snap a child's arm like a twig; he could crush a boy's skull with one fist.

Could he shoot a ten-year-old girl with a bullet?

The thought charges at me, stark and unstoppable. *No!* That's impossible. Utterly unthinkable. I dismiss the idea instantly – not least because if Dom were guilty, he would surely be in prison now. But still it feels like my bones have fossilised; I can't move, my body turning rigid as I allow my shocked mind to absorb the truth: *I'm scared of my husband.*

The Dom I've remembered from the past feels different from the man I'm living with today. Now, for the most part, he's subdued, contained, distant – cold but not angry, aloof but not disdainful. Tragedy has changed him, as it's changed us all, I acknowledge. Only violence casts a long shadow. Rows are normal in any marriage; I know that. But fear isn't. Or it shouldn't be. There's still so much I've forgotten, but this I do remember: things weren't right between us. Dom hit me once – did he hit me again?

Did he hurt my children?

I can't be sure, but I can't take the risk. I see Dom's arm drop as he turns away, his handsome face as white as his son's. His eyes are narrowed over his pinched cheeks, and his shoulders hunch as he slopes out of the room, a jagged shard of glass in one hand and a bent miniature bronze golf club in the other.

Hide!

Aidan drags himself towards the piano in the corner of the living room and curls up beneath it, knees pulled up to his chest. As he sobs into his folded arms, I know with a conviction I cannot place that this reprieve is only temporary. I have to pack up and go. Anywhere. To Lucy's? It doesn't matter. I just need to get out of this house.

And I have to take my son with me.

FOURTEEN

I can't find my keys. Or my phone. Where can they *be*? I've been religiously avoiding contact with the outside world and have no sense even of when I last looked at a screen. I try not to panic; I make myself concentrate on practicalities first.

I woke up knowing exactly what I have to do, and I waited with jittery impatience until the house was quiet – until Dom had put Aidan on the bus to school and headed off to his office. Then I set about searching, going round and round the house, repeatedly looking in the same places until I felt like I was going mad. I was desperate to get out, to escape, to run away with my son to a place where no one could hurt us ever again ... A place of safety.

The second Aidan comes home from school, I'll be ready. Only I can't find anything and now I can't even remember where I've looked or how I got to be sitting on the floor of my bedroom with an open suitcase in front of me. It's the big one we take on our holidays to Cornwall, and it's full to bursting with my clothes – leggings, tunic tops and cardigans – and the children's. Usually, we manage to squeeze in Dom's stuff as well, but there isn't so much as a Ralph Lauren polo shirt in sight. I root around in the corners – nothing. The case is packed just for the three of us, which in itself is odd: Annabel's clothes are in the suitcase as well, so I must have packed this before she died. Had I been planning a trip? Why would we have been going on holiday without Dom? Where on earth would I have been taking the children during term time?

I look around the bedroom as if a clue might spring up and provide the answers. Everything looks the same as ever: the big double bed that almost fills the small bedroom; the heavy mahogany furniture pressed along each wall; the Tiffany bedside lamp that was an anniversary present from Lucy, the telephone . . .

The red light is flashing. There's a message. Scrabbling towards it, I press play: *Hi, sugar, it's me. Miss you, can't wait to see you all soon. I'm waiting for you* . . .

Max. I recognize his quick, deep voice immediately. He sounds almost exactly the same as his younger brother except that his speech is much faster, without the London edges smoothed off. How odd that he would call me 'sugar', though – and I'm sure we're not close enough for him to say he's missing me. And what does he mean he's waiting for me? What is he talking about? I'm not going anywhere; I haven't been anywhere since we buried my daughter.

Was Max at the funeral? I don't remember. Come to think of it, I can't recall seeing him for weeks, months – I don't know how long. That's odd. He *always* used to be round here, whether I'd invited him or not, stopping by after his shift at the gym, claiming he was *just passing*, even though the Ivybridge estate where he lives is a good couple of miles in the opposite direction. He'd just dump his backpack, stretch out on the living-room floor and start playing on the Xbox with the twins, often spending the whole evening with us.

I know Dom resented it, but I've never seen any harm in his

brother. Max has never married and I know he gets lonely; he's a bit of a loner, I suppose people would say. He's good-looking but intense, which might explain why he's never had a girlfriend: his fierce intelligence goes hand in hand with a rather direct manner. As Dom once said: his brother lacks self-awareness. While Dom has charm to soften his arrogance, Max can be blunt and over-bearing. But the twins always found him funny. There's something childlike about his sense of humour, his silly jokes; he's always been perfectly at ease hanging out with two young kids for hours on end.

I allow other memories of Max to wash through me, a flash-flood of images: snapshots of lazy afternoons playing cards at home, fun trips to the park with the kite, Max loping ahead with his arms hooked around the twins' shoulders. Yes, he adored them, especially Annabel. While Dom always treated his daughter like a princess, I suspect he preferred hanging out with Aidan, teaching him ball skills in the garden or building Lego with him at the kitchen table. He indulged his daughter, but he treated her more like a doll than a feisty almost-pre-teen with a mind of her own. She, in turn, became more animated, more *effervescent*, the second her dad walked into the room, as if trying to gain his approval by living up to the frivolous image he had of her.

I was sure Dom had it wrong when he said that I always came down heaviest on her, but she certainly reserved the heftiest share of backchat for me. Lucy used to say it was nature's law for girls to seek the approval of their fathers and boys to want to protect their mums. I stop hunting through the suitcase and try to remember our last conversation on the subject; something about it is pricking at the back of my mind . . .

'Well, I'll agree with you about the boys, at least. Jasper and Aidan are both proper gentleman,' I'd told Lucy as we sat watching the twins and Jasper fly a kite in Bushy Park, after collecting them from a community play rehearsal.

Max had joined us. Lucy had bumped into him at the gym, where she took a yoga class every Sunday morning, and mentioned that she was heading to our house afterwards. Never one to wait for an invitation, Max had tagged along, saying he needed to go for a run, anyway, and he knew an ideal route through Bushy Park.

'Curious character, isn't he? Not a bit like Dom. Apart from physically, of course. Can't deny both of them were blessed in that department. My new Saturday girl definitely has a crush on them.'

'Well, I guess appearances can be deceptive, and siblings can be as different as they are similar. Look at the twins – almost identical to the naked eye, yet complete opposites in personality,' I said, smiling as I watched Aidan and Jasper getting tangled in the kite string and spinning round like lost puppies.

'True.' Lucy grinned too. 'You certainly picked the right brother, that's for sure.'

'You think?'

'Don't you know?' Lucy's smile turned to a gentle frown. 'I know you've had your problems. Things are OK now, though, aren't they?'

'We're getting by. All marriages go through rough patches. You know that.'

'I do. But I got out of mine. Dom is nothing like Matt was, though. Or ... He's never hit you, has he? Sorry, don't take that the wrong way, and tell me to mind my own business if you like. But you would say, wouldn't you, if you were—'

'I'm fine. But thanks.' Suddenly I didn't feel fine, but it wasn't the sort of thing I could blurt out in the middle of the park, surrounded by kids and dog walkers.

'Look, why don't we treat ourselves to a night out? Or come round to the flat one evening and I'll cook. We can chat. Better still, let me know when Dom's working late and I'll come to you. Jasper could always sleep over with Aidan. That way we won't have to worry about babysitters. Bottle of wine and a good old whinge is what you need,' she teased, but I could see the worry in her clear green eyes.

'That sounds great. Thanks, Luce. And Dom is out most nights, so take your pick. It's only me who's the *lady of leisure*.' I rolled my eyes.

'God, you mustn't let him put you down like that! I have no idea how you even manage the twins, what with all their clubs, and the afternoons you spent helping out at the school every week. You've turned your back garden into something out of the Chelsea Flower Show, and all the time keeping an eye on that batty neighbour of yours. Poor old guy would never have left his house since his wife died, if it wasn't for you.'

'Mr Cooper is a sweetheart,' I said, laughing.

'Have you thought about training as a TA?' she said suddenly. 'I know it's probably too much to go back to full-time teacher training right now, but you're brilliant with kids. They loved it when you used to help out in the classroom. Mr Grant always said that. Maybe you could qualify as a teaching assistant. You'd be fantastic and any head teacher would bite their hand off to get you. Honestly. Even the one at your posh new school,' she added, grinning.

'I did look into it last year, actually. But, well, Dom's right: my brains have probably rusted by now, and there's not much time for studying with those two monkeys at home to take care of,' I said, nodding at the twins.

'You mean who would pick up his Armani from the dry cleaner's and make sure his dinner is on the table on time. What *is* it with some men? Soon as they get a ring on your finger they want to shackle you to the Aga.'

'Barefoot and pregnant,' I said, with a sad smile, wondering how I'd mistaken Dom's possessiveness for teasing irony all those years ago.

'But I thought you couldn't . . . ?'

'No. I can't,' I said, reading her thoughts. 'I was just remembering Dom's marriage proposal.'

'Don't tell me, the marriage vows included "till death or a broken washing machine do us part", hey?' She threw her head back and laughed, drawing smiles from other parents loitering around their children in the park, their eyes flicking longingly to the still enormous queue at the coffee hut.

'Ha. Funny. I'd still have said *yes*, though,' I said truthfully.

'*I do*, you mean. I do take thee to be my lawfully arrogant lord and master. Huh. I don't really blame you. Dom's not an easy man to say no to.'

'I'm not sure I've ever tried,' I said, frowning at the slight edge to Lucy's voice. 'Have you?' I found myself holding my breath.

'Won't catch me walking up any aisle again. Except the champagne one at Waitrose,' Lucy said, bumping my shoulder with hers and laughing.

I laughed too before becoming distracted as Annabel came twirling and sashaying across the grass, skinny arms aloft as she dragged the rainbow kite through the sky. Face upturned to the sun, she executed a perfect grand jeté, conker hair trailing behind her on the breeze, mirroring the glistening tail of the kite.

'Beautiful, love,' I called out, feeling goosebumps prickle on my skin at how ethereal she looked. 'You're like a will-o'-the-wisp! Watch out or the wind might pick you up and carry you off!'

'Just like this,' Max said, finishing his run and sauntering over to us, catching Annabel up in his arms and spinning her round and round until she cried out that she felt dizzy. Instantly, he placed her back on the ground as gently as he would a fragile glass figurine.

'Come on, Aid. Race you up the slide!' Annabel said, frowning and shoving forcefully against Max's sweaty vest. 'Can't catch me, Jasper March!' And with a feisty glance over her shoulder, she was off.

I remember how Max watched her flit like a moonbeam across the park. I'm sure it was her daintiness – in such contrast to his heftiness – that entranced him. I often marvelled at Annabel's fairylike qualities myself, loving the way she fluttered through life. Max seemed almost mesmerised by her. His eyes shone when he watched her perform on stage; he was always buying her books on ballet, along with bendy dancing dolls from all the latest musicals. I don't think she had the heart to tell him that she'd grown out of playing with dolls years ago, but I found several of them jammed into the back of the shed, their vacuous faces viciously scribbled on and their hair jaggedly cut off.

Max would have been gutted if he'd known. He must have fallen apart when Annabel died . . .

Realisation crashes over me like a wave.

I haven't set eyes on Max once since we lost her – *where is he?*

FIFTEEN

Hesitantly, I wander out of my bedroom and trail round the empty house looking for clues – a forgotten tracksuit top or pair of trainers; a stack of video games waiting for Aidan to make his selection. But there is no sign of Max, which seems weird.

Perhaps he has stayed away because – like our neighbours and friends – he has absolutely no idea how to be in this dark space where Annabel once burned so brightly. He must have been devastated by her death. Buried beneath my own grief and so preoccupied with how Aidan is coping, I realise I haven't yet spared a thought for Max or how *he* might be suffering. I feel a rush of shame for not thinking of him until now.

He could have come to see me, though, if he'd wanted to. Or *has* he visited and I've just blotted it out? One more memory my traumatised brain has obliterated, along with the identity of my daughter's killer, the wailing police sirens shattering the peace of our quiet, tree-lined road on a beautiful summer's day ... the horror of Annabel's funeral ... I can't remember any of those things; I'm not ready even to *try*. But I *am* curious about Max. I can't think of a single reason why he would have stopped coming to our home. Annabel is no longer here, but he loved Aidan too – why wouldn't he want to see his nephew, comfort him?

I make my way slowly back to the bedroom, options whirring through my mind: he's been hounded by gossip since our family tragedy, and he's had enough and left the area; he doesn't know what to say to his grieving brother and has kept his distance; he's shocked by my actions and cannot bear to look me in the eye . . .

He killed my daughter and he's behind bars.

I'm becoming hysterical. Suspecting first Dom and then his brother. The idea is ludicrous. What possible reason could Max have to hurt either of my children? Why would he ever have wanted to force me to *choose* between them? He'd never have thought to persecute me like that. Dom might have niggled me about Aidan being my favourite, but it wasn't true, and I'm sure Max didn't think so. He was around us even more than Dom, and he loved *all* our family. I saw that with my own eyes, almost every day. There was hardly an evening when Max wasn't at our table.

I think back to the last such occasion I can remember, turning over the details, sweeping for any clues that might explain why Max seems to have abandoned us all . . .

'Cool suit.' Max pushed away his plate and pointed with his steak knife as Dom stalked into the kitchen, rubbing his hands tiredly over his face.

'You here again?'

'Not much call for fancy suits in the gym, of course. Tracksuits don't need to be hand-stitched on Savile Row. But I know my—'

'Max walked the kids home from school for me today.' I jumped in anxiously, sensing Max was about to launch into one of his quirky monologues; I could already see irritation tightening Dom's jaw. 'I – uh – I had a bad tummy ache.'

I rubbed my stomach, keeping up the pretence. It was actually my ribs that were hurting from where Dom had all but crushed them the night before, returning home late from the golf club and insisting it was about time I performed my wifely duty, for once. I still felt numb with shock remembering it. His mocking laugh when I mentioned the migraine I'd had since cleaning the house from top to bottom that afternoon, prompted by Dom's raised eyebrows as he trailed one finger deliberately along the dusty dado rail in the hallway before leaving for work. His angry grunt and the tight anger on his face when he finally realised I was serious about having a headache and rolled off me. I'd lain awake most of the night, worried he would make another move towards me; I'd had butterflies all day waiting for the sound of his key in the front door.

'Oh, did he, indeed? Stick the kettle on, Maddie. I'm parched.'

'There's some dinner left in—'

'I ate out.'

The twins were watching TV in the living room. Max had suggested a game of cards, at which point they'd exchanged glances and disappeared before he managed to find the pack they'd deliberately hidden at the back of the dresser drawer. He picked them up now and started shuffling them, over and over, looking between me and Dom. I stopped spooning coffee into the cafetière and watched him, sensing tension.

'*What*, Max? Spit it out,' Dom said, noticing his brother staring at him. He pulled out a chair and sat down at the kitchen table.

Max leaned back, crossing his arms. 'Heard you're going to Westfield in the morning. Just wondering if you're taking Maddie too. I picked up a new game for the kids, didn't I? Thought I could hang out here with them while you two shop. Play some football, watch a movie, show them—'

'Nope,' Dom cut in tersely. 'I'm meeting a client afterwards.

Potential partner, actually, so we'll probably talk business at the champagne bar. Maddie would be bored.'

Maddie would be in the way, I translated mentally.

'Oh. Is that right? You know they serve more than eighty different champagnes at Searcys. They've got a Krug that's over a grand a bottle. You've always had a taste for the finer things in life, Dom. Bring some back for us, why don't you? Seeing as we're not invited.'

'We?'

'Maddie. Bring a bottle back for your wife.' Max's big fingers started drumming on the table.

'It's fine. Really, Max. I don't want any.' I just wanted him to stop drawing attention to me. If Max didn't back off, Dom was going to blow a fuse. In my direction.

'Shame,' Max said, picking up the cards and starting to shuffle them again.

'What's a *shame* is that I'm so busy I have to do business on a Saturday,' Dom said, 'but I don't suppose that occurs to anyone.' As I placed the cafetière on the table, he pushed the plunger down with force, coffee seeping through the lid and on to the white tablecloth. '*Damn*. Clumsy . . . Just mop it up, OK?' He flicked a glance up at me and I reached quickly for the kitchen roll.

'I thought you were looking for a new golf bag tomorrow. You didn't mention a meeting,' I said quietly, dabbing at the steaming brown patch.

'Didn't I?' Dom didn't bother to explain himself. He lifted his head to look over my shoulder towards the dresser. I knew he was looking for the whiskey bottle; I'd hidden it.

'You missed a bit,' he said, his hand shooting out to grab my wrist, forcing it back to the table, grinding my hand into the hot patch.

'So you'll be out all day tomorrow,' Max said, his dark eyes still watching his brother.

'Yes. No. I don't know. What is this, twenty questions?' Dom stood up and rooted irritably through the kitchen cupboards until he finally found the bottle of Jack Daniel's, pouring himself a large tumbler of the golden liquid and knocking back half in one slug.

His sigh of satisfaction drew a frown from Annabel, who had wandered in to get a glass of water. 'OK if we stay up a bit later tonight, Mum? We want to finish this film.' Annabel's wild hair tickled my face as she leaned close to my ear to whisper her request.

'OK, love. As it's not a school night. Just this once.' I rubbed my wrist, trying to ignore the pain where Dom had squeezed bones that were already bruised.

'You always say that! And then you'll say it again next Friday night, and then the next, and the next, and ... ' She curled into the crook of my arm like a kitten.

'Well, aren't you a lucky girl?' I said, winding a lock of her hair around my finger and tickling her freckled nose with it.

'Not *too* late, though!' I said, as she drifted back towards the kitchen door, rubbing her eyes sleepily.

'Yes, missy. It's well past your bedtime already,' Dom cut in, pouring himself another whiskey. 'I'll come and tuck you in later,' he added, patting her backside as she passed his chair.

'S'all right,' she told him, twirling away. 'I don't need tucking in. And you'll be driving Uncle Max home, won't you?'

'No. I won't,' Dom told her firmly. 'He's big enough and ugly enough to get the bus. Aren't you, Max?'

'Guess so. If it's too much trouble to give your only brother a lift after I've looked after your kids all afternoon. Helped them with their homework. Taught them how to do long division and everything.'

'I'm sure we've more than repaid you with dinners,' Dom said, looking pointedly at Max's empty plate. 'And no doubt you'll be here again for Sunday lunch.'

'Cheers. I'll do that.'

'It wasn't an invitation.'

'Aren't Lucy and Jasper coming on Sunday?' Annabel said from the doorway.

'You still there, princess? Not earwigging, are you?' Dom said. 'Because if you are, you'll have to answer to the Tickle Monster.' He reached across and pulled her on to his lap, tickling her ribs until her laughter turned to a coughing fit.

Annabel resisted, sliding away and pulling awkwardly at her short purple nightie. Usually so happy to be the centre of attention, I registered her self-consciousness as new. She was really growing up, I realised; it wouldn't be long before pre-teen body awareness kicked in and cuddles were completely out of bounds.

'Yeah, they are,' Aidan said, wandering in with his DS in one hand and an empty bowl in the other, his eyes scanning the worktop for more snacks. 'Jasp said his mum's taking him to Westfield tomorrow morning to buy new football boots because he did so well in his maths test.' He found a box of cereal and dug into it, bringing out a handful that he shared between his bowl and the kitchen floor.

'That's nice, love,' I said, turning away to do the washing-up so he couldn't see the blush I could feel creeping up my neck, and the rush of tears filling my eyes. Could Lucy and Dom really be meeting up secretly behind my back? Jasper would be with them, so they could hardly be planning a quiet, intimate drink, but even so it hurt that I hadn't been told, wasn't invited.

'Thanks for the steak, Maddie. It was top. I'll see myself out,' Max said, breaking into the awkward silence.

'No problem. Thanks. See you later.' I forced myself to turn around and smile.

'And don't worry about Sunday. I'll stop by in the week. Bring that new game round for the kids. Catch you later for our poker rematch, hey, Bel?' Max added, squeezing past her in the doorway.

'Give your uncle a kiss goodnight, then, Annabel. Come on. I'm sure the school teaches better manners than that for four grand a term,' Dom said with a heavy sigh, reaching again for the bottle in front of him.

'Sorry. Night, Uncle Max,' Annabel said quietly.

Max rested his big palm on the top of her head. 'Night night, sweet dreams, sugar.'

SIXTEEN

I stare again at the phone next to my bed, as if it might yield more clues to Max's whereabouts. I'm still none the wiser and can't stop thinking of him and puzzling about his message, until it dawns on me that something's missing from my bedside table.

On the day the twins were born, once I'd been patched together and wheeled back on to the ward, the midwife reappeared with an even bigger smile and a Polaroid camera and took the first ever photo of me with the twins. It's a snapshot that means more to me than my entire wedding album. I would not only run back into a burning house to save it, I'd crawl across the proverbial hot coals. I keep it next to me, always, at my bedside, displayed in a simple white wooden frame inscribed with the word 'Love'.

And it's not there.

My eyes dart around the room, but something at the back of my brain pulls them back to the suitcase in front of me. Slowly, I rifle through the clothes, my hand pushing deeper, seeking out the compartment at the bottom of the case. My fingertips find the zip and I draw it back, then carefully I lift the flap, sliding my hand underneath, patting inside the soft fleecy space until I encounter something hard . . . wooden.

My precious photo lies in my lap and I want to dive into the picture, scoop up my babies, be that woman again: dizzy with love for my new husband, our simple happy life, our brand-new family. But it's gone. All of it. Gone for ever. I trace my fingers over the slightly faded images of the twins, wishing I could bring them to life in my hands, wishing I had a pair of magic ballet shoes to transport me back to that moment, the best day of my life. I press the frame against the sob tightening my chest.

Something pricks my skin. Something is poking out of the edge of the frame. I unhook the tiny latches, releasing the plywood back, opening it wider until an envelope slips out. I slip my thumb under the flap, hooking out the contents: train tickets.

Destination: Brighton.

Date of travel: the twins' birthday.

Date of return: open-ended.

Passengers: One adult and two children.

I freeze for countless moments, my mind blank with confusion, and when I finally manage to focus again on the tickets in my hands I hear a shuffling noise. Footsteps. I hold my breath, my skin prickling and goosebumps chasing up the back of my neck.

Someone is in the house.

Hastily, I look around for somewhere to hide, and shock ripples through me as I see a pile of colourfully gift-wrapped presents piled up in the corner of the room. The living room.

What am I doing back here?

I must have blacked out again. My mouth is dry; my eyes are foggy. Disoriented and still breathless with fear, I strain my eyes to look more closely at the mountain of gifts. I see a purple balloon taped to a ribbon around one of them, and it bobs back and forth, swaying in a breath of breeze. I hear wind chimes and the sweet, melodic high notes of a recorder, but I cannot pay any attention to them because I'm transfixed by the printed message on the balloon, gently nodding at me as if to say: *That's right, you read the words correctly.*

HAPPY 10TH BIRTHDAY!

It doesn't make any sense. Why hasn't Dom cleared away the twins' presents? They never got a chance to open them on the morning of their birthday, but surely they haven't sat here all this time; I would have noticed. Or is it coming up to Aidan's eleventh birthday and Dom hasn't bothered to buy new balloons – has time slipped so unnoticed through my fingers that I've missed his special date? *His birthday will forever fall on the anniversary of his sister's death.* My poor, darling boy.

The balloon nods encouragingly at me. It's purple: Annabel's favourite colour. This pile of gifts is not for my son. It is—

Another noise: a creak on the stairs; a scraping, tapping sound at the front door. I can hear my heart thundering and look over my shoulder, waiting for the door to swing open and for *him* to sweep into the room. I'm suddenly convinced that whoever killed my daughter has come back for me; that he's playing mind games with me.

In the next heartbeat I tell myself it's not logical: no one murders a child and then gets to wander the streets of suburbia at will. I try to tell myself not to be so paranoid. I'm not in any danger; there isn't a killer in my home. I'll just walk calmly around the house and prove to myself that no one is stalking me; it's just another symptom of post-traumatic stress. It's Monday morning, Aidan is at school, Dom is at work, the house is empty. It's just me here alone with my nightmares.

But who put the twins' birthday presents back in the living room?

I glance at them one last time as I creep across the room, creaking the door ajar. I peer out into the hallway, squinting against the bright sunlight pouring through the glass front door. My heart seems to slow down and then rapidly speed up as I remember the bulky silhouette blotting out the summer's day. Swiftly, I turn my head and stumble up the stairs, no longer trying to be stealthy, just desperate to get away from that front door: the window into hell.

My feet seem to know where they're heading and within moments I'm sitting on Annabel's bed. My brain obviously draws a direct line between the possibility of an intruder and my daughter; any sense of threat pulls me to her like a magnet. Or, at least, to where her presence still lingers.

I sink down on her bed, listening for noises in the house. Below the silent stillness there is a low hum. I frown, unable to identify it. I wait to see if it stops but a faint electrical thrum still hovers in the air. There's nothing threatening about the soft, resonant drone. Houses make all kinds of strange noises, I reflect. No one has come to get me; no one is lying in wait to hurt me. There is no need to check cupboards, or behind the curtains, or under the bed . . .

But I do anyway, and instead of a bogeyman or a gun-toting monster, I find something almost as terrifying: Annabel's diary.

I sit holding the hardback book, its cover a glossy photograph of dewy white roses, for long moments. I sit with the knowledge that my daughter shared her innermost thoughts within these pages – her hopes, worries and fears . . . and no doubt all the stuff and nonsense that most nine-year-olds spend hours picking over.

I bought this diary for Annabel because it had a pretty cover and she always loved to write, but I never gave it another thought. I certainly never went looking for it, and something makes me hesitate now. Do I really want to see inside the mind of my dead daughter, when there will never be a chance to ask her about anything I may read within these pages?

I realise I'm scared of finding out that I didn't know her as well as I thought – or perhaps that she knew *me* too well, and saw into my own heart far too clearly. Painfully, I acknowledge that my clever, intuitive daughter may have sensed that cracks were appearing between her father and me. It would hurt me so badly now to know that she worried about it. I'm sure I never told Annabel or Aidan in so many words that I was unhappy, as I'm beginning to realise I was, even before domestic unhappiness was blown out of the water by the complete and utter destruction of my world. Death trumps divorce, always.

Was that what was going on? Is that what those three open-ended train tickets mean? That I was leaving Dom and taking the children with me – on their *birthday*? The date seems so significant. Why on their birthday? Or was it just that I could only manage to hold on for one more day, until they'd enjoyed their special moment – blown out their candles before I snuffed out their happiness and took them away from their friends, their home, their father ...?

But why Brighton? Do I even know anyone there?

I remember Annabel's sparkling eyes as she leaned over the end of the pier, and I remember the appointment I was trying to keep. I sense the shadow of someone, am aware that there was a person I was planning – or hoping – to meet during the May half-term break. But I have no recollection of any name; I can't picture anyone's face. My mind draws a complete blank. Perhaps there was no connection; maybe I wasn't meeting anyone that day and Brighton was simply somewhere new, unknown. Perhaps that was the point. Maybe that's exactly what I wanted: to run away and make a fresh start, somewhere no one would think to look for me; somewhere we would never be found.

A place of safety.

The thought echoes in my brain. Safe from Dom – yes, I can see that now. I was scared of him; perhaps the kids were, too. Maybe that's what tipped me over the edge – seeing my children look at their father with wide, frightened eyes, hiding under the piano, waiting for the axe to fall . . .

I wouldn't have told them; I know that. I would have hidden those tickets in the suitcase, tucked inside the photo I would never have left behind. I would have tried to protect them from the truth, not because I worried they might betray my secret to Dom, but because *that's what mothers do*: they keep secrets from their children when those secrets can destroy their entire world. I'm sure Jasper has no idea that his mum is secretly in love with her best friend's husband. Because she is, isn't she? And her son has no idea that his happiness is teetering on the brink – that his mother could pull the rug out from beneath his safe, happy world at any time.

Somehow I know this – and I know that's what I was about to do. And I suspect Annabel may have guessed my secrets. She was the smartest girl I've ever known, while Aidan was the most empathic, most intuitive. Did they both know? And did that knowledge break my daughter's heart? That I was going to take her away from Dom, her beloved daddy. *Daddy's princess . . .*

There is only one way to find out. I open the diary and turn to a random page, somewhere near this summer.

Matthew Jones is an idiot. He thinks he's cool, but he's so not! Why does he keep picking on me? What have I done to him? Just because I told him to stop teasing Aid about his hair.

I smile and relief shudders through me. I hadn't realised how nervous I was. My fingers are still trembling but this isn't as bad as I thought. I keep turning the pages, smiling as my eyes catch phrases here and there. Then a lump forms like a rock in my throat.

> Mum wore lipstick and perfume today. She smelled like angels. I love her round the stars and over Mars. If she was reading this she'd say she loves me more. But she can't. I love her best of anything that exists in the world, the universe, space and heaven.

It takes long moments for any joy to surface through the gut-clenching guilt and heartache. I remember wondering if I chose her because I thought she didn't need me – or if I loved her less than Aidan. How could I have been so blind, so stupid? I adored her; I know I did. Yes, she was often challenging and we had our differences. I was angry with her sometimes – there were days when, if I'm honest with myself, I've hated being a parent – but I simply can't believe there was hate in my heart on the morning of the twins' tenth birthday.

Her words tear my heart to shreds. I want to bury myself in them and weep. *My darling girl.* I wish you were here now to tell me not to cry, not to be so soft. I keep turning pages, barely taking in the words, doodles and cartoon drawings of her teachers and a couple of her friends' dads, until another entry catches my eye. I want to hide in Annabel's bed, my face under her pillow, and never come out as I read:

> Mum hasn't smiled for a week.
> Aid hasn't laughed for a month.
> I may never stop crying for ever.

What was going on that day? I check the date again: it means nothing and I haven't the heart to read any more entries. I start to push the diary away from me when three words draw my attention: *his disgusting touch*.

It's out of sync with the otherwise light and girlish narrative, and I flatten the pages, skim back to the beginning of the page, and start reading again.

> I wish he'd stop looking at me. His eyes follow me round the room like the posters on my bedroom wall.

Is this Matthew Jones again, I wonder, being a pest at school? I continue reading, heart thumping. That boy ... why did no one ever sort him out?

> Making creepy eyes is one thing. But now he wants me to do things. I keep saying no to his disgusting touch. How can he do this to me? He's a grown-up!!

What the ... ?

> He's getting cross with me for telling him no. I know he's not going to give up. He's going to keep coming after me until he gets what he wants. And if he doesn't ...

SEVENTEEN

I know that it's a physical impossibility to suffocate with nothing over my face, but the sensation is exactly how I'd imagine it. I gasp – no, I *bite* at the air, gulping it in and swallowing fat pockets into my lungs to stop myself from blacking out.

No! No! No!

Denial rips through me, but the truth lies in front of me in Annabel's own childish words, written with too much feeling to be made up – not that Annabel ever told fibs. I trusted her absolutely – Aidan, too. I always told them that there was no truth so bad that I would ever stop loving them, and that it was far better to *tell* that truth so that I could do something about it. Help them. But I didn't help her; I didn't know.

She didn't tell me . . .

Why didn't she tell me?

I rock back and forth with the agony of what her silence implies about our relationship, as much as the terrible truth it concealed. The thought that she felt, for whatever reason, that she needed to keep this awful thing a secret from me, her mum, cuts deep. I failed her. I failed her not once, but twice. And now it's too late to put it right, any of it ...

But I need to go on; I need to know *more*. Who was the monster that did this to my daughter? Frantically, I scan the pages, skimming through them at speed, my eyes glancing here and there across my daughter's curly, looping handwriting, desperately looking for a name, a clue ...

There is nothing.

I try not to crumble beneath the sense of failure that presses down on me. All this time I thought I was unpicking *my own* story, but I've been looking in completely the wrong direction. Eyes down, thoughts inward – methodically, step by step, I've been trying to piece everything together, building a neat tower of all the fragments I've managed to pick out of the heavy haze in my traumatised mind, all the tiny clues that I've winkled out and stacked up, higher and higher, hoping that at some point I will be able to climb right to the very top and look down, see the complete picture of what happened, where I went wrong ...

Now the tower has come crashing down, fragments scattering in every direction, and I can't even begin to think how to piece them together.

Think!

Start at the corners and work inwards; that's what Aidan always does, and he builds the most beautiful, elaborate jigsaws. He'll be an engineer for sure one day.

Stay focused! Run through the facts ...

My bag was packed and I had bought train tickets.

My marriage was unhappy.

Max was leaving messages on our phone.

Someone was trying to touch my daughter ...

*

Maternal instinct, like a powerful magnet, finally sucks all the pieces together; scattered neurotransmitters begin to collide, synapses whispering messages, connections forming at lightning speed. I think of Annabel lying so coldly beneath the rose bushes, her eyes staring up at the night sky. Her beautiful eyes gaze in one direction and the stars seem so haphazard, sprinkled randomly in a sprawling shapeless constellation. She turns her head slightly and a pattern emerges: shape, definition, identity . . .

I close my eyes and reach out to my daughter in her flowery grave, and I feel a shockwave of recognition: the man – the monster – who was trying to entice my daughter must also be her killer. I feel it like a lightning bolt shooting through me. There was no tragic coincidence at play. Call it instinct – I simply don't buy it. This wasn't some random stranger who turned up on the morning of the twins' birthday to spoil their day, to steal our lives. He was dressed in military fatigues, but he wasn't a terrorist; he didn't kill my daughter in the name of any religion or politics: it was strictly, deadly personal.

'It's always someone close to the family, isn't it?' I remember Lucy saying when we were talking about a high-profile murder on the news one day, after dropping off the kids.

How bitterly ironic that conversation feels in hindsight; I would never have imagined in my worst nightmares that my own family would become another such talking point at the school gate.

'I know what you mean,' I replied. 'They all sit there at the press conference, looking tearful and devastated, making their heartfelt pleas; and we're all thinking the same thing: *The husband did it!*'

'Awful, aren't we?' Lucy said. 'I'm sure it's not always the case. Murders are sometimes committed by completely random lunatics on the rampage.'

'Of course. Otherwise we'd all be checking our garden sheds every night for sharp implements, wouldn't we?' I'd tried to make light of the subject, feeling a shiver down my spine at the terrible contemplation of a death in the family.

'Still, it's remarkable how often it turns out to be someone right under their noses,' Lucy added, shaking her head.

Right under my nose.

Yes, that was exactly it.

But *who*? What would drive *anyone* to commit the unspeakable crime of hurting a child – a tiny, beautiful girl with skinny chopstick arms, a smile more luminous than the moon as she danced on the threshold of her life? The horror of this is so beyond humanity that anything seems possible. It defies logic; the normal rules of life simply can't apply in such a situation.

I wish I could remember, but trauma has cauterised huge chunks of my life, anything that is too painful to recall. And I've felt so fragile that I haven't been able to bring myself to ask Dom to remind me of that day and what came after. All I've been able to do is look back to the past, hoping that would lead me to some kind of understanding. But it's not enough. I need to know who did this, and I need to know *now*. He didn't just take my daughter's life; he made it a living hell. And then he killed her to protect his own guilt; to stop her telling tales about what he was doing to her behind closed doors.

Why didn't she tell me?

Maybe she *did* threaten to tell, and that's why he finally took action. Yet such a cowardly act could have been committed in secret. He didn't have to wait for an audience; there was no need to stage a public execution. For that is clearly what it was. And he *made me choose*. He punished *me*, too, by making me complicit in his sickening crime. *Why?* Who would want to hurt *me* in such a dreadful way? And how could he even know I would choose Annabel, conveniently covering up what he'd been trying to do to her? It doesn't make any sense.

Think, Madeleine, think ...

I flee out of the room, wildly throwing open doors – my bedroom, Aidan's room, the bathroom, airing cupboard – unsure what I'm looking for but just desperately hunting for something, a clue of any kind, anything that might jolt some kind of understanding into place. Almost flying down the stairs, I burst into the living room, eyes darting around, my fraught gaze resting on the piano, the sideboard, the sofa, the coffee table – the wood burner full of cold ashes ... I need to find a newspaper, or my computer. Or my phone. I need to read my own headlines – the ones I've avoided, too terrified to know the full truth – and finally read in black and white what happened on the twins' birthday.

You have to do this.

You owe it to Annabel – to Aidan ... Stop hiding and start living again!

But Dom has done his job well: he's cleared the house, eradicating any possibility of chance encounters with distressing news stories. He's protected me, just as he's shouldered all the responsibility for dealing with the police, Annabel's funeral, caring for Aidan ... and meanwhile I've just fallen apart. I've remembered my fear of Dom, but I've forgotten his strength. His love. For me, and for our children. I've been so wrapped up in my own torment that I've overlooked *his*. But I *have* seen his agony; I've watched him plodding through the days since we lost Annabel, putting on a brave face for Aidan, keeping an icy wall between the two of us – patient, subdued, a shadow of the man he used to be ...

The stars realign, the pattern shifts, and I see the picture from a different angle. Dom has been punished too. Perhaps *he* was the one the killer wanted to hurt, not me. After all, he has lost both his precious daughter *and* his wife: I've been swallowed up by grief, our marriage hollowing to an empty shell. I try to think of anyone who might have a grudge against him. A disgruntled client? A vindictive rival? A neighbour he's offended – a *teacher*? I grasp at straws, desperately needing to make sense of this senseless crime, because to live with the idea that Annabel's death was just a meaningless, random act of violence by a complete stranger is beyond anything I can bear.

But I'm sure there's something I'm missing. My head is so jumbled I'm overlooking something right in front of me. I go back to the corners, trace around the edges, try once more to fill in the missing pieces. I retrace my own steps, think about the suitcase, the photo, the phone message ... My heart starts pounding as I remember that message. Something about it bothers me.

I'm waiting for you ...

And Annabel's words, written days before her tenth birthday: *He's going to keep coming after me until he gets what he wants.*

Someone full of longing and desire, who wanted something so badly he wouldn't stop until he possessed her – or destroyed her. Someone like the kindly uncle who idolised the beauty of a child he didn't have himself, and became angry when she rejected him ...

EIGHTEEN

My bedroom is quiet. I am exhausted, weightless, floating; I let myself fall into the darkness until it absorbs me. Softly a hand strokes my forehead and it soothes me. I burrow deeper into the cool sheets, their whiteness draping around me like a silken shroud, tighter and tighter . . . I let the dress slide down my arms, brush across my waist, clinging briefly to the curve of my pregnant belly, already full and hard at five months along.

Twins!

My mother was a fraternal twin, so I should have been prepared for the possibility, but it still seems like a miracle. I peel the cool ivory silk away from my hips and roll it down over my thighs, nerves fluttering into excited butterflies as my beautiful wedding dress ripples into a moonlit pool at my feet. I step out of it and look up into Dom's blue eyes, loving the way they widen as he glances down at my ripe body pressing against him.

'You are the most beautiful woman I've ever met. You're all mine now, Maddie, and I'll never, ever let you go.'

He takes hold of my left hand and holds it gently, then presses it firmly so that I feel the platinum band ('Only the best for my wife!') dig into my flesh. He twists and turns it, pushing it on, taking it off, rotating it round and round my finger. Fingertips caress upwards to my neck in long, languid strokes. A hand circles my throat; I feel the unexpected coldness of the skin and I frown. The pressure tightens and I can smell something acidic; it makes me cough. My body stiffens, all sense of peace and pleasure evaporating. I'm choking, gasping for air; I can't breathe and I can't call out. Pain screams in my head, as I see a bright light and hear a loud bang like an explosion; a blinding white flash burns across my eyelids. Breathless with fear I open them, and I'm buried in darkness.

And I am alone.

Realisation unlocks my fear: *I was only dreaming.*

I lie rigid, trembling as I tell myself that I must have fallen asleep, exhausted from the emotion of reading Annabel's diary and trying to work out who pursued her, hounded her – and then took her life. It was just a nightmare, but tattered remnants linger, caught in my skin like thorns. I can still feel the hands around my throat, squeezing, and my heart is racing as my memory fast forwards to the present day: missing Annabel, yearning to hold her.

What time is it? Are Dom and Aidan home yet?

I've given up completely on the idea of leaving. The suitcase lies open next to my bed, but I don't have the energy even to move. Despair weighs me down and I feel empty inside, and more lost than ever. I just need to see Dom. I need to ask him – I need him to tell me ...

I battle to stay awake, but my eyes can't seem to stay open. I hear the sound of Aidan's recorder and I struggle to sit up, my heart leaping at the thought of seeing him. They must be back.

I want Aidan. I miss Annabel. I need to hold my son.

But memories claw at me once more, dragging me back again to the past.

NINETEEN

'You shouldn't have booked the leisure centre for the party.' Dom was sitting upright in our bed, his broad shoulders hunched like a cliff face next to me. 'I can't afford it. The kids' school fees are due this week. What the hell were you *thinking*?'

It was the morning of the twins' birthday, just before dawn. I wasn't sure Dom had slept at all; I certainly hadn't, and my body felt lethargic but also wired, on high alert. I could sense his agitation even in the semi-darkness. I'd been aware of it most of the night, lying next to him as he'd tossed and turned, my eyes firmly shut, body rigid as I tried not to give away that I'd heard him come in.

'I was *thinking* that I wanted to give the twins a lovely party for their tenth birthday. With their friends. And do you know what's really sad?' I tried to keep the bitterness out of my tone but it rankled that he was making a fuss about the cost of the party. He hadn't shown the same frugality last night, judging by the way he'd lurched around our bedroom, bouncing off the walls when he tried to sneak in during the early hours. I could still smell the alcohol evaporating from his pores.

'No, but you're going to tell me, aren't you?'

'What's sad is that every friend they've invited is from their old school. No one but the kids they've grown up with – the ones you don't want them to have as friends any more because they haven't got the right background, or the right sort of parents, or enough money to go to a posh school.'

'Annabel loves that school,' he insisted, rubbing his hands tiredly over his eyes.

'Does she?' I said, letting scepticism coat my words. *Does she? I* thought anxiously, wondering if this was one more thing she hadn't felt able to tell me.

'Yes, she does. She told me so,' he said, and I could hear the smug undertone.

'When?' My voice was faint now.

'What?'

I could make out the glint of his eyes in his shadowy profile.

'*When* did she tell you? Where were you? What were you doing?' I said more confidently, certain he was making it up to hurt me. I tried to think when Dom might have had a tête-à-tête with our daughter. He was hardly ever around these days.

'Oh, the other day. Whenever. Stop interrogating me, for God's sake!' he barked.

'Shh! You'll wake them up. This is supposed to be a special day for them, remember?' I reached out a pacifying hand but withdrew it at the last moment, suspecting he might slap it away.

'For them – or for you?' His voice sliced through the air.

'Surely for us both – and you – *all* of us, Dom,' I said wearily, bracing myself for the row that seemed inevitable now but having little energy for it. 'What happened to us being a family? You're never here any more, you're always angry, you just don't seem happy at all. Dom, this can't – *we* can't go on like this.'

'I'm sorry.' His voice softened unexpectedly, blowing the faintest whisper of hope across my despair. 'It's just . . . I so want to give you all the best of everything. It's all I've *ever* wanted.' His frown was plaintive.

'I know. I know you do. Look, let's just try to have a happy day, shall we? Just get through one more day without a fight. Celebrate the twins' birthday – they deserve a bit of fun after—'

'After what?' A chink of light through the curtains caught the glint of his blue eyes as he angled his body to loom over me, his steady gaze challenging me to answer truthfully.

'After how difficult things have been. These last few months,' I said, hearing my own breathlessness but willing myself not to look away. It had taken me a while, but eventually I'd learned my lesson: maintain eye contact; betray no fear. Sometimes that stopped his anger from boiling over. I had to be honest with him, but I also needed to keep things calm. Meet him halfway without riling him or humiliating myself further.

'Difficult, you say? You been paying any bills lately, then? Because they're sure as hell not paying themselves.' He rubbed his hands over his face again and for a second I thought he was going to drop the subject and back off.

'I didn't know money was so tight. Why didn't you *say*?'

'Why didn't you ask?'

'That's not fair. You've always told me that you manage the finances and I manage the kids. That's what we agreed, isn't it? And besides, the party isn't costing much.'

His hand shot out and grabbed my wrist, taking me by surprise; immediately I felt the blood pulsing in my constricted veins. 'What bit don't you get?' he said, his voice hard again. 'I – can't – afford – a – party.' He spelled it out with a bone-snapping squeeze to my wrist after each word. 'We're practically broke. The business is sinking. We're in danger of losing the house. That meeting in Manchester I told you about, after the party, is actually a job interview, and if I don't get it, we're screwed. The bank will repossess the house.'

I was so shocked I could barely speak. 'Why didn't you *tell* me, Dom?'

'And what exactly would you have been able to do about it? It's not like you have any head for business. Not like Lucy. She knows—'

'*Lucy?*'

'Yes. *Lucy.* But don't worry; she won't be conveniently around the corner from my office if I do get offered this job. We'll have to move to Manchester.' His voice was flat and hard.

'But I don't want to move. The twins are settled here.'

Leave my home, go to a place where I wouldn't know anyone – without any friends to support me, trapped with a husband who—

'You don't have a choice. Look what happens when you make the decisions! You've booked that scuzzy leisure centre for the kids' party. I don't like them swimming there. It's full of old pervs. I thought you'd have more sense.'

'Your brother works there!' I said, trying to pull my wrist away. I was starting to get a dead arm.

'Yes, well, *quite.* I'm surprised they haven't sacked him, after that incident last year. I spent the best part of last night in The Bell Inn listening to all his usual trumped-up twaddle. Said he wanted to talk to me about something. Only I had to buy him at least seven whiskies first, of course, before he'd actually tell me what it was. Same old Max. Same old shit. He's surpassed himself this time, though.' He finally let go of me and sagged forward to rest his arms on his raised knees, his shoulders slumping.

'What incident? What *is* it? *Tell* me!' I wasn't interested in pub talk, but I did want to know if something bad had happened at the pool where I'd booked the twins' party. A chill ran through my body. There were far too many secrets. Dom had clearly stopped telling me anything of any importance, and Annabel had stopped confiding in me, shutting me out of her world. The former shocked me, but the latter was devastating. 'Dom, I read Annabel's diary last night,' I said, when he remained silent. The words sounded thick, my voice deeper than usual; I was struggling to get my breath now.

'*And?*' He raised his eyebrows, mocking my concern.

'And I think something bad has been happening. Something truly awful.' My throat was so tight I could barely speak.

I hadn't been going to tell him. Annabel had refused to talk to me when I'd sat on the end of her bed and gently asked about her diary. Rage and despair had been ripping a hole in my heart all night, but Dom and I had long since stopped sharing our pain. I'd lain in bed thinking of nothing else, trying to work out what to do, and now my agony was bursting out of me. I had to tell him. He needed to know; something had to be *done*.

'Don't be so overdramatic. Give the girl a break. You're always so hard on her.'

'I am *not!*' I said, my heart aching.

'Go on, then, what is it? No, don't tell me: she's been smoking. Or she tried a sneaky cider at the drama club disco. Come on, hit me with it. What shocking secret have you discovered about your sweet, innocent nine-year-old daughter?'

'I'm serious, Dom. I think someone has been trying to ... to touch her. Or make her touch them. I don't know. Just ... something. Something isn't right. I tried to ask her about it last night, but she refused to say anything.'

'What *did* she say exactly?' His big body stilled; his eyes bore into mine.

'I told you, nothing. That's the point. She just said nothing. That she's fine.'

'So what's the problem?'

'The problem is I don't believe her.'

'See, this is your trouble, Maddie. You always think you know better than everyone else. The perfect mother who is right about everything, and everyone else—'

'Dom . . .'

'You just sit there on your high fucking horse, and you can't bear anyone or anything that tarnishes your halo. You worship Aidan because he's a soft mummy's boy who does everything you ask. But you come down hard on Annabel because she challenges you. Because she wants a bit of independence and doesn't want you poking into all her business. And that makes you feel like you're not *quite* the perfect parent. She makes you angry, doesn't she? Go on, admit it. She infuriates you and you hate that about yourself – about her.'

He whipped back the duvet and twisted round to sit on the edge of the bed. I turned away, not wanting to see his naked body, too upset to allow that intimacy between us.

'That's not true, and stop changing the subject all the time. This isn't about me, it's about *Annabel*!'

'No. It isn't. It's about you needing to appreciate what you have in your own life, concentrate on our marriage for once and stop living vicariously through your daughter. Let her go, Maddie. *Let her go.*'

He stood up and reached for his jeans and shirt on the chair, yanking them on but leaving his shirt hanging open; it was so hot in the bedroom. I watched him fasten his belt. I wanted to get up, too – get up, out and on with the day. Clearly, neither of us was going back to sleep now, even though it couldn't have been much after five. Only I wanted to wait until he'd left the room.

I was trying really hard not to cry – Dom found that just as infuriating as my daring to disagree with him. When had he stopped seeing me as the most beautiful woman in the world? When had I stopped seeing him as my hero? Perhaps we'd hit the top of the slippery slope years ago; certainly the events of our ninth anniversary had been a low point. But it seemed to me that things had really begun to slide when Dom decided the twins needed to go to private school.

Yet Dom had been the one to insist on it. *The best of everything; never settle for second best.* That's what he always said, and we'd all paid the price for his pride. His arrogance. He was buckling under the pressure of expenses he couldn't meet and aspirations he couldn't afford. The last nine months had been a fast track to hell, I acknowledged bitterly. Dom had become increasingly absent, and whenever he was around he was fraught with stress. And now I realised why. With his business struggling, the self-imposed burden of the school fees must have been the last straw.

If only I'd known ... But he'd never told me; he'd just taken his frustration out on me, with sarcasm and aggression. I'd grown more and more quiet and withdrawn, terrified of provoking his moods. Aidan, too, seemed to be shrinking into himself. Only Annabel had managed to keep a smile on her face, but it wasn't genuine. I knew then that it had been an act, and I'd missed all the signs. Missed them because I was too busy scrabbling around in the scattered wreckage of my marriage.

I had to put it right; I had to *do* something about it. All of it. Before it was too late.

'Let her go. What, so you can turn her against me and have her all to yourself?' I said, knowing I was playing with fire. I didn't want bruises on the twins' birthday. I just wanted them to have a special day; a birthday they'd never forget.

'Fuck you,' he hissed.

'Just leave me alone, Dom. Please, just leave me alone,' I said, my throat aching with the tears I refused to shed in front of him and the effort of keeping my voice low. The twins were still asleep; I didn't want them to hear us rowing – again.

'Is that really what you want? For me to just . . . step aside?' Just for a second he looked sad, and I wondered if it was still possible to reach him – the old Dom. 'Because it's not what *I* want,' he said, before I could answer, and his voice sounded strangled. 'I've given everything I've got to this family, and I'm not letting you all go. Not without a fight.'

'I really thought you'd be happy about the party, Dom,' I said quietly. 'And it honestly didn't cost much. Max got me a discount on the booking, and he's going to help me set it all up. He's coming at ten, and—'

'No surprise there.'

'Lucy helped with the party food,' I said, ignoring his usual sarcasm about his brother. 'The twins are so excited about their big day. I thought you'd be happy.'

'You thought? You *thought*? But you didn't *ask*, did you? You didn't ask me what I wanted. You just went ahead and—'

'That's not fair. You always leave the kids' stuff to me. You don't have the time and I'm better at it – that's what you always say.'

I could hear desperation in my voice – a mute plea for him to remember that we used to be a *team*, each fulfilling our own role so that we complemented the other's: work, home, school . . . We each played to our strengths, and we were happy. At least we had been, once. After what I'd read in Annabel's diary, I wasn't sure I'd ever be happy again.

Dom crossed the bedroom in one long stride and knelt on the bed, looming over me, his face so close to mine I could see the beads of sweat on his morning stubble and smell the expensive aftershave he doused himself in so liberally. I'd left the bedroom window open last night, but the air was still stifling with summer humidity. I could feel heat coming in angry waves off Dom's broad chest, and with scared eyes I tracked the dark arrow of hair arrogantly pointing down towards the waistband of his jeans, the

121

bulge at his crotch. With his arms braced either side of my head, his biceps also bulged, taunting me with the leashed power in his body. I pressed myself back into the pillows, heart slamming against my ribcage, praying that he wouldn't launch himself on me.

Not today. *Please, not today, of all days.*

I held myself rigid as he leaned in closer still, his knee sliding forcefully between my legs and pressing painfully against me, his breath hot on my face. 'I was just trying to make you feel better about having turned into such a useless fucking *passenger.*'

'You bastard,' I said on a shocked intake of breath, and was as surprised as Dom when my hand seemed to jerk of its own free will towards his face, the slap ringing loudly in the quiet of the dawn.

'Bitch,' he spat, his punch bouncing like a piston off my cheekbone, jolting my head back with almost neck-snapping force.

I turned away and buried my face in the pillow, waiting for more blows, praying no bones would be broken this time; hiding a cracked rib while trying to be jolly decorating the Christmas tree with the twins had been excruciating. But Dom's body weight shifted and a gust of air rushed through the room, followed by the sound of the front door slamming moments later. The whole house seemed to shake.

'Mummy?' Annabel's voice from the next room was sleepy, uncertain.

'It's all right, angel. I'll be there in a second. Try to go back to sleep.' Weak with relief, I tried to swallow around the lump in my throat and keep my voice steady. My cheekbone was throbbing, the pain so sharp I thought I might black out.

'Was that Daddy going out? Has he forgotten to get our present? Has he gone to the shops? When is he coming back?'

She appeared suddenly at my side of the bed, unable to wait for answers. Her hair was gloriously wild and her purple nightie was endearingly crumpled and didn't quite reach her knees.

'It's OK, darling,' I soothed, reaching for her. 'He's just popped out. He'll be back in time for your party, I'm sure. Daddy wouldn't let his little princess down, now, would he?'

TWENTY

Fear shoots like electricity through my brain until I'm convinced it's about to explode. I hear buzzing and bright lights seem to flash in front of my eyes – first the left one, then the right. There is a sharp pain in my left arm; I feel like I'm having a heart attack. I twist and turn, fighting it – battling horror and heartache, fear and suspicion. I force my sleep-deadened legs to move, running out of my bedroom and down the stairs, desperately looking for something – someone – to help me.

I hear footsteps again, somewhere in the house, and I freeze, looking frantically around me. I see faces swimming in front of my burning eyes: the twins' teachers, past and present; coaches at their clubs; other parents; our neighbours . . . Max. *Dom.* But each time I hone in on one, my fingers twitch and clutch at thin air and I remember clawing my way through clammy soil, my arms scratched by thorns, blood soaking through my clothes and vomit filling my mouth as my arms reached out for Annabel.

There is only one thing I'm clear about: Aidan lived, Annabel died, and *I made the call.* I know this because I've seen my guilt branded on Aidan's face for all these months. I've heard every silent roar of blame that Dom is managing, for once, not to bellow in my face. Traumatic shock may have stolen my voice, but their icy silence tells me everything I need to know, as does my heart that is dying inside me, crushed beneath the weight of the only dreadful fact I know for certain . . .

My daughter is dead, and the killer – whoever he is – may have pulled the trigger, but it hardly matters who he was, or why he did it, because *I let Annabel go*, and I hate myself for it – and my husband and son hate me too. I've lost everyone I've ever loved, and it's all my fault.

I open my mouth, and I scream.

PART TWO

TWENTY-ONE

Someone is stroking my hand. I remember that touch; it feels familiar, comforting. But my whole arm feels bruised and battered. I hear the bell-like tinkle of wind chimes and it reminds me of hazy autumn afternoons in my garden, the ashy incense of bonfire smoke catching my throat as I sweep up golden drifts of leaves, the twins laughing as they throw handfuls at each other. A ripple of cool breeze brushes against my cheeks; my eyes are tightly shut but a bright light burns through my eyelids.

I'm close. I can feel it. The sunlight is strong on my face, the bright light urging me onwards, upwards. I'm almost there; I've almost surfaced.

Is this death? A bright light at the end of the tunnel?

Don't be soft, Mum. There's no such place as heaven.

Then how will I ever see you again, Annabel? If there is no heaven, I have no hope left at all.

Calmness seeps through my veins like a liquid drug; the clouds part and the sun is shining brightly. Only it's not the sun: it's an angular metal lamp, its harsh white bulb directed straight into my eyes. Suddenly the powerful beam shifts to one side, but my eyes are still blinded, my retinas dazzled by the burning brightness.

'Mrs Castle? Can you hear me?'

I try to place the voice, but no connection registers. Is it my next-door neighbour? What is Mr Cooper doing in my house? Was it his footsteps I heard on the stairs, following me round the house?

I try to turn in the direction of the voice but my head feels like it's caught in a vice. My eyes ache but they at least move, and through dim, shadowy vision I can just about make out dark hair, a white coat, a solid masculine form. My mind tries to stencil the outline of this tall, lean shape on to the hunched and elderly figure of my neighbour. I close my eyes as I realise it's not a fit. This isn't Mr Cooper. Mr Cooper is eighty and squat; he doesn't have this commanding upright stature of a soldier or a—

I force myself to open my eyes again, squinting against the bright light above me, and I see an unfamiliar room. I'm not at home, then. And there is something shiny hanging from the stranger's neck. Is that a . . . my brain fumbles around for the word . . . *stethoscope*?

'Mrs Castle, my name is Professor Hernandez and I am a doctor. Can you hear me?' he repeats.

Such a calm, soothing voice. But what is that accent? It's not London – it's not even English. I frown, trying to identify it, and the man clearly takes it as a sign that I can hear him; he nods approvingly at me, reminding me more of the twins' new headmaster than our GP. And in any case, our regular doctor is a woman. So who is—

'That's good. Well done. Take your time. You're going to feel very strange at first, so please try not to be scared.'

He places a syringe on a small metal tray and then moves closer, leaning towards me, blocking out the light and filling my entire field of vision. I see brown skin, a neatly buttoned white shirt and tightly knotted navy tie beneath the white coat. Closer still – I can hear him breathing, his chest rising and falling steadily. He's older than he sounds, I think. His hair is greying and there are lines around the black eyes that observe me steadily from beneath low, dense brows: clear, alert, unblinking.

Scared? Why should I be scared when these gentle eyes are here to watch over me? I was scared at home, I remember. But not here.

Where is *here?*

I look around, blinking until the blurriness sharpens into clarity. Apart from the lamp over my bed, the room is dimly lit. I make out two doors, one at the end of the room and one to the side; there is a curtained window to my right and a collection of machines, monitors and digital displays to my left. A fan purrs gently on a side table, making the vase of flowers next to it shimmy and sway as if dancing to the tinkling tune of the wind chimes hanging nearby. I notice a clipboard hooked over the end of my bed; the frame is white metal, the sheets are white, the walls and ceiling are white.

The stark room triggers a decade-old memory of lying in the West Mid postnatal ward, surrounded by new mums, desperately trying to block out the sounds of chattering visitors and crying babies, staring at the ceiling and whispering over and over to myself the names of my newborn twins: *Annabel and Aidan; Aidan and Annabel.* One hand hovered over them constantly as I anxiously watched their every breath, never quite letting go of the plastic crib at the side of my hospital bed; the other grasped the metal bedstead and squeezed hard as I battled waves of cramping pain after the complicated delivery and subsequent operation that lasted hours but still left me with no hope of having any more babies. *Annabel and Aidan.* They would be my only children; they were already my whole world.

I absorb the memory and peer curiously once more around the

room. So am I in hospital? Is that what this place is? Did I faint, black out again? I remember running wildly round the house – did I fall? Who found me – *Aidan*? Questions crowd my mind and I feel the first stirrings of panic, worried that Aidan came home from school and found me collapsed on the floor and was scared. I can't remember what happened, but it must have been pretty bad for me to end up in hospital for only the second time in my life.

'Try to stay calm.' That husky, mellow voice at my side again; a gentle hand on my arm. 'I know you must be feeling confused, so I'll try to explain the situation as simply as I can. Please do your best to lie still, just for the moment. We're taking good care of you. You are completely safe. There is nothing for you to worry about now except getting better.'

Getting better? Nothing to worry about? Has no one told this man that I've lost my daughter, that I was on the verge of leaving my husband, and that my world has shattered into a million pieces?

'Mrs Castle,' he continues, before I can correct his assertion that my life is a bowl of cherries, 'you are a patient in the neurological rehabilitation centre here at the Royal Buckinghamshire Hospital. I'm a consultant here, and I'm in charge of your care. I'm happy to tell you that you're showing excellent signs of making a good recovery.'

Neurological. I did bang my head, then. I wonder if that was before or after I screamed . . .

I remember the scream being torn from my throat – an actual, audible sound in the real world not just echoing inside my mind – and ponder whether something as simple as a blow to the head has finally knocked my selective mutism for six. Maybe something – *what?* – has literally knocked the sense back into me – real, physical trauma to the skull jolting my stubborn amygdala out of auto-freeze mode.

I open my mouth to test this theory but frustratingly no words emerge, even though the voice inside my head is loud and insistent. It's like someone has cut a wire, pulled a plug: I'm jabbering in my mind but no sound is coming out. I feel cross with myself. I can't just lie here; I had something *important* to do.

What did I have to do?

'You've suffered a head trauma and have been in a coma for some time.' The man's speech is careful, measured and unhurried, in stark contrast to the wild, panicky voice still screeching inside my head.

Coma? From a bang on the head – a fall? For some time?

I close my mouth, which feels parched, and give up trying to speak. Listening is so much easier than battling; it's far less exhausting to give in and do as I've been instructed, to just lie here and let this kindly stranger talk to me, even if his words don't make any sense.

I've been in a coma?

I watch his mouth as if lip-reading might help. But I'm not deaf – I can hear perfectly – I just don't understand what he's telling me. I can't feel any connection to the information he's relaying, the person he's describing; it's like he's talking about someone else.

'Emergency surgery was carried out at the West Middlesex Hospital in Isleworth. Once you were stable, they transferred you here for rehabilitation.'

Still nothing clicks. I understand the words individually, but I can't fit them together into a recognisable meaning. He reaches for the clipboard and consults his notes, and I'm impatient to get a closer look, wondering if they might help me grasp the situation more quickly, but when I try to lift my head it feels as though it's weighed down with rocks. I can't move. I'm not exactly in pain; I'm just . . . numb.

Am I paralysed?

Fear darts through me and I know I'm holding my breath as I

make a deliberate effort to twitch my fingers and toes; I only release a deep sigh of relief when the sheet rises up slightly where my feet must be, and I see my fingers lifting one by one as if I'm silently rehearsing a piano tune. I notice my wedding ring is missing from my left hand, and I frown.

'Movement may prove difficult at first, Mrs Castle,' the doctor goes on, more softly now, his steady gaze observing my down-turned mouth. 'Think of it this way: your body has been asleep for more than three months. You're not simply going to bounce back. There's been minimal nerve damage and you've shown reassuringly limited signs of muscle atrophy, but even so. Physical recovery takes varying amounts of time after a coma. We have the very best facilities here, though. Your recovery programme will include physiotherapy, hydrotherapy . . .'

More than three months?

I zone out, taking in little beyond this one simple fact, and I widen my eyes until my eyebrows can't arch any higher; I still don't trust my voice to work but I need to convey my shock and disbelief somehow. One-sided conversations are so tiring, I think, wondering if I'll ever be able to have a proper two-way communication with anyone ever again.

'You look shocked, and I understand that,' he adds gently, bending to lean closer, blotting out the infernal bright light once more. 'I'm sure it is frightening and very disorienting to discover you've lost such a chunk of time. You did begin to wake up after you arrived here, as a matter of fact, but I'm afraid you became extremely unsettled at that point. I would suggest, however, that such agitation is to be expected in the circumstances.'

Circumstances. Yes, that would be my daughter's murder, then. Thank you for acknowledging that. At last we're on the same page.

'We acted quickly to avoid any potential for cerebral com-promise. A swelling of the brain, and so forth,' he tells me,

134

straightening up, his tone brisk now. 'With your husband's consent, my team and I took the decision to induce a medical coma to allow for the better facilitation of recovery. Hence you have remained—'

Wait – did he just say with my husband's consent?

His voice is almost hypnotically smooth; the words slip silkily across my understanding like oil over polished stone, gone before I can fully grasp them.

Dom has been here? But he hurt me. I was scared he would hurt my son. So I didn't leave him – or something, someone, stopped me? He's been with Aidan all the time I've been—

I rock my head from side to side in agitation now, lost in confusion, wracked with sudden fear – for myself, and for my son. My brain tells me that I'm clenching my fists, but when I look down my hands are flat and unmoving against the sheets. There's a mottled purple bruise where a cannula is inserted into the back of my left hand, connecting me to a drip by a plastic tube that winds its way to a little bag filled with clear liquid, suspended from a hook on a metal stand. I try to press my chin against my chest to examine myself more closely, wondering exactly how incapacitated I am, but again my body seems slow to follow my brain's instructions. Still, I can make out little round pads attached to my chest, a baffling array of tubes and wires wiggling like a child's follow-the-line puzzle towards the flickering digital displays.

'Don't worry about the gadgets and wires,' the doctor says, misinterpreting my distress and abruptly changing the subject as he watches me stare at the formidable collection of equipment. He waves a dismissive hand at them. 'I know they look scary, but they're largely precautionary, for monitoring purposes. They're pretty tame, on the whole. They won't hurt you. And remember they all have an off switch. Man rules machine.' He gives a quick smile.

I have no means of correcting his assumption and telling him that it's not the *machines* I'm worrying about, but my husband. He definitely has no off switch; no one rules him.

Was it Dom who found me? I wonder if he called an ambulance or drove me to the hospital himself. But he was at work . . . I was alone and chasing desperately round the house, looking for something – *what?* I remember feeling like someone was watching me the whole time. Did they do this to me? I force my breathing to slow, my thoughts to be still, to empty and allow memory to resurface and fill in the blanks, but nothing comes.

'They're just sensors so we can make sure your body is responding normally,' the doctor continues, frowning slightly now as I stare blankly at the monitors. I'm not even really seeing them; I'm still wondering about Dom, and how I got here in the first place. 'I have personally been monitoring you, Mrs Castle. It's a relief to see you waking up this evening. I was growing concerned these last forty-eight hours, I'll admit. You were becoming agitated and disturbed again, and your vital signs were showing signs of distress – your heart rate, blood pressure, EEG . . . '

I drift off as the voice lists a whole ream of medical words I don't understand. It's such a gentle voice – the accent is Spanish, I realise. I want to lean into it, close my eyes and sleep—

'Stay with me, Mrs Castle. You're doing really well.'

I feel my eyelids prised back one at a time, but I don't flinch as he shines a little torch into my eyes: my mind is looking inwards. I'm no longer present; I am drifting . . .

'It's very important you don't get distressed. We need to keep you as calm as possible while we give your body and mind a chance to fully wake up. I know this is all a lot to take in, but there's no rush.' He holds my hand while I concentrate on slowing my breathing. 'There you are, just relax. You must take it easy.'

Take it easy. He keeps repeating this as though there's a chance of my leaping out of my hospital bed and doing a quick jig around the room.

'Try to stay calm,' he continues as I glare at him.

Calm. It would be a miracle if I ever feel calm again.

'It is a miracle you are even alive after the injuries you sustained,' the doctor echoes uncannily. 'You are my star patient, let me tell you that much. Even with the absolute best twenty-four-hour care we offer here, very few patients come back to us after being shot in the head.'

TWENTY-TWO

I can hear the wind chimes again; they are close by. My eyes open and I can see that the thin mauve curtains have been drawn back now, billowing like a ship's sail into the room, jangling the chimes. I'm relieved that the blinding lamp over my bed has been switched off; daylight pours through the half-open window and for the first time I notice the whiteboard opposite my bed. There are notes scribbled all over it – diagrams scrawled in dark ink. I recognise them and something clicks into place: *my whiteboard*. No sign of Shay, though. Where's the Ghost of Crushes Past when you need him? I think, and a bitter laugh forms deep in my chest. It hurts, badly.

I must have fallen asleep, overwhelmed by the information given to me by that treacle-rich Spanish voice. I still can't move my head much but I can swivel my eyes to the left, just to check that I didn't imagine the machines, that I'm not back in my living room, waiting for Aidan to get home from school. Every time I open my eyes, the world around me seems to have changed; I don't trust my own brain. But little green numbers blink stoically at me, and there's something comforting about the repetitively flashing digits and silently watching monitors. I'm definitely in hospital, then. I hear a soft electric hum and a familiar low beeping sound.

I've heard these sounds before, I think with a jolt of recognition, surely only moments ago. But I thought they were noises in my *house* – I thought I was at home and these were the everyday sounds of domestic life. I think of the grocery lorry I imagined reversing, preparing to make its delivery to Mr Cooper next door, the beeping warning signal weirdly switching to the back garden. They weren't sounds from home: they are medical sounds, the soundtrack of hospital life, I realise.

So how was I hearing these noises in my living room?

I try to lift my left arm to call for someone, but it's a dead weight. I find I'm able to bend my neck slightly, though, arching it to the left so that I can see the cannula disappearing into the back of my wrist beneath a clean, freshly applied bandage. I can feel liquid flowing into my veins, rushing through my body, waking me up again.

Yes, I am awake; which means I must indeed have been asleep – or unconscious. *For three months?* The doctor's words come back to me in a frightening rush.

'But I—'

'*Buenos dias*, Mrs Castle. Take your time. You've slept very well. All night, in fact. How are you feeling this morning?' The doctor is at my side again.

So he's real too, not just the figment of a bad dream. He's standing in exactly the same place as before and I have the sense that he's been right next to me the whole time, even while I've been sleeping.

Briskly, he takes hold of my right hand and squeezes it – comforting me or testing my physical reactions? Or maybe both. It feels good to have someone hold my hand, I realise, and I'm relieved to find that my brain is still receiving messages from my nerve endings, even if it's having difficulty sending commands in the opposite direction. I may not be able to move, but I can still *feel*. And I've felt his touch before, I'm sure of it. Always so tender, soothing, apart from that one time when—

My voice – it *worked*! Suddenly I register that the doctor *heard* me. He was responding to my words, not just second-guessing my mood and facial expressions. Surprise fills me with elation. 'I can *speak*,' I say, testing my new-found ability again.

'Indeed you can,' he says simply, as if it's not the biggest deal ever. 'You have been extraordinarily lucky, Mrs Castle.'

Lucky? That's not a word I feel much connection with.

'I don't feel lucky,' I say croakily, reminding myself to speak the words aloud.

'Perhaps not. But as my mother would say, *al fin es debido el honour*. All's well that ends well,' he translates with a quick smile, picking up the clipboard from the end of my bed and studying it.

'This isn't my idea of a happy ending.' I close my eyes, remembering Aidan and Annabel jubilantly shouting out in unison 'The End!' as we finished each bedtime story.

'You have survived. You have woken up. It is a positive outcome, Mrs Castle,' he says firmly, a stern father rebuking a stubborn child. 'That is what I mean by lucky. And all the signs are very positive for a complete recovery. In fact, you won't be needing *these* hideous beasts much longer,' he says, pointing to the machines with his ballpoint pen before writing something else on his clipboard. He hangs it back over the end of my bed before efficiently changing the drip bag.

'Injuries,' I repeat, trying to remember what he told me before I went to sleep. *Something important.*

'Your surgeon did an excellent job. Thankfully, there has been no lasting brain damage. As I say, lucky. We'll continue to monitor you very closely, of course,' he adds, stepping up to the whiteboard where he jots more notes in small neat handwriting. 'We'll help you find the happy ending you're looking for. *I'll* help you,' he says, throwing a quick, preoccupied smile over his shoulder before turning back to his notes.

For a few seconds, I watch his hand move fluidly across the whiteboard, underlining words, jotting down new ones.

Nothing makes any sense.

I thought that whiteboard was only in my mind, a memory of university lectures that I resurrected to help me process my thoughts and bring them to order. But here it stands, identical in all respects. How very strange. It's like I've walked into a living dream. I look around the white room wondering what or who might appear next.

'Annabel,' I whisper, breathing her name from the depths of my soul. *'Aidan!'* I say more loudly, urgently. Immediately I want to say it again, just for the pleasure of hearing it, just to marvel at how wonderfully, banally familiar my voice sounds, as if it's no big deal to be talking to a strange doctor; as if I could easily have spoken at any time.

But I haven't been able to talk to my son; that much I *know* was real.

Does Aidan know I'm here?

'Who's Aidan, Mrs Castle?' The doctor puts down his pen and turns to look at me.

'My ... he's my son.' There's a lump in my throat; my words barely manage to scrape over it.

'Ah, yes. I remember now. Your husband did mention taking your little boy to visit you at the West Mid after your surgery. He said it would be too upsetting to bring him here, though. Children often find hospitals scary, it is true. It's often best they don't visit until a patient is recovering fully.'

141

Aidan visited me. Was it him playing the recorder? Trying to wake me up?

Annabel would have teased him. *Mum hates that squeaky noise, Aid!* But that was obviously the point. My clever boy. If he'd played his violin, the beautiful sound would probably have sent me deeper into the coma; but the piercing notes of his recorder could penetrate even the sleep of death. Annabel would have been proud of her brother. She would have given him one of her quick hugs, her sparkling smiles . . .

'And I believe the new school term has just started. So Carol, my nurse, tells me. Your husband is probably trying to maintain the normality of daily routines while you recover.'

'Just started. So it's September? And I've been here for three months?' Dates whirl through my mind. 'I've been here since the twins' birthday. The end of May,' I say breathlessly, watching the doctor check his notes.

'That is correct.'

'But that means . . .' Everything is a muddle and there's something important that I still can't grasp. Something that keeps sliding away from me. It feels like my mind is frozen and as it gradually thaws, my thoughts are melting and trickling away into a dark puddle.

'Take your time.'

'So Dom visited me *here*. In hospital. In this room.' My voice is a dry, croaky squeak and my throat feels raw.

'That's also correct,' the doctor says and pours a glass of water from a jug on the bedside table. He holds it to my lips and encourages me to take a few sips. I struggle a little and he grabs a tissue, pressing it gently to my mouth and chin afterwards.

'But I've been at *home*. My husband has been at work. Aidan has been at school. I was looking for something. I thought someone was following me round the house, that they had come back to

142

hurt me. But I was here all this time? Ever since Annabel . . . Ever since—'

'Coma is a fascinating phenomenon,' the doctor says, interrupting me and resting a calming hand on my arm. 'I'm sure your brain has been unravelling a lot of things while you've been unconscious. Processing memories from the past, perhaps. Retrieving scenes and conversations you believed were taking place in the present moment but were, in fact, all recollections from various incidents in your life. Trauma does strange things to the brain, Mrs Castle. There's plenty we don't yet understand about it.'

'That doesn't help me much,' I say, feeling a sigh roll up through my chest.

He smiles. 'I'm sure it all felt very real, as dreams do.'

'Dreams? Memories?'

So how do I know what was real and what was only in my imagination?

'Reality is often a matter of perception,' the doctor continues, pulling up a chair and sitting down next to me. 'Truth is often something we rewrite in our heads over time. We have a memory of a certain day, perhaps, or a particular event, but sometimes it is only that we've seen a photo of it. Our brain has constructed an entire narrative around a single image. It's quite remarkable. One snapshot can conjure up a whole sequence of events that may or may not have taken place. Smells can often trigger the same process in the unconscious mind. Sounds, too.'

'The wind chimes.'

'Your husband brought them. To remind you of home, he said. You like them?'

'Very much. And I heard them.'

'But of course. You have been unconscious, but your brain – your senses – has remained very much alive. This is not uncommon,' he says, watching the frown I can feel creasing my brow.

143

'You mean I'm not just some kind of freak of nature.' I remember how Dom teased me all those years ago; I *don't* remember him sitting at my hospital bedside.

'Far from it. A high proportion of patients who experience unconsciousness report that they remember a great deal about what took place around them during that time. They also indicate having had an *emotional* response to those occurrences. Think about a person with visual impairment, for instance. Their hearing often becomes acute. When consciousness is impaired, as in coma, the *un*conscious mind sometimes comes into a life of its own. The human brain is a beautiful creation.' His eyes light up as he talks about what is clearly his life's work.

'But I bet it looks freaky as hell. No wonder Dom has stayed away.'

'Grown-ups can find hospital visits as upsetting as children, of course. My nurse told me that she found your husband trying to shake you awake. Poor man. In some ways coma is harder for the relatives, you see. You are asleep, but they have to stand by helplessly watching you.'

'He's coming back, though?'

'He hasn't returned since that first visit, which I must confess is pretty normal. As I say, these situations can be distressing. But we've kept him in touch with your progress, and I've contacted him personally to let him know you're awake.' His dark eyes are alert to my responses, flicking watchfully over my face and body as he pushes back his chair and stands up, hovering calmly at my bedside, a white-coated guardian angel.

I close my eyes, imagining Dom trying to shake me awake, and I remember hands squeezing my neck, twisting my wedding ring, fingers digging into my collarbone. Was that actually Dom trying to wake me up? I thought I was dreaming.

'Will you call him? And ask him to bring Aidan to see me?'

I feel a tear roll down my face. 'I miss him so much. I miss my *daughter*.' As I say the word, my voice cracks and I half squeak, half sob, the worry burning in my chest. 'Aidan must be so lonely, so devastated.' Tears roll freely now, and my breath comes in choking gasps.

'I do understand, Mrs Castle. I know that to imagine a child's pain is the hardest thing for any parent. Or any doctor,' he adds. 'Looking after children is one of the most rewarding but also one of the toughest parts of my job. Sadly, it's often a relief when pain stops and they are at peace. Death is devastating, but it brings relief from suffering.'

'Then I wish I hadn't been so lucky. I wish I'd died too.'

TWENTY-THREE

'Please don't upset yourself, Mrs Castle. I don't want anything to cause you more stress. Your body and mind have endured a tremendous ordeal. You must take your time. Try to stay calm. Don't rush to grasp everything at once.' The doctor sits back down next to me, taking hold of my hand. 'I'm right here and I'm not going anywhere.'

I do as he asks and force myself to relax, let the pain of my grief subside. As I feel calmer, I try to make sense of everything he's told me – that I've been dreaming this whole time; that I haven't been at home, watching my husband, my surviving child – that I've just been locked in my memories, reliving the past, imagining that what was happening was real when actually I've just been some kind of ghost in my own life.

I haven't just walked into a living dream; I'm emerging from one . . .

But even as my mind protests that it's crazy, that the doctor is wrong and doesn't know what he's talking about, tiny details click into place. The way I've been sitting in one room but then seem

146

to end up in another, without any memory of moving; the way I would think about a subject or a conversation and then suddenly Dom and Lucy and Aidan would appear and start talking about it – school, the park, Aidan's swimming trophy . . .

'But I saw them. Right next to me. I *heard* them.'

'As I say, our unconscious mind absorbs far more than we know. It's possible you overheard your family talking around you when they visited you in ITU at the West Mid,' the doctor says, leaning forward and resting his elbows on his knees.

'Lucy and Dom in the kitchen.' I close my eyes, remembering listening to them talk from my hiding place on the stairs.

'Sorry?'

'I heard them. My husband and my best friend. But I thought they were at *home*. So was that real or a memory?' I ask, shaking my head, struggling to grasp that I wasn't even there; that I was *here* the whole time.

'Perhaps a bit of both. Maybe you heard them talking at your bedside after the surgery. Your brain then transplanted what it was hearing to a more familiar context. Such as your kitchen table,' he says with a quick smile. 'It would be logical.'

'Logical. It all sounds crazy to me.'

'Dreams can take us to the most unexpected places. The mind is incredibly powerful; the unconscious mind equally so. It processes thoughts and feelings without you even being aware of it, often contextualising them in unexpected ways. You might, for instance, dream of running for a train. Perhaps that is an incident from your daily life, or perhaps it is your brain's way of encapsulating tension you're experiencing. A feeling of stress. Being unable to keep up.'

'But it was all so *real*. So ordinary. Just my everyday life, my family.' Again I have that sensation of having stepped out of a dream into a parallel universe, and the sensation is disorienting.

'Nothing was different? Peculiar or unexpected?'

No one ever looked at me, or noticed me; my son has been ignoring me.

He wasn't ignoring me; I wasn't even *there*, I realise. I had vanished completely.

I feel more tears trickling out of the corners of my eyes, rolling towards my mouth. I taste saltiness and it's the first physical sensation I can remember in a long time. No, that's not true: lately I've been becoming more aware of my bodily senses. I've been waking up, I realise. The doctor said my brain activity had become agitated – *because I was starting to remember more*, I realise. As memories returned, my brain was kick-starting itself back to life. Back to my family.

Aidan – my darling boy. Mummy's here now!

I close my eyes and think it through slowly, step by step, trying once again to fix the details in my mind. I have been in a coma, and my unconscious mind has incorporated all the noises and conversations happening around me into scenes from my own life, at the same time conjuring up real memories and trying to process them, trying to make sense of what's happened to me.

What has happened to me?

'You said ...' I clear my throat and try again. 'You said I've been ... that I've been shot. I don't understand ...'

'Your case notes indicate that your injuries were not insignificant,' he says in a quiet, steady voice, sitting back and looking around for his clipboard. 'But as I say, my team and I are extremely pleased with your progress.' He reaches out and squeezes my hand as if in congratulation, but I've done nothing good; I deserve no praise.

'But there was only one gunshot.' My head aches, partly with shock at speaking the raw, violent word aloud, partly with panic: I feel frightened and confused as horrific shadowy images suddenly rise up to surround me in the bright, white room. I turn my face into the pillow, trying to hide from them and also find some relief from the throbbing in my temples. When I open my eyes again, the doctor is still watching me.

'One bullet is generally enough.' A dark eyebrow lifts quizzically.

I remember clawing my way through the rose bushes, my hands tangling in my daughter's hair, my whole body soaked in her blood . . . so much blood.

It was my blood too, I suddenly realise.

'Unless you're lucky,' I say bitterly, wishing it was Annabel lying here in this hospital bed, not me.

'In surgical terms, there is indeed much to be thankful for. The fact that the bullet penetrated the very tip of your right frontal lobe, towards the forehead, meant that only minor clinical damage was caused. Your surgeon could explain this in more detail, but the essence of your good fortune is that the bullet passed through no vital brain tissue, nor any vascular structures. There was a per-forating wound, of course, but that is healing nicely.'

'I was shot in the head. And I didn't die.' My thoughts drift away from me like clouds.

'It feels like a miracle, yes?'

'It feels wrong. *Unjust*,' I say forcefully. 'I deserved to be the one to die. It should have been *me*,' I say, and my throat feels raw; my whole body aches as if crushed beneath a heavy weight. I close my eyes against a sudden image of Annabel lying deathly still beneath the roses, white petals floating on a crimson pool.

'There we must disagree. No crime deserves such retribution. And I'm sure you've committed no crime, in any case. You're not under arrest, are you? You were brought here for recuperation, not punishment,' he says gently.

'But who . . . ? *Why?*' The words stick in my dry throat, and the doctor helps me to take more small sips of water.

'Ah, there I can't help you, I'm afraid. Perhaps it's best you save those questions for the detective, yes? He should be here at some point tomorrow, or the day after. As he requested, we've kept him fully in touch with your progress.' He stands up now and moves round to the other side of my bed, checking the monitors one last time. 'Try not to dwell on things too much till then, OK?'

There is a clipped edge to his voice now – the no-nonsense manner of a consultant in charge. I feel tiny hairs prickle in a shiver of relief up my arms. He makes me feel safe, and my mind relaxes. I want to sleep; I'm so very tired.

'I'll come back in a little while,' he says, clicking his pen and tucking it in the breast pocket of his white coat. 'Your vital signs are much stronger this morning, but we still need to be cautious. There's no rush. Recovery takes as long as it takes. The most important thing is that you *allow* yourself to heal. Everything else must wait. There's time enough for more talking. For now, *rest*. Understand?'

He glides around me again like a velvet curtain, pausing only to readjust my pillows. I smell antiseptic on his hands; a tangy acidic aroma I know I've smelled before. Was it his hands I remember stroking my hair? A touch so gentle – it can't have been my husband. And Dom has only visited me once. Just one time in all these weeks.

Why hasn't he come back yet? *Has he abandoned me here?*

As the doctor closes the curtains, dims the lights and shuts the door softly behind him, panic suddenly tingles through my body. I have been alone in the darkness – no, it wasn't dark, I think; it was blinding bright ... I've been trapped in that bright-dark for such a long time, but it's only now that I realise exactly how alone I was – how lonely and adrift, and how scared. I feel safe now, but only when I hear this doctor's voice next to me, anchoring me. Everything is so confusing. I have so many questions but I don't even know where to start ...

I try to calm myself down by thinking through what I *do* know. I understand that the bullet that killed Annabel must somehow have injured me too, and that I have been in a coma, and that Dom has been too distressed to visit me. I know that this doctor has been at my bedside for weeks, and that the bright light in my home was in fact the lamp angled over this bed, or perhaps the beam of the doctor's torch examining my eyes; that it was his needle flooding me with numbness, calming my panic when I became too distressed . . .

I have been on a journey through my unconscious mind, and Professor Hernandez – along with his whiteboard – has been my silent companion. I thought his notes were my notes, and so they were, in a way. I understand that as I began to surface from my comatose state, my senses were alert to flashes of the outside world – and, just as in dreams we incorporate a sudden noise or the voices of people around us, so too the hospital and everything around me became part of my inner world.

I feel tearful with relief to know that I have finally left behind that cold, fractured place that was so dark yet also blindingly bright. But I am also afraid. Everything I thought I had seen, all that I had unravelled about my life, my family, turns out to have been an illusion – a trick of my shattered mind. Which means that I may be recovering physically, but I am still lost. In the bright-dark, I believed I was beginning to piece together everything that led up to the morning of the twins' tenth birthday: the day I lost Annabel. In the true light of day, I realise the picture is still just a handful of fragments. I cannot trust my own mind – so what, or whom, can I trust?

As my mind and body finally surrender to exhaustion, I battle to hold on to one thought, repeating it over and over in my mind: *I need to see my son . . .*

TWENTY-FOUR

'Please, please try to contact my husband again. Did you call his mobile as well as the landline? I just want to see Aidan – I need to see my *son*.'

'I know; I do understand. I'll try both his numbers again, I promise.'

Carol speaks patiently, even though I've asked her the same question – growing increasingly frantic – a hundred times already today. She fusses efficiently around my bed, encouraging me to eat a tiny bit of my early supper before giving me one last sympathetic smile and bustling out of the room to continue her rounds.

I know she thinks she's leaving me to rest, as Professor Hernandez instructed, but I'm not getting much sleep. I managed to nap fitfully during the day yesterday, my mind turning over my conversations with the doctor, but I lay awake most of the night. It's not the hospital environment that's bothering me – the glaring artificial light, the sporadic nocturnal activity and random sounds. They're all strangely familiar; my brain seems to recognise and accept them as normal. After all, as I've finally reconciled myself to, it's been filtering them for three months.

It's not the world around me, and it's not even the aches and pains of my body. It's just that I can't rest until I know what's happening with Dom and Aidan – where they are; *how* they are. What they are thinking; how they are coping without me, without Annabel. It's all I care about. More than getting better, more than seeing the detective and finding out the answers to all my questions, *I just want Aidan.*

I'm in a constant state of jittery panic and Professor Hernandez has begun to anticipate my first question each time he enters my room. Each time he's simply shaken his head with a small frown. I can't tell if he's cross or apologetic; he's so serene and unflappable, his presence almost soporific. This morning, I pressed him more urgently, waiting until he'd worked systematically through his tests and observations before telling him that if no one could bring my son to me, I would discharge myself and drag myself home on my hands and knees, if that's what it would take.

'Well,' he said slowly, regarding me steadily, 'I think we'll give it a go unhooking you from these charmers this morning' – he pointed at the machines with his ballpoint pen – 'cut the electronic apron strings, as it were, and see how you fare. But I'd recommend at least a *couple* of physio sessions before you attempt to crawl back to London on your hands and knees.' He smiled. 'Let's hope it doesn't come to that, though. We will keep trying your husband, Mrs Castle,' he said more seriously.

'I just don't understand why he hasn't come to see me yet.' I let him help me sit up in bed so he could start carefully disconnecting wires and removing sensor pads.

But even as I said the words I realised I *did* know.

Our daughter was dead, Dom blamed me for it, and he couldn't bear to see me.

There could be no other explanation. I might have been scared of Dom, but he despised me, and he had absolutely no intention of coming to see me. The hospital could ring as many times as they liked; Dom wasn't coming back.

'I do recall he mentioned his work: something about too many irons in the fire. But we've left several messages now,' the doctor said, pausing to look at me. 'We've even written and emailed.'

'Could he have . . . ? Maybe he's taken Aidan to stay somewhere else? Or moved house, do you think?' I asked, clinging to any shred of hope. 'No, of course not. What a stupid idea, he'd never do that,' I said, talking more to myself than to the doctor, who carried on pushing buttons and taking notes, clicking, unclipping wires, lifting first my left arm, then my right. I felt like a child being dressed for their first day at school. I watched him blankly, conflicting thoughts chasing round my mind: Dom had moved house, unable to live any longer where Annabel died, and he didn't know I was awake. Either that or he'd abandoned me in disgust.

'We haven't received any notification of an alternative address. But, look, I'm sure there's a perfectly reasonable explanation. Maybe he's gone away. For a business trip, or perhaps a short holiday to take a break from the stress and worry. I can't imagine he would stay away for no good reason.'

He pressed his hand reassuringly on mine, saying he would be back again after he'd checked on his other patients. Selfishly, I wished there weren't any. From the second he left the room, I was anxious for him to return; I didn't want to be left alone with thoughts of exactly why Dom might have decided to abandon me and withhold our son.

No good reason.

There was one very good reason, I realised. *Annabel.* And it

154

was pure torture lying there alone, agonising over the thought that Dom might *never* come back. How would I ever get to see my son again?

It's the only explanation that fits, I think now. I doubt very much that Dom's absence has anything to do with a holiday. He *never* takes time off work. Two weeks in Cornwall each summer is the most he's ever agreed to, and even then he's always timed it around his clients' priorities and has remained glued to his phone the whole time we're away. He's always talked of finding a business partner to share the load, but he's rejected every potential candidate over the years as not up to his standards.

No one ever lives up to his expectations. I guessed long ago that it's an issue of control, and that his parents' deaths probably hold the key to this. The suddenness, the randomness of their cancer . . . I suspect it left him desperate to retain more power, more control over his own destiny. I asked him about it once. Annoyed that I was trying to *psychoanalyse him*, as he called it, his furious reaction taught me not to ask a second time.

Is that what his silence is all about? He's demonstrating his power and control over *me*, as a punishment for not saving Annabel? I try to tell myself I'm being paranoid; he was obviously traumatised by his first visit and can't face another. He was trying to shake me awake, the nurse said . . . he must have been so desperate. So worried. And concerned about inflicting the battered and bruised sight of me on our son, letting him see the scary machines, the wires all over my body . . .

I need to get better fast; I need to get home and find out for myself. But the doctor was right: I'm not fit to go anywhere yet. So far I've managed to take only a few short steps, with a great deal of help, across my room to the en suite bathroom, and I feel constantly panicky and paranoid. In just this short space of time

155

I've become completely dependent on the doctor's presence, only feeling safe when he is at my side.

Was I always this needy? I feel like I've woken up in a different body, like I'm having to get to know myself all over again. I've been asked what music I like to listen to, what food I like to eat ... I have no idea, and I don't want to think about any of these things. There isn't room in my head. It was already overloaded with horror and grief at losing Annabel, and now it's approaching bursting point as I wonder if my husband has simply left me here to rot.

Meanwhile, I'm still grappling to get my head around the fact that I've been asleep all these weeks, drifting backwards and forwards through my life in a dream state. In between my sporadic naps yesterday, Professor Hernandez sat by my side again, patiently explaining that the conversations and incidents I remembered in my coma most likely *did* actually take place in my past – my unconscious mind was just trying to process them. But how much was true and how much was a distortion of the facts?

I know he's right that we replay our waking lives in our dreams, but I also understand that our underlying worries colour them differently. I know, for instance, that Lucy really has spent hours at my kitchen table over the years, enjoying time with my family – but did she ever flirt with my husband? Or was it just that I always felt secretly jealous of their relationship and in my unconscious, dreamlike state that jealous insecurity tarnished my memories, my mind replaying them in such a way that I genuinely believed Lucy and Dom were in love?

I want to know – I need to speak to Lucy as well as to Dom – but when I requested a phone to call my friend, her landline was disconnected and I kept getting a 'number not recognised' message on her mobile.

No Dom. No Lucy. No Aidan.

I'm trying hard not to think the worst: that with me stuck

156

here, out of the way, they've seized their chance to be together. I force myself to banish images of the four of them: Dom, Lucy, Aidan and Jasper playing happy families without me. Professor Hernandez is right: there will be a perfectly reasonable explanation. I know Lucy has been looking to move out of her rented flat to somewhere bigger. Perhaps she's found somewhere and has finally moved; perhaps she's changed her mobile number.

Perhaps, perhaps ... All these questions with no answers are driving me crazy – but not as crazy as I feel at not being able to see Aidan.

'I just want to see my own son! Is that too much to ask?' I announce to the empty room. The wind chimes jingle; I hear voices somewhere along the corridor outside my room and the revs of a car engine through the open window. I stare at the white walls and long to hold Aidan, hoping that he's safe, hasn't forgotten me, doesn't hate me. I thought I was at home with him and Dom, and that they were ignoring me because of what I've done, the terrible choice I made. Tolerating my presence but unable to bring themselves to talk to me. Only I wasn't really there and—

My heart pounds faster as it suddenly occurs to me that maybe they *don't* know. It's possible, I suppose, that Dom doesn't. He wasn't there on the morning of the twins' birthday; he stormed out after our row and I haven't seen him since. But Aidan was right there next to me in the garden. What did he see? What did he hear?

Who did this to Annabel, to me?

I lie back and stare at the ceiling, tussling with endless questions. I want to ask Professor Hernandez again, but he doesn't seem to know anything about my broader situation: he didn't admit me to hospital, or operate on me. His responsibility is for my rehabilitation alone.

And I get a terrible sinking feeling inside when I think of revealing my guilt to him: coma may have changed me in some respects, but I haven't woken up with a conscience wiped clean. I long to talk about Annabel, to tell the doctor how much I regret what has happened, how much I miss her. But I can't do so without explaining the choice I made, without confessing what a terrible mother I am. I betrayed my daughter, I let her down, and I hate myself for it. I deserve condemnation but I'm not strong enough to bear it. Professor Hernandez's gentle understanding is all I have; he is my lifeline, the only person keeping me going, and I couldn't bear it if he too turned away from me in disgust. Then I really would have nothing and no one.

So I remain lost, my thoughts whirling endlessly in circles, only two things completely clear in my mind: being ordered to choose between my children, and then crawling beneath the rose bushes, scrabbling through blood-soaked grass, desperately trying to reach Annabel's body. They are the two terrible, absolute truths I can hold on to, but as for the rest . . .

TWENTY-FIVE

'Need some help?'

'Oh, hi. I'm fine, but thank you,' I say and do my best impression of someone who can stand upright and walk in a straight line without bouncing off the walls.

Carol returned after my supper with no further news of Dom, and seeing how upset I was she suggested that I have a go at a little walk along the corridor outside my room, just to the water cooler and back. Divert my mind and build up a bit of strength in my legs. The effort this required certainly proved distracting: it's taken me ages to shuffle only halfway, supported by the kindly nurse. Now she's left me to take an urgent phone call and I'm stranded here leaning heavily on the wall, gripping on to the handrail that runs along the middle of it, no doubt designed exactly for situations like these.

'You don't look fine, if you don't mind my saying. You look knackered. Nice pyjamas, though. Navy polka dots are definitely your look.'

I brace my shoulder more comfortably against the wall and turn to look in the direction of the voice. A young girl of maybe sixteen or seventeen is standing in the middle of the corridor, leaning on a stick, tapping one foot impatiently. She has long, dead-straight, silky black hair that Annabel would have envied so badly. I look down at her feet and am amused to see giant fluffy bunny slippers.

'I prefer *your* look,' I say, smiling at her.

'Mum's idea of fashion,' she tells me, grinning back. 'Or maybe I offended her in a past life. Or this one. Which is entirely probable as I seem to spend most of my time offending *someone*. I talk too much. I know. I've been told. What can I say? I like chatting to people.'

Her voice is quick and loud; she has a strong accent that reminds me of Max's. She's from London too, then, I think, wondering if she's still at school, wondering how Aidan is getting on at his school without Annabel . . .

'Well, speaking as a mother myself, I think your slippers are adorable. So don't shoot your mum just yet.' *Damn*, bad choice of words, I think, and my knees almost give way.

'You OK? Seriously, you look like hell. C'mere, lemme give you a hand. You c'n'ave your pick – this one, or this one.' She holds out each hand in turn, swapping the stick from one hand to the other. 'This is my best one, though.' She holds up her right hand. 'The bones were only slightly crushed in this arm, as opposed to mangled out of all recognition the other side.'

'Oh, gosh, that sounds—'

'Crap. Yep, pretty much sums it up. Although according to my consultant, it's a miracle I'm even alive!' She imitates an accent and pulls a face. 'Even with the facial scarring, speech loss, one useless arm and a permanent limp.'

Ah, I hear the slurring in her voice now. 'I'm sorry to hear that,' I say gently. 'You must be very brave to— Hang on a sec, is your consultant Professor Hernandez?' I ask, the accent and the word 'miracle' ringing bells; he pronounced exactly the same verdict on me. How many miracles can there be in this place? Hundreds, probably, I think, realising there must be lots of other consultants too. I haven't ventured further than my own room, so I don't have a sense of the wider hospital world.

'Yep. Spanish dude. A voice that can send me to sleep in a second.' She leans heavily on her stick again, trying to shift her weight from one leg to the other.

I smile. 'How funny. We share the same doctor.' It feels good to make a connection, however small, with another person. I've started to feel selfish, self-absorbed, wrapped up in my own pain and oblivious to others. Carol and the doctor devote all their energy to caring for me, yet I know next to nothing about them as people. Such self-absorption is unlike me. I think. Or is it? I'm not quite sure what sort of person I am any more; I feel like I left parts of myself behind in the bright-dark.

'He's leaving soon, I heard. Going back to Spain. I reckon they should try to keep him. I'd have given up by now if it wasn't for him,' she says, shifting her stick once more to the other hand.

'Oh, I'm sorry,' I say, noticing that she seems in discomfort.

'Yeah. It's a shame, right?'

'No, I didn't mean about Professor Hernandez. Though that *is* a real shame. I meant I'm sorry for keeping you standing here talking. Shouldn't you be resting? Were you on your way somewhere?' I rest a hand lightly on her arm, hoping it's not the one she mentioned as having been mangled.

'Nah, just enjoying an evening stroll, the scenic tour, innit.' She winks.

'*Very* scenic,' I say ironically, looking up and down the empty, windowless corridor.

'My name's Stash, by the way.' She thrusts a tiny hand towards me.

'Interesting name. I'm Maddie. Pleased to meet you, Stash.' I smile as we shake hands, but I'm feeling tired myself now and really just want to get back to my room, check in with Carol just in case it was Dom on the phone.

'It's Natasha, really, but my baby sister could only manage to say Stash and it stuck. Mum says it suits me. Read into that what you will,' she gabbles on. 'You got kids?'

The walls close in on me; the floor seems to shift and dip beneath my feet. I should have been prepared for this question; I should have had an answer ready. But I've been so deeply immersed in my own pain, I haven't given a thought to the curiosity of others. That's different, too, I think, wondering how else my personality might have changed. It's like I fell unconscious as one person and have woken up as another.

But I'm still Aidan's mum.

Nothing can change that.

It hits me that I'll probably be asked about the twins as soon as I go home; there can't be many people in west London who haven't heard my story. But here at the hospital, miles away from Hampton, I've felt anonymous: just another patient recuperating after trauma. No one here knows anything about Annabel. I can't bring myself to talk about her – the pain, the shame of her loss is far too raw.

When the nurse has talked about her own three children, I've spoken only about Aidan. But I gave birth to *twins*. They are inseparable in my mind; I will never be able to think of one without the other. I've read that people who have lost a limb sometimes feel like it continues to itch or ache, as though it's still attached to them. *I still feel Annabel.* I still feel that three-way knot of love and need that bonded the twins to me from the second they were born: the knot I tore apart but which continues to wrap itself around me. I never want to be released from it.

Suddenly I can't hold it in; for ten years I've talked about my children almost non-stop. I want that time back – I want *them* back, I think agonisingly, trying to swallow over the lump in my throat.

'Two. I have two. Boy and a girl. Both ten,' I blurt out, unable to resist indulging the pretence, just for a moment. I can't bring myself to say that my daughter is dead; I don't want to admit it to the world and have to explain and watch this young girl's face crumple in shock and horror. There is something about her that reminds me a little of Annabel – her pretty, pixie-like face and a vivacity despite the awfulness of her injuries. I want to savour the reminder a little longer. I want to enjoy the twins' names on my lips just one more time: 'Annabel and Aidan,' I say softly, and my voice sounds thick and unrecognisable.

'Twins! Hey, cool.'

Stash notices nothing wrong. My acting skills are clearly better than I'd realised. Outwardly I must be giving the impression of being completely normal. How deceptive appearances can be, I think.

'Their friends think so. Twins always stand out, don't they?' I say.

'I bet they love visiting you here, playing with all the machines, bugging the nurses. They're a riot, aren't they?' She still doesn't bat an eyelid, completely oblivious to the emotions crashing through me. She just winks again and reaches into her fluffy pink dressing-gown pocket to show me a glimpse of a gold packet.

'Scenic route indeed. You're off to hang out with the secret smokers. Don't worry, I won't lecture you,' I say, my heart still thumping in my chest as I realise I've spoken my daughter's name out loud.

'Oh, don't hold back on my account. Lecture away. Everyone else does. I've memorised a whole list of stuff that's not good for me. Although they probably should have stuck "riding on the back of drunk boyfriend's motorcycle" at the top. He was always telling me off for smoking, too. But then, you know, he got crushed by a lorry turning the wrong way off Chiswick roundabout. Feels kinda like my last connection with him – the smoking. So I'm not giving it up any time soon.' Her shoulders dip and her long hair falls over her face.

'Oh, Stash. That's just . . . I'm so sorry,' I say. I push myself off the wall and take a jerky step towards her. 'What a horrendous tragedy.'

'Yeah, well, this place is full of 'em. I'm sure you've got your own tale to tell,' she says, wiping her eyes.

I touch the tender wound still covered by a light bandage on the right side of my head. I feel so lucky to have escaped the lingering damage Stash is enduring; Professor Hernandez was right to call it a miracle. My thoughts come a little less fast now, and there are still gaping black holes in my memory; I can't remember if I prefer toast or cereal for breakfast and whether I'm usually so grumpy in the mornings or these mood swings are entirely new – or circumstantial. But I can't deny that the round-the-clock care I'm receiving is working wonders. I will never take my life for granted again, I think fiercely. *Or my son's.*

'Fancy one?' Stash offers, breaking into my thoughts. She pulls the gold packet out of her pocket.

'Not for me. But thanks.' I glance around protectively, wondering if Stash is about to get rumbled. There are 'no smoking' signs everywhere.

'Wise woman. Hope your kids don't, either. I started when I was ten. Mum was always so high on coke that she didn't notice, and by the time she did, I was addicted. Not to mention pregnant.' She shoves the cigarette packet back in her pocket but continues to fiddle with it.

164

'Pregnant?' I say, genuinely shocked.

'Yeah. That baby sister I mentioned? Actually my kid. Only we don't tell the neighbours on the estate. Mum is raising her – cleaned up her act pretty fast once she realised I wasn't getting rid of it.' Her small, pointy chin juts out proudly, and she looks sideways at me as if to judge my reaction.

'Good for her. And good for you,' I say immediately. 'I mean that. From one mum to another.' I rest a hand on her shoulder and she tries to look tough but I can see she's pleased. I have no doubt that it's been a rough ride for both Stash and her mum. It makes me appreciate my own home even more. I know Dom has always been ambitious for something bigger, better, *more*, but all I've ever wanted is for the four of us to be happy, healthy and . . . safe.

'Introduce me to your kids next time they're in, yeah?' Stash says, her dark eyes lighting up at the thought. 'I'm a walking advert for all the things *not* to try as a teenager. One meeting with me, they'll be set on the straight and narrow for life. You'll be thanking me.'

'Sure,' I say faintly, glad that she's already shuffling away from me along the corridor so that I don't have to explain that my daughter will *never* be able to visit me, and that my husband, for some unfathomable reason, seems to have vanished off the face of the earth – along with my best friend and my son.

TWENTY-SIX

'Please don't panic, Mrs Castle; everything is fine. It's Professor Hernandez.'

I feel a gentle hand on my shoulder as I wake with a start. 'What time is it?' I open my eyes and peer groggily at him. I hadn't even realised I'd fallen asleep.

'Still early. Not much after seven. I'm sorry to wake you. You must have really tired yourself out going walkabouts last night.' He smiles. 'You did very well, by the way. Excellent progress.'

'My family?' The doctor is always telling me to rest; he must have a good reason for waking me up, I think, my heart beating faster as I struggle to sit up in bed, wide awake now.

'We've managed to get hold of your husband. I thought you'd want to know immediately,' he tells me, helping me prop myself up against the pillows. 'I just spoke to him and he's setting off from London right now.'

'Oh, thank God. And my son? He's bringing—'

'He coming alone, he told me. To avoid too much drama and distress.'

'Oh. OK. I guess that's sensible. Thank you.' A burning ache of disappointment tightens my chest. I have to force myself to breathe in, breathe out, in again. I can see Professor Hernandez is pleased to be able to give me some good news, so I try not to spoil it by letting my mood crash.

'He'll be here in a couple of hours. Depending on traffic.'

'A couple of hours. So soon. After all this time it feels a bit strange,' I say, but don't expand on my sudden rush of nerves when the doctor raises his eyebrows encouragingly at me.

Instinctive, habitual loyalty to Dom makes me reluctant to admit that it's actually Aidan not my husband I'm desperate to see. It took a while for my brain to remember the tension in my marriage, but now those images have returned, they won't budge. I *do* want to see Dom, but I'm also scared: of what I've remembered, and of what he knows – or doesn't know . . .

'A good husband will understand that,' is all the comment Professor Hernandez offers.

'A good husband would have visited before now,' I snap. 'Sorry, I just can't believe I'm still not going to see Aidan.' I desperately want to cry, but I don't want to have to explain my tears.

'And your daughter, too, I imagine.'

'Sorry?' The deafening sound of my heartbeat roars in my ears, blood pulsing through me in a sudden hot rush.

'You have twins, yes? I've just come from another patient of mine who mentioned bumping into you on your walkabout yesterday. She's quite a talker and was beyond excited at the idea of twins. Told me off for not knowing anything about them.' He chuckles. 'Although come to think of it, I do recall you mentioning a daughter once – or perhaps I've got that wrong?' he says, and I feel guilty about the look of concern pinching his face as he watches the blood drain from mine.

'No, yes, it's just that—'

'I'm so sorry. It's unprofessional of me to share personal information between patients. Please, accept my apologies. And don't worry, I know the mother–daughter relationship can be very challenging. I'm not married myself, but Carol tells me she often has – how shall I put it? – differences of opinion with her daughter. She finds it hard to talk about their relationship too,' he says kindly.

'If only it were that simple,' I say, sighing heavily, kicking myself now for having mentioned the twins to Stash.

'Well, how about this ...?' He pulls up a chair. 'When your husband arrives, I could suggest we set up a Skype call. That way you get to see your children, and they'll get to see and talk to you without ever setting foot inside this abominable place.' He smiles, and I want to reach out and hug him for being such a genius. 'Well, now, that *is* a happy sight.' He gestures at my face with his ever-present ballpoint pen, and I realise I'm smiling back at him.

I'll have to explain to him about Annabel later, I realise. I at least owe him that honesty, painful as it will be. But for now the thought that I might soon be able to speak to Aidan has sent a thrill of excitement through me. I know it won't be an easy conversation; I know Aidan must be distressed and worried. My unconscious mind has been playing out exactly how sad he must be feeling, but there are two important differences now: *I'm awake. And I've found my voice.*

'I do believe that's the first time I've seen you smile, Mrs Castle.'

'Please, do me a favour and call me Madeleine,' I say, on a sudden happy high. 'Or better still, Maddie. Just so I know you're not cross with me.'

'Maddie.' He smiles again. 'And the only reason I'll be cross with you is if you don't rest and take proper care of yourself,' he says, sounding amusingly like a bossy parent. 'As long as you do that, and if it makes you feel more comfortable, I'm happy to break a few rules and be on first-name terms. My name is Sebastián. Pleased to meet you, Maddie.'

He shakes my hand formally and then, still smiling, he clicks his pen and picks up his clipboard, scribbling on it. I wonder if he's jotting down a reminder to use first names. I've never met anyone so conscientious and methodical; he never stops making notes. I want to borrow them and crib up on my own life, which is still such a mystery to me.

'Oh, no. That won't do at all. I can't call you by your first name – you're a *doctor*.' I feel my jaw dropping and wonder if I look as horrified as I feel.

'Professor, actually.'

'You wear a white coat. And a stethoscope,' I say pointedly.

'This is true.'

'So if I call you Sebastián, that feels like we're equals. And I need you to be much more than that – more than me. *Better* than me. To make me better, I mean.'

It occurs to me that in normal life I would be waving my arms around, gesticulating in explanation. But I have still recovered only pieces of myself: my voice, physical sensations, some movement and a handful of fractured memories. I'm not sure anything will make me completely whole again; without Annabel, that simply isn't possible. But the prospect of speaking to Aidan holds out at least some hope.

'I see.' He cocks his head to one side.

'You do?' He's clever; perhaps he does. I don't add that I need someone to look up to – someone I can rely on – and that it's frightening to feel so powerless and vulnerable, and I want some-one to tell me everything's going to be all right. My parents were always elusive, and then they died, and it was Dom who became my rock, until trust crumbled beneath his aggression and my fear. I've surprised myself by being able to put my faith in another man at all, as I have in Professor Hernandez, and I'm not sure whether that's down to his fatherly manner or simply his official-looking doctor's name badge.

'Yes. I understand that calling me Doctor and seeing me wear a white coat and stethoscope reinforces your confidence in my medical abilities.' He gives a soft chuckle. 'I wish I'd known patient care would be that simple before my parents invested in twelve years' training at Europe's finest med schools. I could have just visited a fancy dress shop and saved them a fortune.'

'Ha. You're very funny. For a professor,' I tell him, pulling a wry smile.

'Nice try, but you can do better than that. I've seen you,' he says, pointing to his own broad grin.

It takes me a moment. 'Oh, you mean ...' It dawns on me that his teasing is just another way of assessing my mental faculties; my smile is a demonstration of fully functioning nerve processes. He's not trying to be funny; he's still monitoring my recovery. 'I'm not sure I have much to smile about right now, but I'll let you know when I feel one coming on,' I tell him, feeling tired and anxious again. 'Tick it off your whiteboard anyway, though. Makes me feel better seeing ticks rather than a list of crosses.'

'In that case, you get a gold star, Mrs Castle.'

I glare at him.

'Maddie,' he corrects after a long pause. 'Apologies, I forgot.'

'And I thought I was the one with amnesia,' I say. And smile.

'Aha, that's better. Now, try to eat some of this delicious breakfast Carol has left for you, yes?' A dark eyebrow quirks comically as he glances at the tray on my bedside table and then back at me. 'As for your amnesia, it may be temporary. We are only at the beginning of a long and winding road. Try not to worry about bridges yet to be crossed. One thing at a time, Maddie. *Baby steps.*'

TWENTY-SEVEN

'Mrs Castle? Maddie?' Carol pops her head round the door, and even though I know I'm *supposed* to be resting, I feel embarrassed that I haven't moved since the doctor left me.

Lie-ins have been a rare luxury since the twins were born; I feel bizarrely guilty that this motherly, uncomplaining woman is having to do so much for me. I watch gratefully as the nurse pulls open the curtains, letting in bright morning sunshine. I thank her as she helps me sit up in bed, propping the pillows comfortably behind my back. She smooths back my messy fringe and then tucks a stray strand of her own mousey-grey hair back into its neat bun, tutting as she catches sight of my breakfast sitting untouched on my bedside table.

'Sorry, Carol,' I apologise, with a rueful smile.

'Not to worry. I'll bring you some toast and tea in a while. But first you have a visitor,' she says, picking up the plastic tray and pulling a face at the bowl of congealed, soggy cereal.

My heart leaps in trepidation before I realise it's too soon for Dom to have made it here. It's still early and the doctor said it's a couple of hours' drive out of London.

'Detective Chief Inspector Watkins is here to see you. I'll show him in, shall I?' She balances the tray on one rounded hip, hesitating as she rests her other hand on the door handle. Her brown eyes widen; doubt furrows her usually smooth, high forehead.

'Yes. Thank you,' I say, feeling a riptide of inexplicable guilt surge through me, followed by tingles of excitement that at last I'll be able to find out more facts, real information. Surely this detective can help me fill in the missing pieces, the last frustrating gaps in my memory. I take slow, deep breaths and try to stay calm as Carol props the door open, waving in a man wearing a long, dark wool coat.

Automatically, I reach up to tighten my loose ponytail and sweep aside the fringe that now hangs over my eyes, tentatively touching the bandage on the right side of my head. I must look awful, and suddenly I feel self-conscious. Carol told me I will most likely always have a scar, and I'm glad: I want it to remind me. The feathery wisps of shaved hair on the right side of my head, beginning to grow back, also remind me of Aidan's shorn curls, and I wonder if his hair will be longer now. In my memories, it was sometimes shaved and sometimes wild and curly – which was baffling at first but makes complete sense to me now I understand that I was recalling scattered snapshots from different moments in time.

'Good morning, Mrs Castle.'

The detective brings with him scents of the outside world. Cocooned in this sterile environment, my senses are alert to subtle changes: the chill of autumn air that lingers on his coat; the oaky mustiness of a damp morning. I wonder if it's raining outside and glance down at his shoes. Immediately I think of big black boots tearing up the lawn, a jagged scar rucking across the lush green grass towards the rose bushes. My heart beats faster at the memory, but I force it from my mind. I need to stay focused now; I need to gather hard facts and not get distracted by way-ward emotions.

I've never met a detective before, but if I'd ever thought about it, I suppose I would have imagined that all DCIs are stubble-chinned, leather-jacket-wearing, wisecracking tough guys. I've obviously watched too many American crime TV programmes over the twins' shoulders, because DCI Watkins' boots are the only point of similarity with this maverick image. There is nothing tough or scary about Detective Chief Inspector Watkins of the Metropolitan Police, as he introduces himself.

He may not be a tough guy but I suddenly feel at a disadvantage, tucked up in my narrow, caged bed, unable simply to dash out of the room if the interrogation gets too intense. I don't even know whether I'm to be interviewed as a victim, witness or suspect: *the guilty mother who committed the vile crime of choosing one child over another.* I study his clean-shaven face, looking for clues. His expression gives nothing away. He looks more like a well-dressed civil servant than a detective: beneath his coat he's wearing a dark suit and a grey tie; his black hair is greying at the temples, neatly cut. I wouldn't pick him out in a crowd.

'Welcome back to the world. Good to see you doing so well,' DCI Watkins continues. He smiles but I see his gaze flick over my face and body, assessing me.

'Thank you. I'm feeling . . . I'm doing OK,' I say, not returning his smile, bracing myself for whatever he has to tell me. I try really hard to wait patiently rather than rush in with questions.

Who killed my daughter?

The four words pulse like a heartbeat inside my chest; I'm almost too scared to ask them, frightened that the answer will flip my already spiralling world inside out and upside down once again.

'Good. That's good. I can see you're being very well taken care of. Excellent.'

He starts pacing round the room, looking at everything as if fascinated. Given that it's pretty much an oblong white-painted box with a couple of armchairs and the odd landscape painting dotted here and there on the walls, it doesn't take long. Maybe hospitals make him anxious; the monitors and machines are rather intimidating, I suppose, although I'm used to them now. But I guess it's not every day he gets to meet a woman who's woken up from a coma after her family has been decimated by a crazed gunman – maybe that explains his jittery demeanour.

'I wasn't sure we'd ever get to meet,' he says at last, still pacing. 'Head injuries tend to be unpredictable, in my experience. I knew you'd be in good hands when you were brought here, though. Professor Hernandez has a reputation second to none. He's saved many a lost cause. Some who didn't deserve his expertise, I might add. But I usually find that justice has a way of prevailing.'

'I certainly hope so,' I say, wishing he'd get to the point.

'But I'm very glad indeed to have the chance to speak with you now,' the detective adds politely. 'Just a formality, of course.'

'A formality?'

'That's right. A couple of questions we'd like to ask you before we officially close the case.' The detective checks his notepad, and again I feel frustrated that he seems to be dragging his feet.

'Close the case? I don't understand. Why is it even still open? You've caught the gunman, haven't you? *Haven't* you?' My heartbeat pounds in my ears as I finally manage to force out, in a harsh whisper: '*Who is he?*'

'Ah. I see.' He stops pacing and turns to look at me, his eyes narrowing. 'You don't know anything at all, do you?'

'I've been in a coma, Detective.' I'm really losing patience now.

'Of course. Then I'll just bring you up to speed, shall I?' he says, lifting a pacifying hand as I sit bolt upright and start fidgeting irritably. 'My senior investigating officer DI Nick Baxter is outside in the relatives' room. He was the detective who conducted the initial investigation into the incident at your home.'

The incident. I close my eyes and remember clawing my way across the grass, the clammy soil, blood soaking through my clothes as I tried desperately to reach Annabel.

'We didn't want to crowd you, but he's here and you can speak with him afterwards, if you like. Run through any details we don't cover here. He has all the forensic reports, of course, along with witness statements and SOCO's analysis of the crime scene, so—'

'Knock knock!' A petite, dark-haired young woman in a navy trouser suit pops her head around the door.

'Ah, at *last*,' DCI Watkins says, sighing heavily, and I realise why he's been prevaricating. He was waiting for this woman, whoever she is. 'Time-keeping not on the curriculum at Cambridge?'

'Sorry I'm late, boss. Got stuck in rush-hour traffic, then missed my exit off the M25. And there was a pile-up on the A41,' she apologises, shrugging her shoulders as she steps in to the room and heads straight to my bedside, her movements brisk and birdlike.

Immediately I realise the detective was right to leave his other colleague outside: I feel crowded with just *two* police officers filling the small room with their unfamiliar presence. I catch a faint whiff of cigarette smoke from the woman's jacket and wonder if that's the real reason she's late. I must remember to tell Professor Hernandez later that there's nothing wrong with my sense of smell, I think . . . Another thing he can tick off his list on the whiteboard.

'This is Michelle Simpson,' the detective says, nodding curtly at his colleague, 'my family liaison officer. She's just joined the case, and I like her to be present in matters of domestic violence.'

Just joined the case – when it's about to be closed?

'Hi. Please call me Michelle – and is it OK if I call you Maddie?' She pulls up a chair and sits down close to my side; any closer and she'd be in bed with me. 'Before we start, I just want you to know that there's nothing to be frightened of any more. You're safe now.'

'So the gunman ... You were saying ... He's locked up, yes?' I look back at DCI Watkins and realise I'm holding my breath; it's making me feel dizzy. I catch a fleeting glance between the detectives and wonder what it means.

'I'm so sorry for what you've been through,' Michelle says softly, leaning even closer. 'But we're going to give you all the support you need. I'm *here* for you, any time of the day or night. I want you to know that.'

'Mrs Castle, if I might jump in.' DCI Watkins steps forward, huffing slightly and looking impatient. I can see why he needs Michelle to do the touchy-feely stuff. 'To answer your question, no prosecutions have been brought and no further action is required at this time.'

'No further action,' I parrot.

'As the final key witness, though, we're keen to hear your version of events. See if we can't fill in some of the blanks,' he continues.

'Blanks,' I echo again. I thought *I* was the only one with blanks ... I don't need more black holes – I want answers, not more questions!

'We're eager to gather whatever information you can share with us, no matter how trivial those details might seem. What you were doing on that day, what you were thinking – basically your recollections of that morning. It may be that we need to come back and speak to you another time – I don't want to tire you too much in one go. I'm aware this is all extremely difficult for you.' He looks down at his notepad again.

'Yes, you can talk to us at *any* time,' Michelle reiterates, flicking a glance at DCI Watkins that says: *Leave the sympathy to me.* 'I'm sure it will take a while for everything to come back to you. Your memory of that day, and all the events leading up to—'

'My daughter's birthday. The morning of my twins' tenth birthday,' I cut in impatiently. They may have come to me looking for answers, but I don't *have* any. That's *their* job, I think angrily. 'But you say no further action is required. I'm sorry, I don't understand.' I shake my head as if that will make everything suddenly fall into place.

'That's correct. As far as the judicial process is concerned, no further action is required at this time.' The detective is still studying his notepad and I want to snatch it out of his hands and throw it across the room.

'No further action. You mean that the gunman ...? Isn't he in *prison?*' I practically yell the word and wonder if Carol and the other nurses outside my room are hearing all this and looking at each other in shock and curiosity.

'Prison? No, Mrs Castle,' DCI Watkins says, finally looking up from his notepad. 'Your brother-in-law took the cowardly way out. He fired a second shot. Turned the gun on himself.'

TWENTY-EIGHT

DCI Watkins would indeed have made a perfect civil servant – or a politician, I think, my mind looping wildly. He has obviously perfected the art of delivering bad news while making it sound like he's just relaying a weather forecast: his voice is so devoid of emphasis that to begin with I can't quite grasp what he's telling me.

'Brother-in-law?' My voice sounds breathy. I feel lightheaded. 'Max.'

'Yes, Max Castle. The weapon was an ex-army-issue firearm; according to your husband it belonged to his late father. A Smith & Wesson Victory Model, to be precise. Six-shot, double-action military revolver with a four-inch barrel.' He checks his notepad yet again for confirmation. 'Misfired it the first time but was bang on target with his second bullet. Clean shot to the head.'

'He was pronounced dead at the scene, Maddie,' Michelle says more gently, taking hold of my left hand and gently squeezing it.

'Max?' I say faintly. *Max?*

'I'm sorry. This must be a dreadful shock,' Michelle continues, 'but we were wondering ... well, hoping you might be able to cast some light on what might have led Max to do this. We're still trying to get a handle on the immediate aftermath, too. Your husband helped us with our inquiries to begin with, but we have all we need from him now, and he's been in such a dreadful state . . . '

'My husband?'

'Yes, Dominic Castle. Your *husband*.' She's still holding my hand and lifts it slightly, as if to show me the indentation where my platinum wedding band used to be.

Did I take it off weeks ago? I wonder. Or is Professor Hernandez keeping it safe for me until I'm well enough to go home . . . I become fixated on the whereabouts of my wedding ring rather than thinking about the implications of what they've just told me.

'I think we can assume Mrs Castle has no memory or knowledge of events subsequent to being shot in the head, Michelle,' the detective says wryly.

'Yes, of course, sorry, I just meant to say that if there's anything from *before* then, anything she might be able to tell us about . . . ' She breaks off, blushing.

'Dominic – your husband,' DCI Watkins goes on, cutting across her, 'returned home from the golf club to discover the crime scene shortly after the occurrence of the shooting. He was the one who placed the emergency call, and I think it's fair to say he was in an extremely distressed state, and my understanding from colleagues' – he dips his head at Michelle in acknowledgement – 'is that he has remained so.'

'You could say he's a broken man,' Michelle chips in. 'He was frantic with worry for you, and then what with the shock of it being his brother—'

'His *brother* did this. Max?' I repeat, in a stunned daze.

My eyes glaze over as I think back to that day, trying to recall any signs that it was Max beneath the army fatigues, the balaclava. The shock is devastating, although a voice inside my head reminds

me that I had wondered about Max, back in the bright-dark –
before I woke up and realised that I might have been dreaming,
but my nightmare was only just beginning.

'There must be some mistake,' I say, even while acknowledging
it's unlikely to be a case of mistaken identity if they found Max
lying shot in our back garden. A shiver runs up my spine as phrases
like 'dental records' and 'blood groups' float across my memory.
There is a metallic taste in my mouth and I reach blindly for the
glass of water on my bedside table then hold it in front of me,
forgetting to drink it.

Max. The twins' big, loud, quick-talking crazy uncle ... It's
not that the idea hasn't crossed my mind before; it's just that the
reality of the confirmation is so ... catastrophic. Because if he shot
Annabel, the gun misfiring as the detective said, so the bullet hit
me too, that surely means Max's guilt goes even deeper than the
police know ...

I remember my fierce conviction that the man who murdered
Annabel must also have been the one grooming her – killing her
to ensure her silence. It still seems the most logical explanation,
but in the cold light of day, neither crime seems to fit with the
Max I knew.

The detective seems certain, though: Max fired the fatal shot
and then turned the gun on himself. Which means I need to
accept the terrible likelihood that Dom's brother – the man I
willingly welcomed into our home, to play with and care for my
children – was also a ... a *paedophile*. The word sends shudders of
anger and revulsion through me, and I become aware that tears are
running down my face when I see Michelle reach for the tissues
on my bedside table. She hands one to me, but then noticing how
tightly my white-knuckled fingers are still clasping the glass of
water, she leans over instead and dabs gently at my cheeks.

'But if Max ... If Max was the gunman, does that also mean ...'

I break off, my mind a tornado of confusion as I try to grasp this repellent scenario.

I remember the way Annabel had started to avoid taking lifts from Uncle Max, and how upset she was when he, not her dad, came to watch her in the drama club show. I remember her complaining that he was always at our house, and hiding the playing cards so he couldn't suggest yet another game of poker with her. But they were such small, innocent, childish things. Were they *really* indicators of something far more toxic?

I open my mouth to voice the question, but then I look at the machines next to my bed, the whiteboard at the end of the room, and I hesitate. I'm no longer certain how much I can trust my own memories: I thought I was awake, watching my son and husband struggle with their grief, yet all the time I was here, unconscious. I was wrong about that – what if I was also completely wrong to believe that Annabel's stalker and her killer were one and the same?

I think of Dom. *A broken man.* He would never recover from the shame of such a revelation. His brother a paedophile; our daughter the object of Max's perverted desires. I think of Annabel lying dead and cold, murdered by her uncle . . . Nothing will bring her back. Slandering Max won't help her now, no matter how much I loathe him and want his name to be publicly denounced for the evil crime he's committed. No, I can't speculate about such a terrible thing without being more certain . . .

But if it *wasn't* Max grooming Annabel, who was it? And if Max's intention wasn't to silence her, why else would he want to kill my daughter? Was it all just about punishing *me* – forcing me to *choose*? If so, what possible reason could my brother-in-law have had for bearing such malevolence towards me? I was never anything but kind to him. *Too* kind, in Dom's eyes.

Nothing adds up. The detectives have presented me with the

missing pieces of information I craved, but I still can't shape them into a meaningful picture.

'It *must* be a mistake,' I repeat. 'Surely Max ...' My mind freezes, my voice dies; I sink back against the pillows and slide into emotional shutdown.

'There's no mistake. I'm sorry,' the detective adds, when I finally manage to meet his eyes. 'But you were about to say something else. Can you remember?' he prompts, pen poised over his notepad. 'Do you have any idea why your brother-in-law might have done this?'

DCI Watkins' steady gaze locks with mine. I have a sense that he's waiting for something specific from me. *But what?* I'm not the one on trial here. *Am* I?

'As I said, no further action is required,' he continues, 'so effectively it's a moot point. Max is dead and the weapon was found in his hand. Your husband is the only other witness to the aftermath, and he has an alibi at Fulwell Golf Club. No one else saw anything.' He flips his notebook shut, as if the matter is settled.

Run!

Hide!

Don't look back!

'It isn't unusual for the perpetrator of a crime to be so close to the victim's family, of course,' DCI Watkins says, almost conversationally.

They're always right under your nose ...

'But we'd still like to pull together as complete a picture as possible. Anything you can remember about Max Castle that may give us an insight into his state of mind, his attitude towards your family, would be very helpful.' He checks his watch and stands up, clearly impatient to leave now he's not getting anything useful from me. 'Michelle?'

'I'll leave all our cards with the nurse, in case you think of anything,' Michelle says, casting me one last sympathetic smile before she hurries out after her boss, patting her jacket pockets. I wonder if she's looking for her business card or her cigarettes.

As the door closes behind them, I feel a surge of fear so powerful I'm convinced I'm going to black out. I think of Dom returning to our home after our terrible row that morning, only to find that his whole world had been blown apart – our son traumatised, his precious girl slaughtered, his wife accidentally shot and his brother dead.

Murderer.

The detective has at last given me a name, but he said nothing about me having been forced to choose; he made no mention of Aidan saying what his mummy did. No one else saw; no one knows . . .

My heart beats faster and my gut clenches in horror as realisation hits me: I'm going to have to tell Dom that although, for some reason I cannot begin to grasp, his brother pulled the trigger, it's as much my fault that Annabel is dead. That *I chose her.*

TWENTY-NINE

The hand on my forehead is gentle, reassuring, lightly brushing to and fro before trailing down to my chin. I hear the wind chimes and think of home, sighing as I turn my face into the palm now cupping my cheek. It feels rough, warm . . .

I frown. The doctor's hands are smooth, cool; they smell of antiseptic.

I smell citrus cologne and then suddenly I can't breathe, my throat closing up as my nostrils begin to burn, and I gag against the hand smothering my mouth, forcing my tongue back down my throat until I start to suffocate. My chest feels like it's being compressed under a heavy weight. I'm drowning; I'm going to pass out . . .

'Stop! Help! Please!' The strained, muffled sound of my voice is shocking. Even now, on my fourth day awake, I can't get used to being able to speak, to the idea that others will hear me – and respond.

'Maddie, what is it? What's wrong?'

I open my eyes to see my husband perched on the edge of the

chair next to my bed where the family liaison officer was sitting surely only moments ago. He leaps to his feet, rushing to my side.

'Dom!' I croak breathlessly. Then, in the next breath: 'Aidan?' I look frantically round the room.

'It's just me, sweetheart. Aidan's fine; it's you I'm worried about. You gave me a fright there. Tossing and turning like you were trying to escape the hounds of hell. Must have been having a nightmare, hey? Last time I saw you it was like you were in a deep freeze. Now you look ... Are you OK?' he asks anxiously, his face close to mine, his blue eyes wide and fearful.

I blink rapidly, battling confusion and panic. 'You're really here. Where have you *been*?' I ask frantically. 'The police—'

'Yeah, I know. I saw them drive off as I was coming in. So you've heard the grisly truth.' He rubs a hand over his face; his voice is a flat line.

'I can't believe it, Dom. I just can't believe that ...' I shake my head, feeling disoriented and tearful. A tight ball of stress seems to be lodged in my chest, constricting my breathing. I must have crashed out after the detectives left; stress exhausts me, as the doctor warned me it would, but sleep hasn't lessened any of the shock and I've woken up feeling like the world has tilted sharply on its axis.

'Seriously, don't even mention that man's name to me.' He straightens up and turns away from me. 'I can't – I'm sorry I haven't come before now. It's been ... I've been ...'

'No, *I'm* sorry,' I say, and tears slide down my face and it feels like they'll never stop. All my fear of Dom, my anger towards him for not being here, disintegrates beneath the bombshell of Max's guilt.

'Hey, don't cry. It's OK. It's not your fault,' Dom says in a soothing voice, turning again to crouch at my bedside, taking hold of my hand. 'All my life he's been a thorn in my side. I just didn't have a clue he was capable of being such a . . . *monster*. He's always tried to take everything off me. Jealousy. Entitlement. Who knows? You're the one with the psychology degree; you tell me. The big brother who felt he deserved it all. Including my family. And if he couldn't have it, he was going to destroy it. Destroy *me*.' His face is gaunt and his eyes are shadowed.

'I know. I can hardly believe it. It's impossible to take in,' I say, squeezing his hand. 'But I meant – I didn't mean . . . I wanted to say that I'm sorry for . . . for—'

'Hush, sweetheart. I'm here now,' he cuts in, and he leans over and scoops his hands beneath my shoulders, crushing me to him so I feel the warmth of his strong chest and the smoothness of his freshly shaven jaw.

I try to inhale without him realising that I'm sniffing his after-shave, to see if it's the same unfamiliar citrus smell that woke me from my dream, but my face is squashed so tightly against his cheek that I can't be sure. I can feel my body starting to tremble at the shock of being this close to him again, after all this time. It hits me with force that I'm alone with my husband for the first time not only since I emerged from my coma, but also since our violent row on the morning of the twins' birthday. I thought I'd been right next to him, watching him, for three months, but it was only from within the confines of my unconscious mind.

'It's so good to have you back, babe. I thought you were completely gone.'

His gentleness puzzles me, contradicting everything I expected of him. I'd been anticipating anger, blame and harsh words. I thought his first visit to me would be full of recrimination and accusing questions: why did I fight with him and make him storm out the house, leaving his family unprotected? Why did I let some-one murder our daughter instead of throwing myself in front of her, giving my life to save hers? Instead, he is conciliatory, concerned.

But something feels odd. Dom has always been so highly charged; brash and quick to fly off the handle. He's a high achiever and works tirelessly to keep himself fit. He has no patience for weakness and has always been intolerant of sickness. I was the one to nurse the twins through chickenpox, while Dom was irritated by their whininess; on the few occasions I've been poorly myself, he's given me a wide berth, allowing Lucy to take over and keep me stocked up on hot lemon drinks and cool, clean sheets. I'm struggling to recognise this man who is being so ... *nice* to me.

He has the same handsome face, the same stylish clothes – yet something doesn't fit. Perhaps it's because I've been remembering him from all the different stages of our relationship, from our first date to our final row. Now I'm firmly back in the present day, I can't quite get a handle on where we sit between those two extremes. The last thing I remember is Dom's hammer punch to my face before he slammed furiously out of the house, and since then our lives have been ripped apart. No matter how hard he's trying to act like everything is normal, I can't simply pretend that didn't happen.

I take a deep breath as he moves to sit back in his chair. I sit up straight and decide it's time to be brave. 'Dom, I need to ask you something.'

'Course. Anything.'

His attentiveness surprises me. I can't remember the last time Dom really listened to me. But he seems to be all ears now. There's nothing like a bullet in the head to finally get someone's attention.

My head is buzzing with so many things, but it's Annabel's diary I keep coming back to, kicking myself for not mentioning it to DCI Watkins. It was such a shock hearing about Max, though; my head was all over the place. But I realise that I *should* have told the detective about the things my daughter wrote. I can't let her death be shrouded in mystery; she died in violence but she deserves to rest in peace. I must get in touch with them; I must remember to ask Carol for their business cards. I need to give the police every bit of information I can, I decide. I'm tired of secrets; they eroded our marriage, our family, and I won't live with them any more.

'Sweetheart,' Dom says, sitting patiently, watching as I work through my panicky thoughts, unable to find the right words or even know where to start. 'Max is gone, you're out of your coma ... We need to get our family back on track, hey? Let's not agonise about the whys and wherefores. It's pointless. Dead men tell no tales, hey? Leave the detectives to do their stuff. The case has been closed and we just need to concentrate on getting you well and bringing you home.' He stands up and leans over to give me another tight squeeze before planting a kiss on my head. I flinch and he apologises. 'Sorry, did that hurt? I forget my own strength sometimes.'

But it wasn't the pain that made me flinch; it was ... memories. Those last terrible nine months or more. All these weeks I've been locked inside my head, remembering hostile silence, violent rows ... They were real memories; I know they were. Dom may not be a killer as I once feared while tunnelling through my unconscious mind, but I *was* afraid of him. And I'm not sure we have it in us to be one of those heroic couples that turn to each other in grief, supporting each other through hard times. We've experienced too many hard times already – and they tore us apart.

I remember the three train tickets. I remember my packed suitcase. Does Dom *know* about them? I push gently at his chest, urging him to take a step back. Eventually he sits down again, and I flick my ponytail over my shoulder and look him straight in the eye, steeling myself to ask him the question I know will crack things open to reveal what's really left between us.

'Dom, was I leaving you?' I say quietly.

'Were you ... *what*? What are you talking about?'

He's out of his seat again, sitting down abruptly on the edge of the bed. Automatically I lie back, my shoulders pressing into the pillows, my hands folded protectively across my chest. Dom rests one big hand on top of them, bearing down so firmly that I can feel my own heart pounding.

'It's just that I remembered something. While I was sleeping.' I clench my fists, digging my fingernails into my palms to help me hold my nerve.

'You weren't sleeping. You were at death's door. I'm not a doctor and I'm sure a million things ran through your head, but I bet most of it was a load of jumbled rubbish. I mean, you took a bullet to the head. You can't possibly—'

'I remembered that I'd packed a case, Dom. And hidden my photo inside it,' I say, trying to keep my voice steady. I know that I don't need to explain which photo, or its significance; Dom will know.

His hand is pressing down harder on mine now. I try not to show any reaction but I can feel the weight of it beginning to constrict my chest, and I wonder if he's aware that he's hurting me again.

'So? We'd been talking about taking the kids away for a weekend. I guess you got a bit ahead of yourself, that's all.'

'When do you ever take time off? Apart from our summer holiday? And we're practically broke, you said so yourself. I do remember that much. I remember us having a massive fight about it on the twins' birthday.' I grit my teeth against the pain of that memory.

'OK, no need to remind me. To be frank, I'm not sure this is the time or the place to be dragging up old rows.' He releases my hands and turns away from me sharply, leaning forward so that his elbows rest on his knees.

'Sorry, I just . . .' I realise immediately that I've made a mistake.

I've said the wrong thing; I shouldn't have brought up the subjects of work and money; they were such bones of contention between us.

'In any case, we're out of the woods now. I've taken on a major new client, and I had a good chat with the bank manager yesterday. It's been a hell of a slog, and I won't deny things got close to the bone. But I've pulled through. We're not going to lose the house. I'm not going bust. It's all going to be absolutely *fine*.'

He stands up and begins pacing up and down the small room, and the scrape of his shoes on the wood floor makes me think of Professor Hernandez's pen scribbling on the whiteboard. I glance towards it and see that it's been wiped clean. Does that mean I'm about to be discharged and sent home now that Dom's here? The thought makes butterflies dive-bomb in my stomach.

'That's good,' I say, falling into old habits with surprising ease: I know I need to placate him before the short fuse of his temper catches light. But Dom remains unexpectedly calm.

'Yeah, it is. So let's stop raking up the past, hey? We've got to think of the future now. We've lost enough. Haven't we?' He stops pacing and turns to look at me, and his blue eyes are clouded with grief; it hurts to look at them.

He's right: we *have* lost far too much. I'm not sure it's humanly possible to survive more. But we can't move forward with lies between us, I think resolutely. If there is any chance at all of us salvaging our marriage and getting through this together, I have to tell Dom the truth, and I have to know the truth from him.

'I found train tickets in my suitcase,' I say, more firmly this time. 'But only three – for two children . . . and just one adult.'

'Ah. Yeah. Fuck.' He sinks back into the armchair as if his legs have suddenly given way, and I'm astonished to see his eyes fill with tears.

'You knew? You *did* know I was leaving you?' I say, watching him, hardly able to believe what I'm seeing. Dom *never* cries. He really has changed.

'I knew,' he admits. 'But it was all my fault – you have nothing to feel bad about. I was having such a shitty run of bad luck. I knew I was turning into a complete stress-head. I lost perspective, I can see that now. I just wanted to give you all the best of everything. Honestly, I don't blame you for finding another guy's shoulder to cry on.' He rubs his palms across his face as he spills out his apology, and then lets his head sink into his big hands.

'A shoulder to … *What?*' A pulse throbs heavily at my temple in shock. I clutch the neckline of my pyjamas, pulling the soft material up to my chin as I slide down into the bed. I want to bury myself beneath the sheets as the implication of Dom's words sinks in. I can't believe it. In all the hours, days, weeks and months of imagining and reimagining our life together, I have never – not one single time – conjured up the thought of another man. I've remembered my early crush on Shay, but apart from my old university lecturer no other man has ever entered my thoughts.

Dom doesn't look up but starts sobbing in earnest now, his broad shoulders shaking. Michelle's words come back to me about my husband being a broken man.

'Please, talk to me. I'm sorry – I'm so sorry I've hurt you so much. I don't remember any of it – packing the bag, buying the tickets … I don't remember turning to anyone. I don't remember any other man …'

Shame cascades through me, chipping away more and more pieces of my self-respect. I know I was unhappy with Dom – I can't, won't deny that. I know now that I wanted to leave him, but I'm shocked to the core to hear him suggest that I was being unfaithful. Can things get any worse?

'Not just any man, Maddie. You were seeing *Max*.'

THIRTY

His low, anguished voice is like a punch to my stomach, and my heart starts beating so fast I feel like it's going to burst. I hear a shrill alarm and feel another flash of recognition. I'd thought that harsh sound was our front doorbell, but it's vibrating from the machine at my side. I stare at the buzzing monitor, one more reminder of how the sounds and smells around me infiltrated the bright-dark, subliminal underworld of my coma.

My panic attack has obviously set my pulse soaring: I'd forgotten Carol hooks me up to this machine for a few minutes each day, to monitor any daily change in my heart rate; she must have connected the wire while I slept. The thin line feels like the only thing tethering me to this life, stopping me from giving up entirely on this painful earthly existence and floating up into the clouds. If only, I think, feeling my last hope of redemption evaporate beneath the heat of Dom's scorn.

I watch as my husband retreats to the corner of the room like a wounded dog, but before I can appeal to him, Professor Hernandez is at my bedside.

'Try to stay calm, Maddie. Don't want you tripping up this close to the finishing tape.' He smiles reassuringly, but I've learned that the doctor has a remarkable ability to look serene while his brain is working at a hundred miles per hour. Even as he looks so utterly calm, I know he's assessing every flicker of response in my physical and mental capacities. 'Am I going to win the race, then?' I ask him wearily.

'You're already a winner. You are alive,' he tells me quietly, his face close to mine as he straightens my pillows and makes me comfortable.

'I'm not sure I deserve any medals, though,' I say sadly. 'In fact, I think I'm due to be disqualified in disgrace.' I can see Dom craning his head, trying to hear our murmured words.

'Your wife needs to remain as calm as possible, Mr Castle,' the doctor instructs as he turns to look at Dom.

'Professor Hernandez? You're needed.' Carol pushes the door ajar and pops her head round it with an anxious frown.

'I'll be there in a moment.' He doesn't move.

'I think it's urgent,' she persists. 'I've got the psych team on the phone.'

'Very well. Remember: peace and rest. No stress.' He looks steadfastly at Dom, still making no move towards the door, and I wonder why the doctor, always so confident, is hesitating.

'Of course,' Dom says smoothly, reaching out to shake Professor Hernandez's hand, and I see the doctor glance over his shoulder as he closes the door behind him.

Immediately, Dom comes to sit on the bed and takes hold of my hand. I don't resist. We've been through so much during our ten years of marriage. Maybe there have been as many lows as highs, but I don't have the heart for any more battles. Annabel's death was hard enough to bear in the depths of my unconscious mind; in the cold, harsh light of day, it's like the pain is stripping the flesh from my bones. All I really have left of her is Aidan. Her twin. I want to hold him close and never let him go – as I should never have let my daughter go. But I can't do it alone. I have to get better, get out of this hospital and home to my son. Whatever doubts I had about Dom, I need to trust him now – and pray that he will give *me* a second chance this time.

'I don't remember wanting to be with Max. I don't remember so much of what's happened. But if you tell me that's the case, I believe you. And I'm sorry.' I squeeze his fingers, feeling tears prick my eyes, and I don't flinch when he closes his big hands around mine.

'I forgive you. Thousands wouldn't,' he adds with a quirk of a smile.

'I'll make it up to you. Somehow.'

'I'm sure you will.' He gives my hand another squeeze, and I notice that his wedding band is missing.

'Your ring?'

'Just being cleaned. Don't panic.'

'I seem to have lost mine.' I glance towards my bedside table as if expecting it to suddenly materialise there.

'Being cleaned too.'

'It is? But how—'

'And maybe this year we'll celebrate our wedding anniversary properly. When you're better, of course. All the painkillers you're on, not sure champagne is such a good idea right now.'

He offers a lopsided smile but I feel sick as the mention of champagne reminds me of the conversation with Max that evening in our kitchen, and of yet another row after Dom did indeed meet Lucy and Jasper at the champagne bar the following morning, as I'd worried might happen. I swallow hard as I suddenly remember, though, that the scene I replayed in my unconscious mind was, in fact, only half the story: Lucy brought a bottle of Cristal to our

Sunday lunch that weekend, handing it to me with a big grin and saying it was a surprise late birthday gift. She'd already given me a present but felt I deserved an extra treat; she'd just needed help picking out the best vintage and knew Dom was the man for the job. I recall this now; I just can't decide whether or not it was the truth. And I'm not certain whether Dom had simply been keeping a secret for my friend, or if he'd wanted to needle me with the paranoia he knew I'd feel.

As more pieces of my memory return, I wonder what other truths I'll unearth – how many more tricks I'll discover that my brain has played on me.

Dad's usually the one who plays tricks.

I remember Annabel saying that to me on our day trip to Brighton. I still have no idea what we were doing there, why I'd bought those train tickets. Perhaps it doesn't matter any more. As soon as I'm better, I'll be going home. To my son. And I'm going to bathe him in all the love I know I felt for his sister too. I won't ever forget that; I won't ever forget her.

'I'm sure half a glass won't hurt,' I say, trying to smile.

'And I'm sure I can lay my hands on a punnet of fresh strawberries somewhere.' Dom grins. 'I'll even give you a back rub, if you like.'

'With a cuppa afterwards.' I force myself to get into the spirit of the moment. Dom looks happy; I've woken up; Aidan is safe at home.

Annabel, my darling girl. I miss you so.

'But of course. Whatever you want.'

'Thank you. For standing by me when I really don't deserve ...' I turn my face into the pillow, but I can't hide the sob that wracks through my chest.

'Hey, come on now. What's all this? Everything's going to be OK. I'm here,' Dom says, slipping a hand beneath my cheek and turning my face to look at him. His eyes are so bright I almost expect to see sparks shooting from them.

'I'm just so sorry. About Max. About . . . everything.'

I need to tell him; I just can't find the words, can't catch my breath . . .

'Forget about Max. You're all mine, Maddie, and I'll never, ever let you go.'

'Oh, Dom. You said that to me once before, remember?' I say.

He loves me; he'll forgive me for choosing our daughter . . .

'Course I do. I never forget anything. Not one single little thing.' He punctuates each word with a tiny kiss on the tip of each finger of my left hand in turn.

'Just me that has trouble remembering, then,' I say, reaching up hesitantly to stroke his cheek with my other hand. 'I really can't remember . . . I can't believe I ever thought of Max in that way. I mean, he was your *brother*.' I close my eyes in shame.

'Sure. Well, he demonstrated *exactly* what little value he placed on family. I mean, for God's sake, he got me to clean and repair that gun!' He shakes his head in disbelief.

'No . . . He did?' The idea is so horrendous I can hardly believe it.

'I got a few bits and pieces from Mum after she died, her jewellery and things, but that gun was the only personal possession Max inherited from our dad. That and his old army stuff.'

'The fatigues he wore that morning,' I say, pressing a hand to my quivering mouth as I remember his bulky form silhouetted in our front door.

'Quite. Anyway, Dad always talked a lot about his soldier days. The gun had a kind of bizarre sentimentality for Max, I guess. But if I'd thought for just one second that he would ever dream of firing it . . . ' He rubs his hands tiredly over his face. 'I thought he just wanted to polish up a family memento. More fool me.'

'You're not a fool. He was the—' I can't bring myself to say what I think of Max. 'He obviously wasn't the man I thought he was,' I say hoarsely, almost choking on the understatement. 'I can't believe I ever considered . . .'

'We really don't have to talk about this now,' Dom says, smoothing my too-long fringe back from my face, his fingertips trailing down my hollowed cheeks, stroking my neck.

'Did you tell DCI Watkins? About me and . . . Max?' I ask, wondering if that's why the detective seemed to be expecting something from me. Perhaps he was waiting for me to confess my infidelity – it would certainly have provided some kind of clue as to Max's motives for wanting to punish me. Perhaps things had turned sour between us and I'd jilted him . . .

'No. Course not.' His big hands circle my collarbone, pressing down lightly. I feel uncomfortable but tell myself I need to let my husband get close to me again. I can't flinch at every touch.

'I think we should tell him. And there are other things I need to—'

'Shh. Don't talk. Just rest some more.'

'But why didn't I go through with it?' I say, still puzzling over the very idea that I could have planned to run away with my blunt, quirky brother-in-law.

He pushes a finger against my lips. 'I guess you just loved me more than you realised.'

'Yes,' I say, and it seems to make sense. Maybe, too, I'd realised I couldn't take the twins away from their father, no matter how unhappy I was. Perhaps, despite everything, I'd decided to give our marriage another go, especially after reading Annabel's diary. Maybe the shock of her words made me *scared* to leave our home. Maybe I just wanted to keep her safe. The dreadful irony of it makes my head swim.

'No doubt about it. We're a team. We've *always* been a team.

Max couldn't compete with that. He never stood a chance of stealing you from me.'

'And do you think that's why he . . . ?' A penny suddenly drops. 'Do you think he was angry with me for backing out?' I say faintly.

'Yeah. I do. I saw him the night before the twins' birthday. Poured whiskey down him in The Bell Inn. Listened to all his crap. He wasn't happy, that's for sure. In fact, he was furious.'

I try to picture Max furious, his big body fired up with jealous rage. But whenever I think of him, I only see his clever, bright-eyed, almost mischievous expression as he lay stretched out on our living-room floor playing video games with the kids. I can't picture him as my lover; I can't picture him with a balaclava over his head and a gun in his hand.

'And *you* were angry with *him*,' he continues.

'Me? Angry with *Max*?'

'Oh, you know, he'd been coming round to our house so much. Every time I put my key in the door, he was there. I guess that accounts for how you came to cry on his shoulder in the first place. I was always working, and Max played on that. But then it got too much. He got too close, too intense.'

'I wanted him to back off a bit and he refused. And I was angry with him for that,' I say, thinking out loud, trying to reconnect with that feeling – turning my thoughts inwards, wondering why still nothing is falling into place. I don't remember turning to Max; I don't remember turning *against* him.

'Exactly. You never seriously wanted to leave me. Certainly not for *Max*.' He all but spits out his name. 'You just wanted to make a point. I should have paid you more attention. I get that. It's unfortunate you chose my brother, but that's life. I can deal with it. I've got broad enough shoulders.'

So did Max, I think. Tall, broad-shouldered, a giant blotting out the summer's day as he came to our home on the morning of the twins' birthday, determined to get revenge, to punish me for changing my mind about leaving Dom to be with him ...

It might be Uncle Max. He said he had an extra-special surprise for us ...

I'd invited him to help us set up garden games for after the pool party, but Annabel was already half expecting him, I remember. Had Max hinted at something? Had he been sitting at home, his anger and frustration building, ready to be released on the day I'd planned to run away with him? The tickets were for that date – but I'd changed my mind, and he snapped.

Only Annabel opened the front door. My darling daughter stepped first into the firing line. How *could* he? Max had always doted on her, wistful eyes watching her whirl through life like a butterfly. I remember the joy he took in her, in both the twins, the endless gifts, games ... *Buying their silence*, comes the thought. Did Aidan know? Annabel made no mention in her diary of confiding in her twin.

'And then there was Annabel's diary,' Dom adds, as if reading my mind.

'I think I'm going to be sick,' I say, clasping both hands to my mouth. I wait for Dom to offer me some water, but he doesn't move and I press my head back into the pillows, closing my eyes, waiting for the world to stop spinning.

'I know I was rough with you that morning, sweetheart. It was such a shock, the things you told me Annabel wrote. I just flipped, I guess.' His big hands run through his hair, ruffling his usually immaculate style.

'I just can't believe Max could – I feel so dreadful, so ashamed that I didn't *know*. That I didn't *do* anything. More than that, that I'd been planning to run away with ... '

'We all make mistakes. You've definitely used up one of your nine lives, though.'

But I can't return Dom's rueful smile. I bite my lip to stop a rush of tears as the final piece of the jigsaw falls into place, completing a dark, shameful picture . . .

When things had seemed beyond repair with Dom, I'd turned to his brother for sanctuary. But he'd come on too strong, and I asked him to give me some space. Then I found Annabel's diary and my world imploded, leaving me frightened to walk away from everything I knew to step into the unknown with Max. He felt rejected; I'd made him feel worthless. And I was also denying him unfettered access to what he wanted most of all: Annabel.

Max wanted payback, and I see now that Annabel's name was always on that bullet; he always intended to kill her, to prevent her from telling tales on him, revealing his sordid secret. But he wanted to make me suffer first by forcing me to make the worst choice a mother can ever face. He took a gamble, but to my shame I simply handed Annabel to him on a plate. I chose her because I was hurt and resentful that she didn't trust me enough to tell me what had been happening and, on top of that, I was angry with her for spoiling what had seemed to be my best chance of escaping my unhappy marriage. If it hadn't been for finding her diary, maybe I wouldn't have lost the courage to leave . . .

When Max pointed the gun at me, something deep inside me overruled all my maternal instincts and, in a split-second of terror and frustration, a moment's unforgiveable loss of reason and control, fury took over and I turned on my daughter.

One victim; two murderers.

I became a desperate, accidental accomplice to a crime that has destroyed my entire family; I inflicted on myself the instant, heartbreaking regret that will plague me for a lifetime. Maybe that's why Max then took his own life: he'd acted on a violent impulse, and he couldn't bear to live with the regret. The detective was right: Max was a coward. He has escaped the pain of living with what he did. But I'm still here, and it's too late for me ever to say sorry, or to make it better; I can never take it back now. I can never bring my daughter back.

So this is what rock bottom feels like.

THIRTY-ONE

'Dom, I need to see Aidan.' I sit upright in my bed, feeling a sob building in my chest, pressing like a rock against my heart. I want to hug my daughter so badly my whole body hurts; I'm overwhelmed by the need to hold my son.

'Later. When you're feeling stronger. Right now, this is the best place for you. Away from all the stresses of home. The gossiping neighbours. I never knew we were such a popular family. So many flowers; they haven't stopped coming for weeks. People certainly love to pop by for a chat when there's a bit of tragedy to pick over, don't they?' he says bitterly, crossing the room to stare vacantly out of the window.

'I guess everyone wants to pay their respects,' I say in a low voice. 'Have you kept the notes?' I ask, the thought of people's messages making my heart leap. 'I'd love to read them. People's condolences. That would mean so much to me.'

I'm deeply touched to hear that there has been a stream of flowers for Annabel, and eager to read what has been written about her. What a beautiful tribute. It's such a wonderful reflection on how much she was liked; how much she's missed. At school, her clubs, by everyone who knew her. She's left a hole not just in my life, but in the lives of others. It isn't a consolation, but it is ... something. The thought of a bundle of letters with Annabel's name on them brings tears to my eyes.

'Sure. I put them somewhere,' he says, turning back towards me with a frown. 'I'd have to look them out. Bit morbid that, though, isn't it? Don't you think we should just move on? Put all this behind us?'

Put our daughter behind us? Never!

'I'm not ready to do that, Dom,' I say, stunned he can even suggest it.

'Well, like I say, just take your time. You're fine here. The most important thing is that you get better.' He takes two long strides towards my bed and rests his big hands on my shoulders, pushing me firmly back against the pillows, leaning over me.

'The most *important* thing is that our family has been ripped apart and that it's *all my fault*. I can't just lie here. Aidan *needs* me.'

'Aidan is fine.'

'He's not fine. He *can't* be fine.'

'Look, let's not argue,' he says, pulling up the chair next to the bed, and I feel ashamed. I remember him accusing me of believing I was the perfect mother, that I knew our children better than anyone. Better than him.

'Sorry. You're right,' I say, taking deep breaths to calm myself. 'I'm sure you're taking good care of Aidan. It's just that I miss him so very much. And I miss our daughter so badly.' Defeat washes over me. I can't make this situation any better. Dom is wrong: nothing will ever be OK again.

'That's just the guilt talking.' He straightens up and starts pacing the room again. 'Because of what she wrote in her diary.

It was a huge shock to both of us,' he says, his voice hard and his mouth a grim line.

I hear the subtext: *I have to cope with this, why can't you?*

'I should have known. I never got to help her. I never got to make it better, or tell her I was sorry.' Tears burst from my eyes and I reach out to Dom, needing his comfort, needing to share this soul-destroying grief with my daughter's father. But he steps back from me, his shoulders hunched.

'What could you have done to make it better?'

'But Max—'

'Max is dead,' Dom barks, and his face is darker than I've ever seen it. 'He's paid his price.'

I struggle again to sit up in bed, and I'm surprised when Dom steps across the room to help me this time, pulling back the covers and lifting me out of the bed, carrying me over to the soft tub armchair by the window. His chest is rock hard with tension, but I feel it gradually leave his body as he places me down in the chair and rests his chin on top of my head, wrapping his arms around me.

'If only she'd told us before,' I say, my words muffled against his chest.

'If only lots of things.' Dom steps away from me for a moment to grab a blanket from the end of the bed, draping it over my legs. The small gesture brings tears to my eyes. It feels like years since there has been any real tenderness between us.

'She must have been so scared. So unhappy. I let her down.'

'It's over now. No one can touch her any more. No one is ever going to get near her again.' He tucks the blanket more tightly around my lap.

'Sometimes it's a relief when the pain stops and they are at peace,' I say softly, remembering the doctor's words and thinking how painfully wise they were.

'Peace. Is that what you're looking for?' His fingertips dig into my thighs.

'I just wish . . . I never even got to say goodbye.' I close my eyes and picture Annabel's face, relieved that the image of it hasn't faded like the photo in my suitcase. I wonder whether Dom has unpacked it, or if it's still sitting in my wardrobe.

'You were unconscious, Maddie. What are you talking about?' He leans closer to my face, frowning, his hands moving up to press down heavily on my shoulders now.

'No, I mean before that. I watched her die right in front of me and—'

'Fuck. *What?* What did you just say?' His big body snaps upright but his fingertips still grip my shoulders; I'm too shocked by the look on his face to cry out in pain. 'What the *hell* are you talking about? God, Max really did a number on you, didn't he?'

'What do you mean?' I say faintly, as once again the world tilts, blood rushing to my head.

'I *mean* I left Aidan and Jasper at home an hour ago, with Lucy. And –'

I stare mutely into Dom's eyes and feel the world spin out of its orbit, shooting off into space.

'Annabel was with them. She isn't dead, Maddie – she's never *been* more alive.'

PART THREE

THIRTY-TWO

'Visual and auditory hallucinations are often significant symptoms of post-traumatic stress.'

The whiteboard is back. Professor Hernandez is looking more animated than I have ever seen him. His usual dignified calm has been replaced by almost fevered excitement as he sketches diagrams and jots down notes on the white screen at the end of my room.

'Hallucinations. I don't buy it. I *heard* Max instruct me to *choose one*. I *saw* Annabel's body fly across our back garden to lie beneath the rose bushes. I *felt* her; I clawed my way towards her, I twisted my fingers into her hair and . . . '

Just saying the words takes me back there and I shut my eyes to block out the horrific images. Nothing stops them, they keep on coming, thick and fast, and my eyes are burning from the tears that also won't stop coming. My throat feels raw from sobbing for hours. I haven't stopped crying since Dom left – crying, laughing, crying, laughing. My emotions are all over the place.

I'm counting the hours until Dom returns. He said enough was enough; I was clearly going crazy in this place. *How could I even have thought the condolence cards were for Annabel?* he wanted to know. They were for *me*, and I needed to be back where I belonged: at home with my family. He promised he'd be as quick as he could; he just needed to collect some fresh clothes for me and get the twins home from school. He needed to prepare them and Lucy for the big news: *Mummy's coming home.*

I reach for my glass of water and take a huge gulp before leaning back in the armchair next to the window, resting my pounding head and closing my eyes.

Annabel is alive.

I feel euphoric, overwhelmed – and completely baffled. It still seems too amazing to be true; I can't stop going over and over in my mind how nothing – and no one – has pricked the bubble of my delusion in all this time. Before he left, Dom explained that Annabel had been too traumatised to visit me after my surgery at the West Mid. Aidan had been equally upset, but he'd had the idea that the familiar sound of the recorder might help to wake me up. I *knew* I'd been right about that; it just never occurred to me to ask the doctor whether Annabel had visited along with her brother.

It never occurred to me, because I believed she was dead . . .

And because I haven't talked about her, no one has asked *me* about Annabel. I've said her name, but I've told no one the grim details of my story. Stash didn't bat an eyelid at the idea of my having a daughter at home, and the doctor simply assumed I wasn't talking about her because we'd had some kind of mother–daughter squabble. Only I knew the truth; and my sadness and shame stopped me telling it.

While I'm sure it made the news when I was shot, *Annabel's* death would have been the story to really grip the media, yet no child was actually hurt. I expect the incident made the local headlines for a time, but no one has recognised my name at this hospital. And why would they? We're miles out of London, weeks after the shooting ... They have hundreds of patients here, and Professor Hernandez said his team had been given my medical case notes, details about my next of kin, but little beyond that. He talked about the bitter-sweet loss when a child in pain is finally at peace, but he meant generally; he had no idea what had happened to Annabel.

But the detectives – they told me she'd been shot ...

No, that's not right, I think. They talked about the first shot being *misfired*, and I simply assumed the bullet had somehow hit me after killing Annabel. I was so distressed during the police interview, I heard only what fitted with what I thought I already knew: that Annabel died and I was injured in the attack. They never mentioned her – or Aidan – because *I was the victim.*

And Annabel is alive.

I close my eyes and allow the thought to sing through me once again. The miracle of it takes my breath away; the mystery of it still bemuses me. Every time I think I'm getting closer to forming a clear picture of what happened, something emerges to shift the perspective, change the angle – and now the picture has been turned completely upside down and back to front.

I need to get home to them all. I want to see them so badly it hurts more than any physical pain I've yet had to endure ...

Even though it's only lunchtime, Professor Hernandez has closed the curtains and dimmed the lights. He sits down in the armchair opposite me, our knees almost touching, and he continues his explanations. I feel like we've been talking for hours; he must be as exhausted as I am, but he looks as alert and interested as ever. I've poured out every detail I can remember about my marriage, Annabel, the twins' birthday, my row with Dom and the events of that terrible morning. It goes completely against the grain of my natural shyness and desire for privacy, but I need the doctor's help to understand: *why* did I believe my daughter was dead?

'Temporary psychosis would not be an unexpected outcome in this situation,' he continues, leaning forward in his chair. 'Especially as you had perhaps shown a predisposition towards this kind of episode. Your postnatal depression was, I would suggest, borderline post-partum psychosis that had remained undiagnosed.'

'You think I was already nuts.' I screw up my nose, feeling like an idiot.

'No. But I do think you've been storing up trouble for some time. Motherhood isn't just a biological experience. Nor purely an emotional or psychological one. Physiological, even. It's a combination of all these things. And then some.' He smiles gently.

'So I was a nut that cracked,' I say wryly. I sigh heavily and shake my head. 'This is all too much to take in.'

'Let's take it more slowly, then.' His voice is low and he frowns in concentration as he explains: 'The trigger was extreme terror, of course. An excessive degree of emotional stress, not to mention the physical injury and neurological compromise resulting from the gunshot itself. These are all factors I would determine as contributing to your misapprehension.' He rests a comforting hand on my knee, but I brush it off.

'My daughter's death was a misapprehension. A *misapprehension*. That won't do; that simply won't *do*!'

'I'm sorry. That was ... Please, allow me to phrase it differently.' He sits back and rubs tiredly at his eyes, the first sign that he's finding this as difficult as I am. 'Your belief that Annabel died was a projection of your deepest fears, Maddie,' he says, speaking slowly. 'You had been feeling extraordinarily guilty about having let her down, and that guilt was greatly exacerbated by fear for her life when the gun was pointed at her.'

'I'm sorry, I still don't get it.' I cross my arms, hugging myself to contain my frustration.

'You don't need to apologise,' he says quietly. 'The brain is the most complex part of our bodies. Even I don't understand all its subtleties, and I've specialised in neurology for almost thirty years. But I will try to put this as simply as I can, OK?' He leans forward again, resting his elbows on his knees and clasping his hands lightly together as he continues. 'How about this: you felt so responsible for not having been able to protect Annabel from an abuser's unwanted attentions that, at the point you were rendered unconscious by the bullet, your brain instantly contorted those feelings into a belief that she had died. You projected your anxieties into a distorted reality.'

'You mean, basically, I made my worst fears come true,' I say slowly.

'In your imagination – your unconscious mind – yes. Exactly that,' he confirms.

'But it was all so *real*. If I close my eyes, I can still see it happening as vividly as if it was just yesterday. All of it.' I rub my eyes as if I can wipe away those images, but I know they will never leave me.

'All of it? Or just Annabel flying away from you, your arms reaching out to save her,' he says, choosing his words so carefully that I know he's making an important point.

'You think that was symbolic,' I say. 'My brain inventing that whole scenario as a visual depiction of what I felt I'd done to Annabel: failed her, let her slip through my fingers.' I look up sharply, convinced that I've grasped it now. I look to his clever face for approval.

'I couldn't have put it better myself,' he says and sits back, smiling gently.

My shoulders slump in relief. At least that's something, even if it's not the whole answer. 'I have wondered ... I haven't ever been able to visualise the gunshot. I don't remember gesturing to Annabel; I don't remember seeing the bullet hit her. I just remember crawling towards her, knowing that I had let her down so appallingly yet again. I put that down to the images being too unbearable for my mind to allow them to come back to me, when all the time it was just – not – completely – real . . .' I cover my face, pressing my fingers punishingly into my eyes. I feel like my mind has tricked me – betrayed me.

'Exactly so. Your mind was full of guilt, and guilt became distorted into paranoid conviction. But you had already been shot, Maddie. You were already unconscious. Your brain just filled in the blanks of what happened, replaying everything over and over until it seemed to have made sense of it. The brain does not like mystery, you see. Where it perceives a black hole, it will fill it with information based on everything it *does* know.'

'Will it ever come back to me? Exactly what happened, I mean? The truth, not what my brain has invented to join all the dots.' I look into his eyes to be sure that he's giving me a straight answer, but his face blurs through my tears.

'Perhaps. Time will tell.' He smiles again and I wonder how I will survive without his gentle honesty; I wonder if I will ever see him again after I leave this place. Stash said he's returning to Spain, and Dom will be back soon, and then I'll be going home . . .

There's a knock on the door and my heart jumps, but it's just Carol, calling the doctor away to another emergency. He doesn't rush to leave; he doesn't hurry me as I share one final thought with him.

'I remember the rose bushes, the thorns. I remember Annabel's hair . . . Something important. There is something important about the rose bushes . . .' I press my knuckles into my eyes again, forcing myself to think, to remember.

'I imagine there is, as your brain has continually returned to the image of them. Something significant has lodged in your unconscious mind. But we cannot know whether that will ever be unlocked. Perhaps it will never come back to you.' He nods curtly at the waiting nurse and then leans towards me, taking both my hands in his, his fingers cool and smooth, his eyes dark with sympathy.

'But my daughter has. Annabel is alive. *She* has come back to me. And that is enough.'

THIRTY-THREE

I find it curious that in the bright-dark of my unconscious mind, I was forever dreaming. And yet now, when my mind has healed and returned to full consciousness, my sleep is dreamless. Tired after my session with the doctor, I decided to shuffle my way back into bed and rest until Dom returned, not expecting to fall asleep. I awake with the stark awareness that I haven't dreamed of Annabel, but I lie here in the dimly lit room thinking only of her.

My daughter is alive.

I understand now that my guilt at letting Annabel down became twisted, distorted by my traumatised brain into a conviction that she'd been shot and killed. And I get that Max wanted to punish me and at the same time bury the truth about his interest in Annabel. What I still don't understand is how it came to be that Annabel lived, and I almost died . . .

I wonder if it means that, in the end, Max was driven more by anger towards *me* than a need to cover up how he'd been pursuing my daughter. After all, he took his own life; he knew he would never be prosecuted for how he'd been grooming her. It didn't matter if she lived; it only mattered that I died. Or perhaps he simply couldn't bring himself to hurt his niece, either through a belated attack of conscience or because he adored her too much. Maybe he pointed the gun at Annabel but changed his mind at the last moment, misfiring it and missing his target: me.

Or perhaps it means I didn't choose Annabel after all . . .

I have no way of knowing. As Dom said: *dead men tell no tales.* And now the police have closed the case because as far as they are concerned, the victim survived and the perpetrator is dead. They can't arrest Max; there can be no murder trial. Only it was never Max's guilt that tormented me: it was *mine.* When I was forced at gunpoint to choose between my children, whose name did I speak?

No favourites; I love my children equally.

Dom has always maintained that I love Aidan best. Ever since the nightmare in Cornwall, it's like he's been obsessed with me having a favourite child. And even though Annabel is alive – perhaps *because* she's alive and waiting for me at home – it feels more important than ever to know how I answered, what I said. I still have no clear memory of what actually happened on the morning of the twins' birthday, and Dom can't help me. Nor can the police.

There were only two witnesses.

I know that my last hope of finding peace again lies with my children: holding them, loving them – and asking them the question that still burns in my mind: *What did Mummy do?*

217

THIRTY-FOUR

'Grab your coat, we're going home!'

I can't stop smiling as Dom hands me my jacket, carefully helping me slip my arms into the sleeves and then supporting me as I make a clumsy lunge into the wheelchair. I take one last look at my room, whispering goodbye in my head to the platoon of machines still standing to attention in readiness for a new patient, followed by a proper thank-you and goodbye spoken aloud to Carol and everyone gathered at the nurses' station.

'I forgot my wind chimes – and I wanted to say goodbye to Stash, too,' I say, looking over my shoulder, but Dom is already wheeling me off down the long corridor, out of the hospital and into the real world for the first time in what feels like an eternity.

It's an amazing place; confined by my fragility to the immediate vicinity of my room, I hadn't realised. I look wonderingly around me and blink back tears as I take in trees, a beautiful garden and a huge blue sky lit up with autumn sunshine. I gasp deep breaths of crisp, fresh air, drawing it greedily into my lungs, closing my eyes and allowing the sense of freedom to soak into me: it feels so good to be alive. To know that my *children* are alive and waiting for me at home, safe and being cared for by Lucy.

My best friend. I feel a pang of regret for the suspicions I harboured about her. All this time she's been living in my home, Dom told me, caring for my children. Despite knowing the difficulties I'd had with Dom, despite how anxious and uncomfortable that must have made her, she put her own feelings aside to look after the twins. Keeping them safe for me until I came home. She'd given up her flat, which would account for the disconnected phone line. It still doesn't explain why I haven't been able to get hold of Lucy on her mobile, though; I make a mental note to ask her when I see her.

I can't wait to see my friend again, but above all I'm fizzing with desperation to see the twins, longing to hold them and reassure them that I'm fine, that we're *all* going to be fine. They must have been in pieces witnessing their mother being shot; I squeeze my eyes tightly shut against the painful thought, hoping and praying they didn't also see their uncle turn the gun on himself. Dom said they've refused to say anything at all about that day, and that he's just giving them time and space and, hopefully, when I'm home, we can talk things through as a family. That moment is all I can think of now.

Home.

This hospital has been my home for more than three months, and while I'm not sad to leave, there is one person I will genuinely miss. I didn't get to see Professor Hernandez before Dom collected me. Carol told me the doctor hadn't yet returned after being called away urgently to see another patient, but he was expected back later. I wanted to wait for him, only Dom was fidgeting restlessly for us to leave. He'd driven like a maniac to get back to me as fast as possible, and he said he just wanted to get me out of there and home where I belonged.

He didn't stop pacing and pointedly checking his watch while

219

another consultant examined me and somewhat reluctantly pronounced me fit for discharge on condition that I see my regular GP in the morning. Dom barely glanced at the advisory leaflets on how to keep up my exercises and the importance of good nutrition before shoving them in his jacket pocket. I could sense his bristling impatience as the consultant meticulously completed all my paperwork, before explaining that he would make contact right away with my GP to book an out-of-hours check-up first thing tomorrow. The consultant was doing his best not to be pressured into rushing, but eventually Dom simply brushed him off.

'That's all fine, then. You've got our details. Now if you don't mind, we need to hit the road.'

I was taken aback by his abruptness. Usually so charming, even smooth-talking, his rudeness seemed uncharacteristic. These doctors had brought me back to life; I owed them everything, and I had expected a little more gratitude from Dom, too. I saw the startled look on the consultant's face and smiled apologetically, putting Dom's brusqueness down to anxiety about getting back to the children. I was just as eager and only wished it had been Professor Hernandez seeing us off. It didn't feel right to leave without thanking him in person.

'Please, tell Professor Hernandez I'll email him as soon as I'm home. Just to, you know, say thank you. And to let him know how I'm doing.' No, that sounded presumptuous, I thought; perhaps the doctor wouldn't have the slightest interest in how I got on once I was no longer under his care. 'If he'd like to know, that is,' I added. 'But mainly I just want to thank him, really. He's done so much for me. I couldn't be more grateful. For everything. I want him to know that. You won't forget, will you?'

'I'll see he gets the message,' the consultant reassured me, shaking my hand. 'I know Sebastián has been particularly concerned about you, and he'll want to speak to your GP after you see her tomorrow. It is rather premature for you to be leaving hospital, by normal standards, and you will need to pursue the physiotherapy programme the GP will put in place. But I appreciate you'd prefer to continue your rehabilitation from the comfort of your own home. I must stress, however, that your treatment *will* need to continue as an out-patient, and—'

'And we're *off!*' Dom said, tipping my wheelchair back like I was doing wheelies, pushing me out of the examination room and back to my own room to collect my jacket and get ready to leave.

I laughed. There was really no reason to delay any longer, and in any case I was buzzing to get home myself. I waved and called out one last thank-you and then gripped the arms of the wheelchair, worried I was going to spill out of it at the speed Dom was pushing me. I smiled at his eagerness, feeling a wave of hope and happiness sweep me along in the wake of his high spirits.

His car is parked on the drive right outside the front doors, in readiness for a quick exit, and while he opens the boot ready to stow the fold-up wheelchair inside, I swivel myself round to look up in awe at the impressive red-brick building, seeing it for the first time from the outside, thinking of the day I was carried up those steps on a stretcher. There would have been no flashing emergency lights, no screaming sirens; I had already been operated on and they'd brought me here to recuperate after my surgery at the West Mid. I must try to find out the name of *that* doctor, I think, wanting to thank whoever had saved my life in the first instance.

It's so strange to think of all that frantic activity happening while I was unconscious, oblivious to everything, already locked deep inside my mind, plummeting back into the past and spiralling through memories. And Aidan, my darling boy, working through every recorder tune he knew, trying his best to wake me up. And it had worked: I *did* hear it.

I wonder if I might have woken sooner if Annabel had visited me. She never came alive to me in my dreams; my brain had well and truly absorbed the fact of her death and made it a reality. I don't blame her for not wanting to see me in that terrible state, but I'm also proud of my son who, for once, had been brave enough to be one step ahead of his sister rather than linger two steps behind. I'm proud of *both* my children and feel so lucky to have them. To be going home to them. My beautiful twins. I can't stop thinking of them.

As Dom helps me into the car and we cruise slowly down the drive, I twist around to take one last look at the hospital and then turn back to stare eagerly at the road ahead, praying for a smooth, trouble-free journey so I can get home quickly to Annabel and Aidan; I am *aching* to see them. Dom mentioned our wedding anniversary, but first we need to celebrate the twins' tenth birthday, I think happily. We never even got to taste the birthday cake I went to so much trouble to make . . .

Lulled by daydreams and the motion of the car, I nod off, but not before vowing to myself that I will never take a second of my life – or my children's lives – for granted ever again. I know Dom and I still have a lot to talk about, and there will need to be some significant changes, but from now on I am going to stop looking back to the past and keep my eyes firmly fixed on the future.

THIRTY-FIVE

'You've turned off too early,' I say sleepily, waking up in time to see that we've come off the A4 and are heading down Syon Lane. 'Better to stay on a bit longer, isn't it, and go direct to Hampton? Twickenham will be solid at this time on a Friday afternoon.' I rub my eyes; they feel gritty and tired, and my legs and back are stiffening up from sitting in the car for so long. I slowly rotate my head to ease out the knots of tension.

'I just need to stop off somewhere first,' Dom tells me, resting a reassuring hand on my knee. 'Go back to sleep for a bit.'

He's got his Ray-Bans on and I smile, remembering how Lucy always used to tease him for wearing them even when it's not sunny. I lean my head against the window and peer out, noticing that as afternoon gives way to evening, it's clouding over, the sky darkening to an oppressive leaden storminess that reflects against the seemingly endless rows of terraced houses, making it feel like we're driving through a dull grey tunnel. We're a long way from the green openness of the Buckinghamshire countryside.

'I think it might thunder,' I say, pulling my jacket more tightly around me. I shiver but it's partly through sudden apprehension: I know Dom and I have some serious talking to do when we're home, and the closer we get, the more I can't help but worry about the conversations to come. I try really hard to put those thoughts aside for now, telling myself to focus on one thing at a time. I need to concentrate first on getting home and enjoying hot chocolate and lots and lots of cuddles with the twins. My eyes mist over at the thought of it; I rub my hands up and down my arms to comfort myself.

'Cold? Don't worry. Not long now.'

'Great. I hope Lucy will keep the twins up for me. What did they say when you told them I'm coming home? I bet Annabel was dancing round the room and Aidan just sat there grinning. But they're happy and excited, right?'

'You know the twins,' Dom says, eyes fixed on the road in concentration.

'I just can't wait to see them,' I say, smiling until I catch sight of the signs for the West Middlesex Hospital. Goosebumps prickle up the back of my neck as we drive past it, and I crane my neck to look at the queue of ambulances lining up outside A&E.

'Hope I don't ever have to set foot in that place again,' Dom says grimly.

'Me too. Not that I can actually remember being there. It's straight on, here, isn't it?' I add as he turns right into Mogden Lane. It's not like him to get his directions mixed up. On any car journey, long or short, Aidan always tries to out-smart his dad by knowing the fastest, most direct route, but Dom is never wrong. He has a brain like a spreadsheet.

'Nope,' he says shortly.

'But this is the way to – ' I break off as I'm suddenly overcome by queasiness. Quickly I lean forward to rest my elbows on my knees, dipping my head to stem the sudden hot, sickening rush of anxiety flooding through me.

'Sit back, sweetheart, I can't see the wing mirror.'

'Why are we going into the Ivybridge estate?' I ask weakly, obediently leaning back but still feeling sick. I try to keep my voice steady, not wanting to admit that my legs are trembling at the thought of going anywhere near the estate where he and his brother grew up.

'Just need to check on something. Sorry, yes, it's at Max's,' he says, glancing apologetically at me before turning back to watch the road. 'But hear me out before you start panicking.'

'But I *am* panicking. Surely you don't expect me to go inside your brother's—'

'It'll only take a second.'

He indicates left and turns sharply into Summerwood Road, the steering wheel making a slithery rasping noise as it slips through his hands when he straightens up and slowly steers the car along the winding road, weaving through the imposing grey tower blocks. I look up anxiously at them as we head deeper into the estate, deeper into Dom's past. This is where he was born; this is the place he was so desperate to escape. He made it, and I know he's always avoided coming back here, and I can't *believe* he's brought me here after what Max did.

I'm shocked into silence, staring mutely out of the windscreen, wondering if I'll actually recognise Max's house, wondering if we'll find it cordoned off by blue-and-white police tape, identifying it as the home of a killer, advertising it as an unoccupied building ripe for looting. I notice a group of seven or eight boys not much older than Aidan loitering under a lamp-post at the junction, smoking and eyeballing Dom's car as we crawl past, pointing at us and jostling with each other. I glance nervously in the wing mirror, watching them disappear into the distance behind us. One of the boys flicks a V sign for no apparent reason, but I don't pay him serious attention: my eyes are fixed on the bend in the road. I'm trying to remember the way in – just in case Dom forgets the way out.

When he pulls up at the kerb in front of a dark-bricked, flat-fronted 1970s-style terraced townhouse, I see that there is no police tape but the windows of the house are boarded up with wooden slats.

'I'll wait for you here.' I can hear the breathlessness in my voice.

'Ah.'

'*What?*' I say impatiently.

'Well, the truth is, there's something I want to show you. *Need* to.' He takes off his Ray-Bans and turns to look at me, his eyes piercing.

'Show me?' Adrenalin is still pumping through me and I feel upset that Dom wouldn't realise how awful it is for me to come here.

'Photos. Family ones. I've only just discovered Max had them and, well, I thought somehow they might help bring us both some closure on what he's done. They belonged to . . . ' He breaks off, rubbing his hands over his face.

'OK,' I say slowly, watching him struggle to get his emotions under control. 'But I'd still rather wait here. If you could maybe bring them—'

'They're framed on his wall. In any case, if I carry you it won't take long. No need to bring the wheelchair.' Without waiting for my response he swings out of the car and within seconds I'm in his arms and we're standing outside Max's front door.

I push against his shoulder in panic. 'Please. I don't want to go in there.'

'All that's missing is a white dress and a veil, eh? Oh, and a bouquet of roses.'

'Sorry? Roses? What?' My heart is pounding so loudly in my ears as I watch him unlock the white PVC door that I can't take in what he's saying.

I glance over his shoulder to see if any neighbours are around, anyone watching us enter the house. I'm suddenly filled with a cold sense of dread: if no one sees us go in, no one will be any the wiser if we don't come out. I try to tell myself that I'm getting in a state for no good reason. But something has definitely shifted in Dom's mood. I remember the signs all too well; back in the bright-dark, I relived every single one of them, and they crawl sickeningly back into my mind now.

'Something old, something new. Takes you back, doesn't it? Me carrying you over the threshold,' he says, striding in to the small, dark hallway and kicking the door shut behind him. It gets caught on the latch and doesn't close properly, so he gives it a final heavy kick with his boot to slam it shut. The sound echoes through the empty, bare-boarded hall.

'Oh.' The sick feeling in the pit of my stomach intensifies. The house is freezing cold and it smells damp and musty, but it's the look on Dom's face that's making me feel faint, nauseous – and suddenly very afraid.

THIRTY-SIX

'Here comes the bride. Perhaps we should check out the master bedroom first. Pretend we really are newlyweds and this is a fresh start for us.' He winches me more tightly against his chest and begins to climb the steep stairs, slowly, one heavy footstep at a time.

'No! Stop! I don't want to go up there,' I say, starting to panic in earnest now as he carries me up the narrow staircase and on to a dingy landing. He doesn't reply but barges open the first door ahead of us with his shoulder, leaning against the light switch inside to turn on a single bare bulb. It must only be 40 watts as it hardly illuminates the surprisingly large square bedroom, but there is enough light for me to see a metal-framed double bed in the middle. A bed with a white mattress and nothing else: no bedding, no other furniture, no curtains or carpet on the stripped floorboards.

And absolutely no sign of any photos on the wall.

'Are you sure, though, Maddie? Because I thought you'd love one last chance to roll around on my brother's bed.'

'Dom ...'

'Make you feel good, did he? Treat you better than I do? Good old Max. Always itching to get his hands on whatever's mine. Always hanging around, ready to step into his brother's shoes.' He tosses me down on to the bare mattress and reaches deep into the right-hand pocket of his trousers. 'Always ready to climb into my bed and fuck my wife.' He roots around for a few seconds more before pulling out a key and striding back to the door.

The grinding crunch of the lock echoes ominously in the empty room; I feel it low down in my belly.

Dom turns to me with a smile on his face and I lurch to the side of the bed, duck my head over the side, and throw up.

'Why, Dom? *Why* are you keeping me here?' I know I shouldn't plead. That's not the way to get through to him. But I can't play his mind games any more.

'To give you time to think, of course.' He stands next to the bed, legs spread, hands on hips.

'About *what?*'

'About everything you've done. What you're going to do next.'

'I don't understand.'

'That makes two of us. I just don't get *why* you thought Annabel was dead. Where did such an idea even come from?' It's the third time he's asked me, jacket off, crisp white shirtsleeves rolled neatly back, looming over me while I cower at the head of the double bed, my back pressed against the cold, peeling, white-painted wall.

'I *told* you, I don't know.' I rub my hands over my face, trying to ignore the acidic smell of vomit in the already stuffy room. Dom doesn't seem remotely bothered by it; he stands like a bodyguard, big body arrogantly upright, shoulders back, watching me with that same small smile.

There is no way I can explain to him how my mind has played tricks on me. It's not that I don't think he'll understand; he's clever. *Too* clever. He's clearly laid a trap for me and he'll turn everything he can against me. One hint of the guilt I'd been feeling on the morning of the twins' birthday – the guilt that my shattered mind transformed into an incredibly powerful, incredibly *real* image of Annabel's death – and he'll have me cornered. I can't admit the choice I made because I know he's going to use every last bit of ammunition he has against me: to confess my deepest shame now would be like handing him a loaded gun.

Yet he won't take no for an answer; same old Dom. I thought tragedy had changed us both. He's been giving a first-rate impression of a concerned, devoted husband. He had me – and everyone else, I think despairingly – utterly fooled.

'You must have had a reason. What did Max *say* to you before he pulled the trigger?' he persists, leaning towards me now.

I press myself harder against the wall, desperate to keep some distance between us. 'He said nothing at all. The twins must have told you that.' It's a calculated risk: I want to know what Annabel and Aidan saw, what they heard. I'm hoping I can bluff Dom into telling me.

'Is that right? Max said nothing. Just wandered in to our back garden with a gun in his hand, a balaclava over his head, and shot you for not running away with him, and then in an agony of guilt and despair shot himself?' His laugh is an angry bark. 'He was more stupid than I thought, then. I can think of any number of ways to punish you that don't involve me ending up with my brains splattered over our rose bushes.'

'But *why* would you want to punish me? I didn't leave you. I'm still here. I'm still willing to give our marriage another go, in spite of—'

'In spite of . . . ?' His face is only inches away from mine; his blue eyes squint accusingly at me.

'Nothing,' I say, not wanting to incite him further by mentioning the physical and emotional cruelty that coloured the last year of our marriage.

'It's a curious delusion, though, wouldn't you agree? I wonder if maybe you were – I'm not quite sure how to put this.' His voice softens but without tenderness; he is taunting me. 'Losing your mind?' His brow creases as he ponders the possibility.

'*No!* I was just . . .' So many words bubble up, overwhelming me; I can't begin to explain what I was. I only know what I am now: frightened, desperate, yearning for my children. If Dom keeps me here, locking me up while he returns to our home, to the twins, that means they will be alone with him – and in the state of mind he's in . . .

Lucy is there too, I remind myself urgently, trying to quell my flash of panic at the thought of the twins being in danger. She won't let any harm come to Annabel and Aidan; I know she won't. But would she really be able to protect them? Is she even *there* – or is Dom lying? It wouldn't surprise me. His behaviour has been so plausible, so conciliatory up until now, but it's clear that it's all been an act. I have absolutely no idea how many lies he's been telling me, and everyone else. What lies he's still telling, or what he intends to achieve with them. He clearly has an agenda; I can't even begin to guess what it is.

I suddenly wonder if there's another, darker reason for Lucy's mobile number not being recognised by the network. But even if it *was* simply a fault on the line, I don't have a phone to call her . . . I don't have anything but the soft Ugg boots, black leggings and grey hoodie Dom brought for me to wear. My oldest round-the-house clothes; it feels somehow symbolic. As if he's reminding me of my place in life.

'I know you've been through a trauma. I understand that.' He's pacing the room now, his footsteps heavy on the wooden boards.

'I'm not mad, Dom,' I say desperately, scrabbling to my knees, guessing where he's going with this. 'You don't have to keep me locked up. I'm not a nutcase, a danger to society – or my children. Professor Hernandez explained to me—'

'Ah, the handsome Spanish doctor,' he says. 'What am I going to do with you? Flitting from one man to the next.'

'That's not fair. He's old enough to be my father, and in any case he's been *helping* me.' My voice is a dry croak.

How I wish I hadn't left that hospital before I'd spoken to Professor Hernandez. But I was so desperate to get home to the twins . . . I was completely fooled by Dom's concern. Three months ago he walked out in anger. I thought he'd returned with an olive branch, but it's just another stick to beat me with.

'What's not *fair* is that you were leaving me.' Legs planted wide apart, he moves to stand at the end of the bed, his finger jabbing accusingly as he lists my crimes. 'You'd packed your bag, hidden your little photo, bought your train tickets . . . You'd been plotting and planning with Max right under my nose. Sneaky, deceitful—'

'I'm *sorry*. I have no memory of any of that.' I hold out a hand to him, but he ignores it.

'So convenient, isn't it, memory loss? And yet I was willing to forgive you. I know I'm to blame for not being the perfect husband, the dream man you fantasised about. But good old Max was, wasn't he? The dark horse. Never saw him with a woman of his own. Turns out he had his eye on mine the whole time.'

'I have no idea what was in your brother's mind, but I'm sure I've never thought of him in that way. I *never* compared you with him,' I tell him urgently. 'If there was anything between me and Max . . . ' I shake my head in disbelief, drawing a mental blank. 'I just can't even imagine it.'

'You can't? The trouble is, I can. All too easily. The bored house-wife stuck at home. Max always coming round, always available to help out while I was caught up in meetings or working late. He lacked my flair, of course. He was rough around the edges,' he says bluntly, 'but some women like that, don't they?'

'He was the twins' uncle. I never thought—'

'That's the trouble with you. You don't *think*. I bet you've never even stopped to ask yourself how *I* feel about all this.' He darts round the side of the bed again and instinctively I lurch away from him, falling back against the thin mattress. He bends over me, arms braced either side of my head.

'Of course I have,' I tell him, trying to stay calm. 'I know how dreadful it's been for you – and for the children. It has for me too. It's like a living nightmare. Being in hospital all this time. Being apart from my children ...' My voice cracks and I fall silent.

His big hands grip my shoulders, shooting pain signals into my brain. I've lost so much weight that my usual curves have all but vanished; there's hardly any padding of flesh to protect my still-fragile bones.

'Surely you don't expect *sympathy* from me? Ha! That's rich. You plot and scheme to disappear from my life, breaking up the family I've done so much for, then you have the nerve to ask me to feel *sorry* for you?'

His voice is getting louder now. I hope he starts shouting; I hope a neighbour hears and comes to investigate. For a second I feel hopeful, then I remind myself that no one ever knocked on my front door in Hampton. The most attention our endless rows ever attracted was a few sympathetic glances from old Mr Cooper next door when I popped round to take him a hot meal. And if no one in my leafy, comfortably middle-class street bothered to find out what was going on behind closed doors, what chance is there of anyone being bothered here – on this unloved estate where families come and go and everybody knows to mind their own business and not ask too many questions?

'I don't want pity. I just want to go home. We can work it out. I know we can.' I try to inject as much sincerity and conviction into my voice as I can, but I shrink away from him as I see his face harden.

'I can't let you do that, Maddie. Not yet.' His voice is soft but his blue eyes are chips of ice. 'You were leaving me. You were *leaving* me and you were going to take the twins with you. Sneak out after their birthday party with me none the wiser, looking like an idiot surrounded by gossips and pity.'

He's glaring at me but at the same time there's that hint of a smile on his face still. I remember this Dom; he feels familiar to me now. He's finally dropped all pretence. The gloves are off.

Smile, punch, smile, punch . . .

'I've raised the twins,' he continues, his big hand jerking out to cover my mouth when I open it to respond. 'I've given them everything I had in me, and you were going to take all that away from me. So I have to be sure, you see? You have to *prove* to me that you're not going to do that again before I let you come back. If you can do that, if you're a good girl and do everything I ask of you, then I might – perhaps – be prepared to let you see Annabel and Aidan again.'

I squirm and choke, unable to catch my breath against the pressure of his hand. I smell cigarette smoke on his fingers; I didn't know Dom had started smoking. The stench of it makes me feel sick again; nausea rushes up into my mouth and everything starts to go black.

'You mustn't worry, though.' Softly now, feeling that my resistance is gone, my body turning limp. 'Lucy is taking excellent care of the kids. They love her, and she loves them. They're safe with *us* now, and that's precisely where they're going to stay.'

He pulls on my ponytail, jerking my head back until I gag on the vomit rushing up into my throat. He waits until I've stopped coughing. Barely conscious, I hear his rasping voice in my ear: 'They don't even know you're awake.'

THIRTY-SEVEN

I'm still invisible.

My first thought on waking up is that I may have *unvanished* as far as the rest of the world is concerned, but *my* world is the twins – and they believe I'm still unconscious, trapped in that unknowable limbo between life and death. As does Lucy, no doubt. And if they don't know I'm awake, they won't be expecting me to come home; they won't know the difference if I *never* come home. No one will know; no one will care.

Will Lucy? For a time, I was suspicious of her, petty jealousy spiralling out of control in my unconscious mind. But now I simply don't believe Dom's hint that they're a couple. I was wrong about my friend – now I'm frightened for her, not knowing where she is or whether she's all right ... Not knowing whether my *children* are all right ...

I start panicking and call out, my heart pounding in my chest as I scream my frustration into the darkness, begging for someone, anyone, to please help me. But there is no one to hear; no one to notice my absence and wonder what's happened to me.

Professor Hernandez. Will *he* miss me and wonder where I am? I'd like to think so, but perhaps I'm kidding myself. I was never close to my own father, but I have a sense of having formed that kind of relationship with the doctor, and it meant everything to me. I think of Stash saying she'd have given up many times if it hadn't been for him, and I feel the same. He saved me. In more ways than one. I was probably just another patient for him, though; I've been discharged and I will be forgotten. There will be another patient in my room now; another poor soul in need of his help. After all, he's an expert in his field . . .

Second to none.

That's what DCI Watkins called him. I think of the detectives and wonder if they will try to visit me again. Will they want to follow up on our interview, check in with me to see if I've remembered anything? Would they be surprised to find I've left the hospital – would they come looking for me at my home? But the case is closed, nothing more to say. What were the detective's words? *No further action is required . . .*

No one is looking for me; there is no way out. I am completely at Dom's mercy. Nobody knows I'm here and I have no phone, no food . . . I'm still too physically weak to attempt any kind of escape, even if I stood the remotest chance of overpowering Dom. I'm not sure I can even get myself to the bathroom and I really, badly need to go. I don't know how long I've been lying here but my bladder hurts. My face feels glued to the rough mattress with saliva, sweat and tears; the inside of my mouth feels like I've swallowed sandpaper. I must have slept but I don't feel rested – I feel crumpled, aching and weak with thirst, hunger, terror and despair.

I try to concentrate on lifting just one leg, but my body feels wooden and heavy. I didn't make it as far as having physio sessions at the hospital, and it's still a considerable effort to move my limbs freely. After the long drive, no sustenance and an uncomfortable sleep punctuated by nightmares, I'm not sure I'll be able to walk without assistance.

'You may as well stop struggling. You're not going anywhere.'

I can't hide the bolt of shock that makes me jump, and I hear Dom's chuckle in response. How long has he been standing there watching me? As I turn my head to look for him, a memory flashes into my mind of the night we first met, Dom staring at me just so from between the bookshelves. I shiver and it takes my eyes a few seconds to adjust to the dark, to be able to make out his tall body tucked inside an alcove where a wardrobe may once have stood. I'm convinced I've never been in this room – in this house – before, but I can tell that everything has been cleared out, all sign of Max erased.

'I need to . . .' I grimace, embarrassed.

'Ah, the little girls' room. I'm not sure my brother went in for luxury toiletries, but then you'd know his tastes better than I ever did. Let's investigate, shall we?' He steps out of the shadows and moves swiftly towards me, digging one arm under my legs and bracing the other behind my back; with the ease of lifting a child, he hoists me up against him.

Instantly I'm reminded of his comment when we arrived, and for the briefest moment I think of the days when there was nowhere I felt safer in the world than cradled against Dom's broad chest: carrying me over the threshold of our first home together; holding me against him as we both cried tears of joy when the twins were born. He used to be my protector, and then he wasn't. Now he's my enemy: every fibre of my being screams out that I was right about him in the bright-dark, and that nothing has changed.

In fact, it's far worse. Max is dead; Dom can't punish him. But he wants to punish *me* for even thinking about leaving him – running off with his big brother . . . The idea still feels completely alien to me, but I know my protests will fall on deaf ears. Dom said he wants to forgive me; I know he lied.

'Please, let me try by myself. I can manage.' I can't bear the thought of him witnessing my humiliation.

'Have it your way.' He instantly releases his hands, carelessly dropping me back on to the bed, knocking the breath from my body and jarring every vertebra in my spine. I groan in pain but he remains looming over me, unmoved by my suffering. Even through the gloom I can see his eyes boring into mine and they are ice cold, hard ... challenging.

There are no ties on my hands or feet, and I suppose I should be grateful for that. I'm not bound up, but I might as well be. It takes every ounce of strength I possess to drag myself to the bedroom door and fall against it, but when I try to open it, I realise it's still locked. I twist the brass knob several more times, turning it frantically from left to right, but still it won't budge.

Dom laughs. 'Silly me. Forgot the key. Now, where did I put it?' He pretends to check all his pockets before finally grabbing the small gold key and holding it aloft. 'Now, how are you going to persuade me to give it to you?'

He grins, stepping towards me, backing me against the door, and his big hands grip my shoulders, thumbs digging deep. I feel a shudder roll through me as he begins stroking the hollow above my collarbone with the tip of one forefinger. 'You're skin and bone, woman,' he says in a low voice that I hear rumble deep in his chest. 'Not sure even Max would find you that enticing now.'

'Let me go,' I whisper, turning my head away from his face, inches from mine.

'Never.'

His arm snakes behind my back and I feel his left hand pressing me closer to him at the same time as he pushes against me, his broad chest smothering my face. His right hand fumbles around, digging into the back of my hip, and I close my eyes and will myself not to scream or show any sign of weakness.

'There. Off you go.'

He cackles and releases me, and as he steps back I see him shove the key back in his pocket. I don't waste a second. I turn immediately and try the door again, awkwardly twisting the knob with shaking fingers; this time it swings open.

'Don't keep me waiting! You've kept me hanging around for three months already,' Dom calls after me as I stumble on to the landing and look frantically around the dark space, blinking as I try to get my bearings.

There are no lights on out here, and when my hands scramble across the wall to find a switch, pressing it in relief, nothing happens. I flick it repeatedly but the flat clicking noise simply echoes in the darkness. Blindly I step forward and my soft-soled boots crunch over something sharp. A smashed lightbulb, I think, looking up to make out something twisted and stringy dangling down from the ceiling. I stretch out my arms again to feel my way along the wall, slowly inching forward, trying to remember where the stairs are, scared I might slip and tumble down them in the dark.

After a few seconds my eyes begin to adjust and I notice tiny slivers of light slipping through the gaps around the panels boarding up each window. I manage to make out that the bedroom where I've just come from is opposite the top of the stairs, and another three doors stand open, leading off the narrow landing. The huge shadowy block looming above me is the underside of a second set of stairs, presumably leading up to another floor, a bedroom or attic space. A shiver prickles the back of my neck in the cold, dank air and I cross my fingers that Dom won't take me up there. My fear is irrational rather than specific: I have no idea what is at the top of those stairs, but locked in an abandoned attic is no way to end my life.

Am I going to die?

I can't force the fear back in its box now it's sprung out at me, but equally I can't bring myself to believe that Dom will actually cause me physical harm. Not seriously. He's angry, he wants me to suffer, but he's not a killer. Max was the one who allowed his temper to get the better of him. Frustrated, intense Uncle Max who always wanted what his brother had – and if he couldn't have it, no one else would. But Dom is the smart, ambitious brother who really made something of his life. He's not going to blow that now; he has far too much to lose. I can't *believe* he would throw away his career, his whole life – his family – just to punish me for an infidelity I don't even remember.

He hurt me before . . .

The thought presses itself forward and I hesitate at the top of the stairs, toying with the idea of shuffling down them and making a bid for freedom. Perhaps, despite my earlier doubts, a neighbour will help me after all – at least let me use a phone, make a call to the police . . . I remember Michelle saying that she'd leave their business cards with the nurse, and I curse myself for forgetting to collect them before we left the hospital. I was so excited to be on my way home to the children, and I realise now why Dom was in such a hurry: there was only so long he could keep up the concerned husband act. He was certainly convincing; maybe that's where Annabel inherited her dramatic talent, I think bitterly.

The thought of my daughter draws my eyes once again towards the stairwell. Every muscle, every nerve ending, is convulsing in fear for my children. But all Dom would have to do is follow me out of the front door and say that his wife is just having a strop. Bit of a domestic. Who would want to get involved? Who would care? Maybe the neighbours will even recognise Dom as Max's brother; depending how long they've lived here, they may also remember him growing up here as a boy. I struggle to convince myself that anyone is going to take my word over his, the suave, well-dressed, articulate businessman who charms everyone – who once charmed me.

Conscious that I need to hurry up or Dom will come looking for me, I shuffle faster around the L-shaped landing, peering into each dark, empty room, squinting and blinking rapidly until my eyes can make out what looks like the bathroom. I've barely managed to use the toilet, get my clothes back in order and feel my way to the sink when I hear a sharp rap on the door.

'Just one more minute,' I call out, plunging my hands urgently into the icy stream of water, bending to angle my face under the cold tap to gulp great thirsty mouthfuls and let the water run over my face, refreshing my sticky, tear-stained cheeks.

'You've had your minute. Time's up.'

The door swings open and I sense rather than see Dom's big arm reach out, his long fingers gripping my arm, squeezing it until I cry out. He drags me out of the bathroom, ignoring my yelp of pain as I misjudge the doorway and bang my right cheekbone on the frame. Disoriented by the unexpected blow, my arms flail around as I try to recover my sense of equilibrium, but Dom gives me no time and my fingernails scrape along the walls, my feet stumbling on the uneven floorboards as he drags me behind him. I'm too shocked even to cry but my cheek is throbbing and my legs are turning to jelly; fear and exhaustion steal what little strength I've managed to recover in the short time since I woke up in hospital. It's almost a relief when Dom shoves me back into the bedroom and I collapse on to the mattress, my breath coming in tearful gasps as I sprawl across it.

'Make yourself comfortable. Just got to pop home for a little while. Couple of small things to take care of. But don't worry, I'll be back soon.'

'No, wait, don't go!' I don't want to be with Dom, but I'm

terrified of being alone here, trapped in this house, this room, where Max lived. I'm caught between the devil and his brother, and I will say or do anything to keep Dom from going home to the twins.

'Sweet. You want me to *stay*. No need to worry; I won't abandon you. I don't run away from my commitments. I'm your husband and that still means something, to me at least.'

'*What* does it mean to you?' I stall for time, frantically trying to think of reasons why he shouldn't go back to the house – trying to think of anything at all that might convince him to stay here, away from my children.

'Oh, I don't know. But just as a for instance, it means that when I marry someone, I don't sleep with their sibling, or plot with that sibling to steal everything that matters to them. Or cook up some kind of crazy, half-arsed plan together to have them *shot*.'

Alone again in the dark, I keep replaying Dom's words, and terror seeps like poison through my veins, making me shudder with revulsion.

Is he suggesting I *knew* about the gun?

Plotting with Max. I have no memory of it; I have no memory of being secretly in love with him, either, or turning to him for comfort when my marriage began to fall apart. So I suppose it's possible I've also forgotten scheming with Max to punish the mocking younger brother who so obviously resented his presence in our home. I was certainly tired of Dom's bullying, and I've seen the news stories: battered wives do sometimes find the strength to take justice into their own hands . . .

An image of a gun flashes across my mind. An old, military-issue firearm that needed cleaning because it had lain in the attic all these years; the attic at the top of the stairs. I try to picture Max there – I try to imagine lying in this bed with him, talking through how it would be. We would make it look like a terrible accident, maybe a suicide, and we would run away together with the children, somewhere peaceful, to the seaside, to Brighton . . . I would go on ahead so as not to arouse suspicion, and he would join me there. Then I read Annabel's diary and everything changed. I felt guilty, vulnerable and on edge; I was too scared to take the risk of leaving our home.

I remember my sense that DCI Watkins wanted more from me. Perhaps it wasn't just my infidelity he hoped to flush out, but the fact that I was an accessory to a crime that went wrong – a murder attempt that quite literally misfired. I can't believe it of myself, but I can't dismiss the possibility out of hand now that Dom has planted the idea in my mind. Maybe I really am a guilty wife as well as a bad mother, and this is my punishment. Max tried to kill me and failed; Dom is going to finish the job his brother started.

I try not to be completely swallowed up by fear. At least I'm not afraid of the dark any more – I've spent enough time trapped inside my own mind – but I *am* frightened of Dom. I've lived intimately with him for so many years and yet listening to him now I barely recognise him. I can't let terror take hold, though, because if I do I think there's a strong chance I might lose my mind completely. Then I will have proved Dom right and he really will have won. But alone in this cold, dark room, there is nothing to divert or distract me, no outward sights to pull my gaze away from looking inwards to the darkness of terror.

Perhaps if I trick myself into believing that I'm just having a weekend lie-in, that this is all perfectly ordinary . . . I remember joking to Dom that I'd give anything for just one night alone in a hotel – one evening when I could have a long, relaxing bubble bath without someone hammering on the door needing to use the bathroom, when I could sleep without having to get up in the night to pull up the twins' blankets or fetch a glass of water, and wake up when my own body clock decided it was the right time. I remember Dom rolling over in bed to give me a lazy, wry smile as the twins bounced into our bedroom, jumping all over the bed and telling me to *wake up, sleepy head, it's fun-day Sunday.* I remember Dom pulling Annabel into the bed for a cuddle, and Aidan offering to bring me a glass of juice . . . I remember my quiet, ordinary, happy family life, and it all feels like a world away and a lifetime ago.

Tears sting my eyes. Everything is such a mess and I'm gripped by an overpowering feeling of having let both my children down, not just Annabel, and I know this guilt will haunt me until my dying day.

Which I'm beginning to fear may come sooner rather than later.

THIRTY-EIGHT

I smell cigarette smoke. And whiskey. The acrid combination teases its way through my nostrils, catching sharply at the back of my throat. I open my eyes to look around me, but there is only blackness. I lie rigid as I feel a hand stroking my hair. I try not to move; I try not to breathe.

Am I going to wake up and this will all be a dream?

I remember the first time Dom visited me in the hospital. I dreamed then of someone smothering me, a rough palm gagging my mouth. Am I having the same nightmare? Or did Dom really try to—

'Morning, sleepy head. It's a beautiful day. Such a shame you won't get to see it.'

The overhead light snaps on and I blink in the weak, grainy glow. Everything comes flooding back to me. Max's house, Dom locking me up in this room before returning home to the twins ... my children who still think I'm asleep in the hospital.

'Annabel ...'

'Missing the kids, are you?' I hear Dom's slow, laboured breaths next to my ear.

He's just arrived – he's out of breath from running up the stairs – I've been here all night – another night away from my children … He's close to me; I can feel the heat of his presence. There are tiny specks of blood on his white shirt collar, and I can smell his citrus aftershave; it mingles with whiskey fumes evaporating from his skin, and I want to shift away. But I cannot move. *Why* can't I move?

'You know I am.' The words are razor blades tearing my throat to shreds.

'That's such a shame. They're not missing you at all. Lucy has taken them swimming, and then they're all going out for pizza with Jasper. We might go and see a film later this afternoon. Plenty of quality weekend time together while lazy Mummy carries on sleeping.'

I shake my head from side to side, wondering why the rest of my body feels trapped, immobile. Have I had some kind of physical relapse?

Dom tuts loudly and in the gloom it sounds like acid on metal. 'You really shouldn't fight it, you know. You can't win.' I can hear the smile in his voice.

I let my body go slack; he's right, there's no point fighting any more. Dom clearly hasn't finished with me yet, and he isn't going to release me until he's said his piece, completed whatever agenda he's working through. I just hope he makes it quick. I will myself to lie still and appear compliant, biding my time.

'When did you get to be so cruel? Why do you *hate* me so much? We still had a chance. We could have made everything right again,' I say persuasively. 'There were good times, weren't there? Don't you remember? Surely they haven't all been wiped out by one stupid decision I didn't even go through with.'

'Is *that* what you think this is all about? Plotting to run away with Max? Is that *really* your only crime?' I could get splinters from his voice.

'I have no idea what you mean,' I say, my mind whirling as Dom switches track yet again, constantly trying to destabilise and confuse me. I have to stay resolute; if I give him an inch, I know he'll take a mile.

'Oh, come off it. *Think*. All those years together – what did you call them? *The good times*? Me out there working all hours to build up my business, you sitting around at home with the kids, Max popping in for afternoon tea and cake, all of you having fun without me, enjoying the home I paid for.' He paces up and down the room as he delivers his bitter lecture.

'Is that how you saw it, Dom?' I'm genuinely shocked. 'That I was some kind of *freeloader*? Not that I was trying to run a happy family home, supporting and looking after you, raising our children—'

'Our children.' He grates out the words, his eyes petrol blue, flashing fire.

'Yes, our babies, Dom,' I say huskily, trying to keep the tremor out of my voice, trying to appeal to the strong paternal instinct I know he has. 'They wouldn't want you to treat me like this, Dom. They love you, I know they do, but they love me *too*. We brought them into this world and—'

'*You* brought them into the world, Madeleine.' He leans over the bed, spitting my name at me, tiny pinpricks of saliva hitting my face.

'Well, if you want to be strictly technical about it, yes,' I say, trying to grasp where he's going with this, old habits kicking in as I try to second guess him so that I can anticipate his complaints and mollify them. 'But we made them. *Both* of us. And they *need* both of us. Please, don't keep them from me any longer.' My resolve cracks and I plead with him even though I know from experience that, once I've started begging, his cruelty will increase, fuelled by his sense of power over me. 'They need me too.'

'Do they?'

They don't even know I'm awake . . .

A wave of helpless fury surges through me and I wiggle and twist my body, more defiantly this time, desperately trying to sit up, move, do anything other than lie here like a lamb to the slaughter while he torments me.

'You can't keep my children from me. I won't *let* you!' I say fiercely, but no matter how much I wriggle and writhe about, I can't sit up.

He tied me up while I slept.

A cold sweat breaks out on my skin as I realise my hands and feet are bound. My threats are empty, and Dom knows it.

'Oh, you won't? That's very interesting. So tell me, what exactly do you plan to do about it?' He reaches out to stroke my hair, his fingers trailing down my cheek, across my lips, pressing inside them to probe the soft flesh inside my mouth. I feel sick at his touch; I taste cigarettes on his finger and it makes me want to vomit.

I wrench my head to one side and he chuckles as he withdraws his hand and straightens up. 'I hate you for this, Dom. If you've hurt them, I will *kill* you! Just stay away from them. They're *mine!*'

So this is what murderous rage feels like, I think, my fists clenching with a will of their own. I squeeze them so tightly I almost think they might snap the cords I can now feel around my wrists. I didn't know I was capable of such fury. Maybe I *did* know about Max's gun, after all. Maybe I—

'You're absolutely right.' His voice is light, almost playful now. He looks down at me, his hands resting casually on his hips.

'Sorry?' I stop writhing, shocked at his capitulation and the low, nasty undercurrent in his voice.

'Oh, don't apologise. That's quite all right,' he says politely, and then he crawls on to the bed, lying down next to my rigid body so that we are side by side in Max's bed, a parody of a happily married couple chatting together before bedtime. We're not touching but he's near enough that every nerve ending in my body screams at his closeness. 'After all, it's true.'

'*What* is?'

He turns to roll his big, heavy body on top of mine, his mouth so close to my ear that his breath fills it, half deafening me so I have to strain to hear his biting words: 'The children *are* yours, Maddie. But they're not *mine*, are they?'

THIRTY-NINE

My eyes burn from staring into the half-light. I grind my teeth together and try to press myself into the mattress, desperate to alleviate the weight of Dom bearing down on me, recoiling from the touch of him on my skin, his hot breath on my face. Memories flash into my mind of him poised above me so many times over the years, his powerful arms braced either side of my head, his hips constricting my legs as he made me wait – a tiger hunched over its prey, taking its time, waiting for the perfect moment to bite.

Crushed beneath him, it takes a huge, bruising effort to draw breath to speak, but when I finally manage to summon up the strength, I find I have no words. I can't think of a single thing to say.

The twins aren't his children?

Then in the next instant: *Is this another of his tricks?*

'I had doubts from the beginning, of course,' he continues, almost conversationally. 'I'm always careful. I may take risks in business, but I've never taken chances when it comes to fucking around.' I feel his fingers dig into my hip bone and my stomach convulses with an involuntarily shudder. He grinds into me and tears of pain and fear slide out of the corners of my eyes.

'What doubts? Why have you never *told* me?' I remember Dom's angry confession that we were almost bankrupt and wonder how it's possible to be married to someone for ten years yet know so little about what's going on in their life, their head.

He wrenches himself off me and the feeling of release is so intense that I cough, struggling to get air back into my lungs. My fragile body still aches from the weight of him; my side hurts so much that I wonder if he's actually cracked a rib. I want to touch them, to find out, but I'm flat on my back, wrists and ankles bound, and all I can do is lie here listening to his deep voice spilling hate into the damp air.

'The twins' hair was a bit of a shock, for starters. I'm not blind and I'm not an idiot. I saw the sideways looks the midwife gave us. You're more blonde than redhead, but at the time I just put it down to genetics – maybe your mother or grandmother had red hair, I told myself. I gave you the benefit of the doubt. I *wanted* to. You seemed like such a nice, polite, middle-class girl. Growing up on this shithole of an estate, I wanted a piece of that.'

'You make it sound so romantic,' I say in a choked voice, shock still rippling through me.

'Romance? So *that's* what you wanted?' He swivels round on the bed to glare at me. 'And there was me thinking I was giving you everything you'd ever dreamed of by working 24/7 to support a wife and two kids that weren't even mine.'

I remember his proposal to me in the Oxo Tower restaurant after we found out I was expecting the twins. I remember my surprise that he was so certain about us getting married immediately. He just wanted what I represented, I realise sadly: a suitable wife, a ready-made family. Perhaps he genuinely believed the twins were his, or perhaps he had doubts. It hardly seems to matter now. By his own admission, he just *wanted a piece of that*.

And yet he's never, over the years, given me any indication of his suspicions. We had a good life, a happy marriage, for the first years of the twins' lives. I know we did. Maybe it was only when our marriage started to flounder that his doubts pressed more heavily on his mind. Maybe when his business started to struggle he felt emasculated, and worries about the twins' paternity began to consume him.

'But, Dom ... there's been nobody else but you. I swear,' I say. 'What makes you think that?' I ask in a hoarse whisper, wishing I could see his face, but he's turned his head away.

'Interestingly enough, it was Max who pointed it out to me. My beloved brother.' He stares straight ahead, his back and shoulders rigid. 'The evening before the twins' birthday. We spent most of our lives barely tolerating each other, but I owe him one for that. For opening my eyes to what was going on right under my nose.'

'*Max?* You're not seriously going to suggest that Max was the twins' father. I didn't even meet him until our wedding. What do you—'

'He'd worked it out. I told you he was clever. Far cleverer than me. I didn't even see it coming. *Meet me in The Bell Inn for a drink*, he said. *I need to talk to you.* So like a mug I bought him half a dozen whiskies and he dropped his little bomb about you two being in love. Idiot that I am, I defended you. *You'd never break our family apart*, I said. And I told him straight: I would never let you take my children away from me. Do you know what he did? He laughed in my face. *Oh, the twins don't belong to you, little brother. Haven't you worked that out by now?*'

'He was talking rubbish, Dom. Absolute rubbish,' I say passionately. 'You've never listened to anything he said. Why did you believe him now?'

'I didn't. Well, not immediately, anyway. I dismissed it all and told him he could rot in hell. But then, you see, I came home and found your suitcase, and I realised he'd been telling the truth. You *were* planning to leave me. You were betraying me with my own brother. It was hardly a big step from there to believing Max was also right about the twins. That I wasn't their biological father.'

Just for a moment, my sense of hearing more acute in the dim room, I can hear the old Dom. I pick up on his pain, the unbelievable hurt he must have felt when Max taunted him that Annabel and Aidan weren't his children. *Daddy's princess*; he's always doted on his little girl in particular. Believing there was no blood tie between them would have been a devastating blow.

'It's not true. He was trying to upset you. I have no idea why, or what he hoped to achieve. But he was lying. I *was* leaving you, and I admit I can't remember whether that had anything to do with Max. But the children *are* yours,' I say firmly. 'Who else could possibly be their father?'

I didn't even bother trying to speculate. Dom had simply misunderstood his brother; I was sure of it. *The twins don't belong to you* ... Max could just have been implying that Annabel and Aidan weren't his possessions – or that Dom had lost his family's loyalty through his aggression. Max had simply been playing games, perhaps in retaliation for the way Dom continually taunted and rejected him. He'd wanted to rattle his younger brother's cage, and he picked his biggest Achilles heel: male pride. I could almost feel sorry for Dom if he hadn't just kidnapped me and tied me up on his dead brother's bed.

'Well, my guess is that lecturer guy you were always mooning over.' He turns to look at me, eyebrows raised.

'Shay?' I say faintly, my thoughts suddenly spinning.

'Scottish guy. Curly auburn hair,' he says pointedly. 'I was your rebound guy, wasn't I? You pretended to be so shy and timid, but your lecturer had already taught you more than a thing or two. *Hadn't* he?'

'It wasn't like that. I wasn't on the rebound. I fell *in love* with you,' I protest heatedly.

'But then he dumped you. So you settled for me. Hard working, well dressed, but not quite *smart* enough, hey? A businessman not an intellectual. And a failing one at that. I haven't exactly set the world on fire.'

'I've always been proud of you,' I insist quietly. 'You're the one who always wanted to conquer the world, not me.'

'But Max was devious. He knew how to get what he wanted. He always did, in the end. He could see things were going pear-shaped between us, so like the attention-seeker he was, he muscled in on my family. And he couldn't wait to let me know all about it.'

'The night before the twins' birthday. When you'd been out drinking,' I recall with a sinking feeling. So that's what Dom was looking for as he lurched and bumped around our bedroom after midnight. Evidence that what Max had just told him about my infidelity was true. And he'd been convinced he found it ... *my suitcase.*

'Drowning my sorrows, I think you'll find it's called.'

Part of me is desperate to plead my innocence, tell him he's wrong, but the other part of my mind is already flying back to that heady week with Shay, after the summer break and before the new university term started. I thought I'd seen the last of him; I had no idea I might have been staring into the beautiful faces of his children every day for ten years. Annabel is so theatrical, so exuberantly animated; Aidan is a big reader, a deep thinker. They both have red hair, but then my hair is strawberry blonde. There are as many differences as there are similarities; I can't be sure ...

I wonder if that's why all my memories of Shay came back to me in the bright-dark, haunting my unconscious mind, and I question

255

myself whether, deep down, I've always had a suspicion that I'd fallen pregnant after sleeping with him – that there had been a perfectly logical explanation behind the confusion about my due date. Had I suspected as much even when Dom proposed to me? He clearly thinks I'm capable of the worst kind of deception, and I'm beginning to feel like I don't know myself at all, or what I'm capable of.

A sudden thought flashes through me: *Shay moved to Brighton ... Was it Shay, not Max, I was running to?*

I remember taking the twins there; I remember my sense that there was someone I was supposed to be meeting. Had I finally decided that Shay *was* the twins' father and made contact with him? I wait for more memories to surface, but nothing comes. I can picture his face, recall his theatrical charm, but I can no more imagine rekindling my old affair with Seamus Jackson than I can envision starting a new one with Max.

'But you don't have any *proof*,' I say, struggling to believe any of this is really happening.

'What makes you so sure? DNA tests are easy, these days. Swab of saliva, pop it in the post, Bob's your uncle. Or not, as the case may be.'

'So have you had one done?' I ask breathlessly. 'They're still your children, Dom,' I say when he doesn't reply. 'In every way that counts, you are their father.'

'Oh, don't throw that "it's just biology" crap at me. If I'm not their real father, I don't give a shit about them – or you.' He swings his legs off the bed and stands up.

'I don't believe you.'

'More fool you.'

Yes, I am a fool. I've believed every kind word, every tender touch, since he came to the hospital. I was so busy beating myself up for my own guilt that I never thought to question his. But he's known about all of this since that first visit, I realise. I remember Professor Hernandez telling me how the nurse needed help to pull Dom off me, how he'd been consumed by distress, shaking me to try to wake me up. He wasn't trying to wake me up, I see now; he was trying to make me to stay asleep – for ever.

My life is going to end in this dark place. I feel it in every trembling part of me. Hope deserts me for long moments until I think of Annabel and Aidan, my babies – always my babies even though they are grown children now. I have to get back to them.

'So what happens now? You can't keep me locked up here for ever. We can start again; we can work things out ...' I begin to panic as awareness creeps over me that our discussion is coming to an end. I feel like Dom has finally said his piece; he's spilled out his grievances, and if the twins really aren't his children, he has absolutely no reason to care about me any longer – *or them*.

My children are in serious danger; everything he's told me crystallises into this one certainty. I shake my head back and forth, frantically rocking my body to see if I can dislodge the cords restraining me.

'That's *good*,' he drawls, moving closer, and then I feel one big hand landing on the centre of my chest, pinning me down. 'I'm glad you're feeling stronger. So you'll be in a fit state of mind to know *exactly* how it feels to lose everything that really matters to you.'

'No – please. Please don't hurt my children! OK, I was leaving you, Dom. That much I believe is true. But you have to understand, I was scared. Of the rows, the bruises. I needed to get out. I wanted to feel safe again. I wanted to know that the *children* were safe.'

'The children? Or just Aidan?' His voice is ice on glass.

'What do you mean?'

'I've always wondered, you see. No favourites, that's what you always said. Always the perfect mother, but such a flawed wife. You deserved punishment for your infidelity alone, for making a fool of me all these years. But that wasn't quite enough. It's not enough for me to win, you see. You have to lose. *Everything.*'

'I've *never* said I'm perfect. And I don't have favourites. I love them both . . . ' He was digging the knife into the deepest, darkest core of my shame. Taking me back to the heart of my guilt, my self-loathing: the choice I made. He'd always picked on me about favouring my son; he was never going to let that go, even now when he believed that neither of the children were his.

'But I knew, you see. You saved Aidan once, and I knew you'd do it again. You're a terrible mother. The very worst. I knew it, and I wanted you to die knowing it. I wanted you to go to your grave knowing you were capable of saving one child and sacrificing another. I wanted you finally to choose one. *Bitch.*'

PART FOUR

FORTY

My breath rasps in my throat and there is a tonne weight of fear crushing my chest as I hear the words I will never forget – because suddenly I know that I've heard my husband say them once before. On a sunny morning at the end of May, the perfect day for a pool party. The twins' tenth birthday.

Choose one, bitch.

And, finally, I remember . . .

I remember it was the day before the twin's birthday and I was as nervous as a cat about to have kittens. My suitcase was packed and tucked away in the back of the wardrobe. Dom was working late – so he said. I knew he was out drinking, as he was most nights; I knew he would be home later, expecting to exert his conjugal rights, followed up with a punch if he wasn't completely satisfied.

I remember Max had stopped by with a new DVD. I'd invited him to stay and watch it with us, but he seemed jittery and said he was meeting someone for a drink. So I left the twins watching the film and trailed nervously around the house, checking a cup-board here and a bookshelf there, making sure I hadn't forgotten anything they would miss. For myself, I could have walked away with just the clothes I stood up in: I was leaving Dom, taking the children to a place of safety, and I didn't care if we were flat broke for the rest of our lives, as long as we were free.

I hadn't told Annabel and Aidan that we'd be leaving after their party. I didn't want to spoil their birthday – and I also knew how impossible they'd find it not to give something away. Dom would pick up on their nervous anticipation, and all would be lost. But he would be going to the train station straight after the party, heading up to Manchester for a meeting, then all I had to do was smuggle the kids and our suitcase out of the back gate, where I'd walk down the alley to meet the taxi I'd arranged to wait for us at the end of the road.

I checked my purse for the hundredth time: I still had the key to Lucy's holiday cottage in Brighton. It was unbelievably gener-ous of her to let us stay there for a while, but she'd insisted it was no problem. She'd bought the cottage a couple of years ago, after inheriting money from a great-aunt, and she'd been renting it out to tourists. It was going to be the place she retired to, she said – since leaving Devon, she'd never stopped yearning to live by the sea again – but as she had to make some more money out of the deli first, she was more than happy for me and the kids to use her cottage as a bolthole.

I'd already met the managing agent in Brighton a couple of times, under the pretext of taking the twins for a seaside day trip, and everything was sorted: train tickets booked, accommodation arranged, taxi to arrive half an hour after the last party guests left ...

Annabel and Aidan would be upset, though; I was worried about that. I'd always taken great pains to hide any bruises, and although I knew they were much quieter around their father than they were around me, I'd put that down to his being that much louder. Most people faded into the background around Dom; it didn't mean the twins were frightened of him. Or did it? I couldn't be entirely sure, and that was the biggest part of my reason for leaving ... I would never let anything bad happen to my children: I'd given them life, and they were *my* life.

I remember looking for something to hide in the suitcase to comfort Annabel on our first night. I slipped into her bedroom and quickly looked around for anything that would bring a smile to her face. She'd been growing up so fast, lately, abandoning teddies in favour of teen magazines, but she was devoted to Panda. I couldn't pack him in the case, though; she slept with his soft, furry body clutched against her every night, and she would definitely miss him at bedtime. It had to be something else – a toy she'd perhaps forgotten about, and would be happy to see again. So happy that it would take her mind off the fact that we were runaways ...

I remember reaching under her bed, my hand sweeping around in search of something, anything. I remember the shock as my palm made contact with the sharp, pointed corner of a hardback book. I remember scooping the book out from under the bed and smiling at the picture on the cover: white roses. I'd bought the diary for Annabel as somewhere for her to write little stories about her life, but I had forgotten all about it. She probably had too, I thought, deciding to have a quick peek inside.

Shock. Devastation ... I remember those feelings and how my body felt paralysed with them. I remember kneeling on Annabel's floor, my hands shaking, nausea churning in my stomach. I reached for Panda and I cried into his tummy, sobbing until my throat hurt, my chest burning with the effort of making no noise so that I wouldn't be heard. I remember trying to talk to Annabel in her room, trying to coax her to open up, feeling desperate, despairing and frustrated when she wouldn't.

And guilt surged through me. I hadn't *known*. I hadn't protected her. I'd failed her. But whoever was doing this to her, I *would* find out. I would do everything I could to make them pay. But only once we were at a safe distance: I had to stick to the plan. I had to get the children away, and then everything would be all right . . . I believed that. I just had to hold everything together until after the party; I just had to act normal, as if nothing unusual was happening, as if everything was completely fine . . .

I spent the evening in a daze, piling up the twins' birthday presents in the living room after they'd gone to bed, attaching 'Happy 10ᵗʰ Birthday' balloons to the pile with ribbons: purple for Annabel, red for Aidan. When Dom came home later, he was drunk and I pretended to be asleep. I remember him stumbling around the room, slamming through cupboards, bumping into walls. I remember the hot, rough hand sliding over my hip; I remember it sliding round to my breasts, squeezing them until I thought I would cry out in pain and betray the fact that I wasn't asleep. His hand shoving me over on to my stomach; his body slumping heavily on top of me: I remember pain – my head yanked back by my hair, a burning sensation between my legs as he spread my thighs apart and jerked violently inside me – once, twice, three times – grunting as he rolled off me.

I remember lying awake in bed all night, just waiting for the light of dawn and the start of the last day I would ever have to put up with this misery. Then, in the half-light, as night surrendered to morning, I remember the row, Dom's anger before he stormed out . . . and everything fast forwards from that point: decorating the cake, chatting with the twins, a smile on my face but my mind frantically rehearsing everything I had to do after the party:

suitcase, photo, tickets … everything that was precious to me. Grab the twins and *go*!

I squeeze my eyes tightly shut, and Max's dark, dank bedroom slides away and I'm right back there, in my own home, on the morning of the twins' tenth birthday …

FORTY-ONE

'I can't believe you actually made that cake all by yourself.' Aidan looked up from his DS to watch me pressing candles into the soft icing, my tongue sticking out of the side of my mouth in concentration.

'No offence taken, love,' I joked. 'But Lucy did give me a hand – it's one of her recipes.'

'Ooh. I might have a bit, then.' Annabel, reclining on the sofa like an off-duty princess, flicking through a magazine, poked her head up over the arm. 'Is she coming swimming too? Or are all the grown-ups going to sit in the café and gossip?'

'Cheeky monkey!' I said, opening a second packet of candles.

'You'll come in the pool with us, Mum, won't you?'

I blessed Aidan for not yet being embarrassed at having his mum hanging around. How many more birthdays until the twins just wanted to do their own thing?

'Course I will, love. Wouldn't miss the chance to dunk you both, now, would I? Mums have to get their revenge somehow for all the trouble you kids cause!'

'You love us really, though,' Annabel said confidently. 'What would you do if you didn't have us to boss around?'

'What indeed?' I exchanged another glance with Aidan: a smiling conspiracy, both of us happily indulging his sister's conviction that she was the centre of our universe. After all, it was true. *Star*. 'And, yes, I love you both loads. You're the best things that ever happened to me.'

'Oh, Mum! Don't be *soft*,' Annabel said, rolling her eyes.

The doorbell buzzed and our laughter died. The twins exchanged glances and I saw in their deliberately bland expressions that they had indeed both heard the row this morning. *Damn.* I saw questions flicker across their pale, softly freckled faces, so similar in features yet so different in expression: Annabel's defiant, chin raised, reluctant to show any anxiety; Aidan's troubled, almost identical blue eyes wide with concern.

Was it Daddy come back to apologise for storming out? Would he be in one of his good moods? Or would he have been to the clubhouse after his round of golf, as he's taken to doing, lately – would he stumble round the house, impatient with every stray toy and un-ironed shirt?

I felt sad for a moment that he'd missed out on our lovely morning. He'd been a good dad, I acknowledged with a sigh; we'd been a happy family for the best part of ten years. But today, for the first – and last – time ever, he'd missed the twins' favourite lemony, sugary pancake breakfast; he'd missed the delicious crackle of wrapping paper as I rearranged the pile of presents in one corner of the living room ready to open later.

'I'll get it, Mum. You carry on, you're doing a great job,' Aidan said seriously as he laid his DS carefully on the coffee table and headed into the hall.

'Hang on a minute, love. You know I don't like you answering the door to strangers.' Sudden breathless fear – not premonition;

I didn't believe in that. Just my mum-radar, as Lucy always called it. Or perhaps simply a legacy of my overprotective neurosis when the children were babies.

'Who says it's a stranger?' Annabel tossed down her magazine and leaped to her feet. 'It might be Uncle Max. He said he had an extra-special surprise for us.'

'Huh.' I rolled my eyes, hoping it wasn't yet another unsuitable DVD. I needed to tell Max to stop turning up with knock-offs he'd got from his mates on the estate. Perhaps I also needed to have a tactful conversation with him about not coming round here quite so often.

I looked at my watch. It couldn't be Max, though. He wasn't due for another half an hour. He wouldn't have had a chance yet to pick up the extra rackets to play tennis in the garden later.

'Just give me one more sec,' I said, thinking it was most likely Dom trying to niggle me by making me open the door for him – forcing me to dance attendance on him after our row earlier. Well, he could wait. And he could damned well say sorry for being so nasty this morning. Plucking the last candles out of the packet, I carefully pressed them into the soft blue icing, sat back and licked my fingers as the last one slid into the cake. *Perfect.* 'I'll be right there!' I called out, feeling anxious now, worrying I'd push my luck if I kept Dom waiting any longer.

I hurried after the twins into the hall, frowning as I saw the bulky silhouette in the frosted-glass-panelled front door. It didn't look like Dom. His clothes were always so stylish, his shape broad but not hulking.

Annabel seemed to read my mind. 'It's the postman, bet you – look at that giant shadow through the glass. He must have the most humongous stack of presents!'

'Hope one of them is a new Xbox,' said Aidan, hovering at Annabel's shoulder as she reached for the front-door latch.

I smiled secretly to myself thinking of the PlayStation in his pile of presents. I'd found it in an end-of-season sale and knew he'd be so excited, as I hoped Annabel would be about the tickets I'd bought her for her first ballet at the Royal Opera House. I'd already asked Lucy to bring whatever gifts I couldn't carry down to Brighton with her when she visited, and I'd hidden a couple of little surprise gifts in our suitcase, too, for the twins to open later – after Dom had headed off to Manchester and we were safely in Lucy's cottage.

'You know your dad's not keen on video games,' I said, trying to measure his disappointment. Dom was so rarely home to play with the kids, and any time he *was* here he spent glued to his phone and laptop.

'That's because he always wants to win and hates getting shot,' Aidan excused his dad, and I heard the edge in his voice even as he rolled his eyes and laughed. I joined in with his laughter. Another conspiracy of smiles. Neither of us wanted to admit we were anxious about Daddy coming home.

For a second, the sunshine completely blinded me as Annabel swung the front door open wide and the bright morning light flooded our hallway with summer warmth. It was the perfect day for a birthday; the perfect day for heading off to the pool with a bunch of good friends, hanging out in the back garden later, chatting and eating cake, feeling glad that the last terrible nine months were behind us. For ever. Soon we would be gone. By the time Dom got back from Manchester, we'd be safely in our new home. He wouldn't be able to find us, and any future meetings would have to be arranged through solicitors, and supervised . . .

I was still picturing Lucy's seaside cottage as my eyes finally managed to focus through the glare, and for a second I couldn't take in what I was seeing: rough, old-fashioned army fatigues . . . a balaclava. A gloved hand reaching out for the twins.

'MUMMY!'

My legs almost gave way and my heart seemed to stop as Annabel was dragged from the doorway, round the side of the house. I stumbled after her, my flip-flops catching on the front doorstep, my scream stuck deep in my throat as I watched Annabel's fingers graze along the pebble-dashed wall, bloodying as she frantically grabbed on to anything that might help her escape the tall, bulky figure, his heavy boots carving a scar across my neat lawn as he yanked my daughter towards the seclusion of the rose bushes. Aidan stumbled after her, his eyes dry with fear and his slender arms reaching out for his sister. His clenched fists were no defence against the powerful gloved hand that grabbed him tightly by his shirt collar, effortlessly lifting him off the ground so that his arms flailed and his legs kicked uselessly.

I needed a weapon – I needed something heavy to strike out with – one of the twins' swimming trophies, or one of Dom's golfing ones that he always polished so meticulously. I looked around me for a spade, a gardening fork – anything. But there was nothing; I had no means of protecting them, and Annabel's screams reverberated in my chest like the tremors of an earthquake as I tried to run, my legs turning to lead, clawing my body through the thick, sweet summer air towards my children.

Don't you dare lay a finger on my daughter!

The gun pointed to each of us in turn and a maelstrom of fear set my head spinning. I clawed my way through the air to get to my children, terror clouding my eyes, the world closing in on me until I was trapped in tunnel vision: the twins seemed to kaleidoscope away from me, achingly vulnerable little people in their cool new birthday outfits, dwarfed by the murderous power of violence.

'Run! Hide! Don't look back!' I launched myself in front of them, throwing my arms wide as I forced the words from my terror-constricted throat.

'*Choose one, bitch.*'

'*Choose me!*'

He didn't hesitate; he fired.

My ears were deafened by the bang. I felt Annabel make a grab for my hand at the last second before she reached for Aidan and pulled him after her, across the grass towards the French windows at the back of the house. My mind filled with an apology I couldn't speak: *I'm so sorry to leave you, my loves.* I felt myself slump towards the rose bushes, my hands reaching out to clasp great handfuls of petals, thorns shredding my skin. They reminded me of Annabel's diary and how I would never get to make things all right now.

My head rested in the soft mulchy grass, and for a split second I saw feet. Trainers. A box of rackets and tennis balls ready for party games. Long legs in tracksuit bottoms; a backpack by his side.

Max.

My fingers squeezed the silky softness of the white roses.

And then there was darkness.

FORTY-TWO

Max arrived *after* I was shot.

Realisation burns across my skin like a fever, leaving a scalding trail of fear that sets my body trembling. Then in the next second, a wave of relief that washes away pain.

I said, 'Choose me.'

I fought for *both* my children. I tried my hardest to protect them. *Equally.*

'I thought mothers weren't supposed to have favourites. That's what you've always told me.' His angry accusation is laced with pained bitterness.

'And I meant it. I *don't!*' I protest, feeling strength return to my body as I finally remember the events of that morning. After all the conversations I had with the doctor about sounds and smells prompting memories, it took only two words to trigger mine: *Choose one.* They crystallise the essence of what it means to me to be a mother: I *didn't choose.*

But suddenly I realise why Dom needs to believe I did.

Because if *I* am capable of choosing one child over another, it means *all* parents are – it means that just because Max was the idolised big brother, Dom was still valued. He wasn't unlovable, a failure; parental bias is normal. For a fleeting moment I feel sad as the realisation sinks in that Dom has projected on to me every last atom of the resentment and childhood insecurity that has never left him. My supposed fatal flaw – my favouritism of Aidan over Annabel – holds the key to Dom's redemption. In order to believe in himself again, he needs me to affirm that I *did* make that choice.

I remember his dogged fierceness as he talked about his family when we first met: *It's not about pride. It's about vindication.* He's finally got one over on his big brother, and he's punished me to justify his actions. He picked a hell of a way to make his point . . . But I refuse to make him feel better, to give him the vindication he's been craving since his parents died without acknowledging that Dom was the strong one, the successful son.

The smell of smoke is strong, drawing me out of my thoughts. I look up and see the bright red tip of a cigarette arcing through the darkness. There is a tall, dark shadow against the wall. It moves, shifting like a ghost through the gloom, edging closer to the side of the bed; a slim beam of light slithers through the gap around the boarded-up window, outlining the bulky shape in an eerie glow. The silhouette twists and glides next to me, bending over me until the sliver of light casts twin glints in his blue eyes.

'Are you quite sure about that? You seemed pretty convinced to me that Annabel was dead,' he mocks me, and I have to strain my ears to catch his words.

If I couldn't see and smell the smoke curling up from his cigarette, I could half imagine it was the voice of my conscience metamorphosed into a malignant spirit, haunting me with what will always remain my darkest secret: the fact that I did believe, even for a heartbeat, that I might have given up my daughter. It shames me, even as I know the truth: the guilt is entirely *his*. But

I have to hold on to that; I can't let him mess with my head any more. It's over; or it soon will be.

'Was I supposed to die?' I say softly, feeling a flutter inside me at the thought that it was Annabel's hand reaching out to grab me at the last moment that meant the bullet only grazed instead of obliterating my brain.

'I'm glad you didn't,' he says, 'because you're going to suffer *so* much more living without your children. Death would have been merciful,' he tells me. 'But I'm not an unreasonable man. I can do mercy. If you ask me nicely enough, I might yet grant you that release. Call it a sort of final tribute to our marriage. A belated tenth-anniversary gift.' He gives me a wry look. 'Funny, hey? I always said I would never let you go, but suddenly I find that I can. Oh, so easily.'

'Stop playing games with me, Dom,' I say quietly, determined not to let him intimidate me any more with sick threats. 'You've made your point and you've dragged me through hell and back. It has to end *here*. You won't get away with this,' I add hoarsely, trying to ignore the shiver running up my spine.

'Oh, but I already have. Max has conveniently taken the rap for me, which is only fair, after all. *I've got feelings for a special lady in your life*, he said. *And I'm sure she returns them.* He sat opposite me in that pub and had the nerve to say he was worried how I'd feel about it – how hard he'd tried to stop feeling that way, how he'd tried to stay away but couldn't resist those blue eyes, that pretty hair, her soft skin ... He looked me in the eye and said he was *addicted to his sugar*.'

'But did he actually say he was in love with me? That we were—'

'You think I'd give him the satisfaction of taunting me with details? The smug look on his face said it all. He was stealing my wife, and he wanted me to know it – to know that I'd lost you, and that the kids were never mine in the first place. He wanted to take everything from me. So I've given it to him: all the blame, and half the punishment. The other half is yours, sweetheart. You just couldn't go a day without seeing him, could you? Not even on your children's birthday.'

'Max was lying. Or you've jumped to the wrong conclusion. You should have *talked* to me about it. But you didn't – you never have. You always just assume the worst about me. You didn't play golf that morning, did you?' I say, my mind replaying the dreadful sequence of events.

'Course I didn't. You'd already told me Max was arriving at ten. All I had to do was change in the shed, and wait. I'd already stashed my dad's old kit bag in there, ready to clean the gun. Just as Max asked me to.' He smirks.

'Your dad's old army clothes. Sitting there in your terrifying disguise. Holding his gun. Waiting for the right moment to—' My voice rises hysterically as I picture it all.

'Max was early. It all happened a lot faster than I intended. I was rushing, or I wouldn't have missed my aim.' His smirk turns into a frown.

'I saw his feet. Under the rose bushes.' I don't need Dom to confirm it. My mind hasn't stopped picturing those rose bushes for weeks, and I knew there had to be a reason they'd lodged so deeply in my imagination. 'You shot me then killed your own brother.'

'He fought hard, I'll give him that. You should have seen the look on his face. He started this fight, but I had the last word. And he *deserved* to die. He fucked my wife and then he taunted me about it. Not as clever as he thought, Max. He really believed that telling me about his sordid infatuation would put me in my place. He underestimated me,' he grits out.

It was supposed to be a double execution: the unfaithful wife, the disloyal brother. My first instinct about punishment being the motive was spot on; I just got the wrong man. It was Dom, not Max, who staged the scene. Max's death was part retribution, part expediency – a means of covering up Dom's crime. I can imagine the look on Max's face all too well. Whatever he said to Dom in the pub, whether he deliberately lied to provoke Dom, or was simply teasing him to get back at his brother, he turned up that morning ready to help the twins have a happy birthday party, and instead he had a gun shoved in his hand and pointed at his head. I know exactly how that feels.

'And now it's your turn.'

He leans closer and something catches the faint beam of light, making it flash in the dark. *A knife.* Closer still. The blade gleams as it slices through the darkness. I grind my teeth together and close my eyes, picturing Annabel's and Aidan's faces, remembering how perfectly their bodies fit into my sides, cuddled safely against me, and how good it feels to stroke their hair and kiss them good-night. I think of them as tiny babies, the heat of their soft bodies as I tucked them into the crook of my arm. I picture them as curious toddlers, kicking their little boots through autumn leaves in excitement. I remember picnics and plays, sports days and swimming galas ... cheering the twins on when they won, comforting them when they lost. My beautiful twins, so similar to look at yet each unique in personality: Annabel daring, Aidan so shy; both hovering on the brink of their teenage years. Little people in the making – *my* little people.

I've heard it said that a person's life is supposed to flash in front of their eyes as they think they're about to die, but it's my children's happily haphazard, precious lives that play in my imagination as I stare at Dom's face and acknowledge the cold, hard, inescapable truth: *My husband is a killer.*

His hand brushes across my mouth and instinctively I turn my face, sinking my teeth into the flesh of his palm.

'You bitch. You fucking *bitch*.' He reels back. 'I shouldn't have called that ambulance. I should have let you bleed to death.'

He climbs on to the bed, straddling me, his weight pressing down; I am trapped, helpless. I want to fight but there is no strength left in me. I feel my body giving up and hear a voice inside my head calling out to Annabel and Aidan, begging them to forgive me for leaving them yet again.

Who will look after them when I'm gone?

My mind feels fuzzy now; his thighs are crushing my chest, his knees squeezing the sides of my head like a vice, and I can scarcely draw a breath. I need to keep fighting: I can't give up . . . but I feel my strength leaving me. Soon, I will vanish once more into the bright-dark. Only perhaps this time there will be no brightness, only bottomless, endless dark.

Come on, Mum, don't be soft, you can do it!

I try to resist as he grabs hold of my bound wrists with one hand and yanks them above my head, but the violent motion wrenches every ligament in my shoulders and the pressure of his fingers on my bones leaves me weak with pain. I cry out but the sound is muffled against his chest as he leans forward, the knife angled upwards. His arm jerks out, a stabbing punch, and there is a snapping noise.

He's cut the cords around my wrists.

My arms drop and I half groan, half wail; sobs wrack through my body and my lungs feel tight with fear.

'I can't take any more,' I whisper, rocking my head from side to side as he cuts the cords binding my ankles. 'Please, it's enough.'

'You're right. But don't worry. There's only one more choice left for you to make, Maddie. I wonder if you will make it.'

'What is it?' There's hardly enough breath in my body to say the words.

'A deal.'

'A . . . What kind of deal?' I don't trust Dom to keep his side of any bargain.

'Turns out I didn't need to go all the way to Manchester to be offered that job. My reputation preceded me,' he brags. 'But I thought I might leave the decision to you. All you have to do is tell the police that you've remembered. That it *was* Max who shot you. Then I'll let you go. You'll never have to see me again. Or – and this is where you need to think carefully, for once, if you can do that – I can leave you here to die. No one knows you're here, and by the time they find you it'll be too late.'

'So that's why you've brought me here. To play your mind games with me, break me down until I give you a way out. But you *won't* get away with this. Lucy—'

'Is quite happy at home with the children, and I'm sure she'd happily keep looking after them after the tragedy of your disappearance – when the police discover that you simply couldn't get over the death of your lover and you wash up on the Thames foreshore.'

'You wouldn't . . . *Lucy* wouldn't. I don't believe you!' I strain my voice to shout the words, as much to convince myself as to denounce Dom for the liar I know him to be.

He's pacing the room now, but suddenly he strides towards the bed, towering over me, hand raised. 'Don't look so frightened,' he says, reaching out a hand to stroke my hair.

I flinch in recognition. 'It *was* you, wasn't it? Stroking my hair, trying to smother me as I slept, telling me that I was just having nightmares when I woke up choking.'

'Twice I almost suffocated you,' he says, looking pleased with himself. 'The first time when I signed the release forms for you to be put into a coma, and then again when I visited you. But then I figured it would be so much more fun to keep you alive, watch you suffer. Watch me and Lucy. We're good together, if I do say so myself. We always have been.' His wink is cocky.

I tell myself he's bluffing. I've been wrong about Lucy, but I won't make that mistake again. I hope she *has* been looking after the twins, but I no longer believe she's been trying to steal them from me. I wouldn't wish my husband on my worst enemy, and I simply don't believe Lucy is that.

She's in as much danger as the children, I think suddenly. She doesn't know I'm awake; she doesn't know Dom was the gunman. Maybe he's been spinning her a line all this time about Max, how worthless he was, how shameful my behaviour. Lucy won't realise she's living under the same roof as a killer. I hold my breath in horror at the thought.

Or perhaps she *does* know. Perhaps Dom has her so terrified that she's forcing herself to stay quiet, play along and avoid lighting his short fuse, just as I did for all those years. He's holding her captive . . .

The twins too.

'You haven't hurt them, have you?' I ask, the words grazing my throat, my eyes drawn to the tiny specks of blood on his shirt collar, surely from shaving cuts. 'If you've laid so much as a finger on my children—'

The fist crashing into the side of my face knocks me sideways and, taken by surprise, I tumble off the bed, landing heavily on the rough wood floor. Everything goes black for a second and I rest my forehead on the boards, trying not to be sick. My cheekbone, already tender from banging it against the bathroom doorframe, hurts so badly I can't believe it's not broken. Pain shoots into my temples; my head throbs.

'You have no right to question me. What business is it of yours *what* I do? You forfeited the right to ask anything of me the day you slept with my brother and lied about the twins being mine.'

'But I didn't . . . I *never* . . .' I can taste blood in my mouth and I'm not sure where it's coming from. My left arm, bruised from taking all my weight when I fell, feels like it's no longer part of my body, and I have to concentrate hard to lift a hand to touch my face. My fingertips come away wet, but I can't tell if it's from my nose or the gash at the corner of my mouth. I look up at Dom and realise the cut must have been caused by his wedding ring. I can't believe he's actually wearing it; he hasn't returned mine to me, and I'm glad. Once, I wore it with so much pride, until it became a symbol of subservience . . . then fear.

I feel almost like I'm floating above the room, looking down at the pair of us. I see myself – damaged body, half-broken mind – and remember my surprised joy when Dom slipped his mother's sapphire engagement ring on my finger, the butterflies inside me as I said yes, the pride and joy I felt as we exchanged our wedding vows.

'You've got till tomorrow morning to make up your mind. I'll be back then for your decision.'

There is no question in my mind: I will do *anything* to protect my children, to get back to them.

Daddy's the one who usually likes tricks.

I look at the face of my husband, the man I once loved so much, and a terrible thought sinks like a stone to the bottom of my heart as he turns away from me and heads to the door, the key turning in the lock as he closes it behind him with a soft thud: *Maybe I'm the last one to die. Maybe they're all already dead.*

FORTY-THREE

I shouldn't have let him leave; I should have kept him here, said yes immediately to his sick deal, anything to prevent him going home to the twins. What if he's lying again? What if he doesn't come back? I'm going to die alone here, barely able to move, starving to death, and no one will be able to help me – help my children. And it's my fault for not stopping him. Surely he wouldn't. It's one thing punishing me, but not the children. I can't *believe* he could hurt a child . . .

Then I remember Annabel's diary. Someone *was* trying to hurt her, and I still don't know who, and I want to read my daughter's words again, to try to work out if there were any clues I missed. But where is it? I remember hunting frantically through the suitcase in the bright-dark, my unconscious mind replaying my desperate search before the birthday party, one last check that everything was packed and ready. But I found only the tickets, the photo, and nothing else. The diary was gone.

Has someone taken it?

I remember my conviction that the man who pulled the trigger had a double motive: to punish me and to silence my daughter.

The police told me Max was the gunman; Dom has schemed to lead me down the same blind alley. It was all a lie: a smokescreen, a cover-up. Now I realise it was actually Dom who fired that bullet, and I was the only target in his sights. Me – and Max. And that changes everything . . .

It means Max was a victim too, guilty of aggravating his brother but not necessarily of grooming Annabel. Maybe someone else was pestering her – a teacher, a neighbour, the parent of a friend. She drew cartoons of them *all* in her diary, and I freeze in horror at the thought that this monster could still be out there, plaguing her to this day.

I wish I had Annabel's diary to help me work out who did this. Max or a stranger. Or someone close to our family . . . It's impossible to know, and I still can't get it out of my head that it just seemed so *logical* for the gunman and my daughter's would-be abuser to be one and the same man. Only the rules of logic don't apply here; everything is being played out by *Dom's* rules. What was it he once said to me, about the first rule of dating Dominic Castle?

Expect the unexpected . . .

Bluff and double-bluff.

Suddenly my heart starts pounding as I come full circle and wonder if my first gut instinct was right all along: that one monster *is* responsible for both crimes. And that can only mean that the man who was pestering Annabel to touch him is returning home right this second, killing time while he waits for me to make my choice, to decide which way the axe should fall.

If it hasn't fallen already . . .

And now there is nothing and no one standing between my husband and my daughter.

Minutes, hours pass. My nerves are in shreds. I try to stay calm. I must think logically. Dom, Max or a stranger – who was harassing my daughter?

I think back to the words I remember from her diary, the *disgusting touch* of the man who was stalking her, his eyes following her round the room . . . Not classroom.

Round the room.

Under our own roof. Surely Max or Dom: it has to be one of them . . . But nothing I remember points to either, and once again I feel that sick desperation that I failed to protect my daughter – that I missed the signs. *Were* there any?

I remember Annabel's increasing self-consciousness. But she was growing up; surely that body-coyness is a natural development. I remember how she'd grown tired of Max's jokes and had started asking friends' mums for lifts home. She rolled her eyes when Max came round, and I remember telling her not to be rude when she asked how long he was staying as soon as we sat down to Sunday lunch one day. But children get bored of adults. There was surely nothing unusual in any of those things.

And Dom. The Tickle Monster. Always pulling his little princess close for a hug in passing, or for a lazy cuddle in bed at the weekends. But I was there the whole time; his affection towards the children was a *good* thing. Or was I just being naive?

Annabel had refused to tell me when I asked. She wouldn't give me a name, and I was loath to press her for details, sensing her distress and confusion. I'd planned to ask her again once we were in our place of safety. Only we never made it, and I need to know if I've just allowed a monster to walk back into my home. One who believes the children aren't his; who doesn't care about them any more.

I close my eyes and empty my mind, and try to allow memory to surface and give up the answer to my most pressing question of all: *Who wanted to hurt my daughter?*

'It's fine, Dom. It doesn't matter. Honest. It's been a long day after a hard week. We're both tired.' I knew I should feel disappointment, but it was relief that surged through me as Dom rolled away from me and stood up. I pressed my head back into the pillows, trying not to move, just waiting for him to go.

'I'll see you downstairs. I said I'd take the kids swimming.' He yanked up his boxers unceremoniously and reached out for his chinos.

It was Sunday afternoon and the twins were watching the entire box set of an American comedy series that Max had brought round yesterday. Seeing how engrossed they were, Dom had gestured to me. It had taken me a couple of minutes to interpret his raised eyebrows; it was a long time since we'd done anything as spontaneously romantic as sneak into our bedroom in the middle of the afternoon. Eventually I'd got the message and we'd headed upstairs.

But I'd felt awkward, on edge knowing the children were just downstairs, and Dom had seemed impatient, almost angry. There was no attempt at seduction: he'd just wanted to lie down on the bed and get on with it. After the briefest rough fumble, though, it had become obvious that it wasn't going to happen. He'd hidden his embarrassment well, but I'd dreaded to think how he might take it out on me later.

'That sounds nice,' I told him. 'It's been a while since we all went swimming together.'

'I said *I'll* take them. It'll make a change for them to hang out in the pool with their dad instead of good old Uncle Max. And I'm taking them to Richmond. Much nicer there. Not so many lecherous old pervs loitering around. Might treat them to pizza afterwards.'

'Sure. Sounds lovely,' I said, feeling excluded but acknowledging that Dom was right: he did need to spend more time with the children.

Annabel hadn't been so keen. 'I want to watch this.' Lying

flat on the floor on her tummy, she didn't take her eyes off the screen.

'The pool will be shut soon.' Dom had all three swimming bags over his shoulder already.

'Come on, Bel,' Aidan said, pausing the DVD. 'You can show off that new dive Uncle Max taught you last week.'

'And we can have a dip in the jacuzzi afterwards, too,' Dom added. The twins always loved the hot bubbles, pretending they were floating on top of a volcano.

'Really? Cool. As long as we don't have to go in the sauna. Uncle Max always makes us go in there after swimming, hey, Bel?' Aidan said.

'Full of sweaty old men,' Annabel said over her shoulder, not looking round.

'You've never mentioned that?' I frowned. 'I'll have a word with Uncle Max. I don't like the sound of that at all. They're not *naked* in there, are they?'

'Don't be ridiculous,' Dom said.

'Well, I don't know, do I? You do change in a cubicle, don't you, Bel?' I continued, thinking I should insist on going along after all. 'You don't get undressed in the communal bit?' She was growing up so fast, and sometimes I didn't think she quite realised it. It was hard to counsel caution without making her overly self-conscious. I wanted her to be safe without making her paranoid. Public pools were such a nightmare of worry for parents, I thought.

'Course I do, Mum,' she said, looking at me like I'd lost my mind. 'Most of the time, anyway. If they're not all full.'

'She can come in a cubicle with me. It'll be fine. Stop worrying,' Dom said. 'Now, kids, no more stalling, grab your things. Last one to the car has to answer to the Tickle Monster.'

The twins scrambled to their feet, leaving me to turn off the

DVD and tidy up the mess of books, games and magazines strewn across the living-room floor. I busied myself for the rest of the afternoon, trying not to worry about the children – they were safe with their dad, after all – trying not to dread the evening, once the children were in bed, when Dom and I would be alone again. It was unusual for him to be home; he was generally out most evenings now, even at weekends, seeing old clients or meeting prospective ones. I hoped he wouldn't be expecting a repeat performance of this afternoon.

Maybe I'd give Lucy a call and see if she and Jasper fancied popping over for an impromptu sleepover and supper ... *Safety in numbers.*

Nothing particularly suspicious springs to my mind. It would be easy to over-analyse and misinterpret, I think, trying not to let fear for the children railroad my imagination into dark, paranoid places. To know that I couldn't protect my children in the outside world is one thing; that I left them vulnerable to harm under my own roof is devastating. If I'd ever seen anything that made me uncomfortable, either between Max and the children or with Dom, I know I wouldn't have let it pass. But Annabel's words had been clear.

Unless her diary was another figment of my imagination, conjured up from the depths of my distress, along with her being propelled backwards across the garden by the impact of a bullet ...

I can't believe I've invented the existence of a whole diary, though. My memory of it is far too vivid; if I close my eyes, I can feel its sharp corners, the bumps and indentations where Annabel's biro had carved into the smooth white pages. I remember telling Dom about what I'd read in the early hours of the twins' birthday; I can clearly recall his shock and anger, too. And I'm sure he mentioned the diary when I was still in hospital, but that seems so long ago now . . .

Once again, I've lost my grasp on where the line between truth and reality lies. Only one person can tell me: my daughter.

But will I ever get to see her again?

FORTY-FOUR

I wake to the sound of laughter: *children's* laughter. It's just my imagination playing tricks on me again, I think. The room is dark; I am alone. For how long? Dom will surely return for his answer soon, and I need to be ready.

I wonder if this is all just another test. He said the choice is mine, but experience teaches me that he's probably already made his decision. He asked me to choose between the children, but it wasn't a real choice: he just wanted me to die believing I'd made it.

Power.

I realise now how disempowered Dom had been feeling. By his own admission, his business was failing; our relationship had also broken down and he was getting increasingly wound up by Max's constant presence and sly taunts. He must have reached breaking point when Max seemed to hint at us having an affair. When Dom found my suitcase, it surely confirmed his worst fears: he was going to lose everything. So he snapped. He's not a psychopath, or a natural born killer: he's an ordinary man who became desperate to the point of crazed, vengeful malevolence.

And he's got me exactly where he wants me now. I should have fought back a long time ago; that is my biggest regret. I loved Dom, and we were good together, but then we weren't, and, in truth, I'd realised after the very first slap that none of my attempts to appease or re-engage with him were going to work. At that point I should have got out, but I held on to hope too long. Lucy was right: I left it too late. What was I waiting for? For Dom to change? For life to get better – or worse? Was I waiting for someone literally to put a gun to my head?

I hear another hoot of mirth followed by a chorus of giggles, and for a second I wonder if I'm actually still asleep and dreaming, or if the shut-off valve in my mind has rescued me from horror once again by diverting my thoughts towards happier places – the park, the playground, with the twins happily playing and chasing each other. Then I hear shouting and realise it's coming from outside on the street. Chattering. Excited screeches and more boisterous laughing.

It's Monday morning, I realise, the back of my neck prickling as the implication of this sinks in. *There are people just a few metres away from me.* If I could just signal my presence to them some-how – bang on the window boards, summon up enough voice to scream. I struggle to raise myself from the bed, but the effort defeats me and I can only fall weakly back on to the mattress, battling tears of frustration as I imagine the parents and school-children walking past Max's front door without a second glance, noticing nothing unusual in boarded-up windows on another empty house, their thoughts focused on the day ahead.

My mind spins with memories of the daily school run, of Annabel and Aidan climbing on to the bus dragging school bags and gym kits, Aidan struggling with his violin case. I remember how I'd walked them all the way to the gates when they first started at the prep school, clutching their hands in mine, trying to encourage them that everything would be all right, they would soon make new friends and they could see their old ones any time they liked. I remember loitering until I'd watched them cut across the lawn and walk into the main building, never taking my eyes off their progress but all the while distracting myself by chatting to whomever I was standing next to, wishing it were Lucy, wishing we were back at the old school gate.

It was Annabel who first suggested they should start taking the bus; lots of the other girls in their class did, she claimed boldly, and she didn't want to look like a baby.

'But don't, like, wear your dark glasses and follow us all the way there, Mum, will you?' She looked up from spreading peanut butter on her toast; she'd taken to making her own snack after swimming club and it was a meticulous process that always made me smile.

'You mean like your own personal bodyguard? You should be so lucky.' I let the comment about my dark glasses pass, clenching my teeth at the reminder of bruises I'd tried to hide. I popped two more slices of bread down in the toaster in case Aidan wanted some.

'Stalker, more like,' she said, laughing.

'Can't you come on the bus with us, Mum?' Aidan asked, wandering in to the kitchen and dumping his bag in the corner before remembering to hang it up in the cupboard under the stairs. Dom didn't like the house *junked up*, as he called it. I encouraged the twins to be as neat and tidy as possible downstairs, with the promise that they could be as messy as they liked in their own rooms.

'Course, love, if you want me to,' I told him, glad to have an excuse to do exactly that. I felt nowhere near ready to trust them alone on public transport and had every intention of tagging along somehow, even if it meant following them from a distance.

I wrapped an arm around Aidan's shoulder as he sauntered back into the room, giving him a squeeze.

'We'll be safe, Mum,' Annabel insisted, rolling her eyes at her brother when he reached over to grab a slice of her toast. 'The stop's right at the end of our road, and James and Sally get on at the corner. If you're worried, just ask their mum to make sure we get on the same bus, and we'll sit with them. They're two years above us. Practically grown-ups.'

'You've got this all worked out, haven't you, smarty pants?' I said, hunting in the fridge for something to cook for Dom's dinner, knowing he probably wouldn't come home to eat it.

'Well, if you got us a mobile, you wouldn't need to worry at all, would you?' was her response, accompanied by a cheeky grin.

'Let's have a trial run, then, shall we?' I gave her a look, refusing to be drawn on that subject; I'd made my feelings clear already. 'I'll speak to James' and Sally's mum and see if you can sit with them. But don't be surprised if you see me lurking on the back seat. At least to begin with. I know the school's only along the High Street, but even so. I don't want to run the risk of you two monkeys getting into any trouble.'

'Trouble? Nothing even *the tiniest bit* dramatic ever happens round here, Mum!' Annabel said, and this time Aidan rolled his eyes in agreement.

I'd asked Dom for his opinion the following morning while he was shaving, and his only comment was that he'd walked to school since he was old enough to tie his own shoelaces, and he didn't know what I was making such a fuss about. The kids were mixing with a better class of families now, he added. Not so much to worry about as when they were hanging out with riff-raff.

Bad things happen to posh people, too, I remember saying in my head, but I'd learned the folly of sharing that kind of anxiety with Dom.

Lucy had been far more reassuring. 'We can't baby them, Maddie. It's hard, God knows it goes against every instinct to let them loose without us at their side, but at some point we have to trust them. We've taught them well. We need to let them spread their wings. At least as far as the bus stop, anyway. And with us walking fifty paces behind them on their first day,' she added, grinning.

'I just feel like I wouldn't be doing my duty, or something. School, clubs, ferrying them around – that's what I'm *here* for. To be with them. And I like it. Shoot me but I like hanging out with my children. I just don't want to turn into one of those – what did I hear one of the nannies say the other day? Helicopter parents?'

'Easy for a nanny to say. Not their child,' Lucy said, pursing her lips. 'Not their heartstrings, not their maternal guilt. I feel the same, Maddie, but you deserve a life too.'

'Don't feel sorry for me, Luce.' I'd tried to be discreet about how things were with Dom, but I couldn't hide every bruise, and Lucy wasn't stupid. 'A life to do what? The twins *are* my life.'

'And what about Dom?' she said quietly. 'Don't tell me, he's made you feel you don't deserve anything else,' she said intuitively. 'You're his personal—'

'It's not that simple,' I said, sighing.

'Isn't it? How many second chances are you going to give him, Maddie? Because he'll take as many as you offer. And he'll keep on taking, until you stop giving.'

'Last night I dreamed of us at the seaside,' I said wistfully, all talk of the school run forgotten. 'Just me and the twins. They were splashing in the sea and I was just sitting there. Watching them. That was it. Nothing more than that. But I was safe. They were safe. We were happy.'

'You only have to name the day, Maddie. The cottage is yours whenever and for as long as you want it. I know only too well what it's like. I told myself Matt would change, but the day he shook Jasper, I realised I was deluding myself. Jasper was only six months old. I'm lucky he's still here. Don't wait till it's too late, hon.'

Too late.

Is it all too late?

I'll never forgive myself if it is. I need to make it up to my children, and I hope with everything that's left in me that they are all – Annabel, Aidan, Lucy and Jasper – safe, happy . . . alive. Even if I can't be with them, I just want them to be OK.

Please let them be all right; please, please don't let them be hurt or in pain.

My eyes finally snap open but I feel groggy, disoriented and tearful as the memories evaporate into the dank, murky air. The sound of children's voices floats towards me again, more strongly now, as if they are indeed passing right in front of the house. Definitely not a dream. I picture the sprawling groups of local schoolchildren making their way through the estate towards Ivybridge Primary School, chatting about what they did at the weekend, what they watched on TV the night before, which boy has started fancying which girl, and whether the teachers will notice if they don't hand their homework in for another week.

The ordinariness of it breaks my heart and a dry wracking sob hurts my bruised ribs. How many times have Lucy and I complained over the years about the busy school days, the rush to get to after-school clubs, the endless quest to keep up, keep in the loop, keep on top of everything? *Go, go, go.* Lucy always seemed to be one step ahead of the crowd; my organisational skills were rather more haphazard, but the twins always said they loved opening their PE bags to find odd socks and a random T-shirt; they said it was fun waiting to discover what unusual combinations I'd packed away in their lunchboxes. It made school life more interesting; it reminded them of me, and they carried that reminder with them like a hug all day.

Small stuff. Tiny pockets of gold tucked inside the beige anorak of everyday domestic life. Dom has taken all that away from me. Maybe there is still a chance. If I ever get out of here; if Dom keeps faith with the deal he offered me . . . Max is dead; it can make no difference to him if I denounce him as the gunman. And I feel no guilt about it: I was never in love with him; there was no affair. I'm now completely certain of that. Either Dom got the wrong end of the stick, or Max was just winding him up. Maybe he was tired of being the lonely bachelor and, after half a bottle of whiskey, the devil came alive in him – exactly like his younger brother – and he tried to cause trouble with a big fat lie, not knowing that Dom would believe him or where it would lead. Well, now it's my turn. The difference is that *my* lie can't hurt anyone, certainly not Max. The police already think he pulled the trigger, in any case. But it will make all the difference in the world to me – and the twins.

My throat is burning and my stomach feels empty, cramping. I cough and it turns into a rattle. Trapped in this cold, damp room with no food, no warmth except my jacket to use as a blanket, I must have developed a chest infection. I constantly feel sick and feverish. I can hardly hold my head up; dizziness makes it feel like a spinning top. I battle to keep my shoulders upright for a few painful moments before my muscles begin to tremble with the futile effort and I sink backwards, losing all hope.

I'm overtaken by a coughing fit so I don't hear the key in the door and shock bolts through me as I hear the ceiling light fizz and open my eyes to see Dom standing in front of me.

'So, do we have a deal?'

FORTY-FIVE

'You found the tickets in my suitcase. Did you find anything else?'
I say carefully.

Dom has at least helped me to the bathroom. He's even brought
me a bottle of water. No food, though; he clearly intends to keep
me weak and unable to make a break for it. As if I could . . . I can
hardly walk . . .

'Such as?' He rests his thumb on the tip of the knife, just
reminding me of its presence.

'You took it, didn't you?'

'It's my get-out-of-jail-free card. Of course I took it,' he says
scathingly.

'What do you mean? How on earth could Annabel's diary
protect *you?*'

'Because she was writing about Max, of course. What father
wouldn't want to protect his daughter and stop the man who was
trying to hurt her?' He smirks.

'Easy to say, now he's not here to defend himself. How many
more crimes does your brother have to take the rap for, Dom? You

can have your deal,' I say wearily. 'But will anyone actually believe me, that's what I'm wondering.'

'I had no trouble getting myself an alibi at the golf club. I'm sure I can find witnesses to corroborate Max's interest in young girls. He was almost sacked for it once. I only have to ask his manager at the gym and he'll confirm the truth: Max was a dirty bastard.'

'Yet you let him into our home. And you didn't tell me,' I say, anguish warring with anger.

'I didn't think even my brother would be idiotic enough to shit in his own nest,' Dom says. 'But when you told me about her diary, I knew instantly. It was him, beyond a shadow of a doubt. One more reason he deserved a bullet in his dumb brain.'

One more reason for Dom to storm out of our bedroom and sit waiting with the gun in his hand for Max to arrive.

'And is this what Annabel has said? Have you *asked* her?'

Is she still alive? Is she OK?

'I don't need to. And neither should you. Where's your mother's instinct now?' He sneers. 'It's all there in her diary. Why don't you take another look? You're lying on it.'

I take a sharp intake of breath as I suddenly become aware that the lump at the end of the mattress isn't just broken bed springs, and I try to scrabble towards it, but my arms and legs are stiff and heavy. The mattress suddenly tips and I roll to one side. Dom slides his arm underneath and pulls out a hardback book covered with white roses. I hold out my hands and my eyes fill with tears at the weight of Annabel's diary on my palms; it feels like I'm holding a piece of my daughter, and as I open the book her words blur in front of my eyes. I'm so caught up in my distress that I almost don't hear the first knock.

But Dom does; I feel him tense beside me.

A louder banging noise almost makes me jump off the bed. Louder and louder; it sounds like someone is trying to break

296

down a door. I clutch the diary hard against my chest, wondering breathlessly if someone else has come to settle a score with Max, only too late.

'Don't. Move. A. Muscle.' Dom's hands shoot out, one grabbing my wrist so hard I think it might snap, the other clamping over my mouth.

'Mrs Castle? Maddie? Are you *in* there?'

I recognise that voice!

'Don't worry, Mrs Castle. We're coming in to get you.' A different voice calls to me from outside the house. Louder. Authoritative. English. It's vaguely familiar but I can't quite place where I've heard it before.

'Make one move and I'll finish you right now,' Dom says gruffly, yanking me off the bed and dragging me behind him, my weak legs scrabbling desperately.

He turns off the light and backs himself against the bedroom door, bolt upright, clutching me against his body. His heart thuds against my shoulder blade and for a moment his left hand curls almost protectively around me, pressing flat against my midriff in a mockery of a lover's touch. Then it slides up to cover my mouth as he reaches behind himself with his right hand. A second later, I feel the tip of the knife pricking the skin of my throat.

'If you can hear me, Madeleine, just hold on tight for a few more minutes. Don't be frightened. Please just try to stay calm ...'

Call me Maddie, I think. And as tears of fear mingled with relief roll down my face, I smile.

FORTY-SIX

'We know you're in there, Dominic. We've been to your house and found it all shut up. Bit of a mess in there, though. Can you tell us anything about that?'

I feel Dom stiffen behind me, but he says nothing.

What has he done to our home?

I can hardly breathe as I try to picture what's happened. Are the children still there? Is Lucy?

My thoughts fly all over the place as I wait for the detective to speak again. I recognise DCI Watkins' monotone drawl now, and I remember how unflappable he seemed during our interview at the hospital, but I can't believe he can be as calm as he sounds. If he's really sure that Dom is here, and isn't just bluffing, then he must also know he's holding me captive and that I'm in danger. Why isn't he yelling at him or breaking down the door, or something?

Because this is a hostage situation, I realise.

I am Dom's hostage.

Immediately I think of news footage I've seen over the years; I think of the twins saying that nothing dramatic ever happens where we live, and I wonder if they're watching the headlines on television right now: a siege situation on a west London council estate. Is Lucy with them, comforting them as they watch in shock and horror?

Or were they all part of that scene of destruction at our home?

I'm desperate to cry out, to alert the detective – to ask about my children. But the blade is pressing against my windpipe and I no longer believe Dom would hesitate to use it. I know that if I cry out, he will slice my throat before the sound of my voice even leaves my mouth.

My breath comes in short, rattling gasps as I try to keep it steady, anxious to know what's going to happen next, waiting to see how the detective will try to appeal to Dom. I can't think of a single bargain he can offer. What kind of deal is there to be done with a man who has nothing left to lose?

But there is only silence now from outside the door. I grit my teeth to stop myself crying, and I can feel my knees locking painfully with the effort of standing rigidly still. My initial rush of relief at the detective's arrival has vanished, and as the silence continues, terror swirls around me in the dark. I'm desperate for him to say more – to explain what's happened at my home, to reassure me that my children are alive. Why doesn't he *say* something? *Do* something? But as at our last meeting, he is obviously taking his time, following his training, working through the appropriate steps. He's doing his job; I should be thankful for that. I just wish he'd do it *faster*.

'I trust you've been taking good care of your wife,' he says at last. 'She should really still be in hospital. Or resting at home, being looked after by her family and her GP. Professor Hernandez here was under the impression that was *exactly* what was going to happen.'

Dom tenses, his chest thrusting out behind me, and I jump.

He tightens his arm around my waist in response, squeezing me harder against him.

'Thankfully, the doctor is an extremely conscientious and uncannily astute man. He'd picked up on something in your mood at the hospital, and it bothered him that he hadn't seen your wife before she left. So alarm bells rang when he heard Madeleine hadn't shown up for her scheduled appointment with the GP the following morning. Why would she miss such an important appointment, Dominic? Can you help me with that?'

I can hear Dom's breathing becoming more agitated, deep and laboured. The detective is getting through to him; I can feel his big body trembling behind me.

'Police work. It's all in the details, you see. Missed appointments, a thank-you email the doctor was expecting that didn't materialise ... An experienced criminal would have thought of these little things. But you're not a master criminal, are you, Dominic? You've just allowed a bad situation to get out of hand. Don't worry, though. We can help you work things out. If you open the door, we can talk.'

I hold my breath, waiting to see if Dom will take the bait. He won't like the implication that there's something he's overlooked. He's established his consultancy on a reputation for thoroughness. I remember the hours he spent coming up with his company tag-line: *Castle Consultancy: a fortress of financial security*. But that was business; this is personal.

The detective is right: Dom didn't intend for any of this to happen. He's been acting on knee-jerk impulses all along, a gut instinct of furious reaction to what he believes to be my lies and his brother's disloyalty. Does he also genuinely believe Max was grooming Annabel? If he does, and it's not just another smoke-screen for his own sins, then it would surely have inflamed his anger when he loaded that gun and sat quietly waiting for Max to arrive: one more person his brother stole from him. His mum, dad, wife . . . daughter.

He's lied to me constantly since he came to the hospital, manipulating my emotions, playing on my guilt to humiliate me further. But I have no sense that he's lying now. There is nothing left between us to salvage; our marriage is over. Dom has admitted his crimes and he has nothing to gain by further deception. Max was the monster in Annabel's diary; I'm finally convinced of it, and I only wish I could share my horror and grief with Dom – the man who, before bitterness and paranoia tipped him over the edge, raised our beautiful children with me. Our twins – or mine alone? I can't be sure, and it shouldn't matter. Getting home to them is all that matters now.

Dom offered me a way to make that happen – a choice – and I want to believe, after all the lies, that it's genuine. I want to believe that, deep down, a tiny part of the man I once loved still loves and cares about me. I can sense the tension in him; he stands frozen to the spot. Clearly there is no grand plan. There is no clever trick up his sleeve for the end game. There is no exit strategy.

'In other instances, the doctor might not have been quite so concerned,' the detective goes on. 'But I did agree with Professor Hernandez when he called me on Saturday to express concern that it was a little odd for you to abandon your wife for so many weeks and then rush her – I believe those were his colleague's words – out of the hospital.'

I'm feeling lightheaded and open my mouth to draw in air, but Dom misinterprets my intake of breath as the prelude to a scream and presses the knife more firmly into my skin, close to the pulse point above my collarbone. I feel a trickle of blood and my knees give way. If he didn't have such a tight grip around my waist, I would collapse. I sag against him and I'm surprised when all of a sudden he seems to have difficulty holding my weight, stooping to mould himself around me until I am enclosed, imprisoned by his big body.

'You can talk to me, Dominic. I do know you're in there. We looked everywhere else, of course, but DI Baxter here had a hunch about this place. We've been here before, you see. Checked it over as part of the investigation into your brother's alleged shooting. I say alleged because naturally we found absolutely no evidence to speak of, and I've always been a little reluctant to close the case. Something just never quite gelled for me. My interview with your wife only consolidated that feeling.'

No police cordon – no further action required . . .

I remember wondering if the police had been here. I was right to, but it doesn't surprise me that they found nothing of any significance; Dom has wiped out all trace of his brother's existence. I wonder when he hid Annabel's diary under Max's mattress, and a shudder of disgust rolls through me at how Max pretended to be the perfect uncle yet all the time was watching, coveting, *pestering* Annabel behind my back.

Addicted to his sugar . . .

The phrase flashes in my mind and in the same instant I remember Max's phone message. *Hi, sugar, it's me. I'm waiting for you . . .* Adrenalin rushes through me, flooding my brain, sharpening my senses and crystallising my thoughts into a stark realisation: Max was trying to confess his feelings for *Annabel*, not me, that evening in the pub.

My thoughts tumble ahead so fast I almost can't keep up with them. Max *told* me he was meeting someone for a drink the evening before the twins' party, and I remember thinking how jittery he seemed, how on edge. He'd wanted to talk to Dom about something, and I don't believe it was me. Max did have a guilty conscience, but it had nothing to do with adultery and everything to do with his niece. Maybe his feelings for Annabel had been preying on his mind; maybe he'd become overwhelmed by them and wanted to come clean before her milestone tenth birthday party ...

It seems crazy, though, that he would take the risk of confessing those feelings to his brother: he was clever; he would have *known* how Dom would react. I shake my head, battling to keep it clear. Perhaps I'm wrong and his mind was on me after all, only not in a romantic sense. Maybe he went to the pub intending to give Dom a piece of his mind about how he treated me. Max always seemed so loyal to me – protective, even, taking my side against his brother. No doubt Dom interpreted that as more evidence of an affair, but Max could have gone to the pub that evening simply intending to ask Dom to back off – to rein in his bullishness, at least for the twins' birthday. After all, Max had no idea that I was about to leave Dom; he couldn't have known he was about to light a fuse that would propel his brother home to discover my plan and blow it sky high ...

I try to imagine the two brothers, head to head in the pub, old rivalries and resentments simmering between them, and I can picture Dom's brusque and condescending response all too easily. Max would have knocked back more and more whiskey, and perhaps then his mouth simply ran away with him. He couldn't get Annabel out of his mind; he'd *tried to stay away*, but he was hooked on her and couldn't stop his feelings spilling out of him. He simply had to talk about her: *those blue eyes, that pretty hair* ... Intoxicated by his infatuation with Annabel as much as by alcohol, he flirted with danger, unable to resist speaking of his secret, forbidden obsession. *His obsession with my daughter* ...

The walls seem to close in on me. I fight the sensation of being swallowed by darkness and force myself not to panic but to think rationally about the Max I've known for ten years. He always adored Annabel; he could never take his eyes off her. I've felt so guilty for not realising that his adoration went deeper than that of a proud uncle; my skin has crawled every time I've thought of him trying to touch her. But have I been blinded by my own maternal guilt? Have I condemned Max outright as a monster when it was simply all in his head? He got too close – I know that much from Annabel's diary – and that is shameful, harmful enough. But deep down I can't shake the sense that Max would never really have acted on his deviant impulses. He idolised Annabel; he wanted to possess her in some way – perhaps not even physically. As Dom once threw at me: *she's the angel on top of the Christmas tree, and she outshines everyone.* Max just needed to be around Annabel. She sensed this, and she was deeply uncomfortable – understandably so. And maybe Max had begun to realise that his fantasies had to stop.

I feel a surge of protectiveness towards Annabel and with it comes the certainty I've doubted so despairingly – that I *do* know my daughter, and I know she *would* have told me if Max had ever actually crossed the line. He invaded her space; he hovered around her like a moth courting the flame that dazzled but would ultimately destroy him. And then he realised he was playing with fire, spending so much time hanging around his niece, and on the day before her tenth birthday – the day he'd wanted to help make so special – his feelings overwhelmed him. Confused, desperate and in turmoil – and then drunk – he turned to the only other man who might appreciate Annabel's bewitching charm, hoping to find some kind of relief, solace or understanding. Perhaps even forgiveness or absolution.

Incredible as it seems to me that Max could have expected any of those things from Dom, a voice in my head reminds me how easy it can be to rationalise guilt and normalise the most unpardonable act: it was only when I believed my children might be in danger that I finally found the strength to leave Dom. Until then,

I'd convinced myself that if my children didn't know about his aggression, it couldn't hurt them. How long had Max been telling himself it was OK to *look* as long as he didn't *touch*? I can almost hear his deep, quick voice talking and talking, trying to convince himself that he wasn't doing anything wrong, that no one was getting hurt . . . He died without knowing exactly how many people *have* been hurt.

Was Max a true paedophile or just a sad, lonely man entranced by the beauty of my daughter's innocence? I'm not sure I'll ever know for certain, but I do know that Dom didn't even give him the chance to complete his drunken, misguided confession. Always hot-headed, he jumped instantly to the wrong conclusion – that Max and I were having an affair – and he charged home to punish me. And then, the following morning, his brother . . .

Dom was right about one thing: Max has paid the price. I just can't bear the thought that Annabel has too – for her uncle's twisted passions, her father's blinkered possessiveness, and my naivety.

It can't end this way; I won't let it.

My heart is pounding so loudly I can hear it echoing in my ears. I turn my head to tell Dom what I've realised – to ask him to give himself up and give us a chance to talk, really talk – but my throat dries as I see the look on his face.

'If I die, you die,' he whispers softly in my ear, his shoulders hunching as he dips his head to the side of mine. The stubble on his chin grazes my cheek.

It's all far too late, I realise. What's gone before no longer matters; the final curtain is about to fall. I tighten my grip on the hardback book, wishing the detective would hurry up and *do* something. From what he's saying I can gather that DI Baxter is out there with him, along with Professor Hernandez. That's three men against one, and surely they will have come armed and prepared. My eyes swivel around the room and I wonder wildly if I should just make a break for it, hide under the bed while the detectives barge in and—

'Perhaps you might be able to help us further with that line of inquiry, Dominic,' the detective continues at last. 'The evidence against your brother was entirely circumstantial. Forensics were satisfied, but I never did quite buy it. No real motive, you see. Turned this place upside down and couldn't find a jiffy to help us, either. It all looks a bit different now, though, I must say. Someone has done a thorough job emptying the place. I hardly recognise it. Your handiwork as well, I suppose? Tampering with evidence,' he says, baiting Dom a little more obviously now as he still refuses to be drawn out. 'We might need to have a little chat with you about that. And about the children.'

My knees give way entirely now and I can't help the moan that curdles deep in my throat. I turn my head to look pleadingly up at Dom, wanting to beg with my eyes for him to give himself up. But his own eyes are fixed and bloodshot, and his head is shaking, very slightly, from side to side. He catches my shocked glance and frowns down at me, pulling me closer against him, preventing me from dropping to the floor by digging his fingers into my ribs until I almost faint with the effort of not crying out.

My children. What about them?

'Come on, Dominic. You can't hide from us. You must know that. We live in a paranoid digital age. Whatever movements are trackable, we track. We have you on CCTV footage right now carrying Madeleine into this very house. Bit of a lucky break for us that your brother lived so close to the pub. Their security cameras picked you out nicely. But we can help you find a way out, Dominic. No need for you to feel cornered.'

Never corner a wild animal.

From out of nowhere, the words pop up in my mind, perhaps

from the twins' favourite wildlife programme or one of their school textbooks. Dom has nothing left to lose. No matter how I might wish things were different, the truth is he doesn't care about me, the woman he's convinced betrayed him, or the twins, the children he believes aren't even his; and from his crazed eyes, I'm beginning to suspect he doesn't much care about anything any longer. The detective's words will be like a red rag to a reckless, angry bull with an almighty grudge and no fear.

'I don't need your help.' Dom's voice is a low growl. 'I don't need anyone. I can finish this all by myself. My family, *my rules.*'

His statement cuts sharper than the knife grazing my skin. Stars dance in front of my eyes, turning the darkness into a hazy, swirling curtain around me. I remember lying rigidly in bed waiting for Dom to come home each night; I remember the loneliness, the humiliation of always trying to pacify him for fear of him turning his aggression on the twins. I think of him thundering home after seeing Max in the pub, never giving me a chance to explain, always believing the worst of me. I feel scorching heat surge through my body, moving steadily upwards through my legs, my midriff, my arms, all the way to my fingertips: an electrical charge of fury shocking me into action.

'*We are not your family!*' The words are torn from my throat; I howl them into the cold air. *I* am the cornered, wild animal; but I refuse to be caged any longer.

I picture the twins' faces and keep hold of that image as I dive forward into the dark room, a scream of anguish and desperation rupturing from my throat as I lurch in the direction of the bed. All I need to do is get far enough away from the door to let the detectives force their way in; all I need to do is put a temporary barrier between Dom and me. That's all I need. A place of safety, just for a few seconds.

'You are mine. You've *always* been mine,' Dom snarls.

He grabs me from behind before I've taken my second step. His big arms circle me and he easily captures both of my hands in one of his, the diary skittering to the floor as he spins me around, yanking my arms upwards towards his chest, flattening my palms against his thumping heartbeat. He dips his head and for a second I think he's about to kiss me. I draw in a ragged breath of horror, straining to pull away from him, my legs collapsing weakly as I realise I'm right.

I hear hammering, loud rhythmic bangs against the bedroom door; I hear the sound of splintering wood. But it's as though I'm in a stupor, cocooned in a bubble with Dom, floating upwards, the floor disappearing far below us. Sounds are muffled and I can't take my eyes off Dom's face as he gently lifts me to my feet, holding me firmly in front of him before lowering his head towards mine. Terror shudders through me; I can't move or breathe. I'm transfixed by his glazed eyes, the quirk of his mouth, so I don't notice when he reaches into his trouser pocket, only glancing down when I feel something cold and hard pressing against my left hand.

My wedding ring.

Suddenly I remember my dream: my wedding dress dropping to the floor, Dom twisting and turning my wedding ring. He was really touching me, I realise; he'd come to visit me in the hospital and tried to smother me, removing my ring at the same time. In his eyes, I'd forfeited the right to wear it, and he wanted to dispose of it, as he wanted to dispose of me.

Almost as soon as I realise that Dom has twisted the platinum band on to my ring finger, he presses the knife into my other hand, and in the same moment the bedroom door bursts open, the violent crash of the door flying off its hinges finally shattering my trance. Torchlight dances across the walls, spotlighting Dom as he draws me closer towards him, hugging me almost tenderly to his chest, pulling me closer and closer against his big body, swaying

from side to side as if to music. He hums beneath his breath. I recognise the tune: it's the song we chose together for our first dance.

'Dom ...' My voice dies as I realise that the knife between us
has sunk deep into flesh. A short, sharp jerk and then it slides in
easily, deeply, fatally. I feel myself sway and I start to black out
as a gush of hot blood drenches me, spattering loudly on to the
wood floor.

I look down and see Dom's big hands still wrapped around
mine between our two bodies, my fingers gripping the steak knife
I now recognise from the kitchen set Max gave us as a wedding
gift ten years ago. The black wooden handle presses painfully into
the palm of my right hand; the long blade is hidden, pointing away
from me, lodged deep inside my husband's chest.

FORTY-SEVEN

The curtains are drawn and the short driveway is empty. I peer out of the car window, looking up and down the street, and I can see that all the neighbours' curtains are also closed against the autumn dusk. A typically quiet Monday evening on our peaceful, tree-lined road. I expected it to feel different, but it's only me that's changed.

And the season. I left this house, this street, on the morning of the twins' birthday at the end of May, the threshold of English summertime; it's September now and the leaves are golden, glowing like embers in the street lamps. We are parked in a circle of light beneath the one outside our house, and I wish DCI Watkins had chosen a darker spot further along so as to keep our presence low-key. But I suppose all the neighbours will know by now; DI Baxter will have knocked on every door.

At least there was no need for flashing blue lights. We crawled through the Twickenham traffic, along Hampton Hill past Bushy Park and onwards to Hampton village, with no siren wailing out a distress signal, nothing to draw attention to our progress or force the traffic to yield before us: no emergency, but a powerful, breath-stealing urgency that made me grind my teeth and grip the seatbelt until my knuckles turned white.

The detective turns off the engine and as the purr of the motor quietens, the only sounds I hear are the occasional crackles of the police radio and the hoarse rattle of my own breathing. I watch from the back seat as DCI Watkins glances in his wing mirror, checks his watch, hooks his notebook out of his pocket and finally turns to look at Michelle sitting next to him in the passenger seat. I try to interpret their silent exchange; I don't want to ask them what they're thinking. I don't want to hear platitudes – or the truth.

I press my hands together to stop them shaking and jump when Professor Hernandez leans across the leather seat to take hold of them both, squeezing them between his own. I flinch as I'm reminded of Dom's touch, but the doctor's gentleness is a world away from my husband's death grip. I squeeze back and the physical contact brings me some comfort, but it can't stop the trembles rippling through my body.

I'm shaking uncontrollably, but I'm not cold. It's warm in the police car, the windows are beginning to steam up, and Michelle loaned me fresh clothes to change into after showering back at the police station: clean, loose black lounge pants and a soft longline maroon sweatshirt. With my hair washed and tidied into a fresh ponytail, I feel slightly more human. Michelle also brought me a flask of hot, sweet tea, a bottle of water and some fruit and sandwiches, which I ate and drank automatically, tasting little but knowing I needed to refuel my weakened body. I swallowed the medicine the doctor brought me, too, hoping it would revive me after what I'd just endured – and give me further strength for what lay ahead.

I'd been in the police station less than an hour before Lucy and the twins were officially reported missing.

*

'There still hasn't been any answer at the house,' DCI Watkins said, leaning one elbow on the desk and rubbing his eyes with his other hand. I wondered how long he'd been on duty. 'We forced entry this morning, of course, and found all the rooms in a real state. I've got the SOCO guys all over it. But there was no sign of the children. Or your friend. We've checked with staff at her deli in Teddington and she hasn't been seen for a couple of days.' He reached for his notebook before confirming: 'Last there on Friday morning, the girl said.'

The day Dom collected me from the hospital and said he just needed to nip home, to take care of a couple of things . . .

'And she didn't think that was odd? Didn't it occur to her to report Lucy missing when she didn't show up all weekend?' I said, irritable with shock, frustration and fear for my children. I leaned over and threw the remains of my sandwich in the detective's wastepaper basket, unable to stomach any more.

'She's only new. Just started working there, didn't you say, boss?' Michelle chipped in.

'Brilliant timing,' I said bitterly, frowning at him as I remember the conversation about the deli I overheard between Dom and Lucy in the bright-dark. 'Sorry, I don't mean to be . . . I'm just so . . .'

'It's perfectly OK. You have absolutely nothing to apologise for. We'll find them, Maddie. We will.'

He tried to hold eye contact with me but I could tell he didn't want to. I'd seen the sideways glances from the other officers we'd passed as Michelle ushered me into this office; I knew what everyone was thinking. I'd been thinking it myself almost since the first moment Dom carried me up the stairs of Max's house and locked the door.

I'm finally back – and my children are gone. Missing. Presumed dead.

'The girl also said she understood Lucy had been moving house. So when she didn't show up, she put it down to her being busy and thought no more of it. Shame, really. Had she panicked and tried to get hold of Lucy, we might have been alerted earlier to the fact that she was missing.' DCI Watkins sat back in his chair, folding his arms across his chest.

I wondered if Lucy had genuinely believed Dom had been changed by tragedy and had offered to move in with him to help with the children, or if he'd *forced* her, and then when he didn't need her any more ... I wished I knew which was the truth, but either way it didn't help explain where my friend was now, or why she'd gone missing – along with Annabel, Aidan and Jasper.

'Your husband's business colleagues have also spoken highly of him. It seems he's been acting quite out of character. But you'll know better than us,' Michelle said. 'Friends and colleagues generally only see what they're allowed to see, not the whole truth.'

'The whole truth. Or something our unconscious mind rewrites for us,' I said, thinking of the doctor's words.

'Sorry?' Michelle and the detective exchanged glances.

'Doesn't matter. Have the children been in school?' I asked, my eyes darting around the office as if clues to their whereabouts might somehow pop out from the posters and notices pinned across the walls of the high-ceilinged room. I stared blankly at a map of the UK stretched across two noticeboards, coloured pins dotted here and there. Was that a record of my movements, Dom's – or another case entirely? My eyes roamed across the coloured tangle of roads, up and down the country and then lingering on the south coast, my heart pounding as the word 'Brighton' seemed to leap out at me.

'Up until Friday. Subdued but present was their teacher's comment. They've been keeping a special eye on them, she told me. Under the circumstances of your being in a coma – which is what

313

everyone still thinks,' DCI Watkins said, glancing at Michelle for confirmation. She nodded, continuing to chew her pencil to a woody pulp. I watched her discreetly pick a soggy, flaky shard from between her teeth.

'And today? Were they at school *today*?' I said, my mind still turning over the road map, grasping at a thought that kept drifting away. 'If they were at school, perhaps they're just round at a friend's house now for a playdate. New friends I've never met.' I'd already given them every name and number I could remember, and they'd checked them all, finding nothing.

'National teachers' strike.' DCI Watkins checked his notebook again for confirmation.

'Fuck,' Michelle said, aiming the mangled pencil stub at the bin.

'Precisely. So no one has missed Lucy at work this weekend, everyone has presumed she's just been busy moving house, and the kids have been at school as normal right up until Friday. Dominic has clearly managed to convince everyone that it's business as usual. And it was only when he came to see you on Friday and for whatever reason decided to escalate matters that his plans changed.' The detective checked his watch.

It was because I told him I thought Annabel was dead.

That's what made him ramp up his next step. He'd realised that his plan had been successful – I genuinely believed I'd chosen between my children – and he'd seized his chance to turn the thumbscrews and make me agree to his escape plan, keeping hold of Annabel's diary in case he ever needed evidence that he'd only acted to protect his family from an abusive monster. Perhaps he even had a line about self-defence already prepared. *He* was the guilty one, but he'd preyed on *my* guilt, which I'd handed to him on a plate. As always, I'd given him the upper hand, and he'd punched me with it.

'Brighton.' I stood up suddenly, a light bulb flashing on in my mind. I shuffled quickly towards the map, reaching out to trace the diagonal orange line of the M23 out of London and down to the A23, my finger urgently tracing all the way to the bright blue of the English Channel.

'Sorry?' DCI Watkins and Michelle spoke as one, both turning to look at the point where my finger jabbed at the map.

'Lucy has a holiday cottage in Brighton. It's a long shot but … she might have gone there. Taken the children. I don't know, but it's possible?' My heart started to thump even faster as I wondered if it could be true. I wanted it to be; I wanted to go there right now and find them all eating fish and chips on the pebble beach, watching the sunset and talking of the day I would come home to them.

'Give me the address,' DCI Watkins said brusquely, handing me his notepad and pen. I wrote it down and watched breathlessly as he picked up the receiver of his desk phone. 'On it,' he said shortly, after disconnecting the call.

'So what's the plan now, boss?' Michelle asked, coming to stand next to me, resting a gentle hand on my arm and urging me back to my chair. 'Try to keep the weight off your feet, Maddie. The doctor said you must take it really easy. He's gone out for more meds, but in the meantime, sit,' she said, her smile softening the bossy command.

'Officer on his way to this address, and we've put out notices to police stations nationwide,' DCI Watkins said. 'Closer to home, I've arranged to meet DI Baxter back at the house in an hour. He's there as we speak, knocking on neighbours' doors, seeing if anyone has seen or heard anything that might give us a lead. I'm going to head over shortly; I want to take another look round the place myself. And after that, we'll—'

'I want to be there,' I cut in firmly.

'Well, I'm not sure if—' The detective looked shocked at the suggestion, his hands lifting in a gesture of refusal.

'I want to *be* there,' I repeated. I looked him straight in the eye, making him stare my agony in the face. 'You're going back to search the back garden, aren't you? That's what you're planning to do. There's no trace of them in the house or at Lucy's deli. None of their school friends have seen them. Your detective is knocking on doors. If they're not in Brighton, that leaves only one possibility I can think of. And you're thinking it too, aren't you?' I said, my chest tightening with sobs that turned into a hacking cough.

I felt like I was burning up. Michelle was right: I really needed to be in bed, probably back in hospital. But there was no way I was going to let the detectives return to my home without me being there.

'It might be better if the guys call us afterwards, don't you think?' Michelle said, grabbing a blanket from a cupboard and draping it over my shoulders. 'I'll stay here with you. Get some rest, let them search. You're not in the best state to be out there, and they'll call us the second they find anything.'

'*No!* I lost my family once and I've just watched my husband die right in front of me. He accused me of being a freeloader, some kind of passenger in my family, a useless—'

'Your husband clearly wasn't in his right mind, Maddie. You mustn't hold on to—'

'I'm *not* going to sit here drinking tea while I lose my children a second time!' I said, only just managing to stop myself stamping a foot in temper.

'Well, I think that settles it, then,' Michelle said, raising her eyebrows at DCI Watkins. 'Back in a tick. I just need a—'

'You can smoke on the way, Michelle. Let's go,' the detective said firmly.

FORTY-EIGHT

'I think it's time.' DCI Watkins turns to look over his shoulder at me. 'As you requested, we'll let you go ahead first and we'll follow after. Are you ready, Maddie?'

Am I ready?

I'm still grappling with what that even means when I hear the clunk of the car door and look up to see Michelle stretching out a hand to me. She helps me out of the car and my legs wobble almost uncontrollably, but I feel the doctor close behind me and know he's ready to catch me if I fall.

My first few steps are so shaky that I wonder if I should have accepted the offer of a wheelchair after all, and I only make it half-way up the short drive before I need to stop. I take a deep breath as I stand looking up at the modest white-painted semi-detached house that has been my home for ten years, where Dom first carried me over the threshold as an excited new bride. So many promises – some kept, many broken. Our marriage began and ended with a dance and a love song; I know that tune will haunt me for ever.

'Thanks for coming all this way to be with me, Doctor. Thank you for everything,' I say without turning round. 'No matter what happens now.'

I can sense his support, his quiet strength, and I try to take courage from it. It was strange at first to see him without his white coat; somehow he still looked like a doctor, though: discreet, professional, trustworthy. It wasn't just the medical garb and stethoscope that gave him such presence as a consultant, I think, remembering how he'd teased me. It was just *him*; he inspires confidence in others through the sheer power of his kindness and honesty. He heals not just with his hands and mind, his medical experience and expertise, but simply by *being*.

'Call me Sebastiàn,' he says. 'We are friends now, not doctor and patient, yes?'

'Yes,' I agree. 'Friends. But I still need your help. I'm not sure I can do this. I'm so frightened. I don't want to lose . . . I wish I could be as strong as you . . . ' My voice trails away. I stare at the front door, willing it to swing open and for the twins to come bundling out, saying it has all been some kind of terrible mistake and they've just been playing happily in their bedrooms.

'There are different kinds of strength, Maddie. You managed to pull yourself out of a dark place once. You can do it again. Very few people come back from the depths of coma you endured. I remember our sessions all too vividly. You went on an immense journey, locked inside your unconscious mind, and there must have been an extraordinarily powerful force drawing you back to life.'

'My children,' I say simply. 'And without them I . . . '

Biting back the thought I force myself to move, to continue walking slowly towards the house, my boots crunching on the gravel. As I approach the familiar glass-panelled front door I notice empty milk bottles underneath the step; a green recycling box sits to one side and a pair of Aidan's muddy football boots stands propped up against the wall, waiting to be cleaned. Signs of ordinary family life; I can't pull my gaze away from them, and my eyes fill with tears as I look closer and notice Aidan's name scrawled inside his left boot.

I feel drawn by a sudden need I can't explain to retrace my steps from the last day I spent in this house. Perhaps that was in Dom's mind too, I wonder, as he re-enacted our wedding dance moments before impaling himself on the knife: one last chance to remember before all is lost. Was he recalling those happy moments from our wedding to comfort himself? Or was he reminding me as one final punishment for my supposed betrayal? He took his own life, but he made me complicit. *If I die, you die.* And a little part of me *did* die with him.

I glance over towards the corner of the house, the narrow foot-path that leads round the side, and I turn away from the front door; I know there will be no answer anyway if I press the buzzer. I start walking again, my head pounding with the thought that this might be my last ever chance to walk in my children's footsteps. I can hardly bear it but it feels like all I have left of the twins: the memory of those final moments before I lost them.

Slowly I make my way along the rough concrete path towards the back garden, every step bringing me closer to my memories of that terrible morning. I trail my fingers along the pebble-dashed side of the house and feel as though I'm walking through a time-tunnel; it's like crossing over into a parallel universe and I half expect Dom to come charging up the path with the twins clutched in his arms.

But there is no one; not a sound. The garden is quiet, dark, sheltered from the street lamps that light up the front of the house. The grass is long and unkempt and I see that the rose bushes are almost completely bare now, their spindly, woody arms pointing in random directions as if to misdirect me in my search for clues, evidence, any sign that my children might be hiding – or their bodies hidden – in this place that Dom knew I loved. He's done his best to take everything and everyone else from me; I'm trying hard not to believe he would really have executed his final punishment and taken the lives of the two little people who matter more to me than everything else put together.

I look up at the stars and then down at the ground, seeing the echo of the night sky in a scattering of white petals fluttering confetti-like across the right-hand side of the lawn. It looks as though a wedding party is about to take place – or a wake. A sweet-sour taste fills my mouth and I have to swallow the impulse to be sick.

'Annabel,' I whisper, barely breathing her name, my eyes searching for her thin, lifeless body beneath the barren rose bushes, even though I know it isn't there – has *never* been there.

I look up towards the bedroom windows at the back of the house: Aidan's room, with Annabel's right next door.

Run! Hide! Don't look back!

That is where Annabel would have run to hide, pulling her brother behind her on the morning of their birthday. Her own private little world; her place of safety. I keep my eyes fixed on the dark window, picturing them crouched on the bedroom floor, their arms entwined around each other, eyes squeezed tightly shut and heads close together as they waited for the horror to pass and Mummy to come and find them. Only I didn't come, and I wonder how long they waited, what they heard, and what they imagined was happening outside in the garden below. They may not have witnessed either shooting, but images would have played out in their minds all the same. I want the chance to wipe out those terrible pictures and replace them with only happy ones.

I step across to the wooden swing bench where I used to curl up with the children on summer days. The Buddha they gave me sits patiently next to the bench; I close my eyes and picture the twins' joy as I unwrapped it after my special Mother's Day breakfast and told them it would bring us peace always. I remember those moments so vividly, even as I remain conscious of the world around me. This is the difference now when I drift off into memories. In the bright-dark, I became *part* of my memories; I inhabited the past, gliding between different times in my life, never realising that I wasn't actually *there*.

Until now, I've never wondered why I always remained inside the house, reliving and replaying all the events of my life but never venturing out here, to the place where the peace I'd promised the twins was destroyed, violence tearing through our safe world, ripping my life apart. Now I understand that my unconscious mind was protecting me. As Professor Hernandez once said to me: *the mind is incredibly powerful.*

I have fought my way back to life, and I *will* find my children, I think desperately, starting to hunt in earnest through the garden now, dragging my hands through trailing wisteria and the laurel hedge along the back fence, plunging my arms into hawthorn bushes, heedless of the thorns tearing my skin. I rip into the huge rhododendron bush in the far corner and yank away branches of spruce overhanging the back of the shed where Dom changed into his dad's old army clothes and sat waiting for his moment. My legs are shaking so much I can hardly stand, but I don't stop: I trample through the flower beds I spent years nurturing, oblivious to the little wildlife statues of my tranquillity garden toppling sideways as I walk round and round in circles, sobbing now, tears running down my face and my heart pounding until I think it will shatter into pieces.

Annabel! Aidan! Where are you?

A ball of anguish chokes me as I whirl around the garden, the stranglehold of hysteria tightening as I search desperately, repetitively, returning again and again to look at the same empty swing where Annabel still isn't sitting, ducking to look underneath the slide where Aidan still hasn't crouched to hide from me. If they are not here, I have no idea where else to look; and if I cannot find them, I wish Dom had taken me with him.

'Maddie, please stop.'

I ignore DCI Watkins' low warning. I know he wanted to search the garden methodically, no doubt to preserve any evidence. I'm disturbing a possible crime scene; I'm making his job harder and he'll be wishing again that he'd insisted I stay back at the police station. But this is *my* garden, *my* children; I *have* to find—

I hear a scraping noise.

Hairs prickle at the back of my neck.

I turn. I look across the garden to see old Mr Cooper from next door shuffling round the corner of the house, leaning heavily on his polished ebony walking stick as he joins Professor Hernandez and the detectives standing wide-eyed at the edge of the lawn. DCI Watkins, Michelle, the doctor and another man I presume must be DI Baxter: the moon casts an ethereal glow over them all; they look like ghosts, pale figments conjured up by my imagination to play yet more cruel tricks on me.

But pressed close to each side of my elderly neighbour, skinny chopstick arms hooked tightly through his, stands a small, freckle-faced, copper-haired child. I blink once, twice, but they don't disappear. A hollow cry erupts from my throat and I lurch forwards. As if made of stone my feet refuse to move: heavily, clumsily, I drag them across the dewy grass, and then I am stumbling, falling towards my children, arms outstretched until my shoulders almost dislocate, every last pain in my body forgotten as I watch the twins simultaneously break free from Mr Cooper and fly towards me.

'Mummy!'

The thud of Annabel's body against my chest is followed a second later by Aidan's, and it feels like they've kick-started my heart, bringing me back to life. I wrap them up and hug them so hard I don't think I can ever let go; I feel their skinny arms work their way behind my back, linking hands with each other, entwining until our three hearts echo with one thumping beat and it's impossible to know where one of us ends and another begins.

'I knew you'd come back for us,' Annabel says at last, turning her soft cheek to rest flat against my chest.

'Always, my darling girl,' I say, burying my face in her golden crown of curls, breathing in the poignantly familiar sweet scent of apples mingled now with the damp-cinder tang of autumn.

'I thought we'd never see you again,' Aidan says, looking up at me with blue eyes shining out from a face that is crumpled and wet with tears.

'Nothing – *no one* – can keep me from you, my precious boy.' I hold him tighter, my throat too choked to say more.

'You have a very kind, wise neighbour, Maddie,' Lucy says, stepping forward, and I look up to see her smiling through her own tears. 'He heard Dom smashing up the house in the early hours of Saturday morning, and the moment he saw his car pull away, he came to get us. We've been playing bingo pretty much non-stop ever since.' She rolls her eyes, and then she is dancing towards us, sobbing and laughing as she throws her arms around me. 'I'm so happy you're home,' she says as she presses her cheek to mine. 'We never knew – all this time Dom told us you were still asleep in the hospital, that it was unlikely you would ever wake up and that we couldn't visit you, couldn't—'

'I can't thank you enough, Lucy,' I say hoarsely. 'For looking after them. You are the best friend I could ever wish for. Now meet my other best friend. Sebastiàn. He helped me find my happy ending,' I say, beaming as Professor Hernandez strides across the grass to shake Lucy's hand, before returning to pump the hand of each of the detectives in turn, ruffling Jasper's hair and then last of all stooping to give a surprised Mr Cooper a big hug.

'As I told this young detective here when he knocked on my door just now, Madeleine has been a life-saver to me since my wife died,' my frail but brave neighbour says, pulling a neatly pressed white handkerchief out of his tweed jacket pocket and meticulously dabbing his eyes. 'I know he came by before. I'm sorry I didn't answer the door. I thought it was, you know, *him* come back for the twins. I've been keeping them hidden in my wife's old sewing room, you see. Just till I could work out a plan. It was the very least I could do for Maddie's little ones. Look at them. Who could ever bear to hurt a single hair on their beautiful heads?'

I look down at the twins, pressing against me as if to imprint their bodies upon mine. They are part of me, as I am of them: a three-way knot that has looped between us since before they were even born, and I will never let it be broken again.

'I love you both beyond life,' I say, treasuring the steady rise and fall of their chests against mine, their synchronised puffs of breath warm against my neck. 'I love you round the stars and over Mars,' I whisper between their red-gold heads.

Annabel looks up at me and our eyes lock in recognition of her words and where she wrote them. I'm almost too blinded by tears to see the shy, anxious smile on her face, but I feel her tiny hand squeeze mine.

'Is it over, Mummy?'

'Like a bad dream. We're going to start living our own dreams now.' I gaze down at the two almost-identical, happy shiny faces glowing up at me. 'My precious twins. I choose *us*.'

ACKNOWLEDGEMENTS

In writing this story I thought a lot about dreams, and I'm fortunate to be able to say that my three biggest wishes in life have been granted: meeting my husband, having our children, and now becoming a published writer. Of course, as you will know, fulfilling dreams takes an immense amount of hard work as well as a hefty sprinkle of luck – and I'd like to say a huge thank-you here to some very special people who have helped me.

Emma Beswetherick – for your unwavering faith in me, your brilliantly incisive but always nurturing guidance, awe-inspiring speed, energy and enthusiasm. And for offering champagne at every opportunity! Quite literally, I couldn't have done this without you, and I feel privileged to have you as my editor. Best phone call from a New York taxi cab ever. *Thank you!*

Dominic Wakeford (infinitely more charming than your namesake!) – for your eagle-eyed insights and answering all my questions so patiently! Alison Tulett – for fabulous copy-editing and pointing out every bloop with such tact! And Fraser Crichton – for catching everything that slipped through the net. Anniina Vuori (and Diane Spivey) – for your super efficiency and friendly patience in demystifying contracts, and because Contracts people are the unsung heroes who genuinely make things happen!

The entire Piatkus team – for all that you do. Which is a lot! From Rights to Production, Sales & Marketing to Publicity, you are a fabulous, incredibly talented bunch of extraordinarily kind, clever and creative people.

Eugenie Furniss – for being so wonderfully fleet of foot in taking up the baton!

Finally, my husband and children – who convinced me to follow my dreams, without realising they've already made the most important ones come true.

Paul – for all the massive, life-changing things. Paying the bills, keeping the children happy and entertained to give me time to write. Never, ever letting me give up. Thank you for being right by my side – always encouraging me, often carrying me!

Hani and Rafi – thank you for filling my every day with happiness, and for putting up with Mummy being glued to the laptop! I could never have written this book without you: it is all because of you, and it is all *for* you, always. You are growing up into such amazing people, but you will always be my babies – and I love you both beyond life.